P9-BYA-872

Disney

FROZEN II

-« THE MANGA »-

Adapted by

ARINA
TANEMURA

VIZ MEDIA

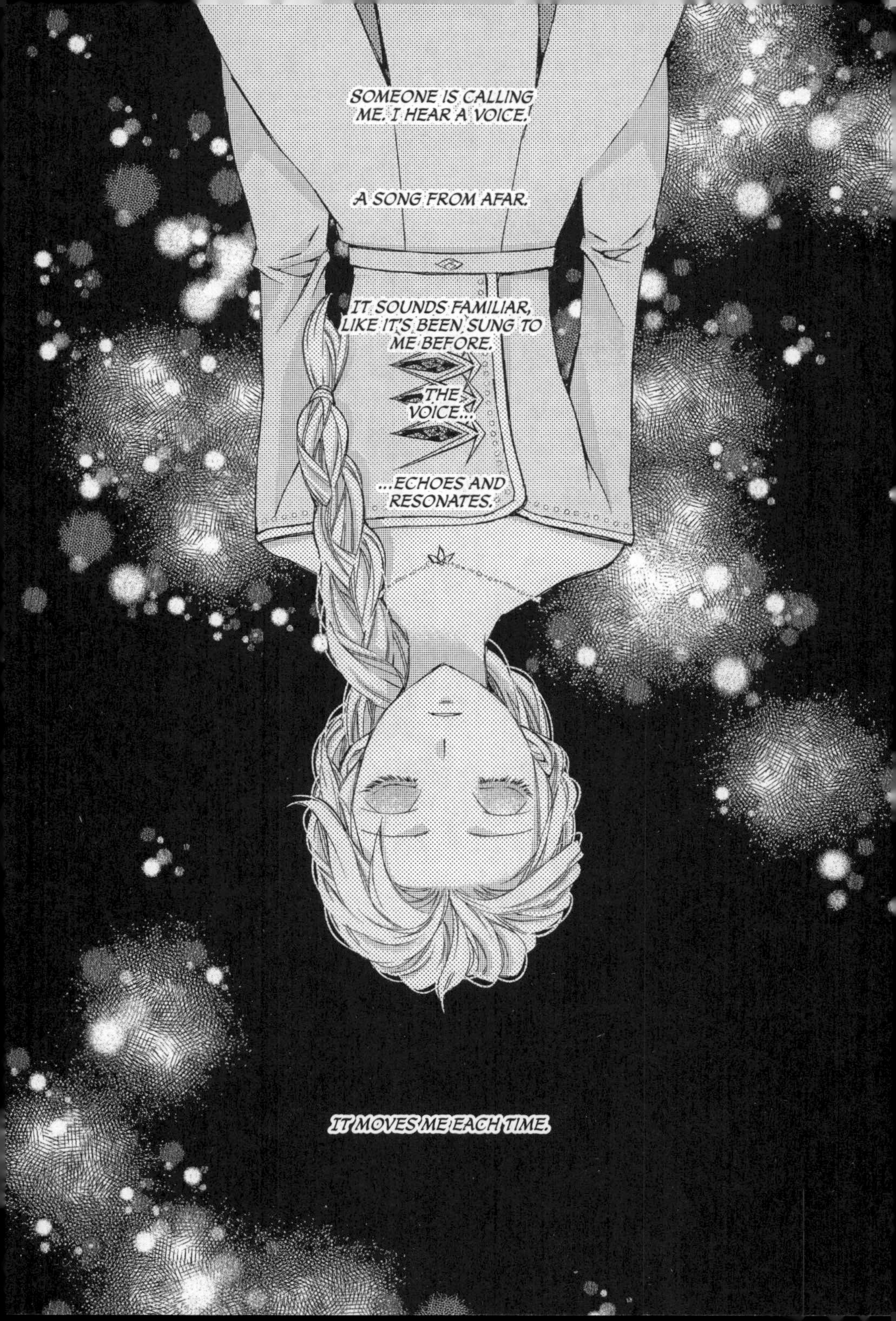
SOMEONE IS CALLING ME. I HEAR A VOICE.
A SONG FROM AFAR.
IT SOUNDS FAMILIAR, LIKE IT'S BEEN SUNG TO ME BEFORE.
THE VOICE...
...ECHOES AND RESONATES.
IT MOVES ME EACH TIME.

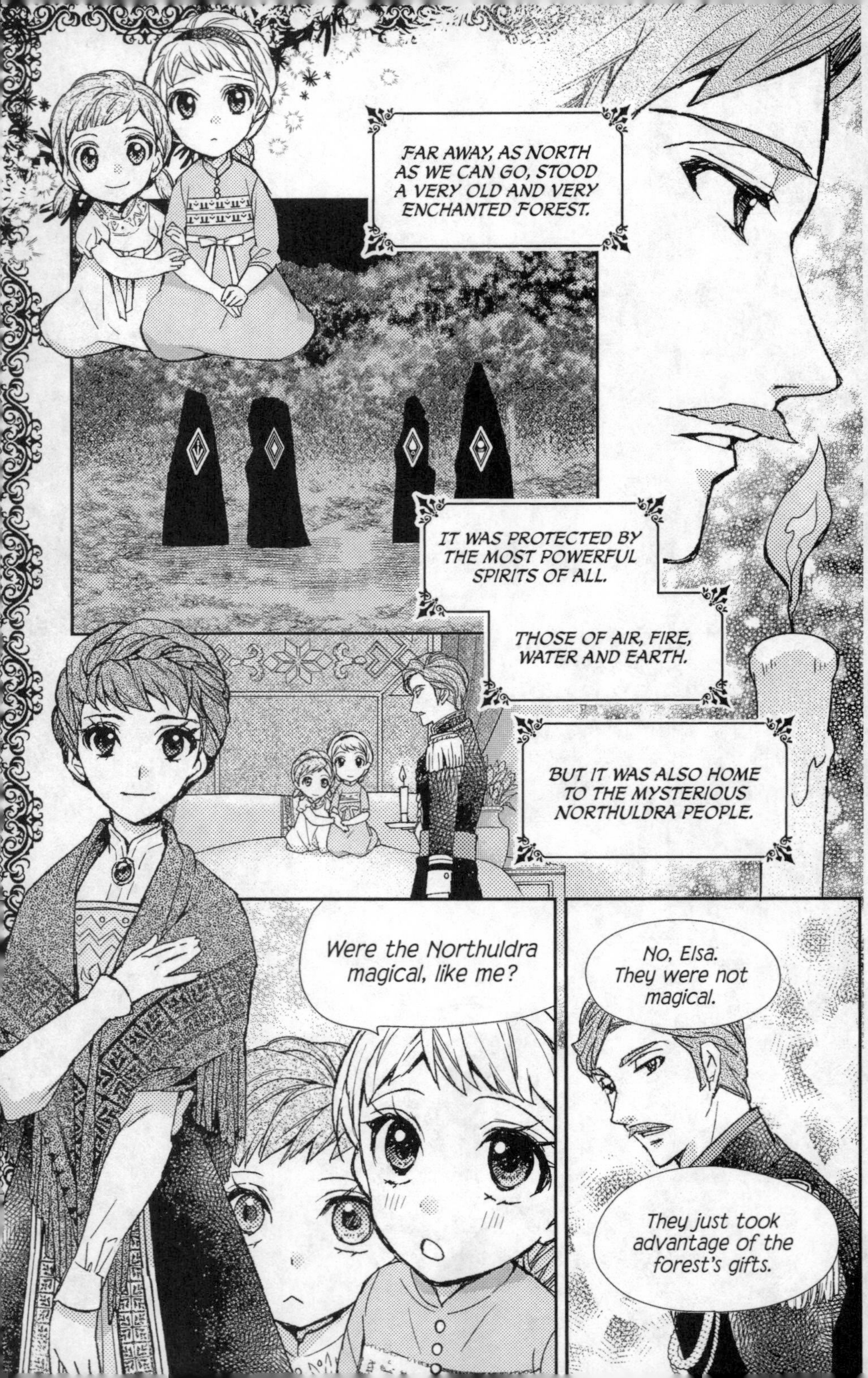
FAR AWAY, AS NORTH AS WE CAN GO, STOOD A VERY OLD AND VERY ENCHANTED FOREST.
IT WAS PROTECTED BY THE MOST POWERFUL SPIRITS OF ALL.
THOSE OF AIR, FIRE, WATER AND EARTH.
BUT IT WAS ALSO HOME TO THE MYSTERIOUS NORTHULDRA PEOPLE.
Were the Northuldra magical, like me?
No, Elsa. They were not magical.
They just took advantage of the forest's gifts.

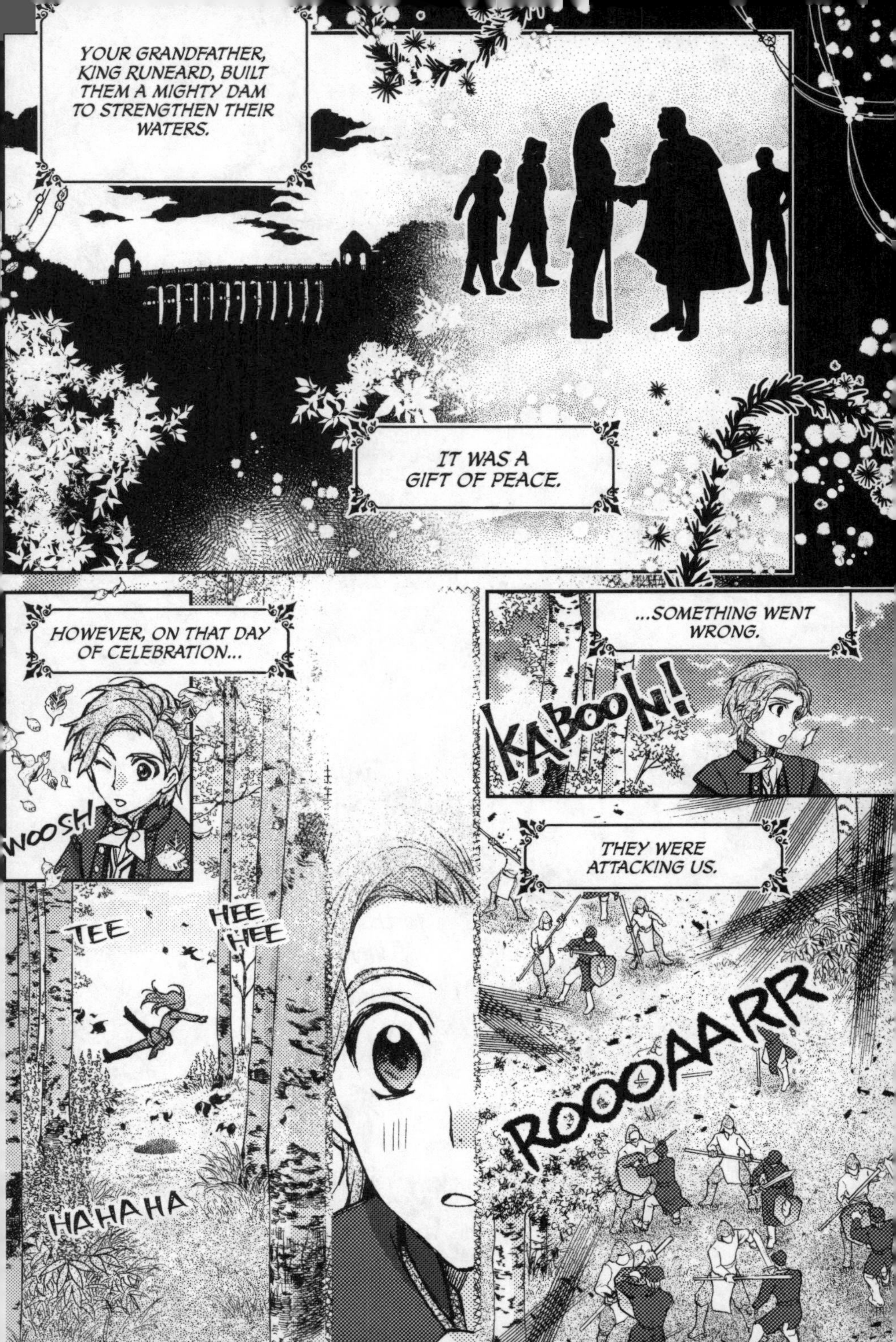
YOUR GRANDFATHER, KING RUNEARD, BUILT THEM A MIGHTY DAM TO STRENGTHEN THEIR WATERS.
IT WAS A GIFT OF PEACE.
HOWEVER, ON THAT DAY OF CELEBRATION...
WOOSH
...SOMETHING WENT WRONG.
KABOOM!
TEE
HEE HEE
HAHAHA
THEY WERE ATTACKING US.
ROOOAARR

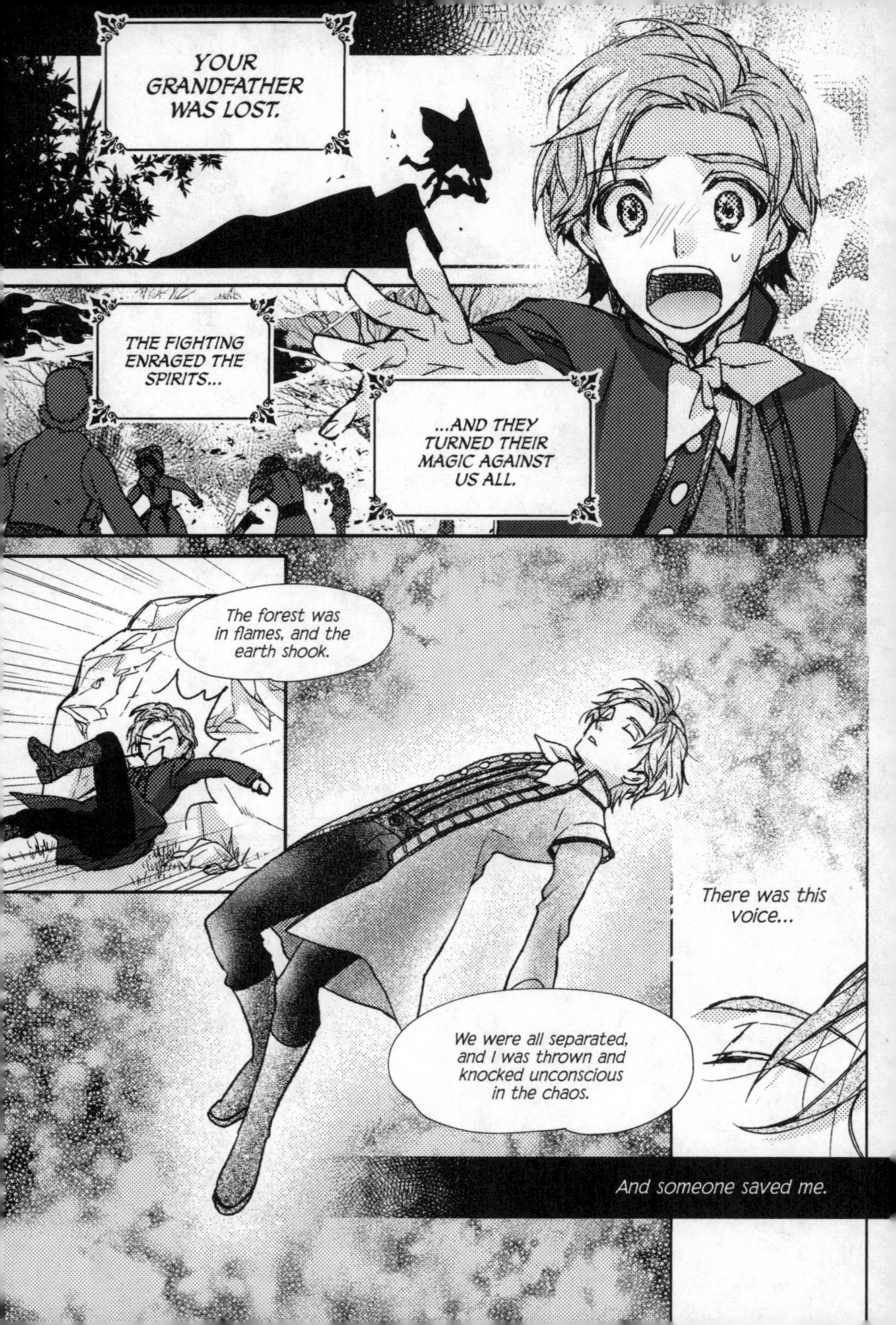
YOUR GRANDFATHER WAS LOST.
THE FIGHTING ENRAGED THE SPIRITS...
...AND THEY TURNED THEIR MAGIC AGAINST US ALL.
The forest was in flames, and the earth shook.
We were all separated, and I was thrown and knocked unconscious in the chaos.
There was this voice...
And someone saved me.

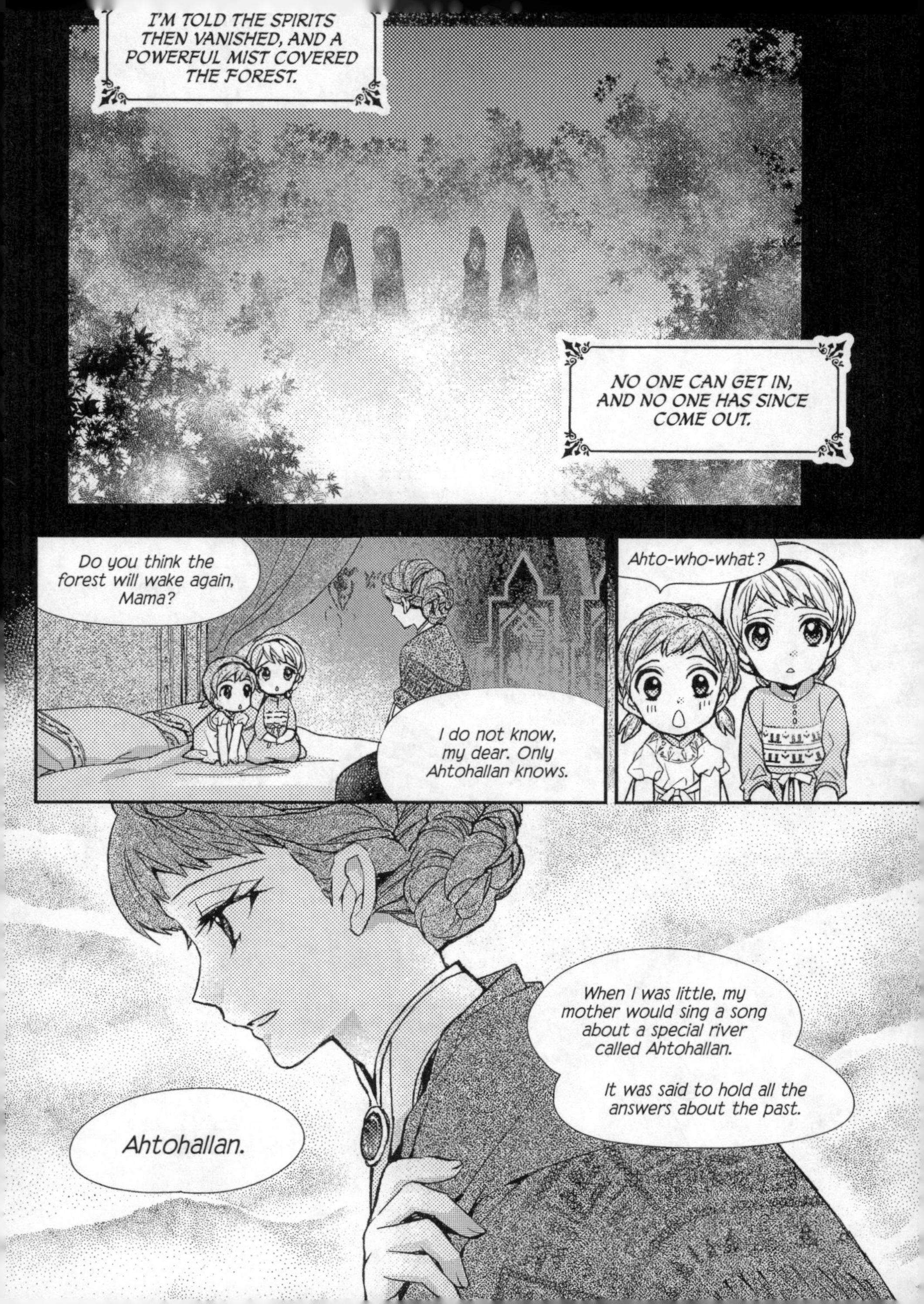
I'M TOLD THE SPIRITS THEN VANISHED, AND A POWERFUL MIST COVERED THE FOREST.
NO ONE CAN GET IN, AND NO ONE HAS SINCE COME OUT.
Do you think the forest will wake again, Mama?
I do not know, my dear. Only Ahtohallan knows.
Ahto-who-what?
Ahtohallan.
When I was little, my mother would sing a song about a special river called Ahtohallan.
It was said to hold all the answers about the past.

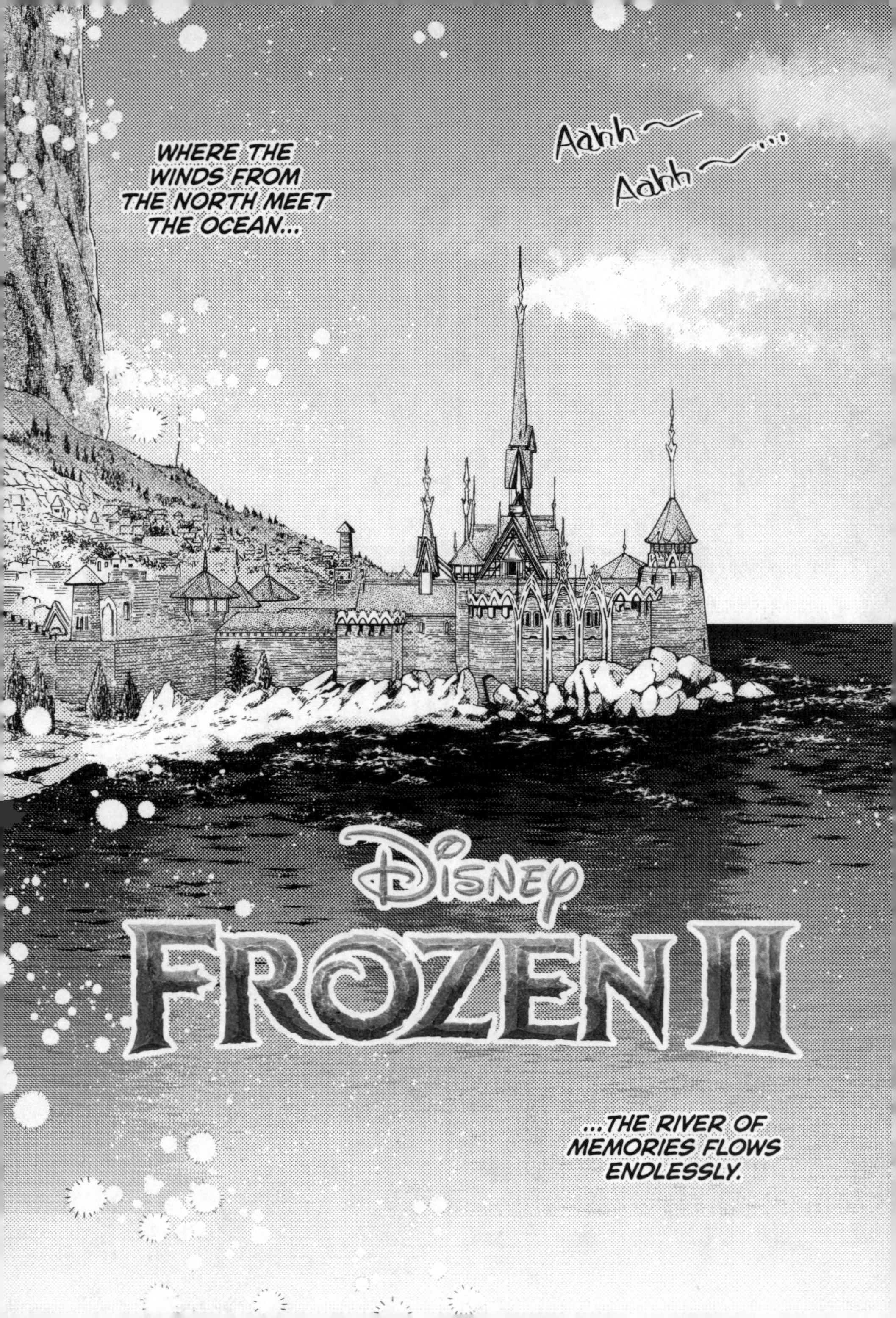
WHERE THE WINDS FROM THE NORTH MEET THE OCEAN...
Aahh~ Aahh~...
Disney
FROZEN II
...THE RIVER OF MEMORIES FLOWS ENDLESSLY.

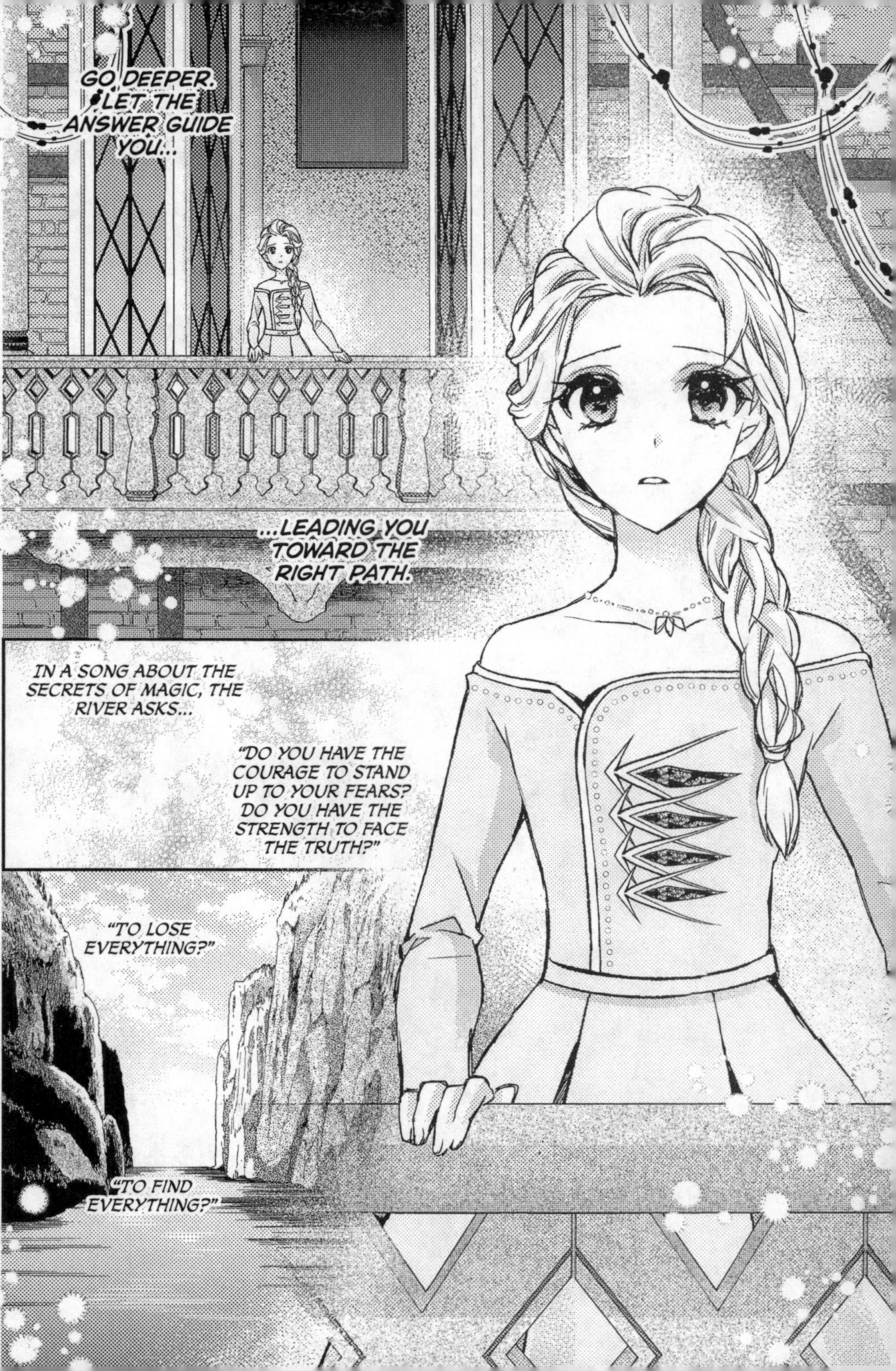
GO DEEPER. LET THE ANSWER GUIDE YOU...
...LEADING YOU TOWARD THE RIGHT PATH.
IN A SONG ABOUT THE SECRETS OF MAGIC, THE RIVER ASKS...
"DO YOU HAVE THE COURAGE TO STAND UP TO YOUR FEARS? DO YOU HAVE THE STRENGTH TO FACE THE TRUTH?"
"TO LOSE EVERYTHING?"
"TO FIND EVERYTHING?"

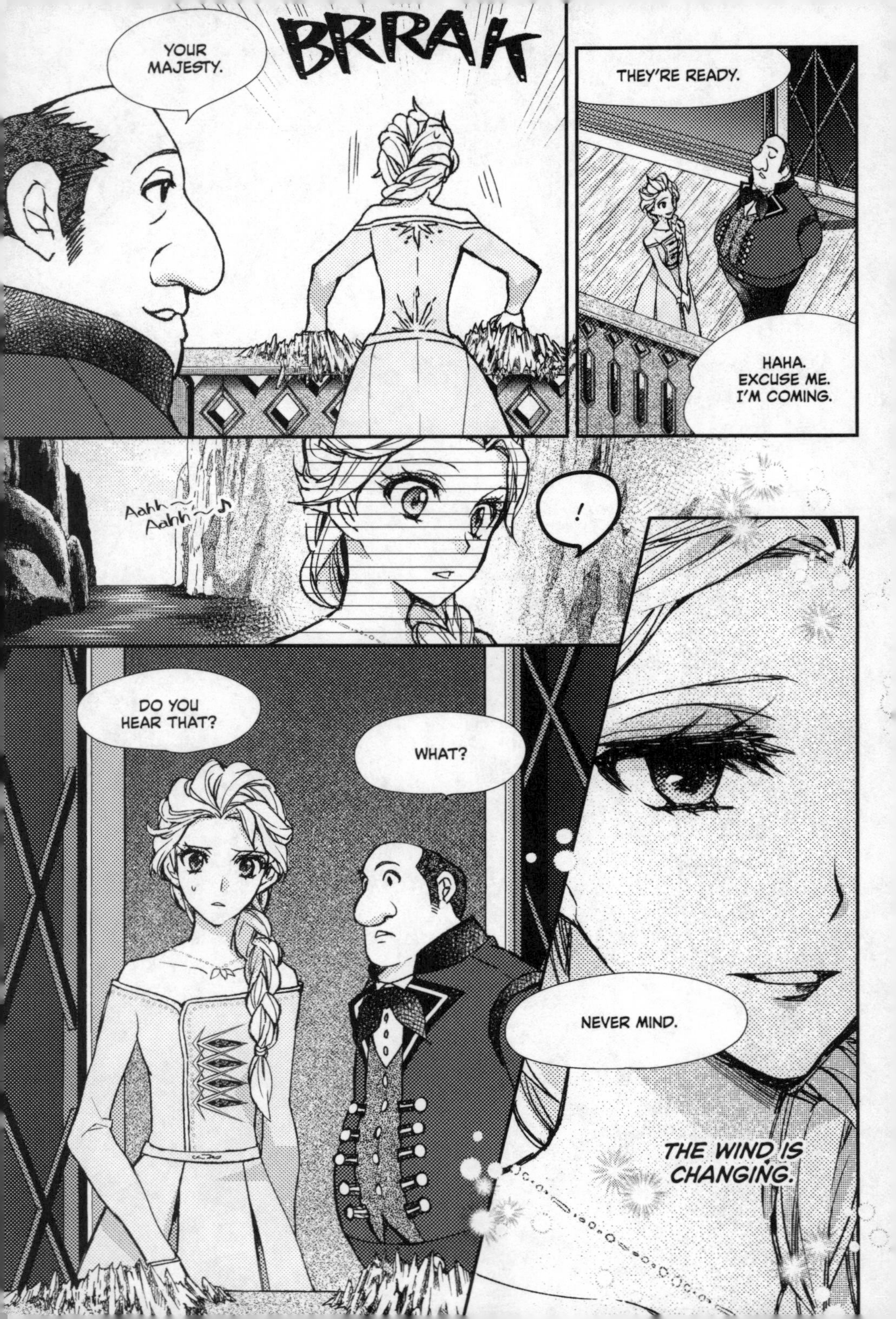
YOUR MAJESTY.
BRRAK
THEY'RE READY.
HAHA. EXCUSE ME. I'M COMING.
Aahh~ Aahh~♪
!
DO YOU HEAR THAT?
WHAT?
NEVER MIND.
THE WIND IS CHANGING.

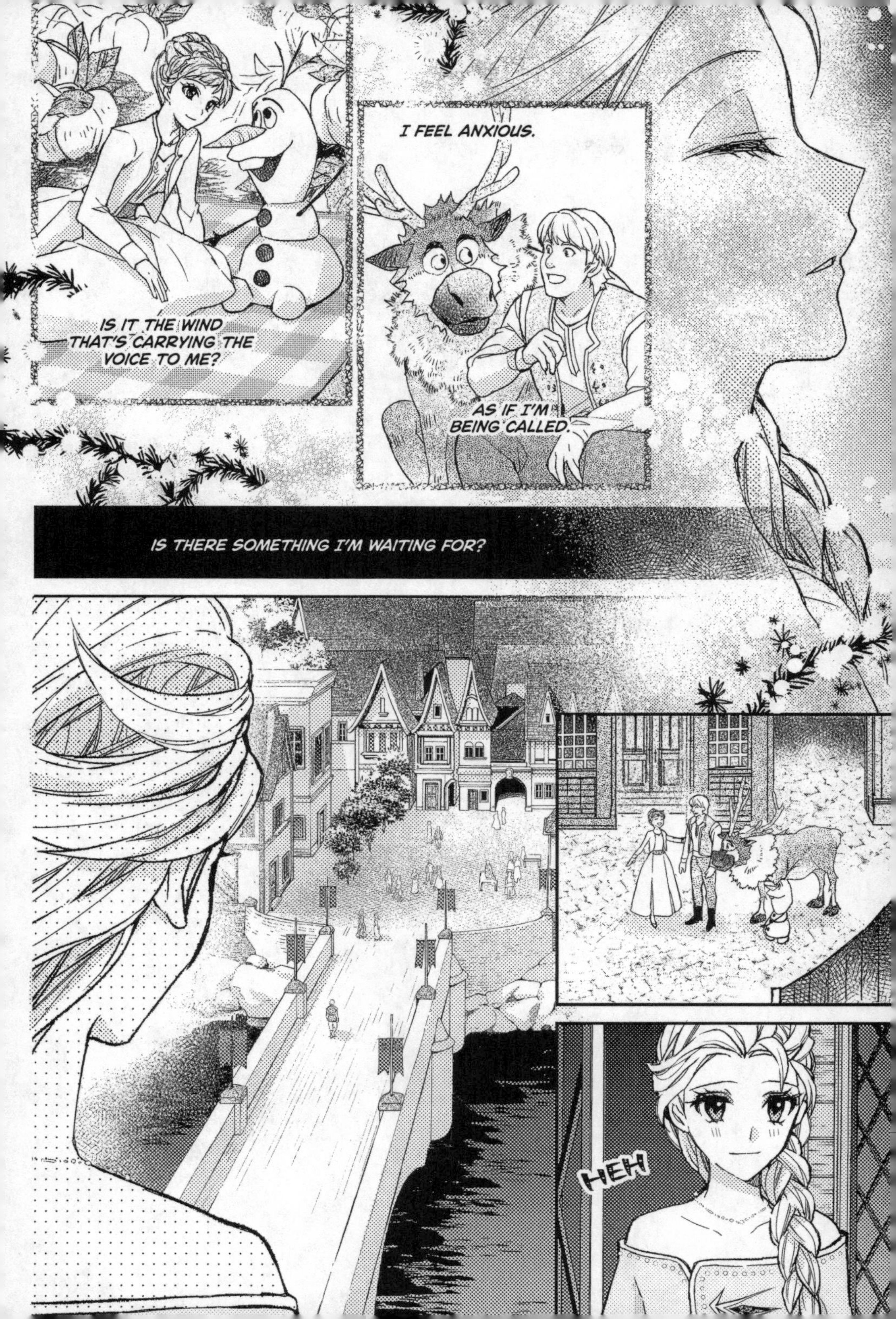
IS IT THE WIND THAT'S CARRYING THE VOICE TO ME?
I FEEL ANXIOUS.
AS IF I'M BEING CALLED.
IS THERE SOMETHING I'M WAITING FOR?
HEH

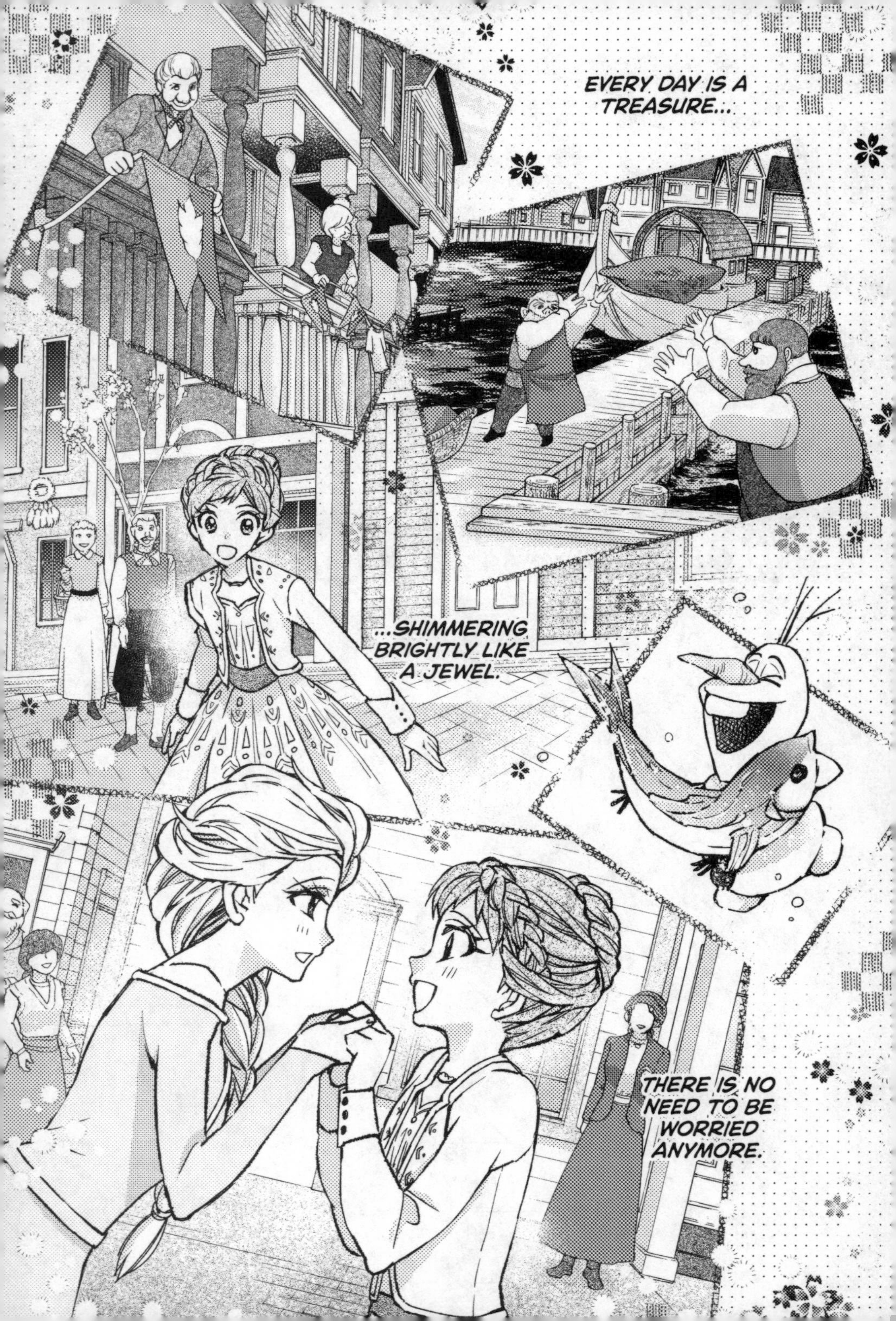
EVERY DAY IS A TREASURE...
...SHIMMERING BRIGHTLY LIKE A JEWEL.
THERE IS NO NEED TO BE WORRIED ANYMORE.

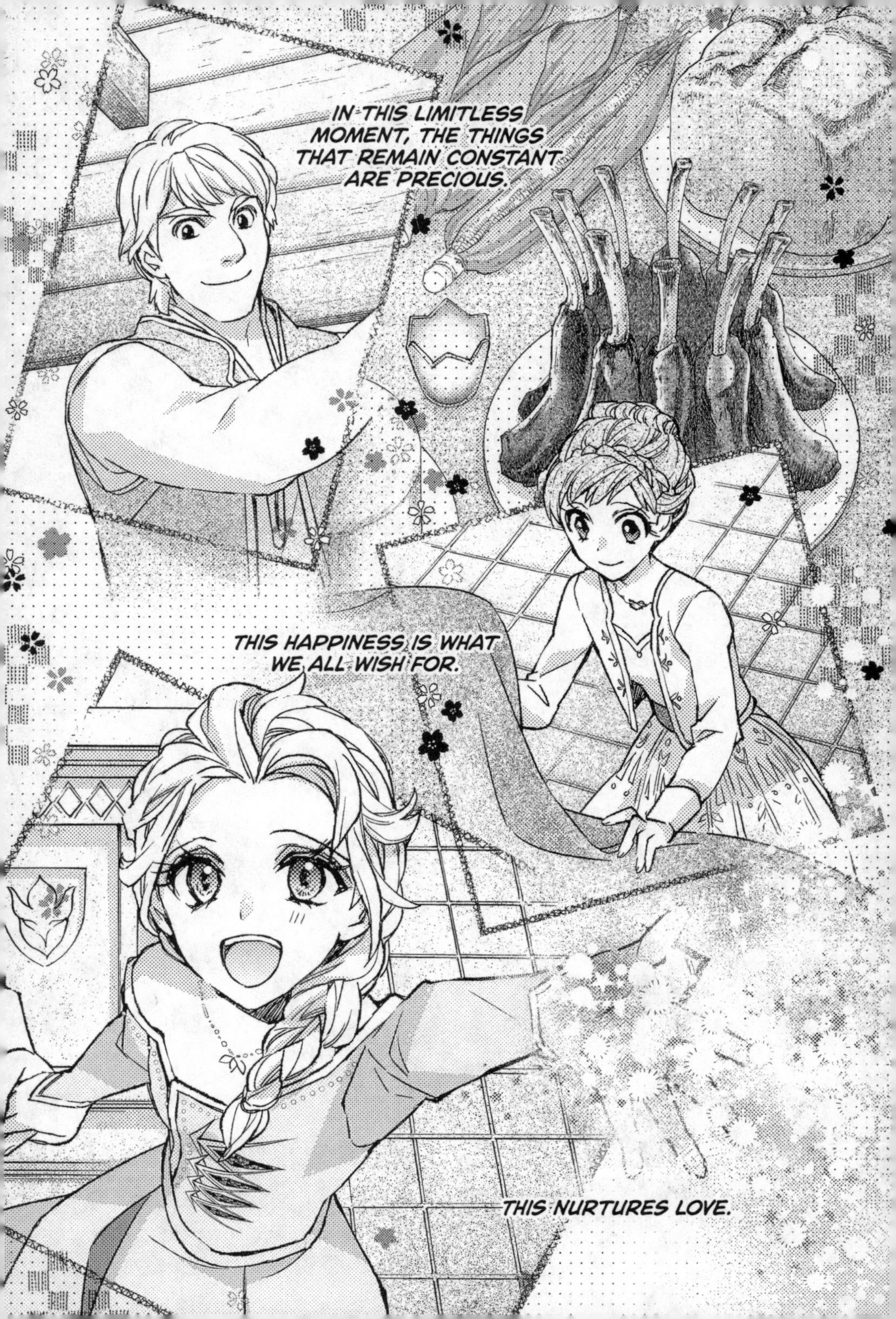
IN THIS LIMITLESS MOMENT, THE THINGS THAT REMAIN CONSTANT ARE PRECIOUS.
THIS HAPPINESS IS WHAT WE ALL WISH FOR.
THIS NURTURES LOVE.

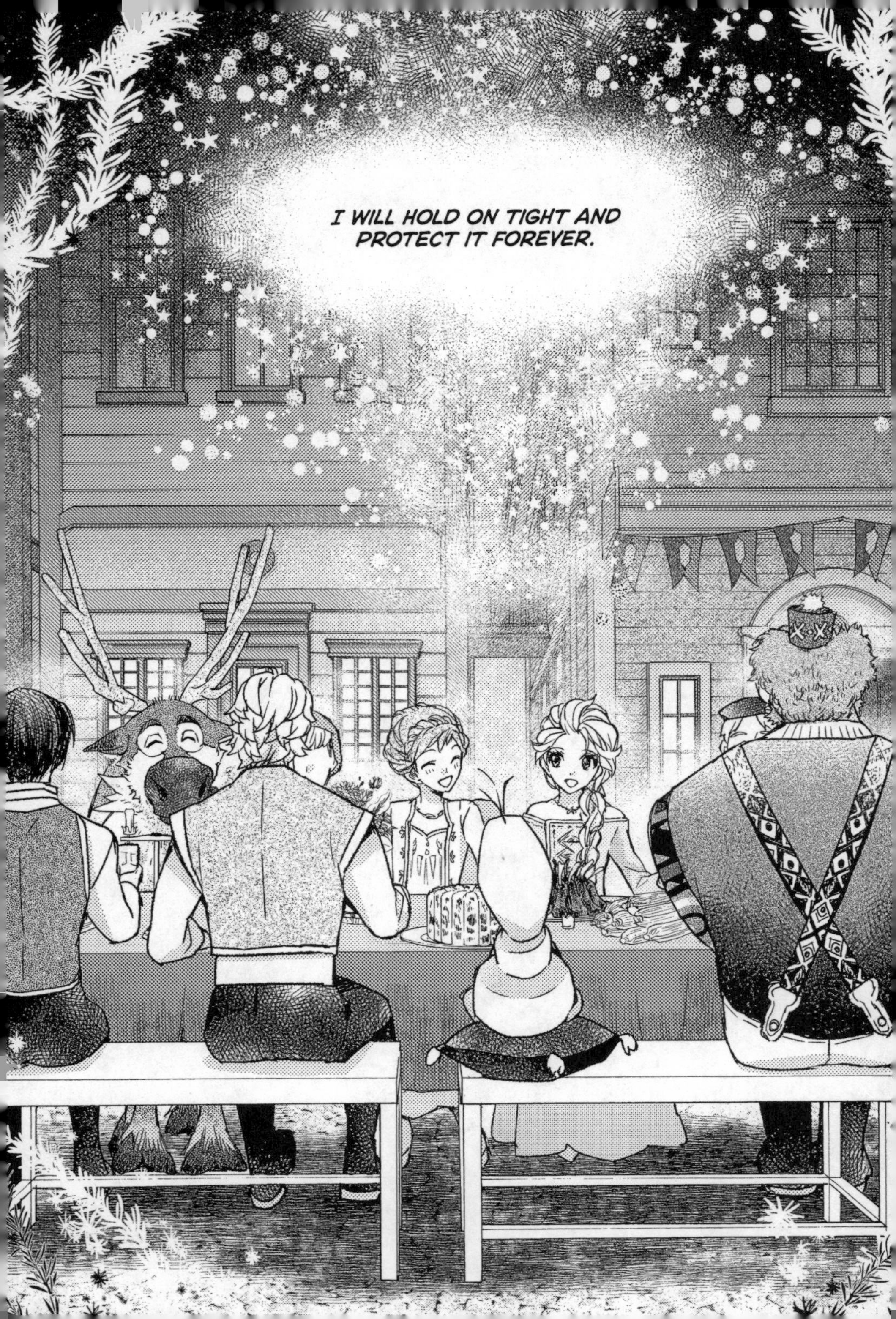
I WILL HOLD ON TIGHT AND PROTECT IT FOREVER.

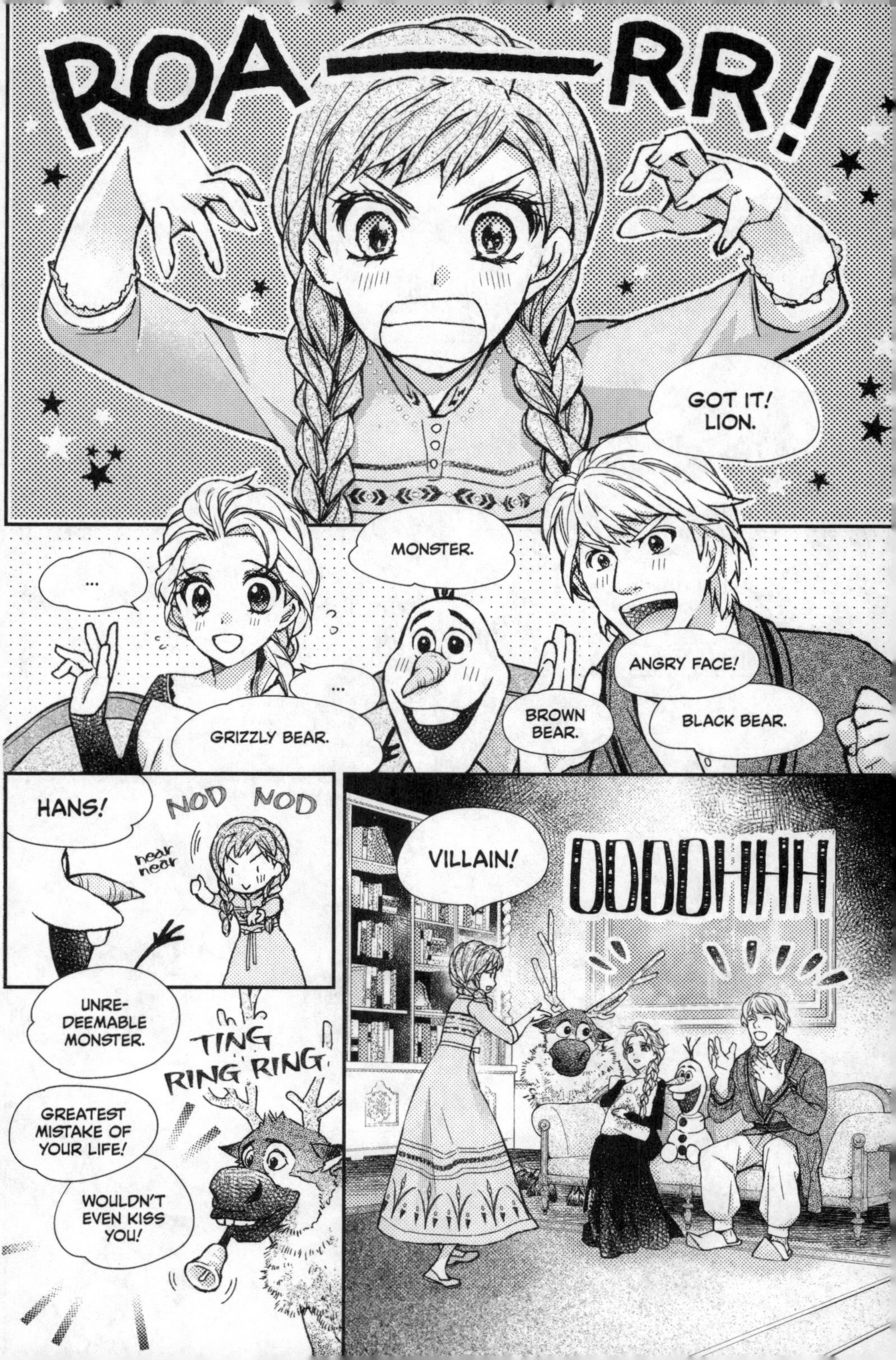
ROA——RR!
GOT IT! LION.
...
MONSTER.
...
GRIZZLY BEAR.
BROWN BEAR.
ANGRY FACE!
BLACK BEAR.
HANS!
NOD NOD
hear hear
VILLAIN!
OOOOHHHH
UNRE-DEEMABLE MONSTER.
TING RING RING
GREATEST MISTAKE OF YOUR LIFE!
WOULDN'T EVEN KISS YOU!

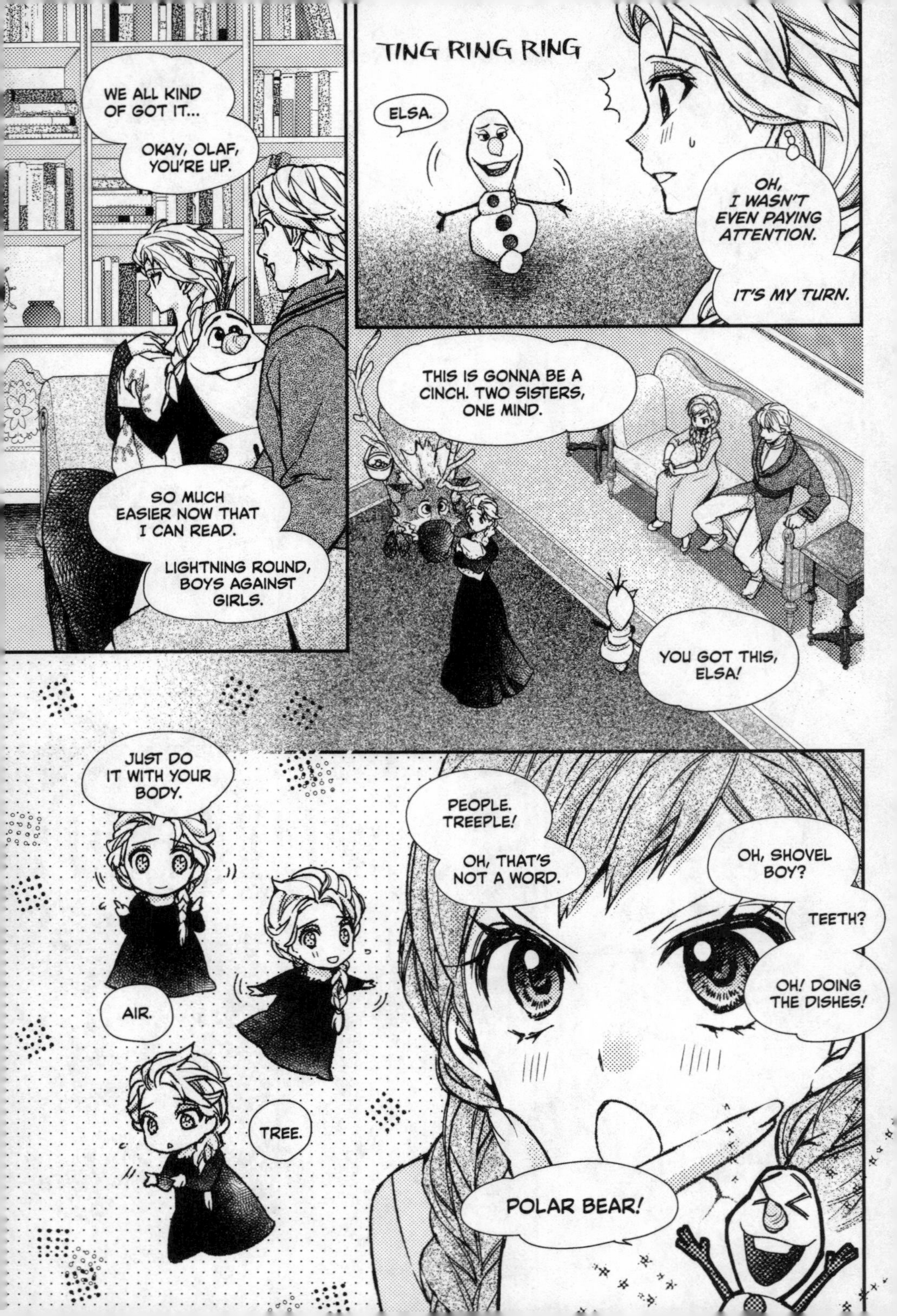
WE ALL KIND OF GOT IT...
OKAY, OLAF, YOU'RE UP.
SO MUCH EASIER NOW THAT I CAN READ.
LIGHTNING ROUND, BOYS AGAINST GIRLS.
TING RING RING
ELSA.
OH, I WASN'T EVEN PAYING ATTENTION.
IT'S MY TURN.
THIS IS GONNA BE A CINCH. TWO SISTERS, ONE MIND.
YOU GOT THIS, ELSA!
JUST DO IT WITH YOUR BODY.
AIR.
TREE.
PEOPLE. TREEPLE!
OH, THAT'S NOT A WORD.
OH, SHOVEL BOY?
TEETH?
OH! DOING THE DISHES!
POLAR BEAR!

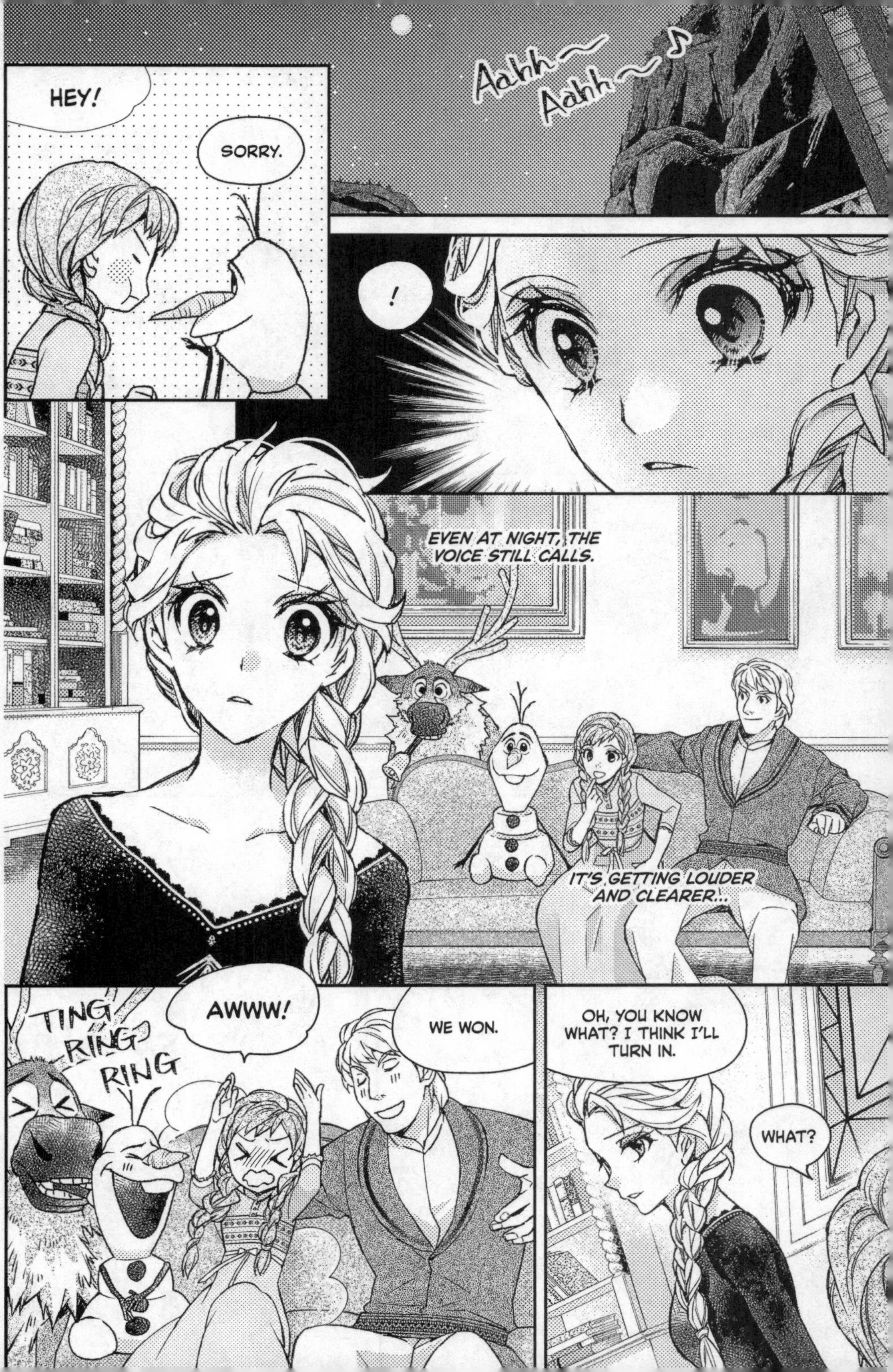
HEY!
SORRY.
Aahh~ Aahh~♪
!
EVEN AT NIGHT, THE VOICE STILL CALLS.
IT'S GETTING LOUDER AND CLEARER...
TING RING RING
AWWW!
WE WON.
OH, YOU KNOW WHAT? I THINK I'LL TURN IN.
WHAT?

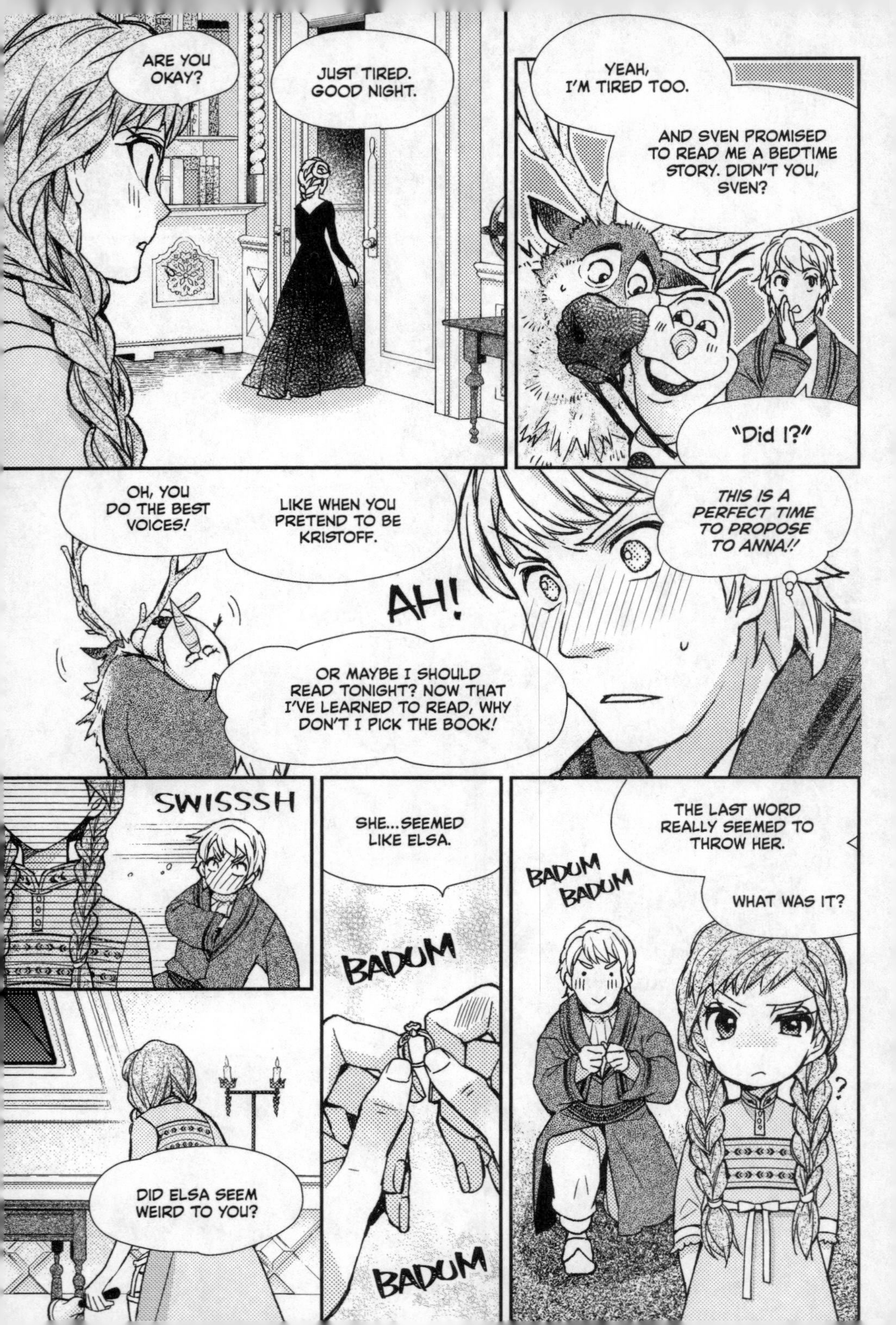
ARE YOU OKAY?
JUST TIRED. GOOD NIGHT.
YEAH, I'M TIRED TOO.
AND SVEN PROMISED TO READ ME A BEDTIME STORY. DIDN'T YOU, SVEN?
"Did I?"
OH, YOU DO THE BEST VOICES!
LIKE WHEN YOU PRETEND TO BE KRISTOFF.
THIS IS A PERFECT TIME TO PROPOSE TO ANNA!!
AH!
OR MAYBE I SHOULD READ TONIGHT? NOW THAT I'VE LEARNED TO READ, WHY DON'T I PICK THE BOOK!
SWISSSH
DID ELSA SEEM WEIRD TO YOU?
SHE...SEEMED LIKE ELSA.
BADUM
BADUM
THE LAST WORD REALLY SEEMED TO THROW HER.
BADUM BADUM
WHAT WAS IT?
?

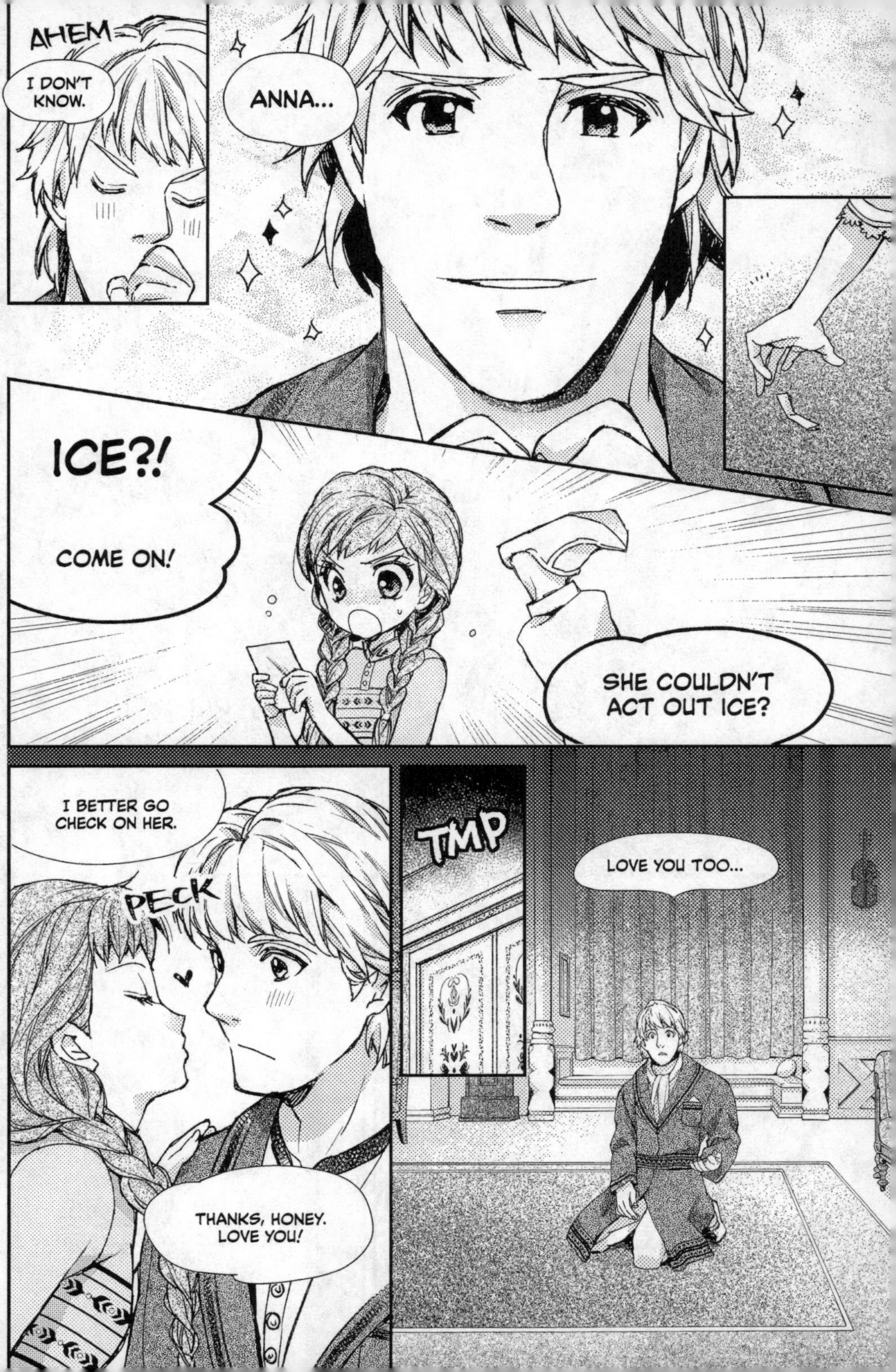
AHEM
I DON'T KNOW.
ANNA...
ICE?!
COME ON!
SHE COULDN'T ACT OUT ICE?
I BETTER GO CHECK ON HER.
PECK
THANKS, HONEY. LOVE YOU!
TMP
LOVE YOU TOO...

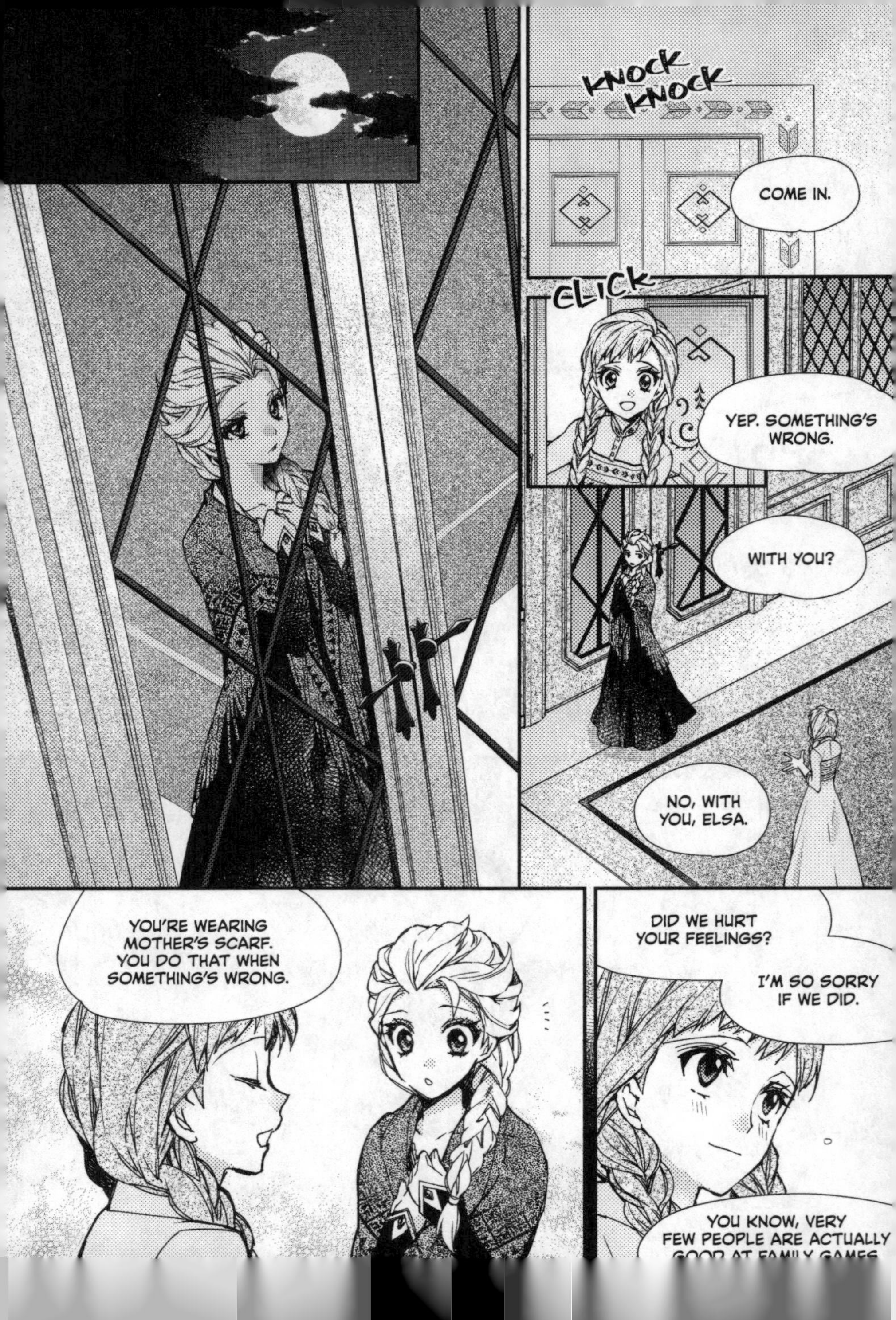
KNOCK KNOCK
COME IN.
CLICK
YEP. SOMETHING'S WRONG.
WITH YOU?
NO, WITH YOU, ELSA.
YOU'RE WEARING MOTHER'S SCARF. YOU DO THAT WHEN SOMETHING'S WRONG.
DID WE HURT YOUR FEELINGS?
I'M SO SORRY IF WE DID.
YOU KNOW, VERY FEW PEOPLE ARE ACTUALLY

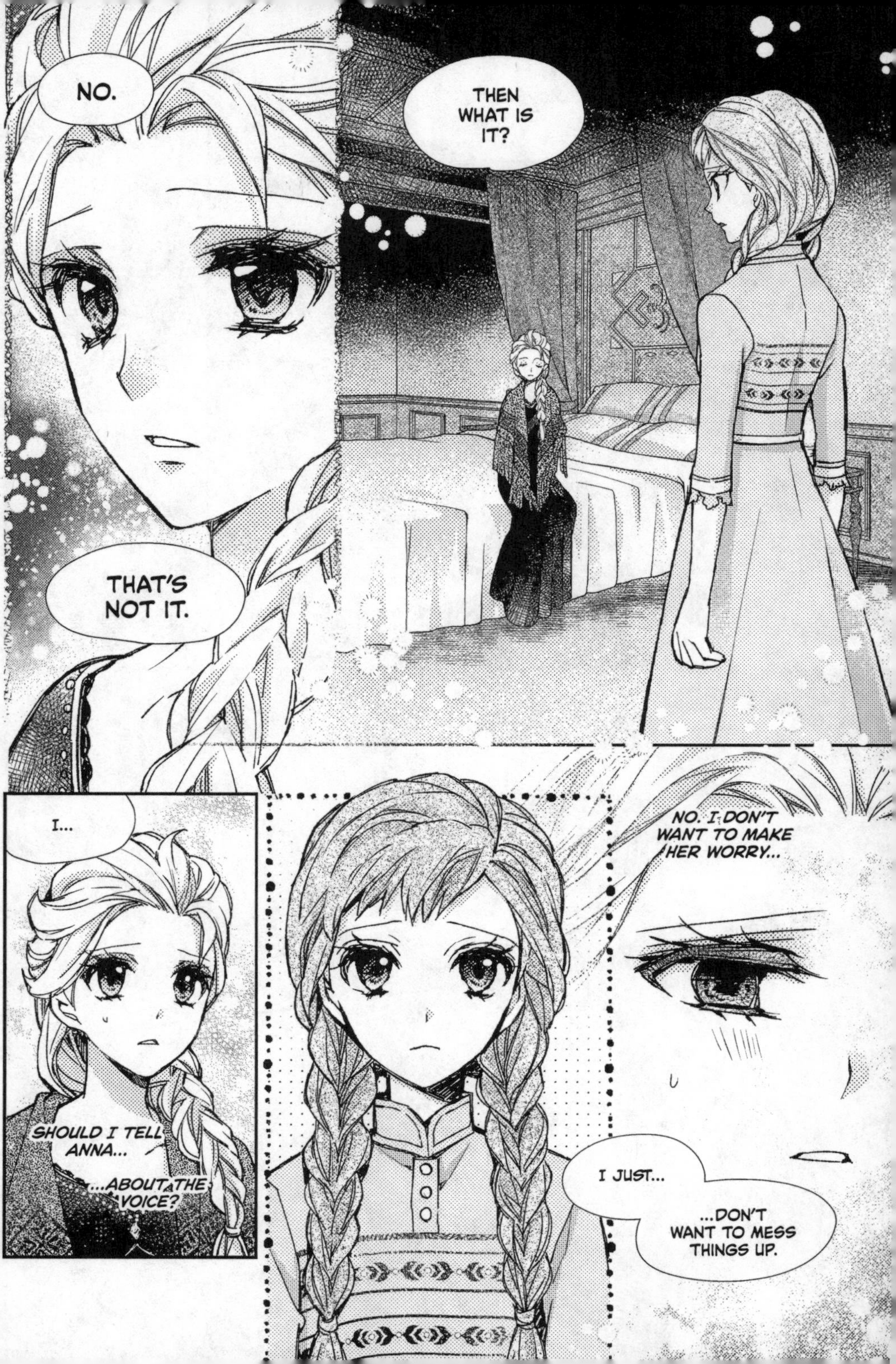
NO.
THAT'S NOT IT.
THEN WHAT IS IT?
I...
SHOULD I TELL ANNA...
...ABOUT THE VOICE?
NO. I DON'T WANT TO MAKE HER WORRY...
I JUST...
...DON'T WANT TO MESS THINGS UP.

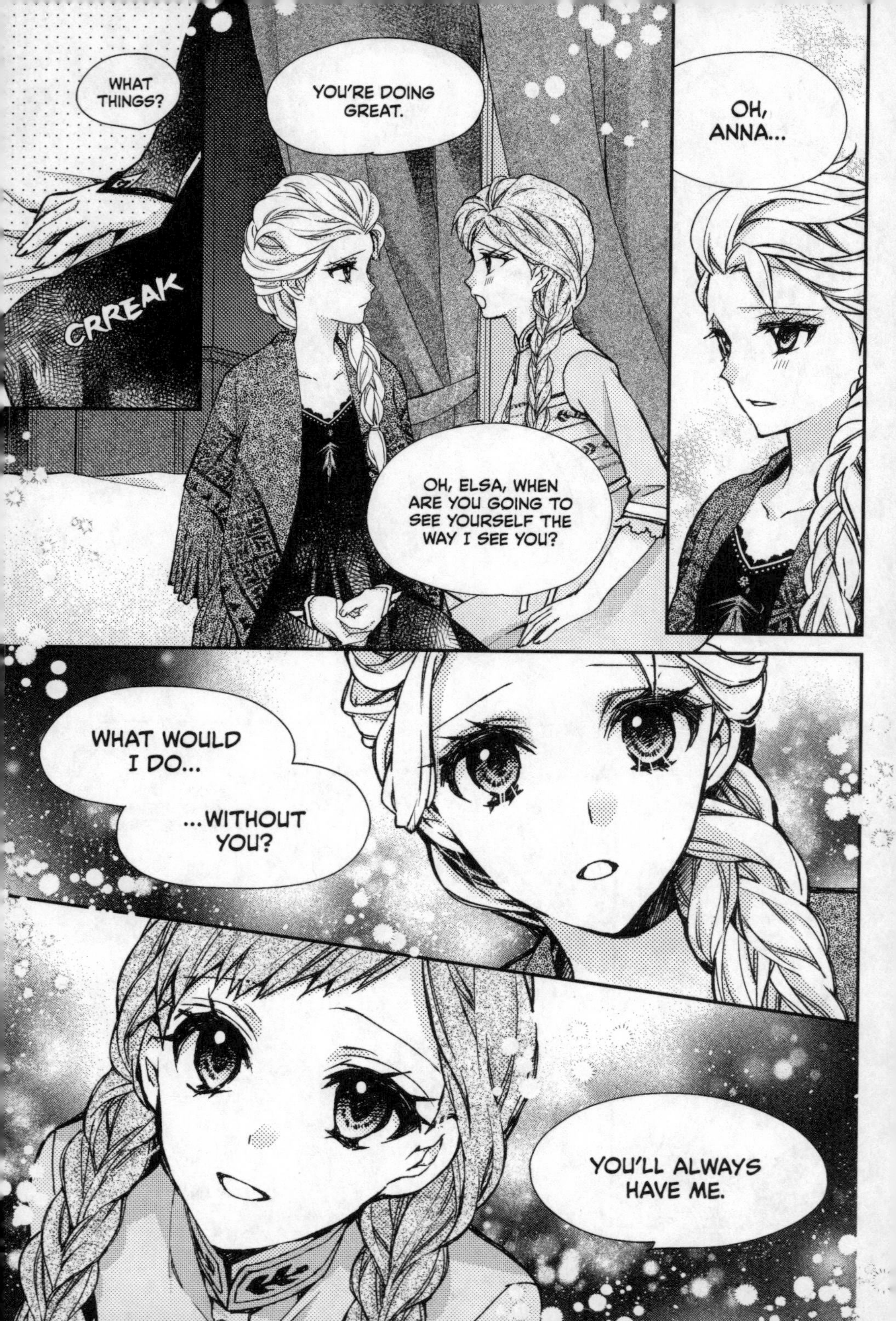
WHAT THINGS?
CRREAK
YOU'RE DOING GREAT.
OH, ELSA, WHEN ARE YOU GOING TO SEE YOURSELF THE WAY I SEE YOU?
OH, ANNA...
WHAT WOULD I DO...
...WITHOUT YOU?
YOU'LL ALWAYS HAVE ME.

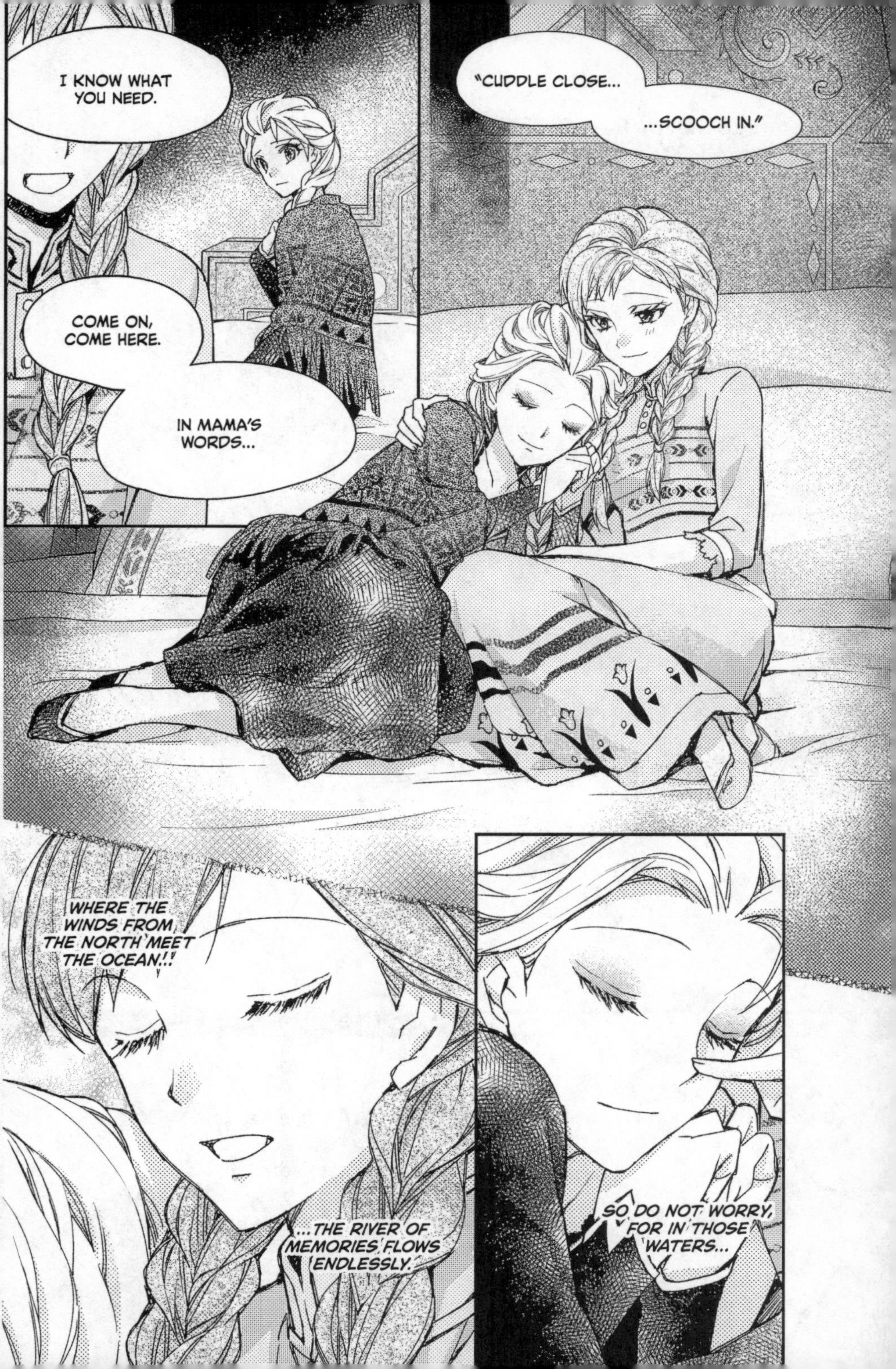
I KNOW WHAT YOU NEED.
COME ON, COME HERE.
IN MAMA'S WORDS...
"CUDDLE CLOSE...
...SCOOCH IN."
WHERE THE WINDS FROM THE NORTH MEET THE OCEAN...
...THE RIVER OF MEMORIES FLOWS ENDLESSLY.
SO DO NOT WORRY, FOR IN THOSE WATERS...

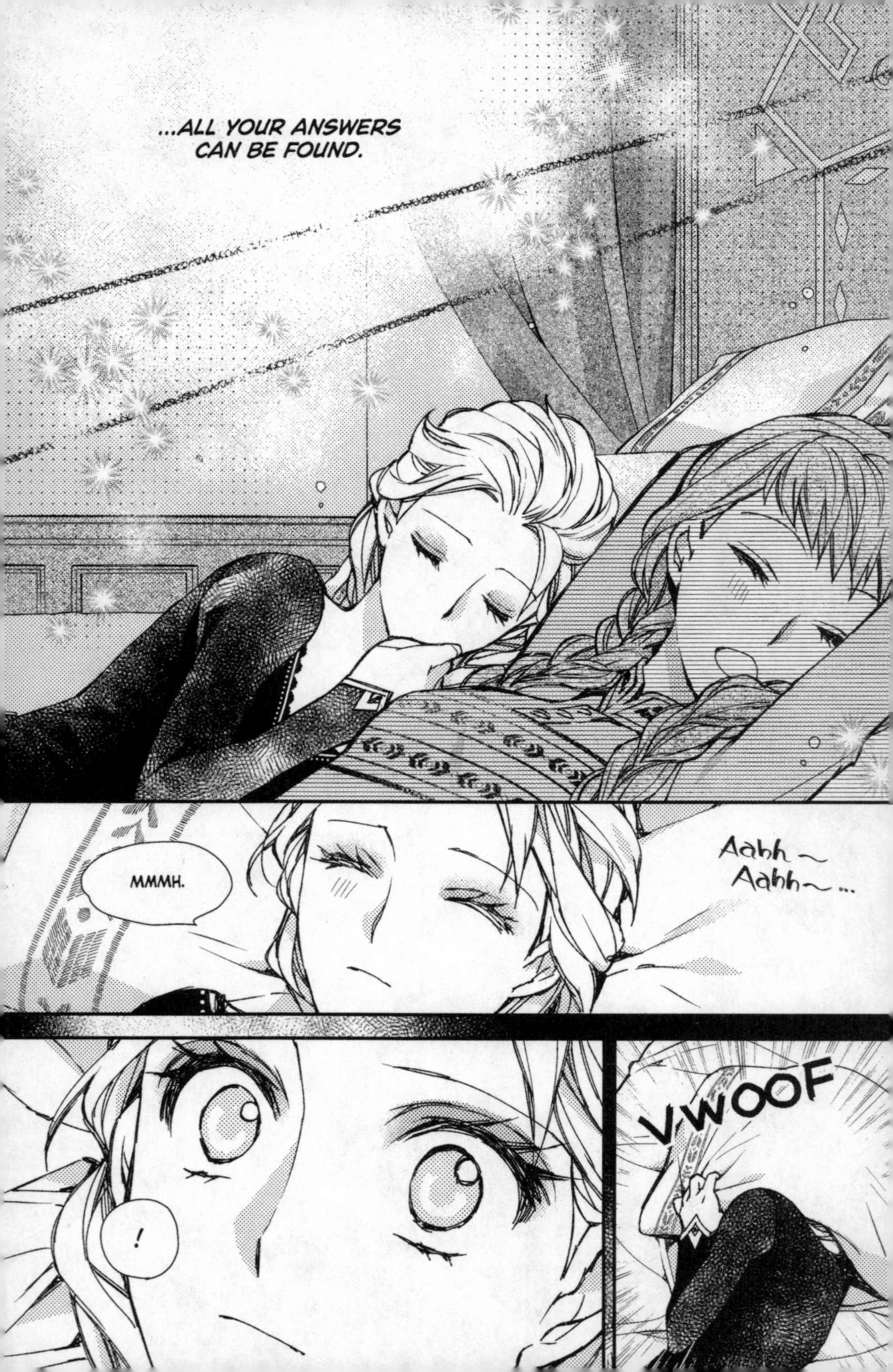
...ALL YOUR ANSWERS CAN BE FOUND.
MMMH.
Aahh~ Aahh~...
!
V-WOOF

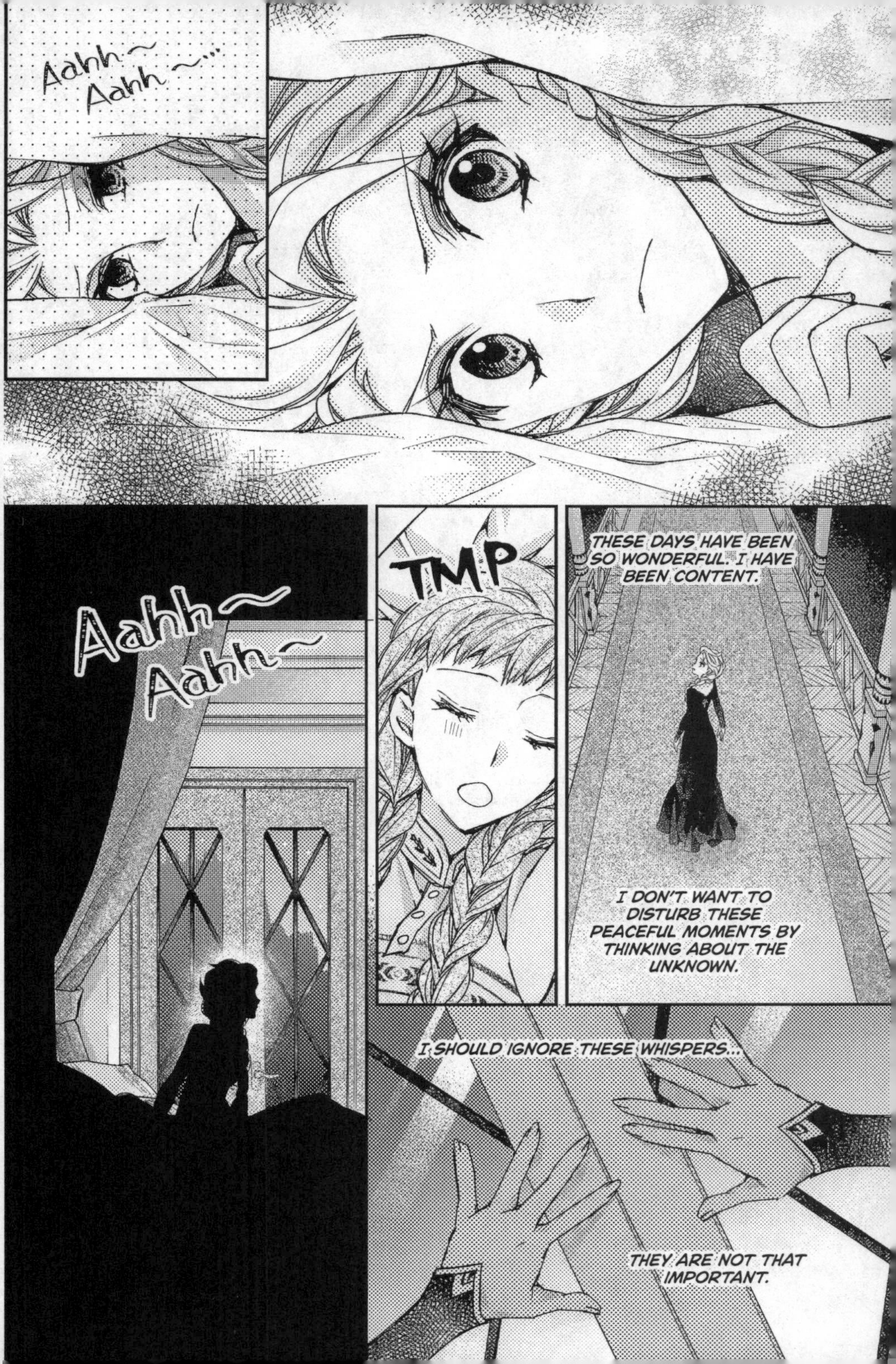
Aahh~ Aahh~...
Aahh~ Aahh~
TMP
THESE DAYS HAVE BEEN SO WONDERFUL. I HAVE BEEN CONTENT.
I DON'T WANT TO DISTURB THESE PEACEFUL MOMENTS BY THINKING ABOUT THE UNKNOWN.
I SHOULD IGNORE THESE WHISPERS...
THEY ARE NOT THAT IMPORTANT.

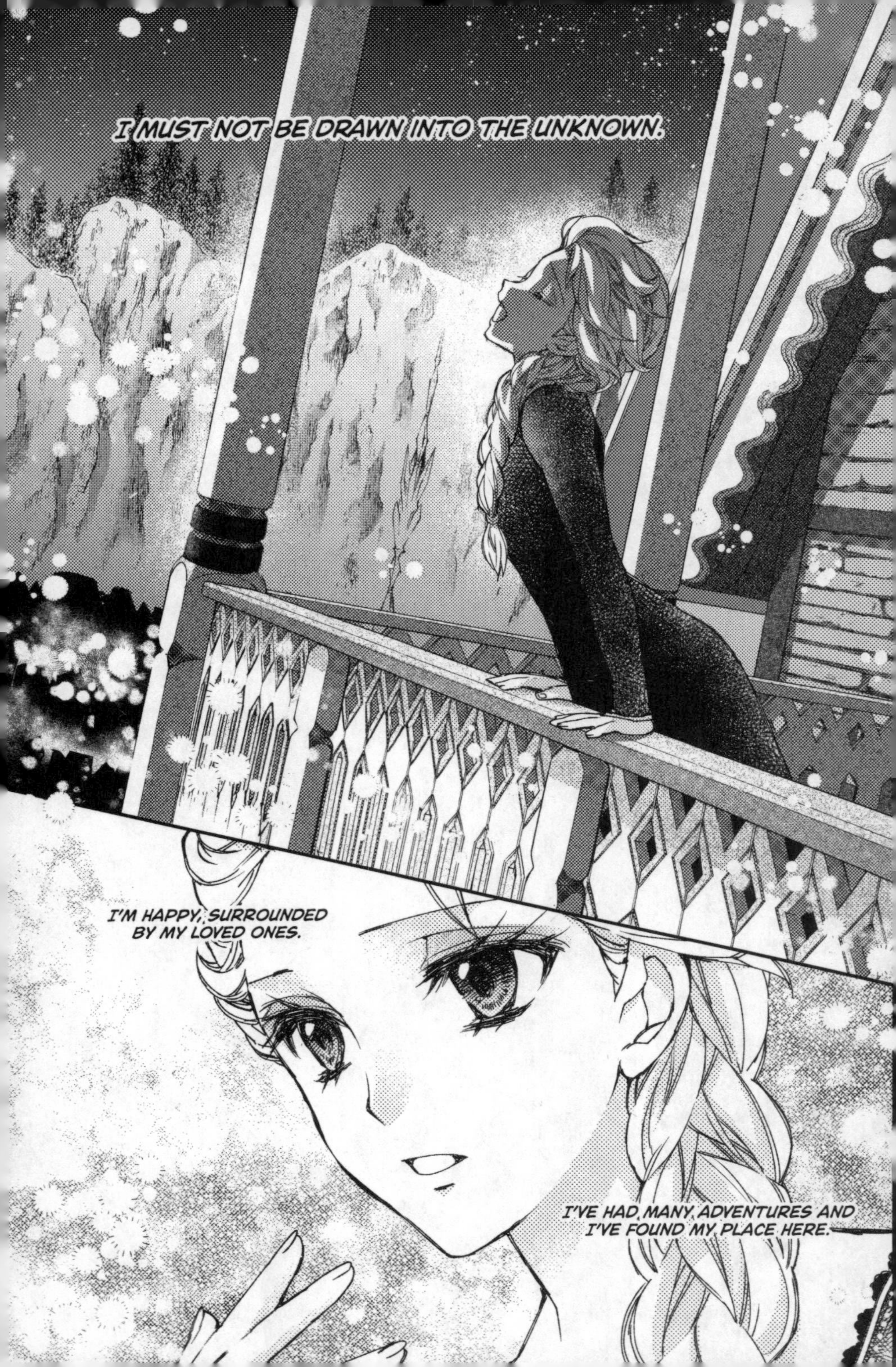
I MUST NOT BE DRAWN INTO THE UNKNOWN.
I'M HAPPY, SURROUNDED BY MY LOVED ONES.
I'VE HAD MANY ADVENTURES AND I'VE FOUND MY PLACE HERE.

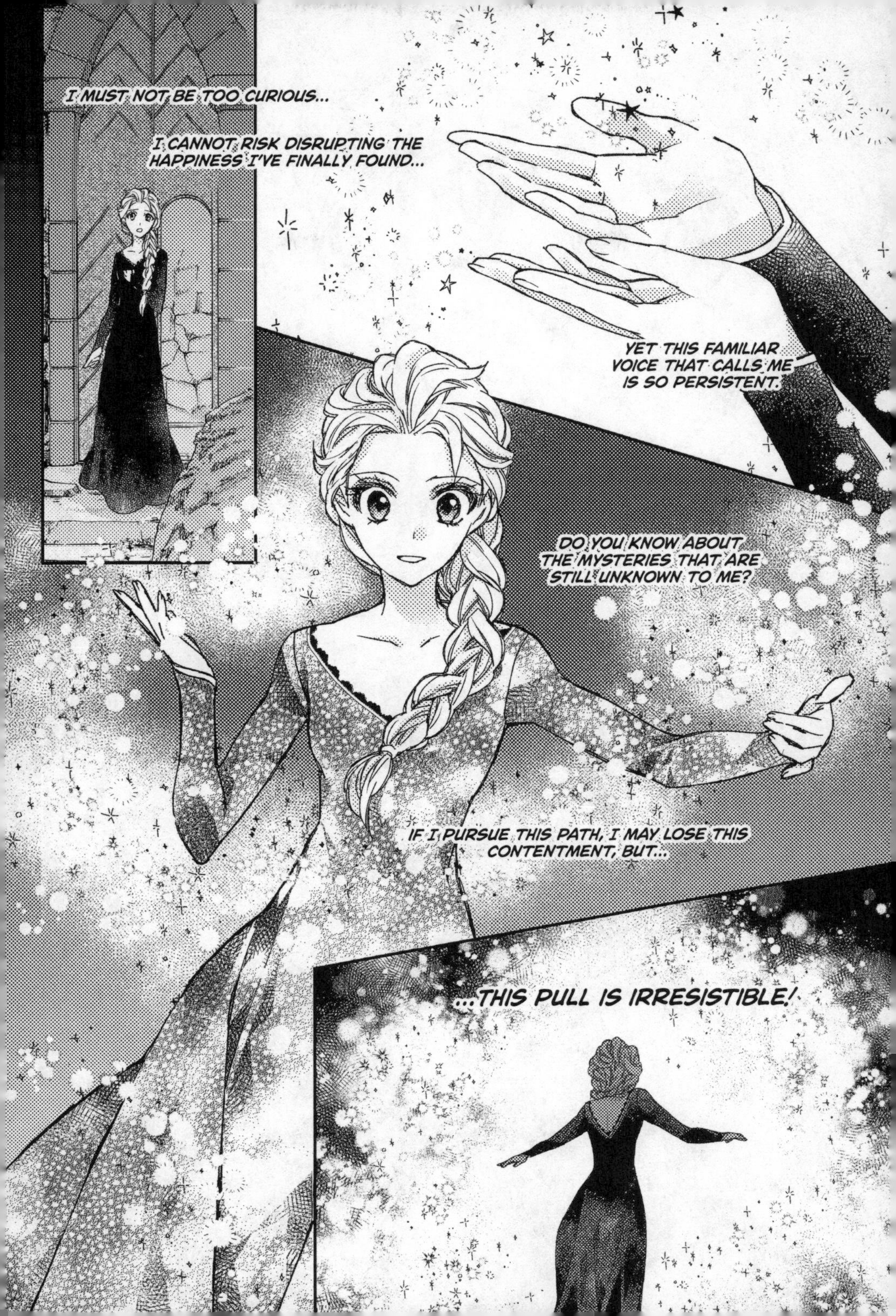
I MUST NOT BE TOO CURIOUS...
I CANNOT RISK DISRUPTING THE HAPPINESS I'VE FINALLY FOUND...
YET THIS FAMILIAR VOICE THAT CALLS ME IS SO PERSISTENT.
DO YOU KNOW ABOUT THE MYSTERIES THAT ARE STILL UNKNOWN TO ME?
IF I PURSUE THIS PATH, I MAY LOSE THIS CONTENTMENT, BUT...
...THIS PULL IS IRRESISTIBLE!

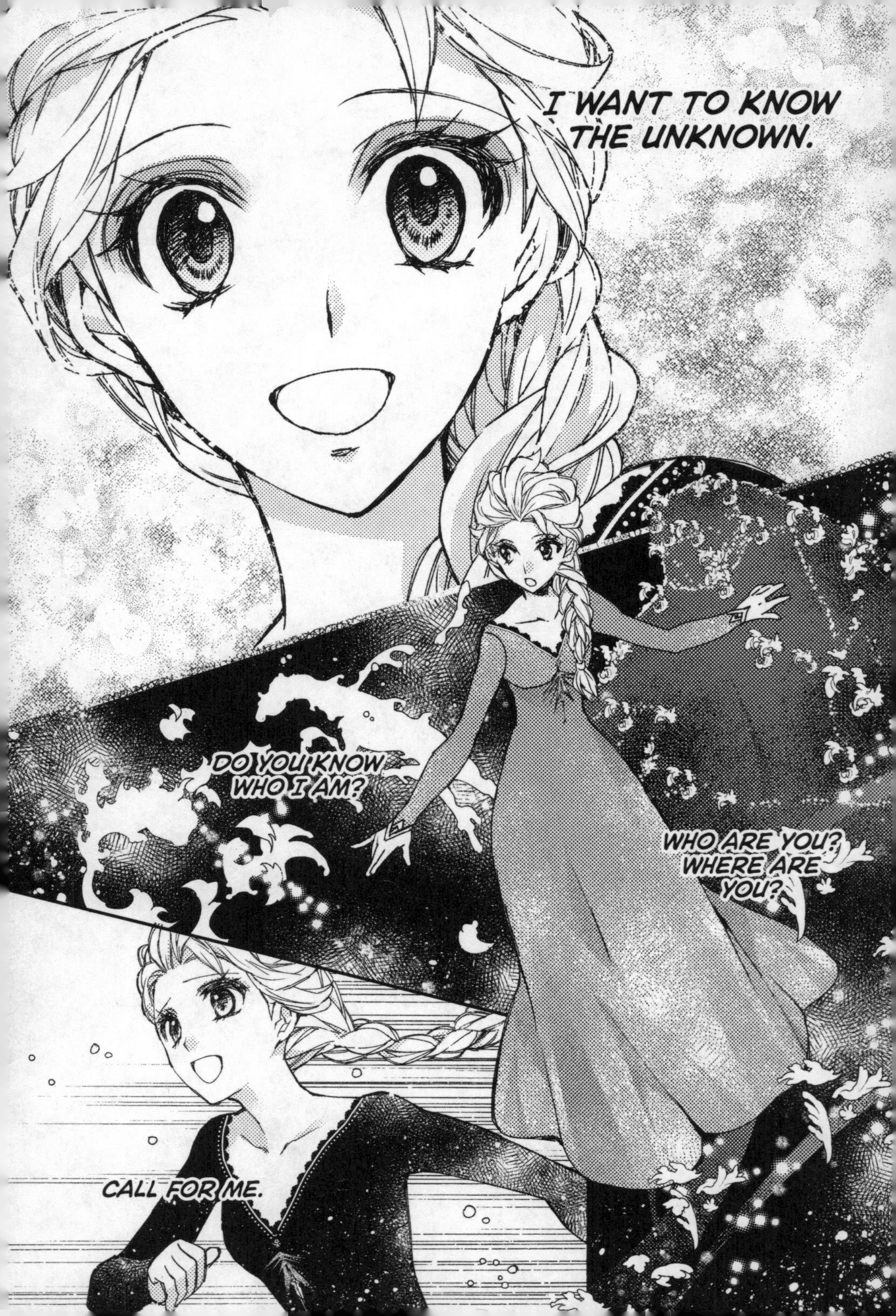
I WANT TO KNOW THE UNKNOWN.
DO YOU KNOW WHO I AM?
WHO ARE YOU? WHERE ARE YOU?
CALL FOR ME.

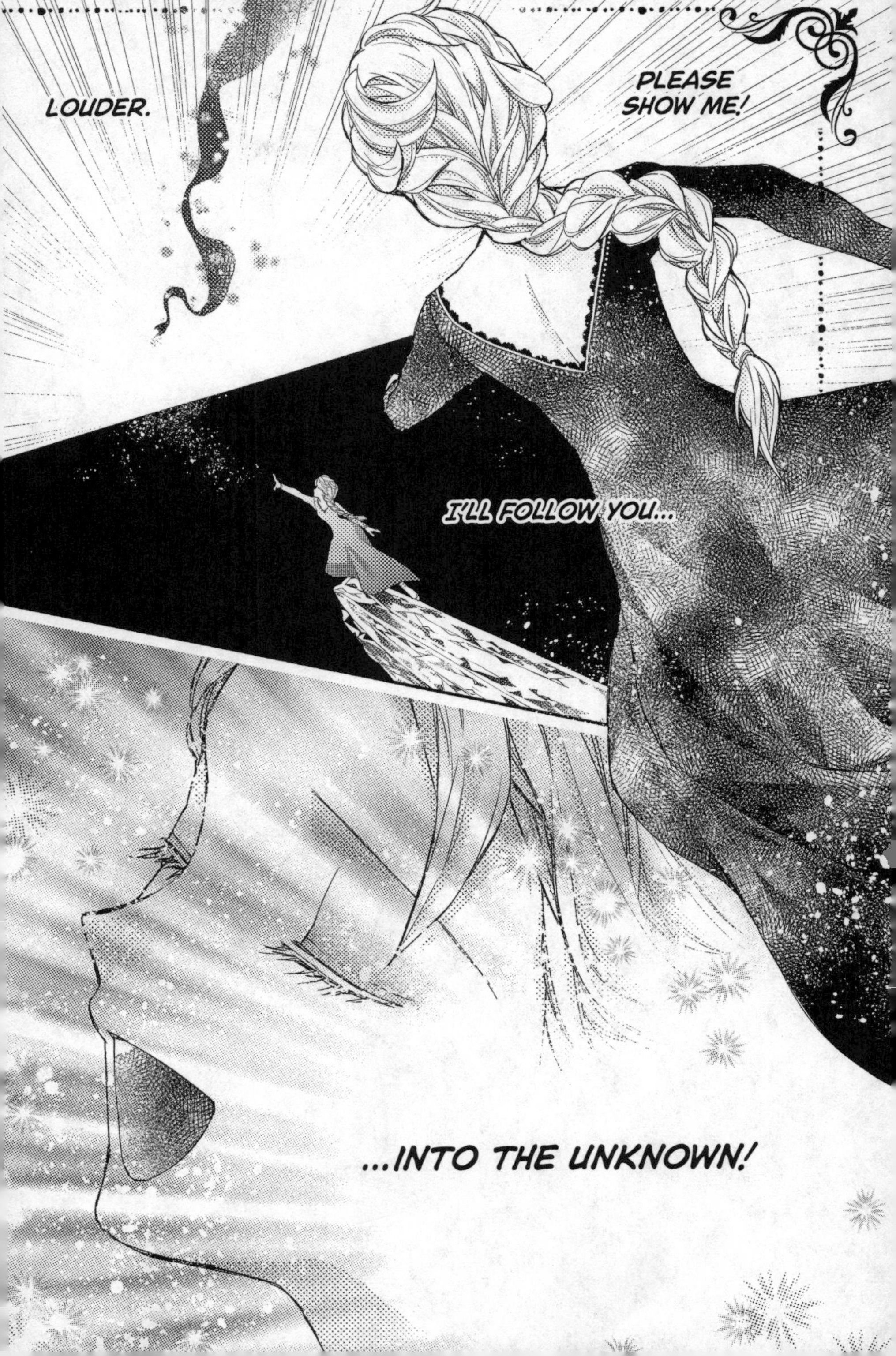
LOUDER.
PLEASE SHOW ME!
I'LL FOLLOW YOU...
...INTO THE UNKNOWN!

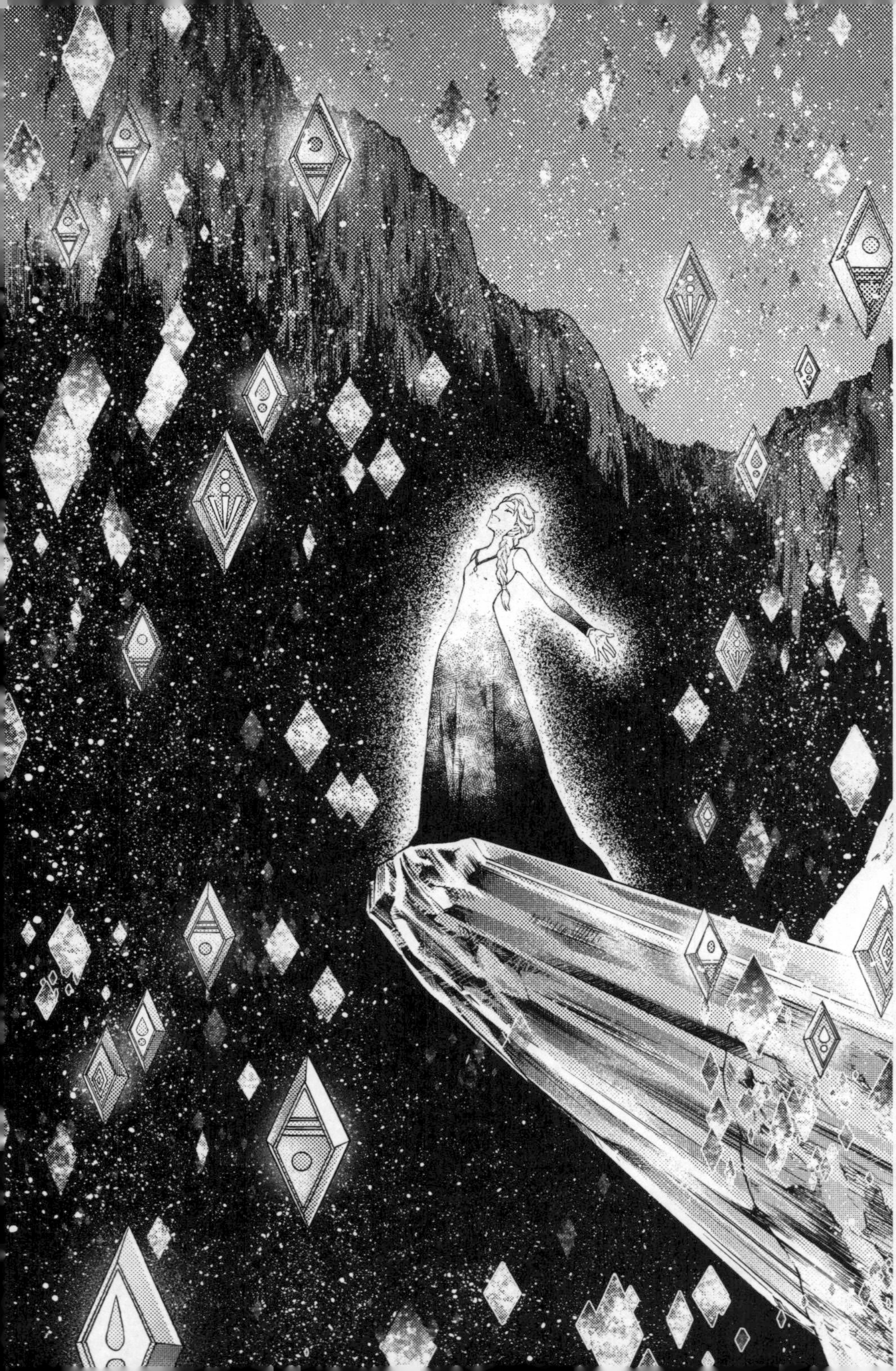

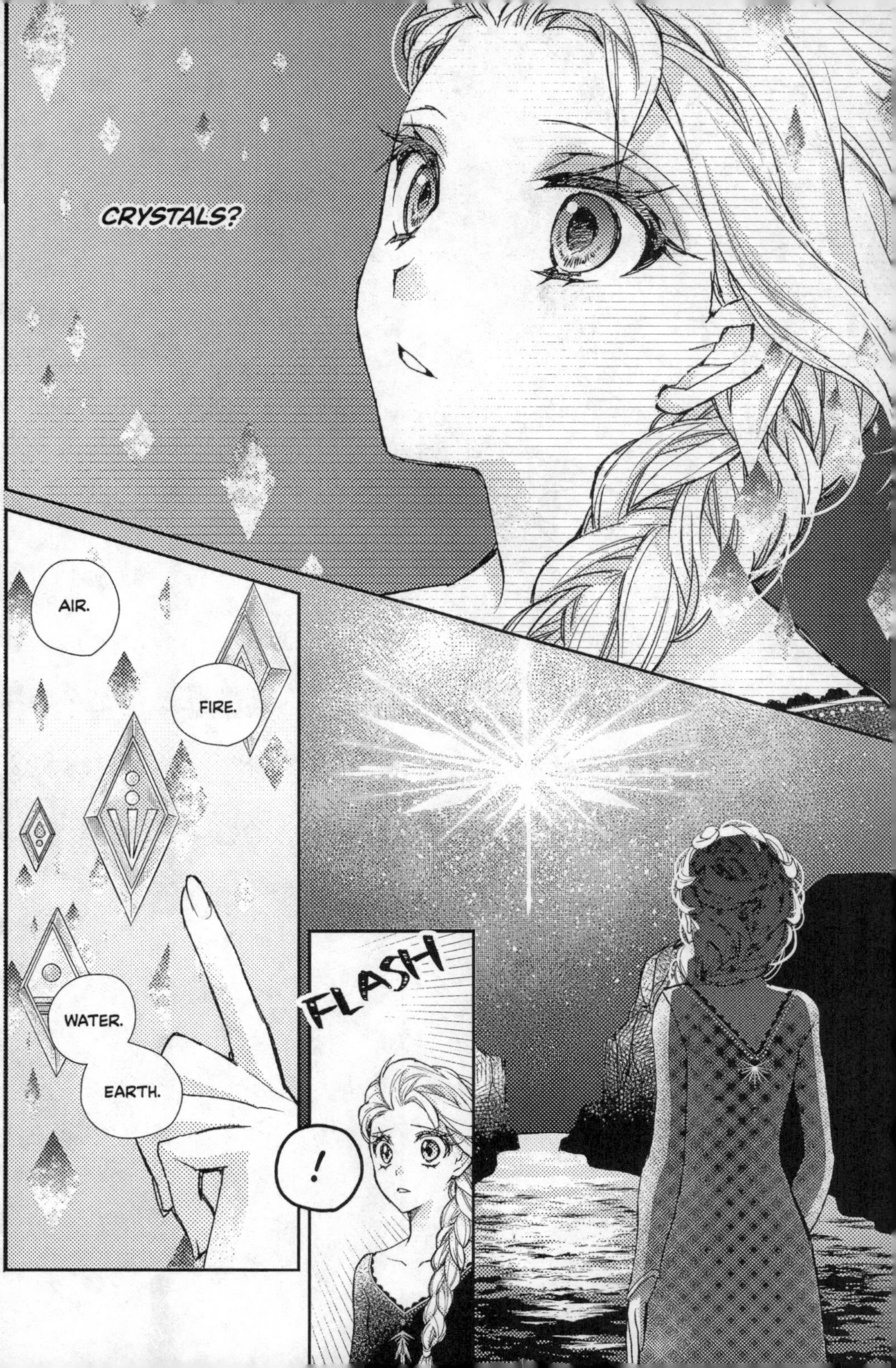
CRYSTALS?
AIR.
FIRE.
WATER.
EARTH.
FLASH
!

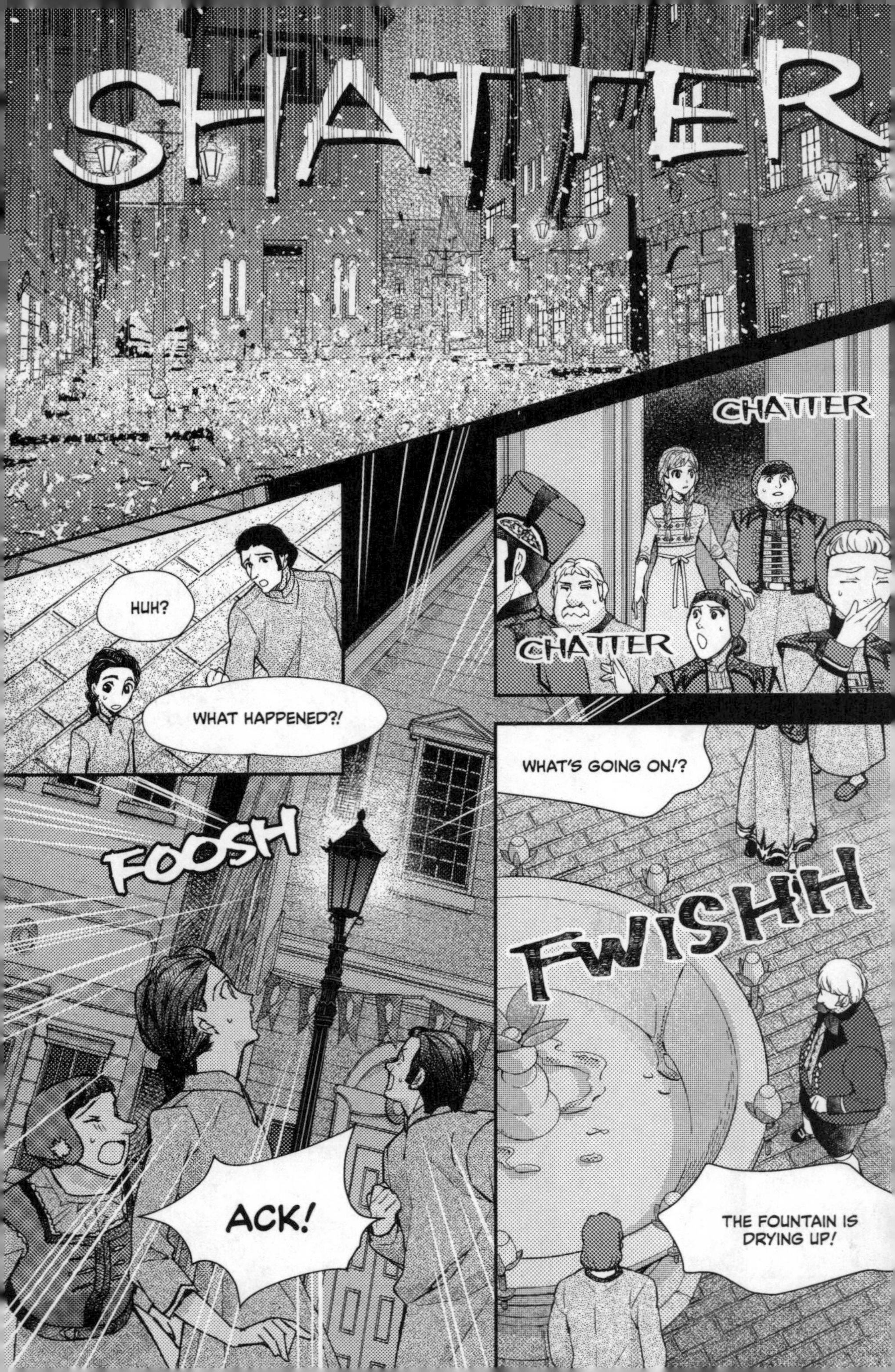
SHATTER
HUH?
WHAT HAPPENED?!
CHATTER
CHATTER
FOOSH
ACK!
WHAT'S GOING ON!?
FWISHH
THE FOUNTAIN IS DRYING UP!

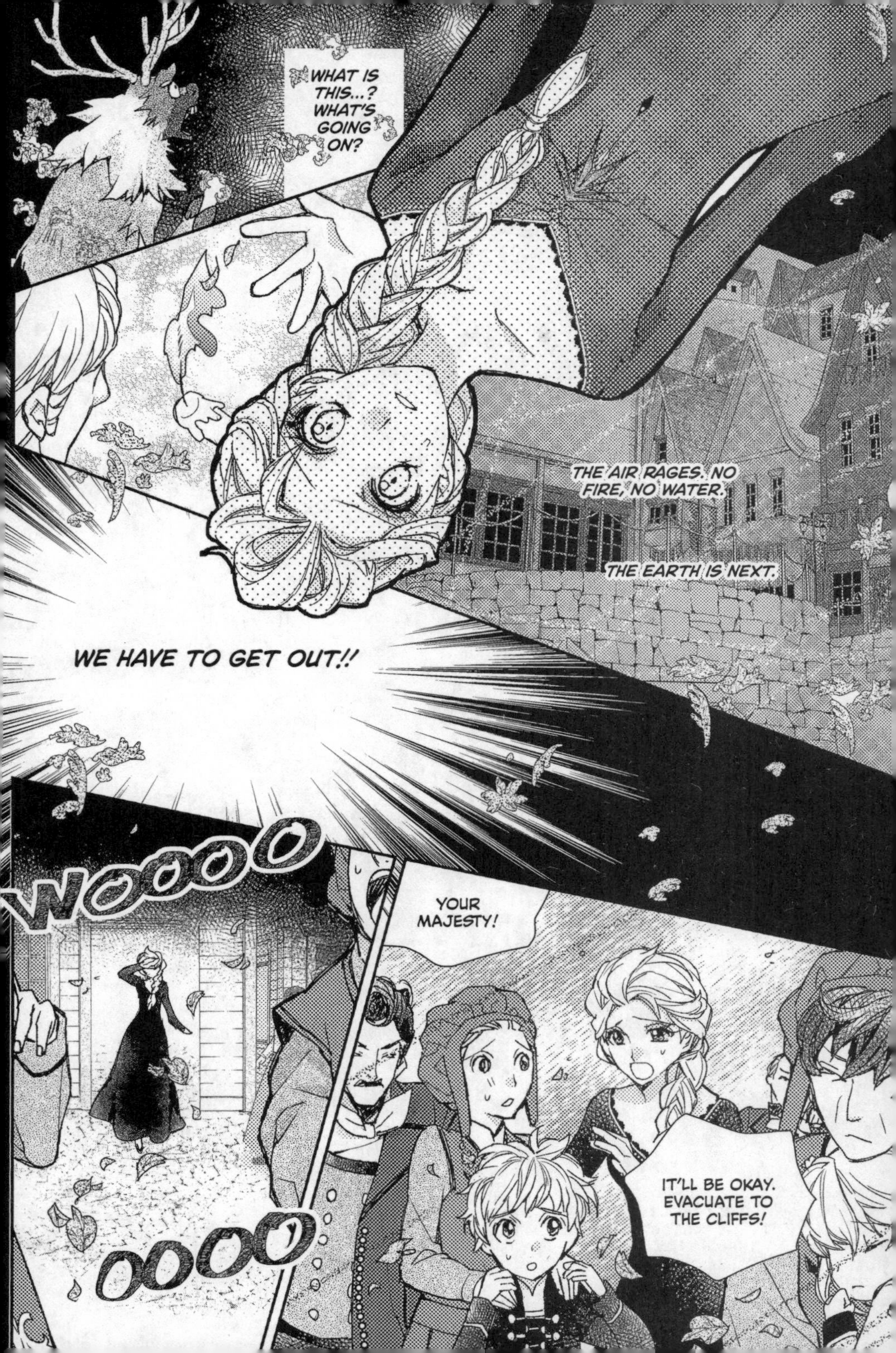
WHAT IS THIS...? WHAT'S GOING ON?
THE AIR RAGES. NO FIRE, NO WATER.
THE EARTH IS NEXT.
WE HAVE TO GET OUT!!
WOOOOO
OOOOO
YOUR MAJESTY!
IT'LL BE OKAY. EVACUATE TO THE CLIFFS!

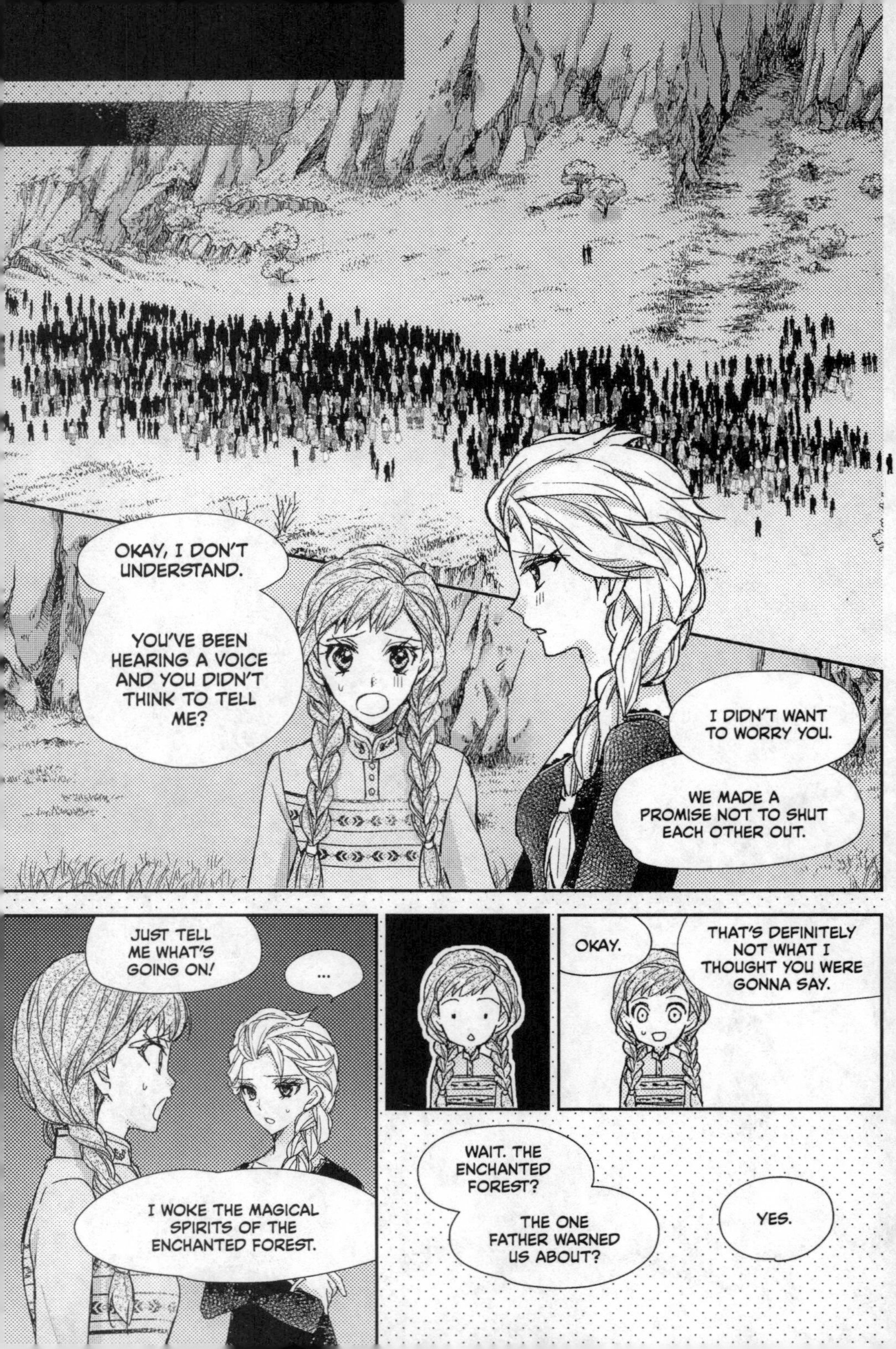
OKAY, I DON'T UNDERSTAND.
YOU'VE BEEN HEARING A VOICE AND YOU DIDN'T THINK TO TELL ME?
I DIDN'T WANT TO WORRY YOU.
WE MADE A PROMISE NOT TO SHUT EACH OTHER OUT.
JUST TELL ME WHAT'S GOING ON!
...
I WOKE THE MAGICAL SPIRITS OF THE ENCHANTED FOREST.
OKAY.
THAT'S DEFINITELY NOT WHAT I THOUGHT YOU WERE GONNA SAY.
WAIT. THE ENCHANTED FOREST?
THE ONE FATHER WARNED US ABOUT?
YES.

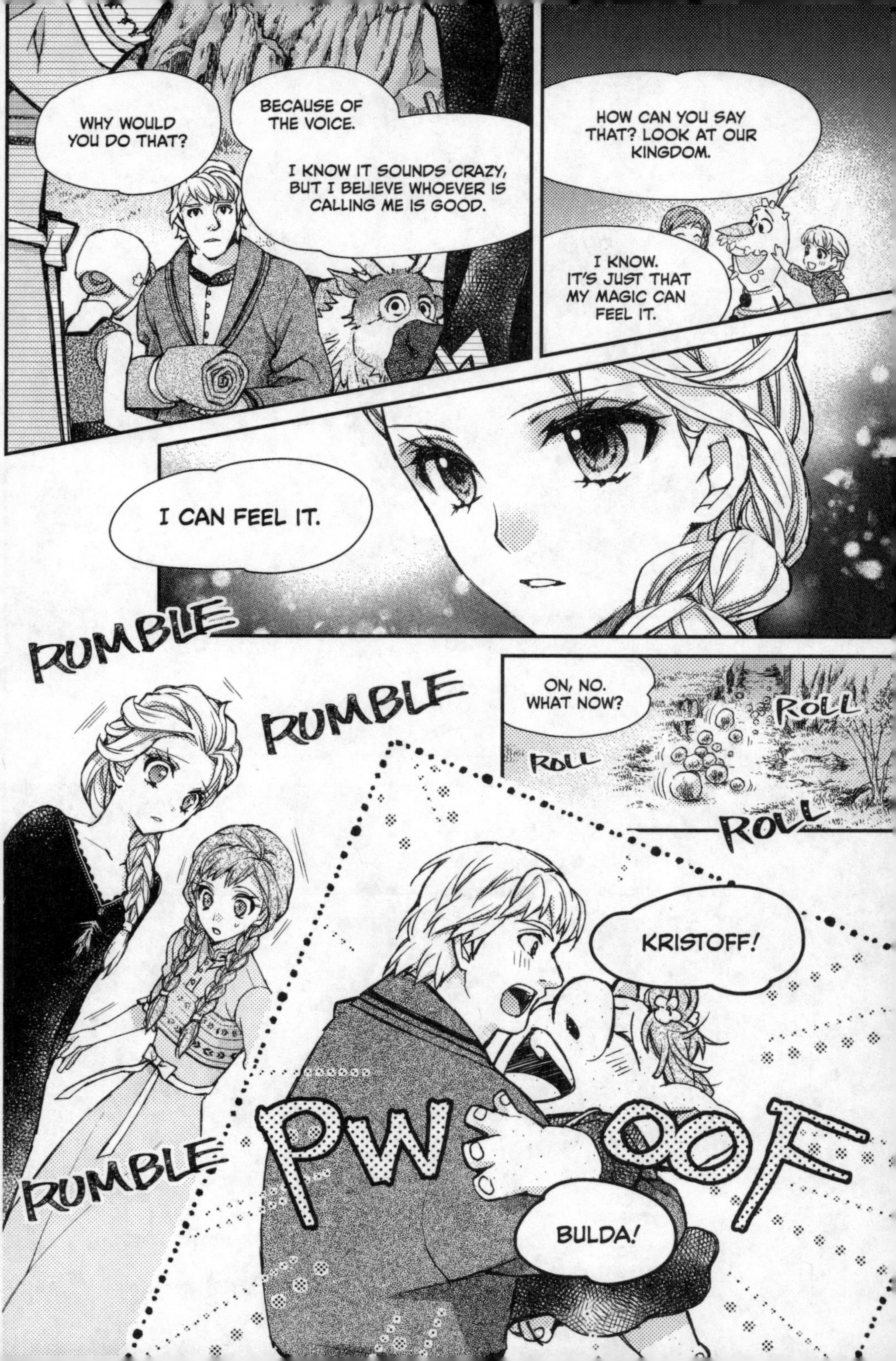
WHY WOULD YOU DO THAT?
BECAUSE OF THE VOICE.
I KNOW IT SOUNDS CRAZY, BUT I BELIEVE WHOEVER IS CALLING ME IS GOOD.
HOW CAN YOU SAY THAT? LOOK AT OUR KINGDOM.
I KNOW. IT'S JUST THAT MY MAGIC CAN FEEL IT.
I CAN FEEL IT.
RUMBLE
RUMBLE
ON, NO. WHAT NOW?
ROLL
ROLL
ROLL
RUMBLE
KRISTOFF!
PWOOF
BULDA!

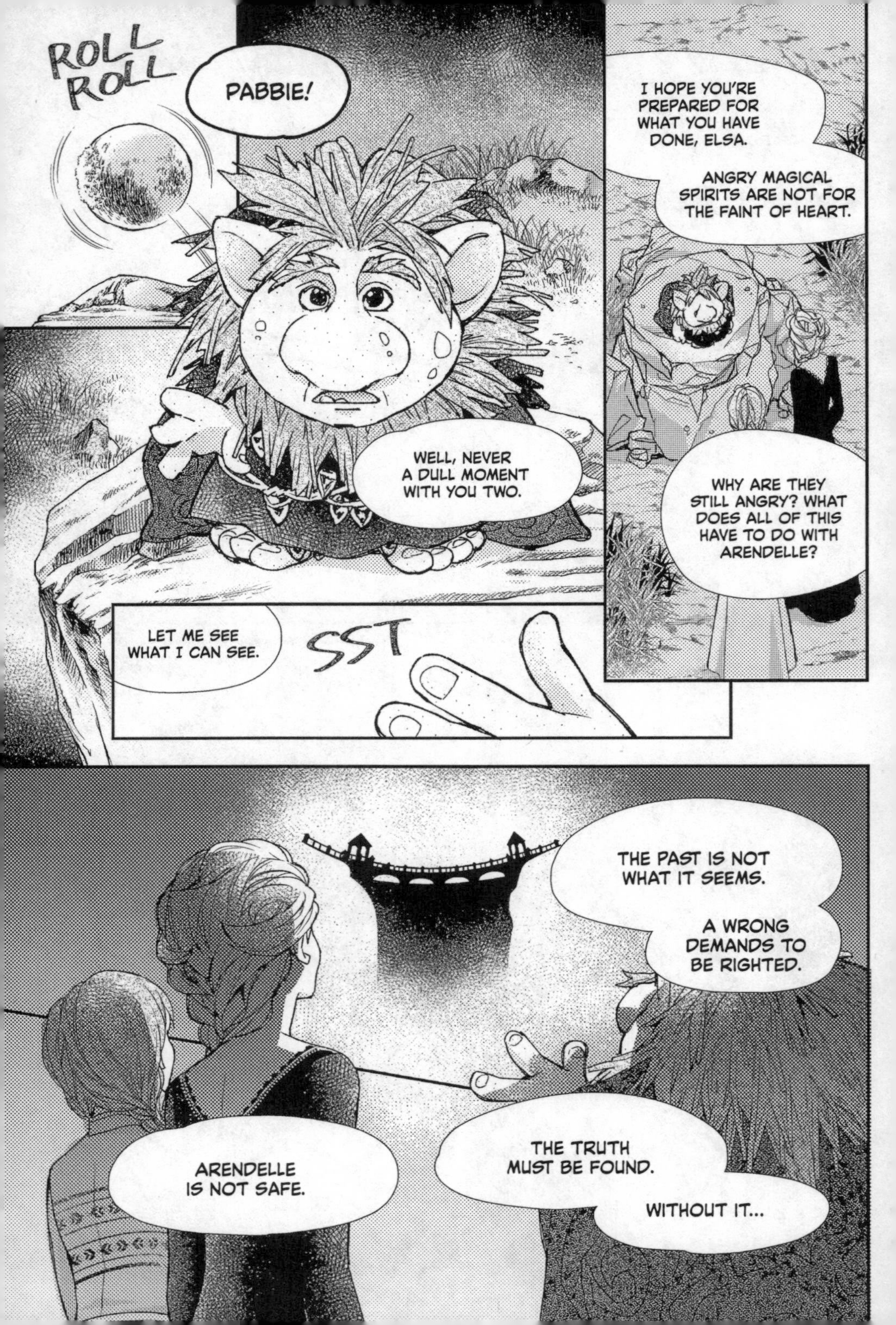
ROLL ROLL
PABBIE!
WELL, NEVER A DULL MOMENT WITH YOU TWO.
I HOPE YOU'RE PREPARED FOR WHAT YOU HAVE DONE, ELSA.
ANGRY MAGICAL SPIRITS ARE NOT FOR THE FAINT OF HEART.
WHY ARE THEY STILL ANGRY? WHAT DOES ALL OF THIS HAVE TO DO WITH ARENDELLE?
LET ME SEE WHAT I CAN SEE.
SST
THE PAST IS NOT WHAT IT SEEMS.
A WRONG DEMANDS TO BE RIGHTED.
ARENDELLE IS NOT SAFE.
THE TRUTH MUST BE FOUND.
WITHOUT IT...

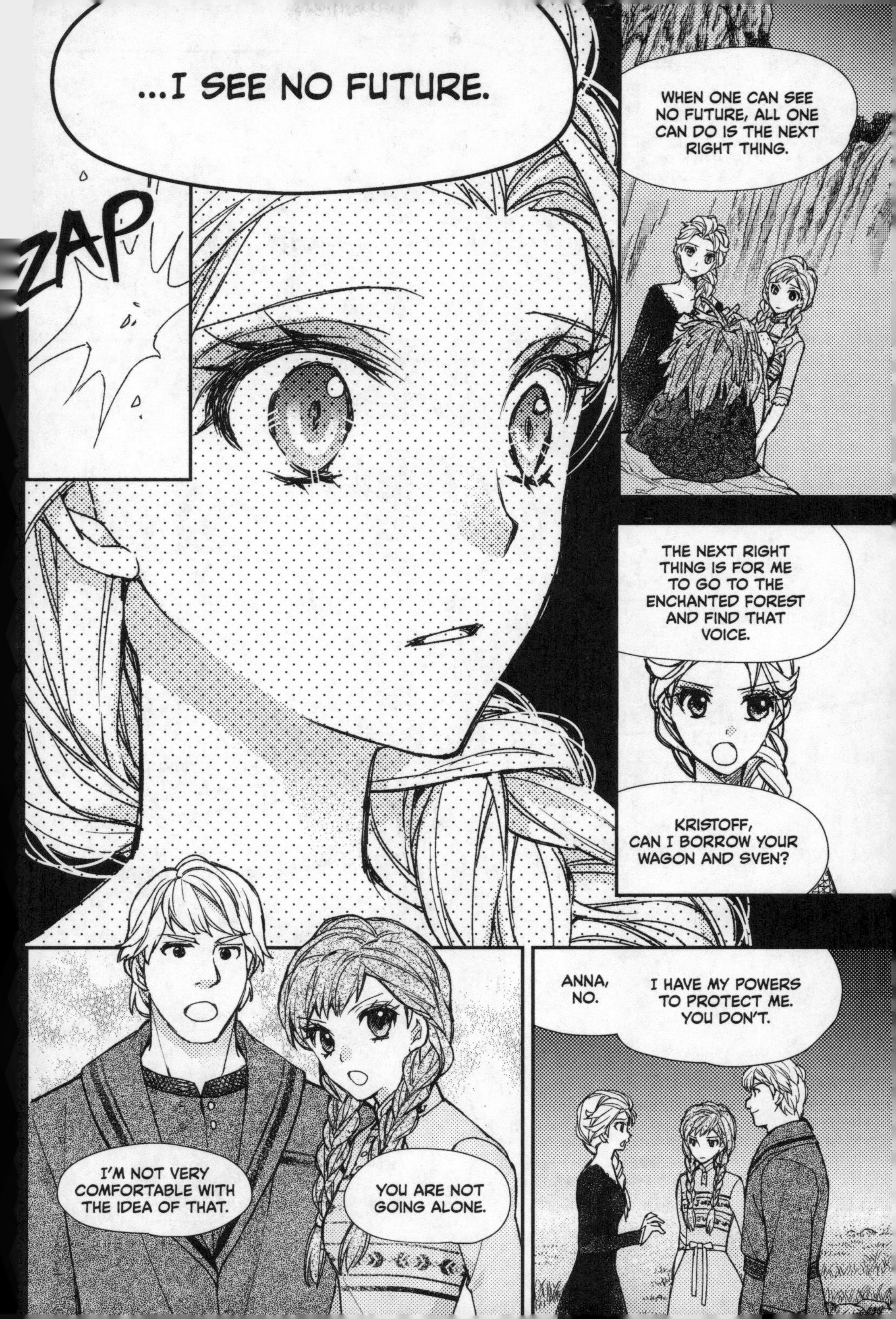
...I SEE NO FUTURE.
ZAP
WHEN ONE CAN SEE NO FUTURE, ALL ONE CAN DO IS THE NEXT RIGHT THING.
THE NEXT RIGHT THING IS FOR ME TO GO TO THE ENCHANTED FOREST AND FIND THAT VOICE.
KRISTOFF, CAN I BORROW YOUR WAGON AND SVEN?
I'M NOT VERY COMFORTABLE WITH THE IDEA OF THAT.
YOU ARE NOT GOING ALONE.
ANNA, NO.
I HAVE MY POWERS TO PROTECT ME. YOU DON'T.

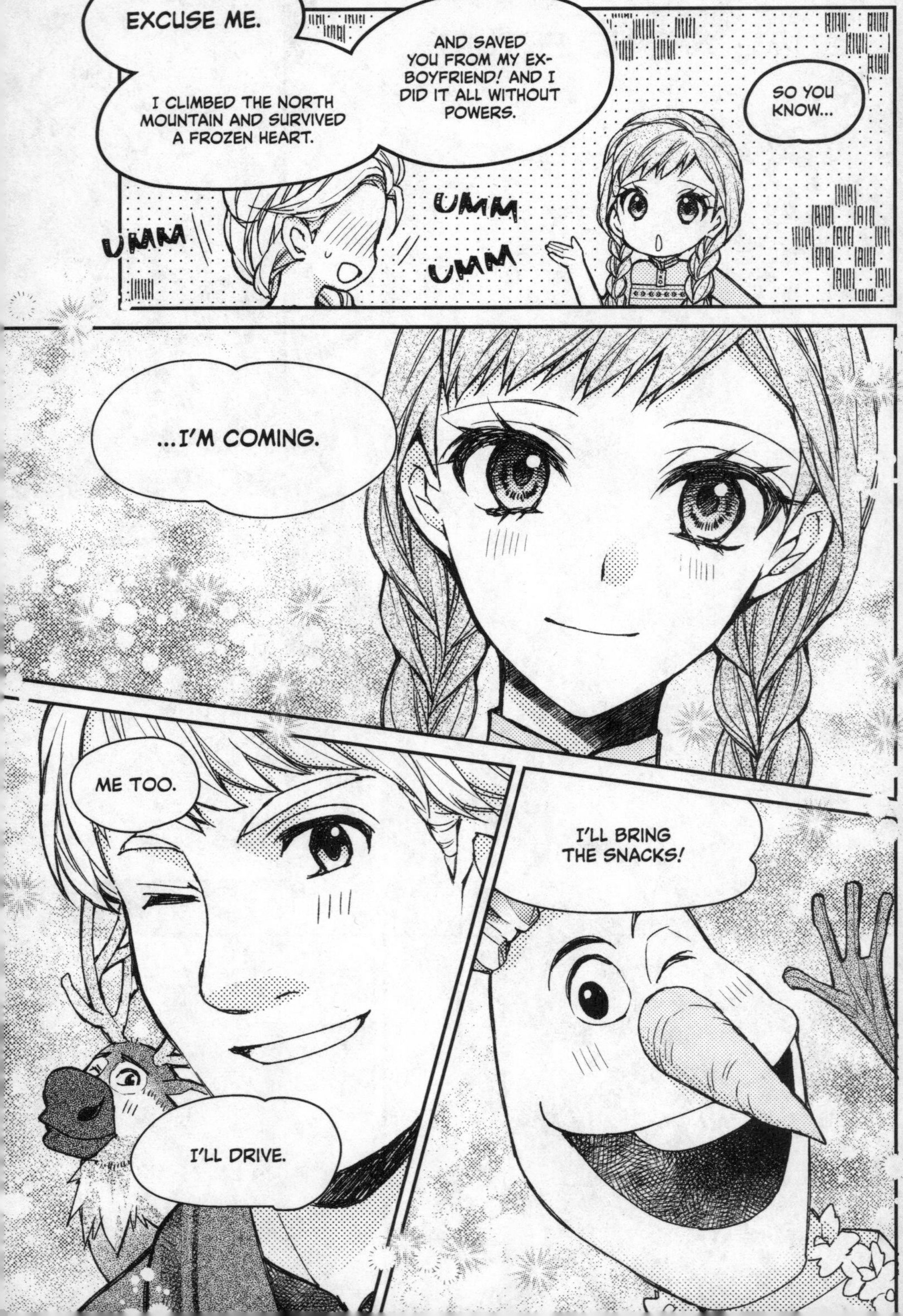
EXCUSE ME.
I CLIMBED THE NORTH MOUNTAIN AND SURVIVED A FROZEN HEART.
AND SAVED YOU FROM MY EX-BOYFRIEND! AND I DID IT ALL WITHOUT POWERS.
UMM
UMM
UMM
SO YOU KNOW...
...I'M COMING.
ME TOO.
I'LL DRIVE.
I'LL BRING THE SNACKS!

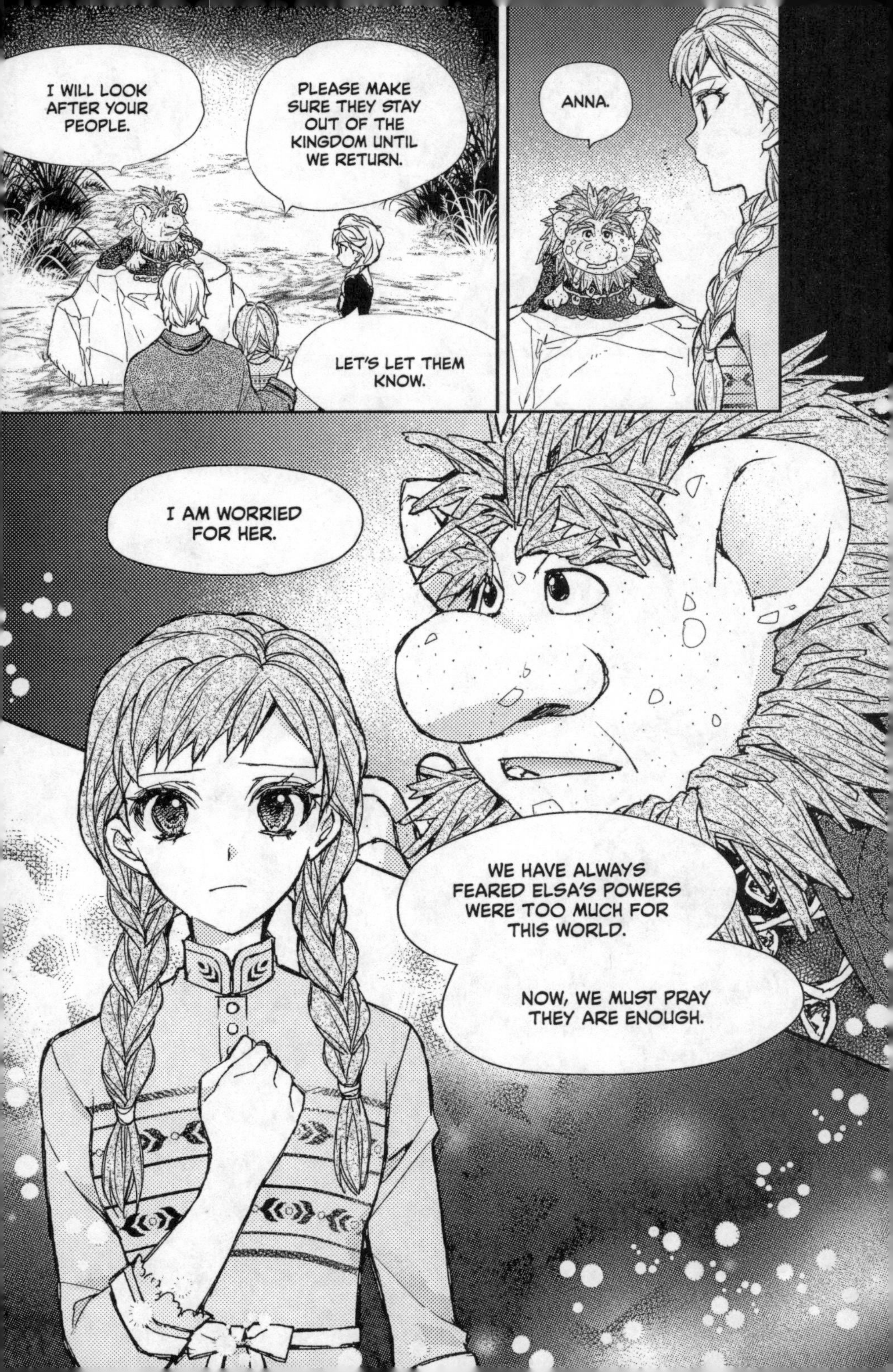
I WILL LOOK AFTER YOUR PEOPLE.
PLEASE MAKE SURE THEY STAY OUT OF THE KINGDOM UNTIL WE RETURN.
LET'S LET THEM KNOW.
ANNA.
I AM WORRIED FOR HER.
WE HAVE ALWAYS FEARED ELSA'S POWERS WERE TOO MUCH FOR THIS WORLD.
NOW, WE MUST PRAY THEY ARE ENOUGH.

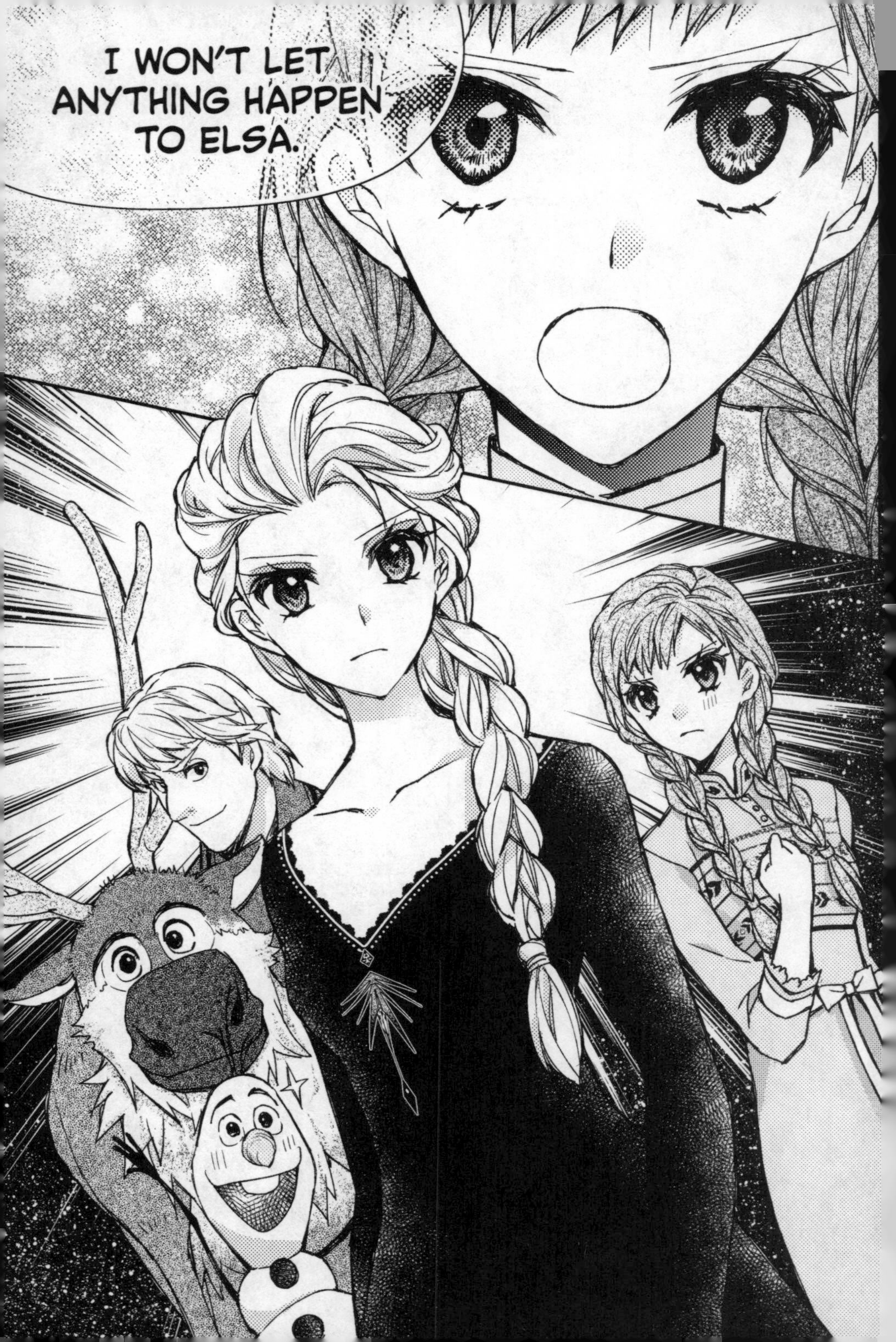
I WON'T LET ANYTHING HAPPEN TO ELSA.

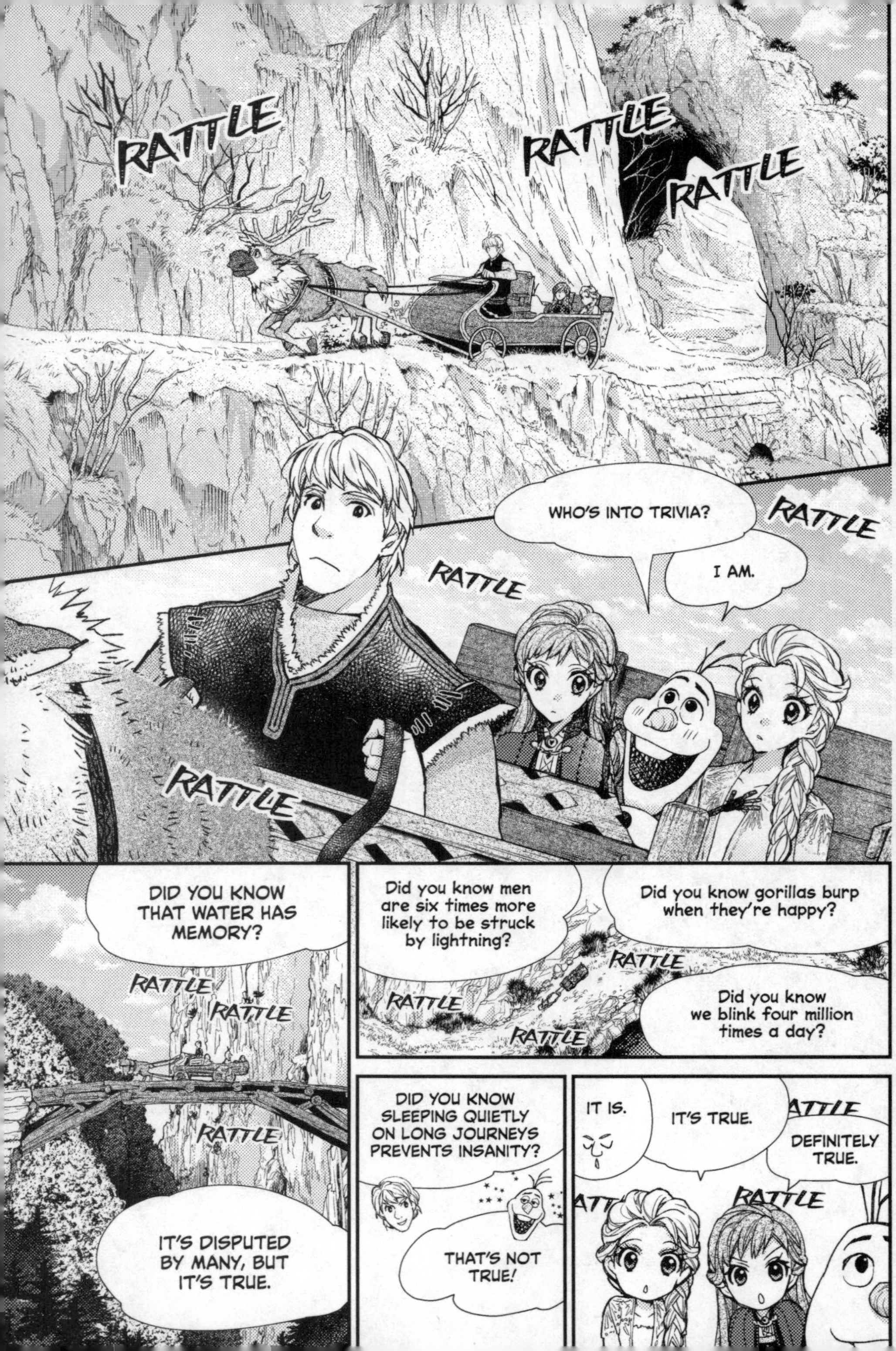
RATTLE
RATTLE
RATTLE
RATTLE
WHO'S INTO TRIVIA?
RATTLE
I AM.
RATTLE
DID YOU KNOW THAT WATER HAS MEMORY?
RATTLE
RATTLE
RATTLE
IT'S DISPUTED BY MANY, BUT IT'S TRUE.
Did you know men are six times more likely to be struck by lightning?
Did you know gorillas burp when they're happy?
RATTLE
RATTLE
Did you know we blink four million times a day?
RATTLE
DID YOU KNOW SLEEPING QUIETLY ON LONG JOURNEYS PREVENTS INSANITY?
THAT'S NOT TRUE!
IT IS.
IT'S TRUE.
DEFINITELY TRUE.
RATTLE

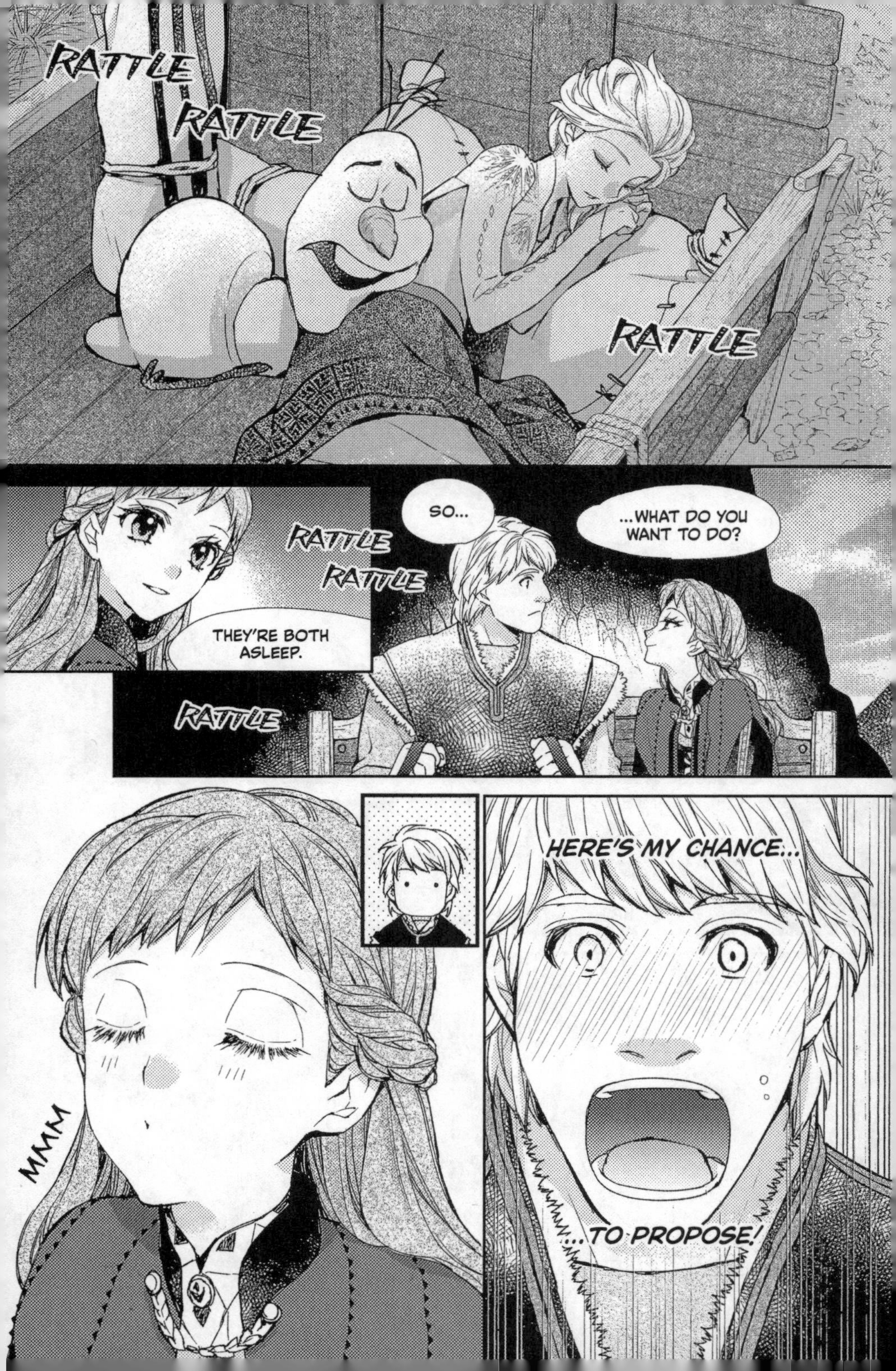
RATTLE
RATTLE
RATTLE
RATTLE
RATTLE
THEY'RE BOTH ASLEEP.
SO...
...WHAT DO YOU WANT TO DO?
RATTLE
MMM
HERE'S MY CHANCE...
...TO PROPOSE!

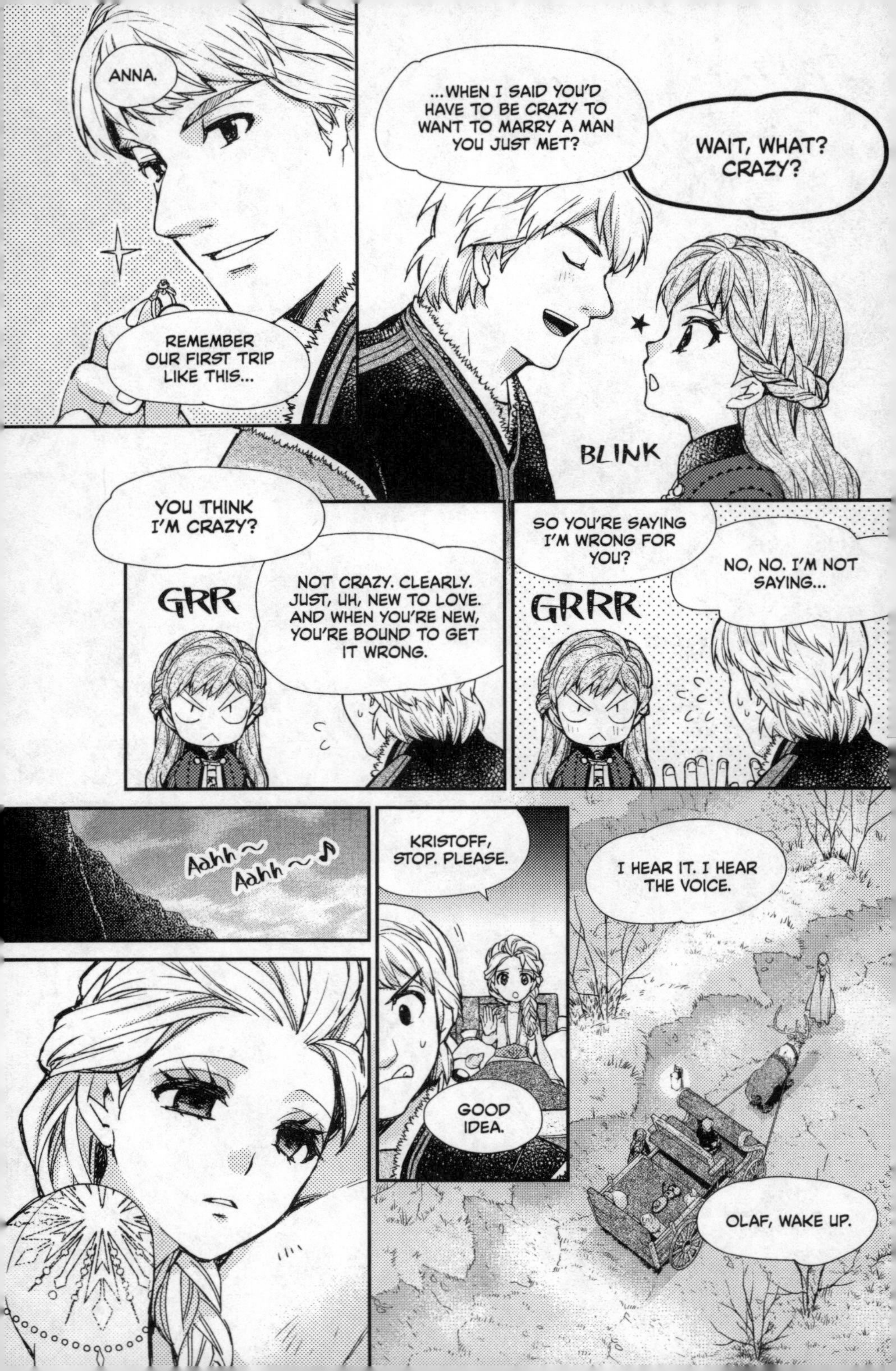
ANNA.
REMEMBER OUR FIRST TRIP LIKE THIS...
...WHEN I SAID YOU'D HAVE TO BE CRAZY TO WANT TO MARRY A MAN YOU JUST MET?
WAIT, WHAT? CRAZY?
BLINK
YOU THINK I'M CRAZY?
GRR
NOT CRAZY. CLEARLY. JUST, UH, NEW TO LOVE. AND WHEN YOU'RE NEW, YOU'RE BOUND TO GET IT WRONG.
SO YOU'RE SAYING I'M WRONG FOR YOU?
GRRR
NO, NO. I'M NOT SAYING...
Aahh~ Aahh~ ♪
KRISTOFF, STOP. PLEASE.
I HEAR IT. I HEAR THE VOICE.
GOOD IDEA.
OLAF, WAKE UP.

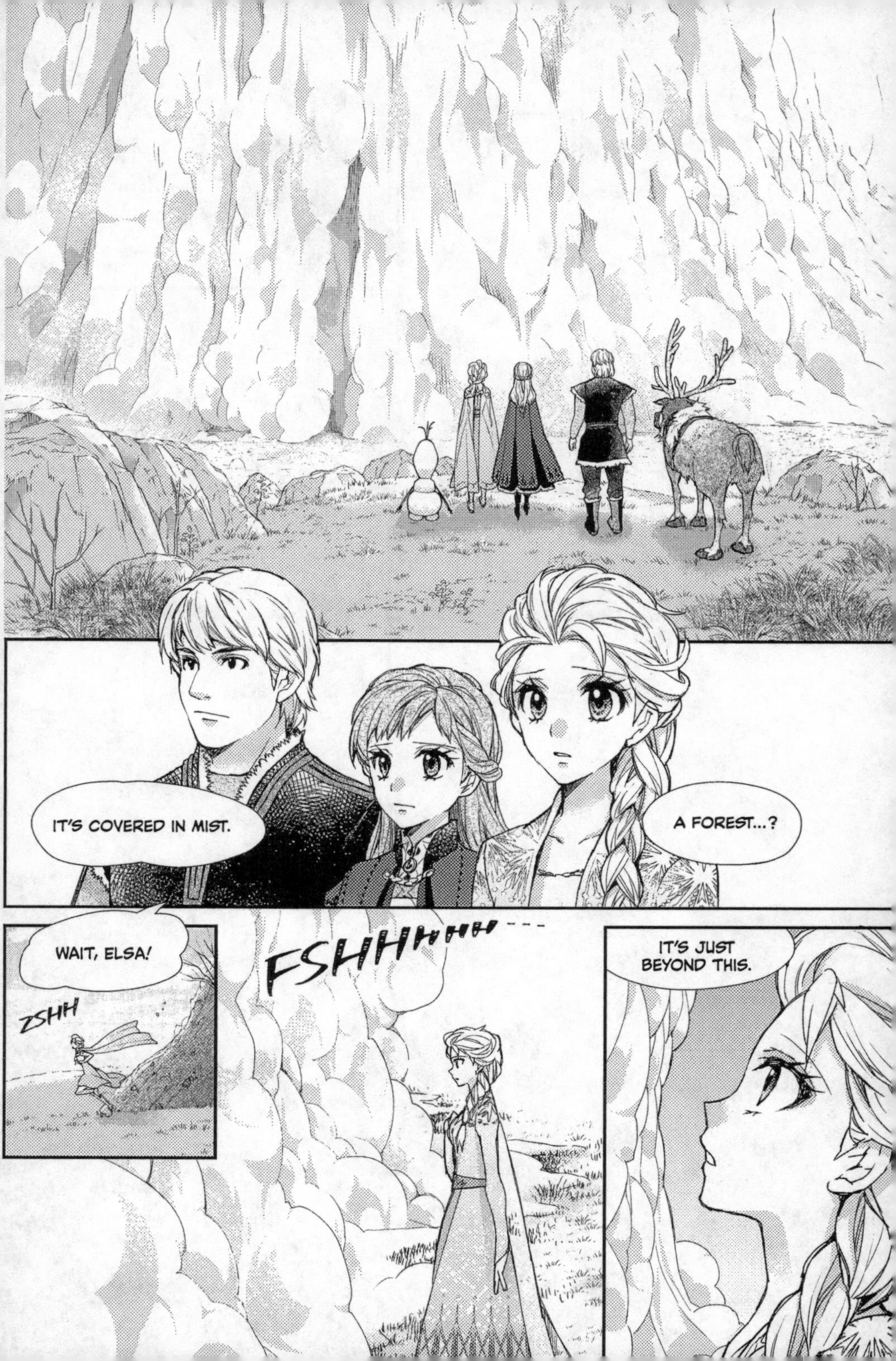
IT'S COVERED IN MIST.
A FOREST...?
WAIT, ELSA!
ZSHH
FSHH
IT'S JUST BEYOND THIS.

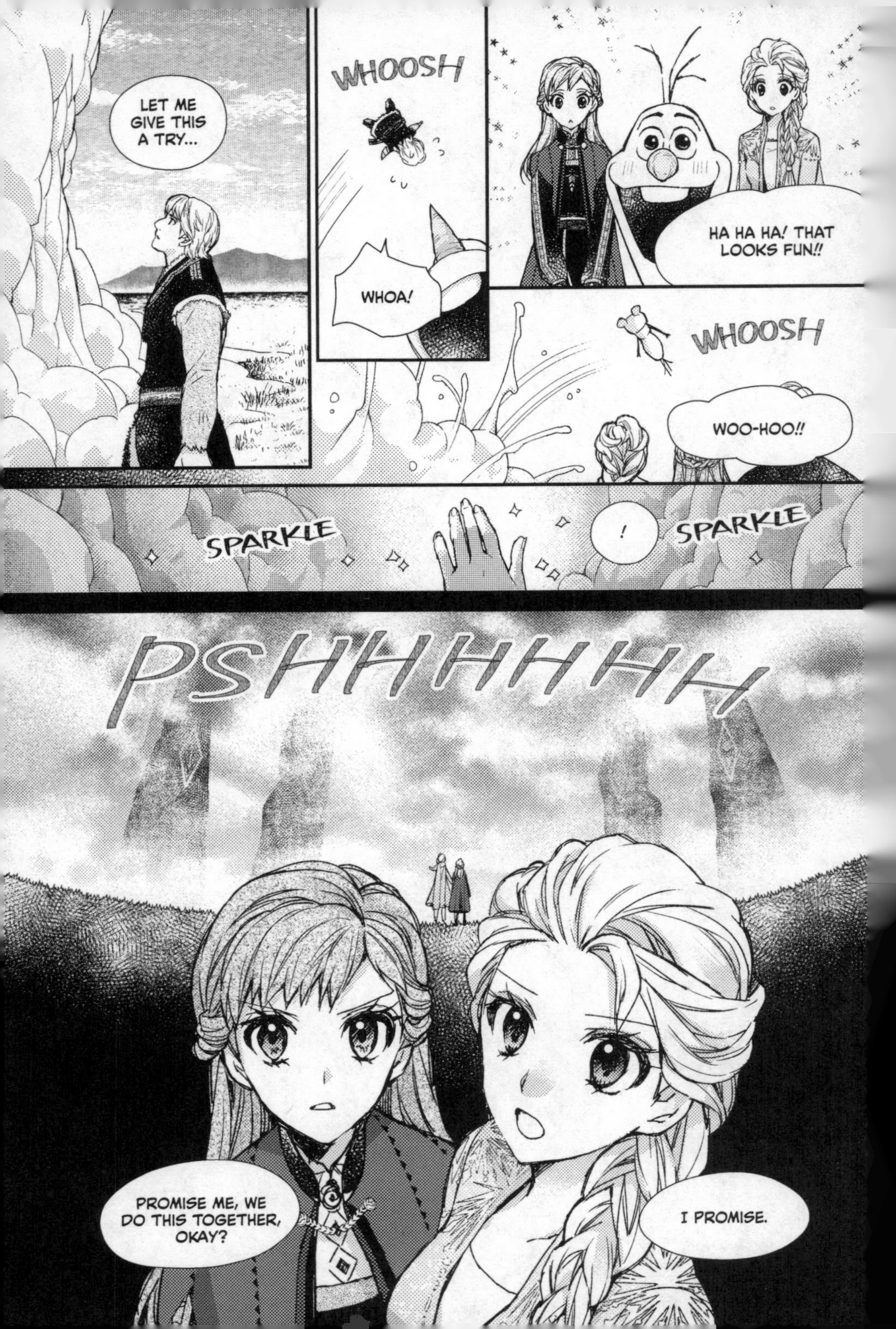
LET ME GIVE THIS A TRY...
WHOOSH
WHOA!
HA HA HA! THAT LOOKS FUN!!
WHOOSH
WOO-HOO!!
SPARKLE
!
SPARKLE
PSHHHHHH
PROMISE ME, WE DO THIS TOGETHER, OKAY?
I PROMISE.

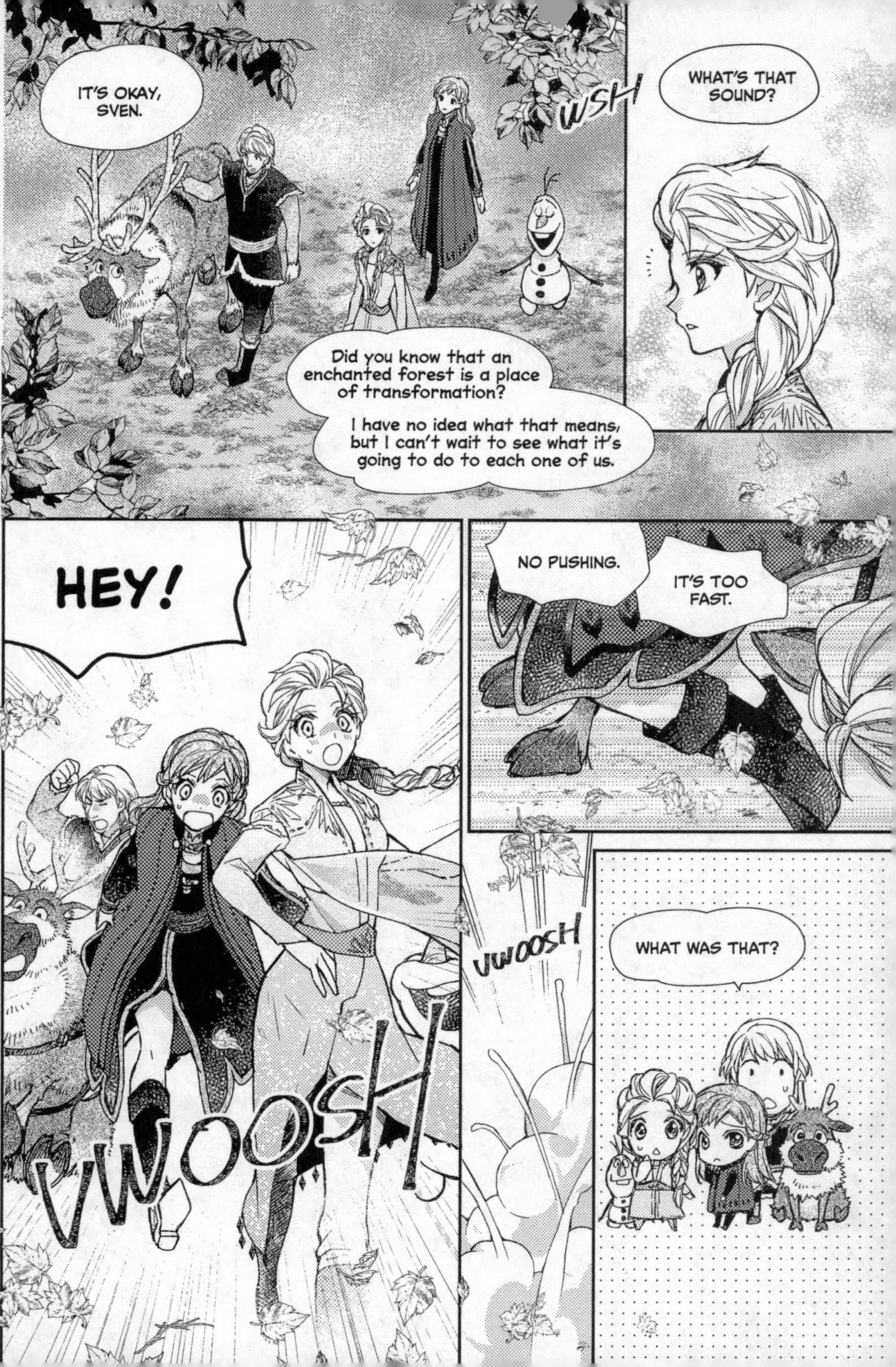
IT'S OKAY, SVEN.
WSH
Did you know that an enchanted forest is a place of transformation?
I have no idea what that means, but I can't wait to see what it's going to do to each one of us.
WHAT'S THAT SOUND?
HEY!
VWOOSH
NO PUSHING.
IT'S TOO FAST.
VWOOSH
WHAT WAS THAT?

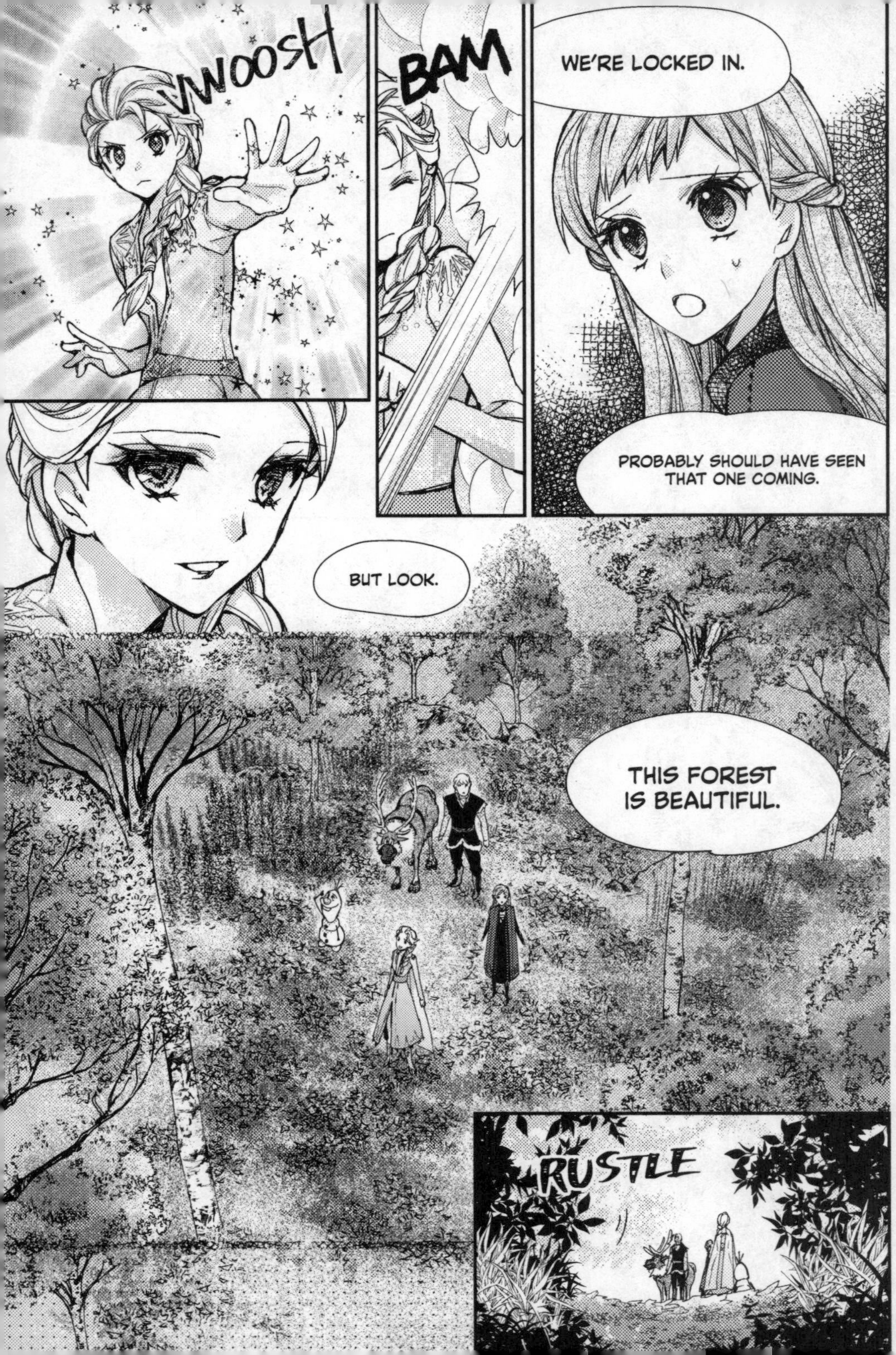
WHOOSH
BAM
WE'RE LOCKED IN.
PROBABLY SHOULD HAVE SEEN THAT ONE COMING.
BUT LOOK.
THIS FOREST IS BEAUTIFUL.
RUSTLE

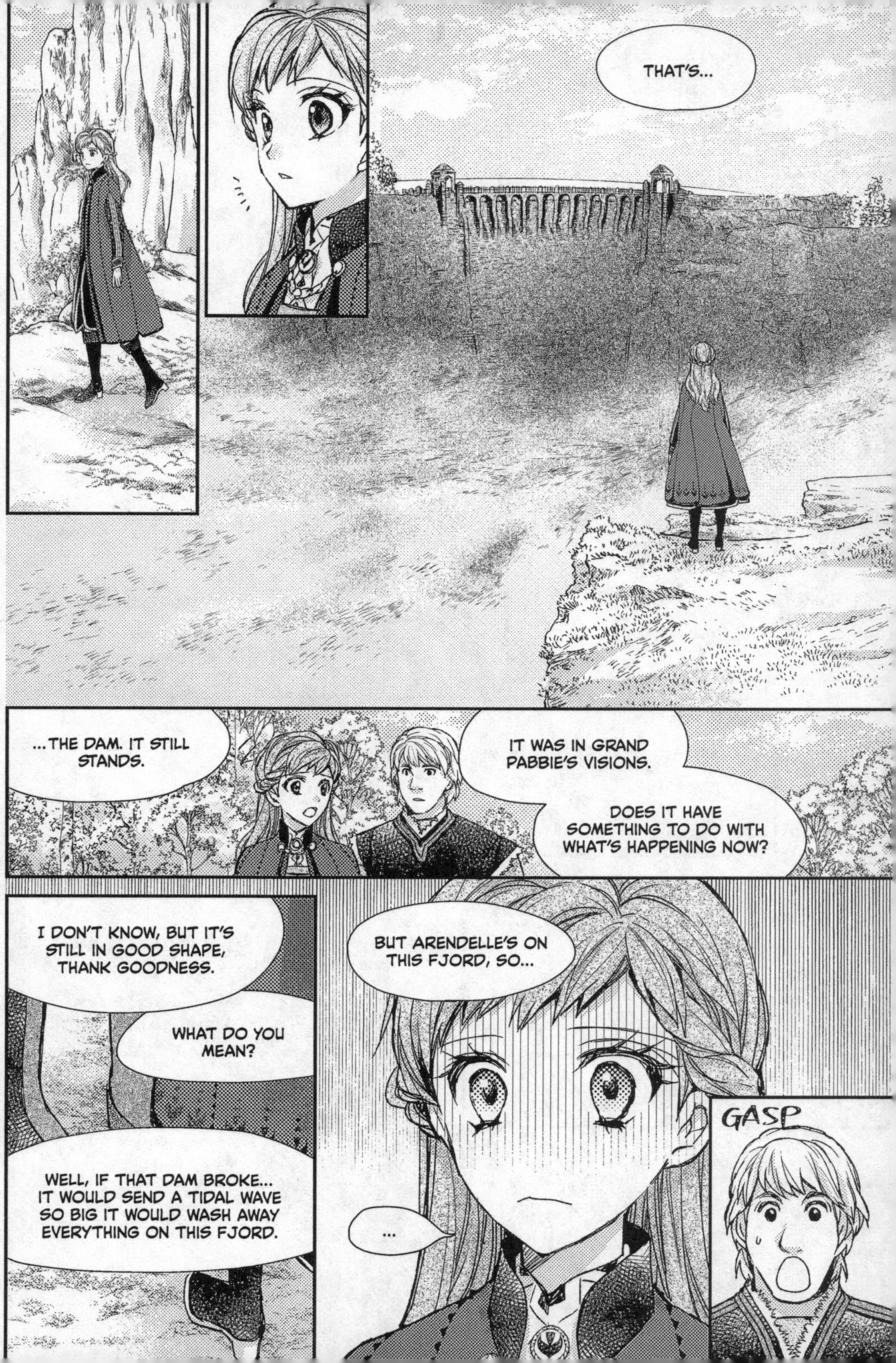
THAT'S...
...THE DAM. IT STILL STANDS.
IT WAS IN GRAND PABBIE'S VISIONS.
DOES IT HAVE SOMETHING TO DO WITH WHAT'S HAPPENING NOW?
I DON'T KNOW, BUT IT'S STILL IN GOOD SHAPE, THANK GOODNESS.
WHAT DO YOU MEAN?
WELL, IF THAT DAM BROKE... IT WOULD SEND A TIDAL WAVE SO BIG IT WOULD WASH AWAY EVERYTHING ON THIS FJORD.
BUT ARENDELLE'S ON THIS FJORD, SO...
...
GASP

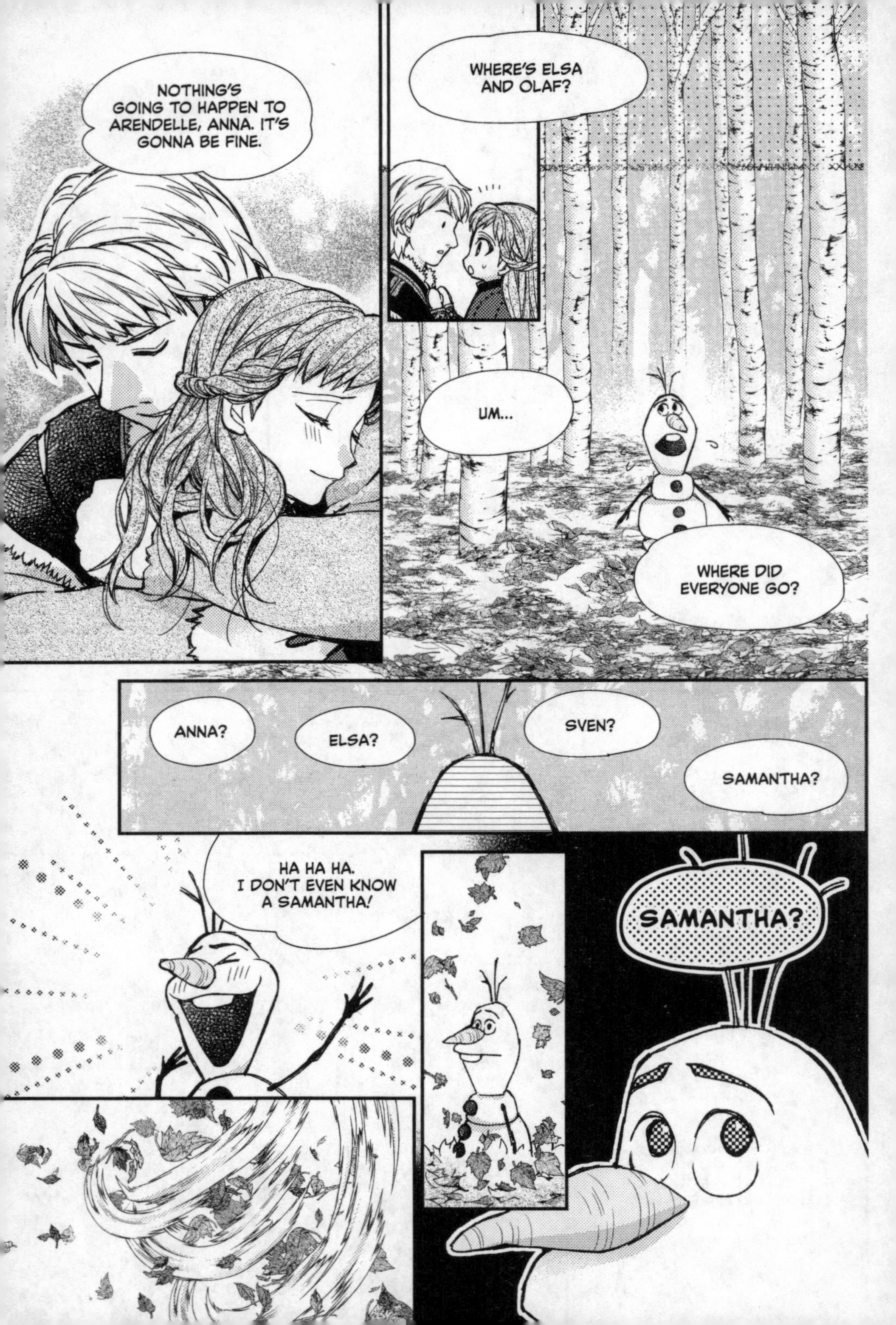
NOTHING'S GOING TO HAPPEN TO ARENDELLE, ANNA. IT'S GONNA BE FINE.
WHERE'S ELSA AND OLAF?
UM...
WHERE DID EVERYONE GO?
ANNA?
ELSA?
SVEN?
SAMANTHA?
HA HA HA. I DON'T EVEN KNOW A SAMANTHA!
SAMANTHA?

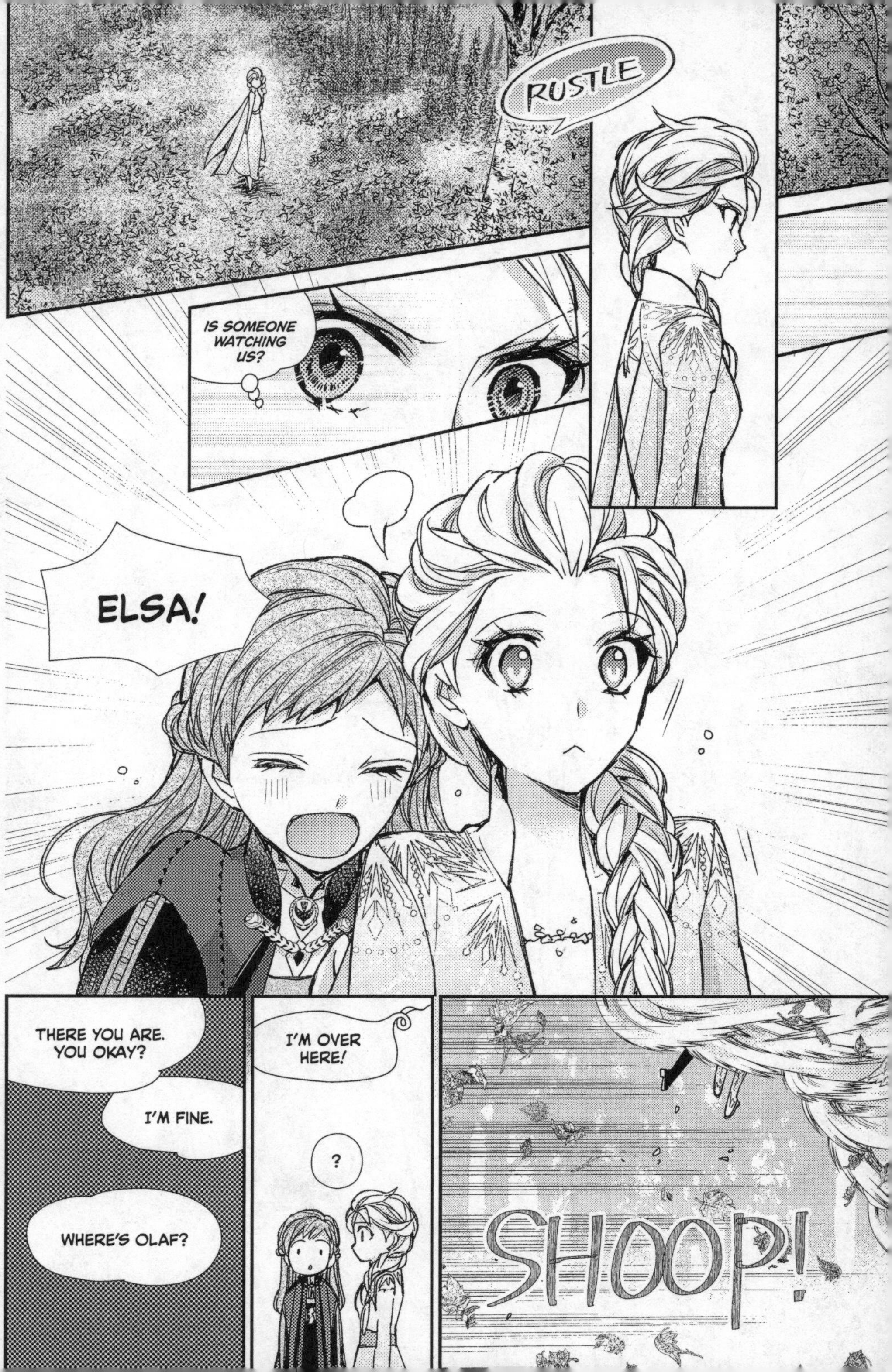
RUSTLE
IS SOMEONE WATCHING US?
ELSA!
THERE YOU ARE. YOU OKAY?
I'M FINE.
WHERE'S OLAF?
I'M OVER HERE!
?
SHOOP!

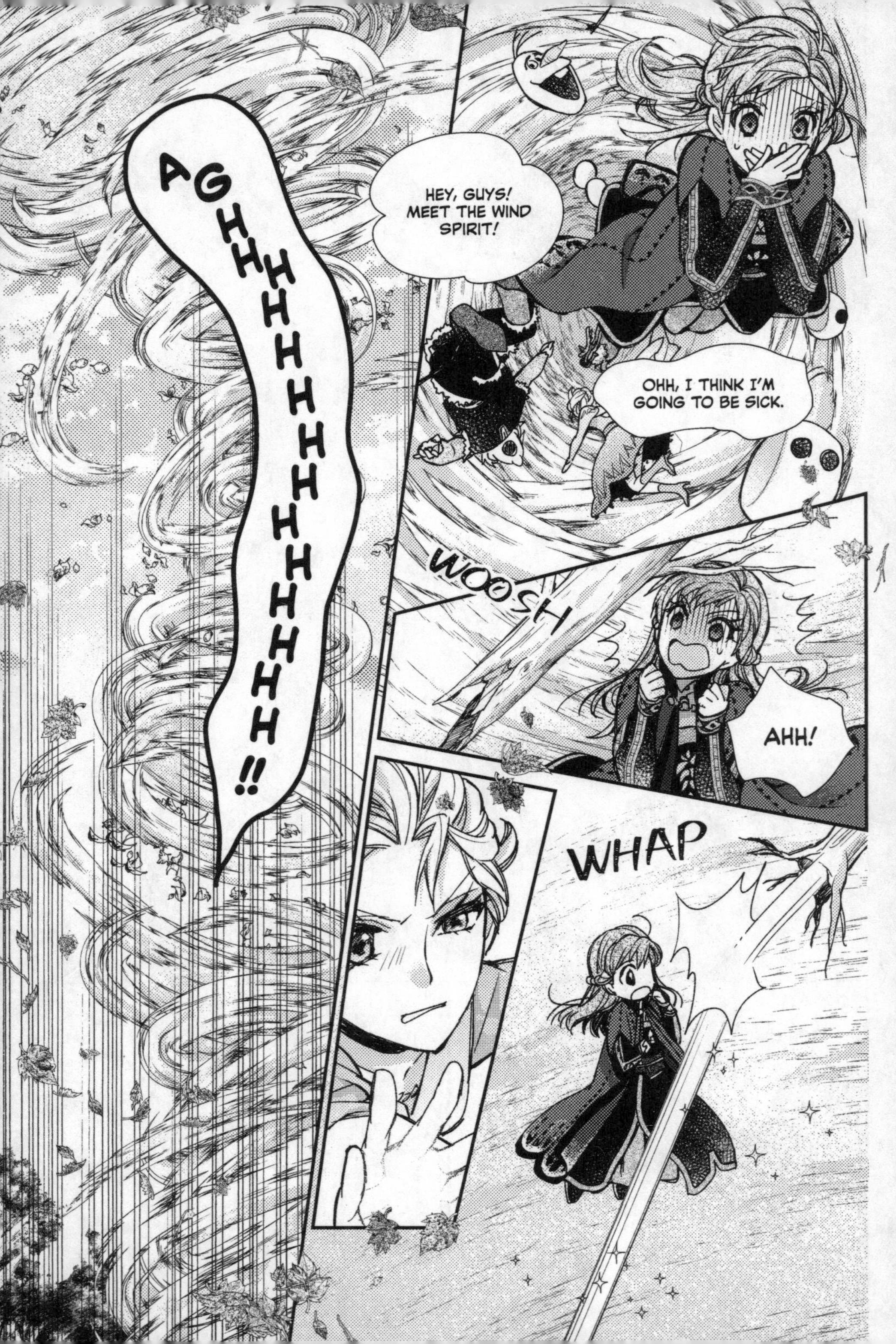
AGHHHHHHHHHHHHH!!
HEY, GUYS! MEET THE WIND SPIRIT!
OHH, I THINK I'M GOING TO BE SICK.
WOOSH
AHH!
WHAP

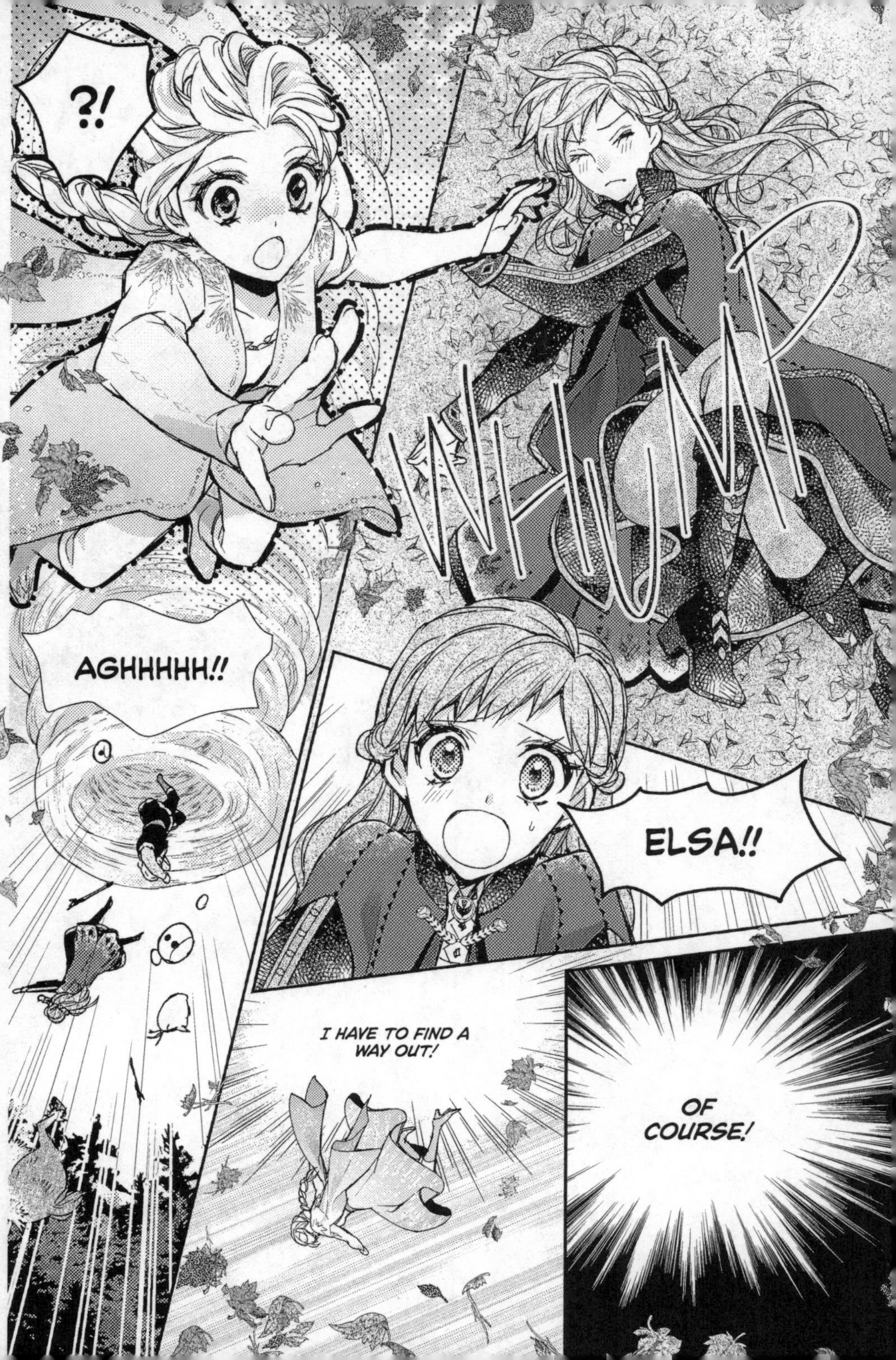
?!
WHUMP
AGHHHHH!!
ELSA!!
I HAVE TO FIND A WAY OUT!
OF COURSE!

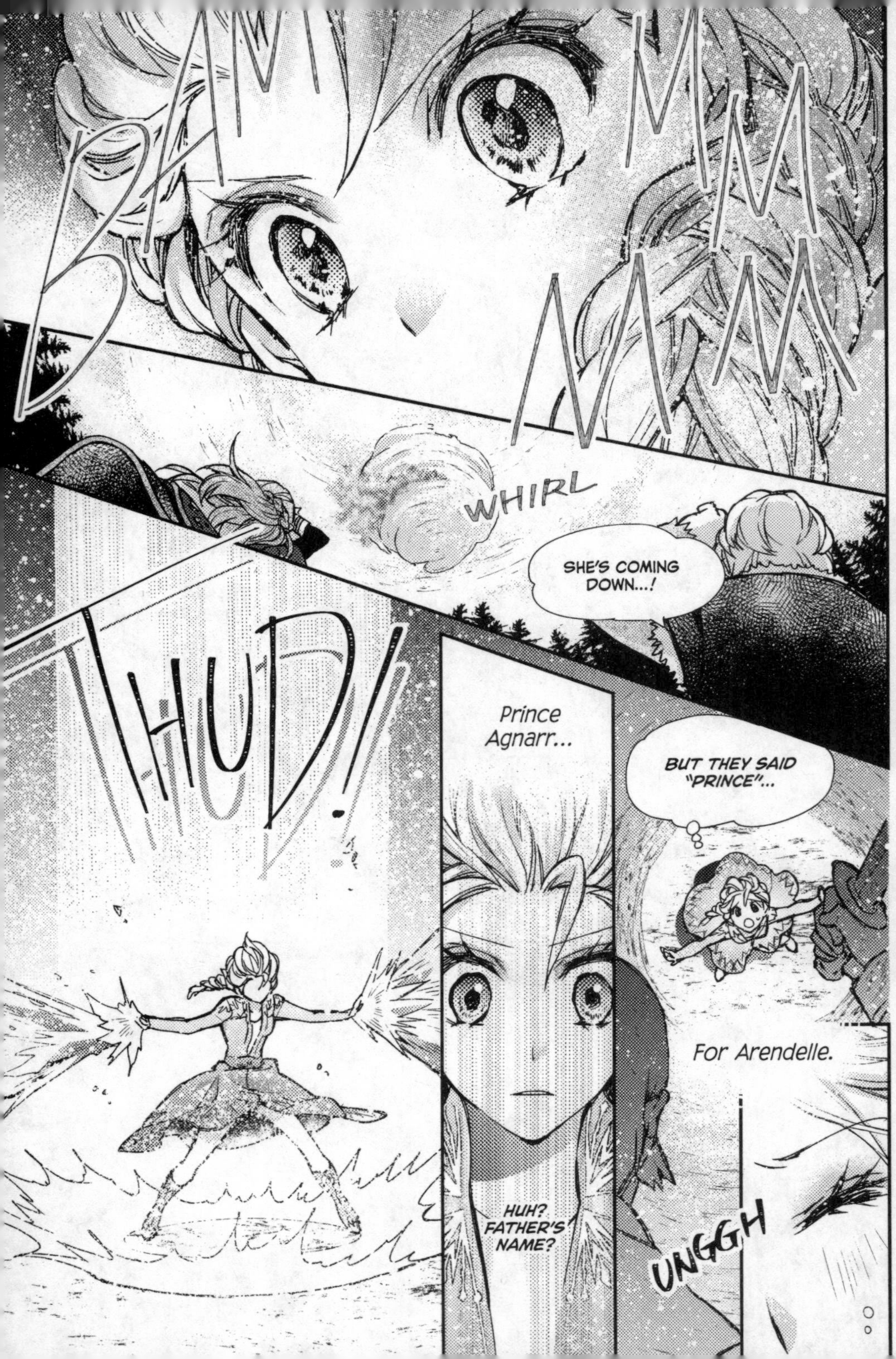
BAMMMMMM
WHIRL
SHE'S COMING DOWN...!
THUD!
Prince Agnarr...
HUH? FATHER'S NAME?
BUT THEY SAID "PRINCE"...
For Arendelle.
UNGGH

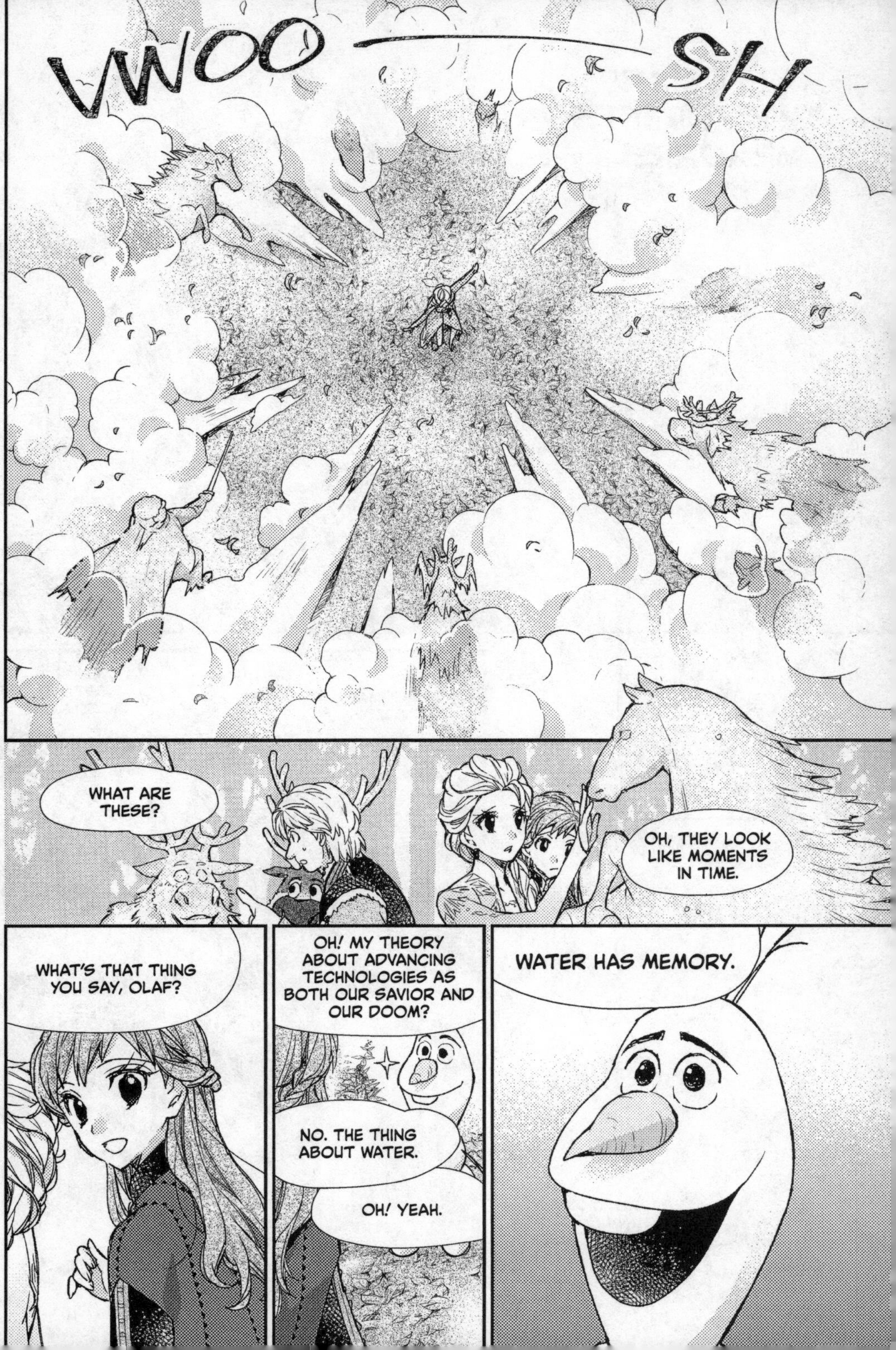
VWOO—SH
WHAT ARE THESE?
OH, THEY LOOK LIKE MOMENTS IN TIME.
WHAT'S THAT THING YOU SAY, OLAF?
OH! MY THEORY ABOUT ADVANCING TECHNOLOGIES AS BOTH OUR SAVIOR AND OUR DOOM?
NO. THE THING ABOUT WATER.
OH! YEAH.
WATER HAS MEMORY.

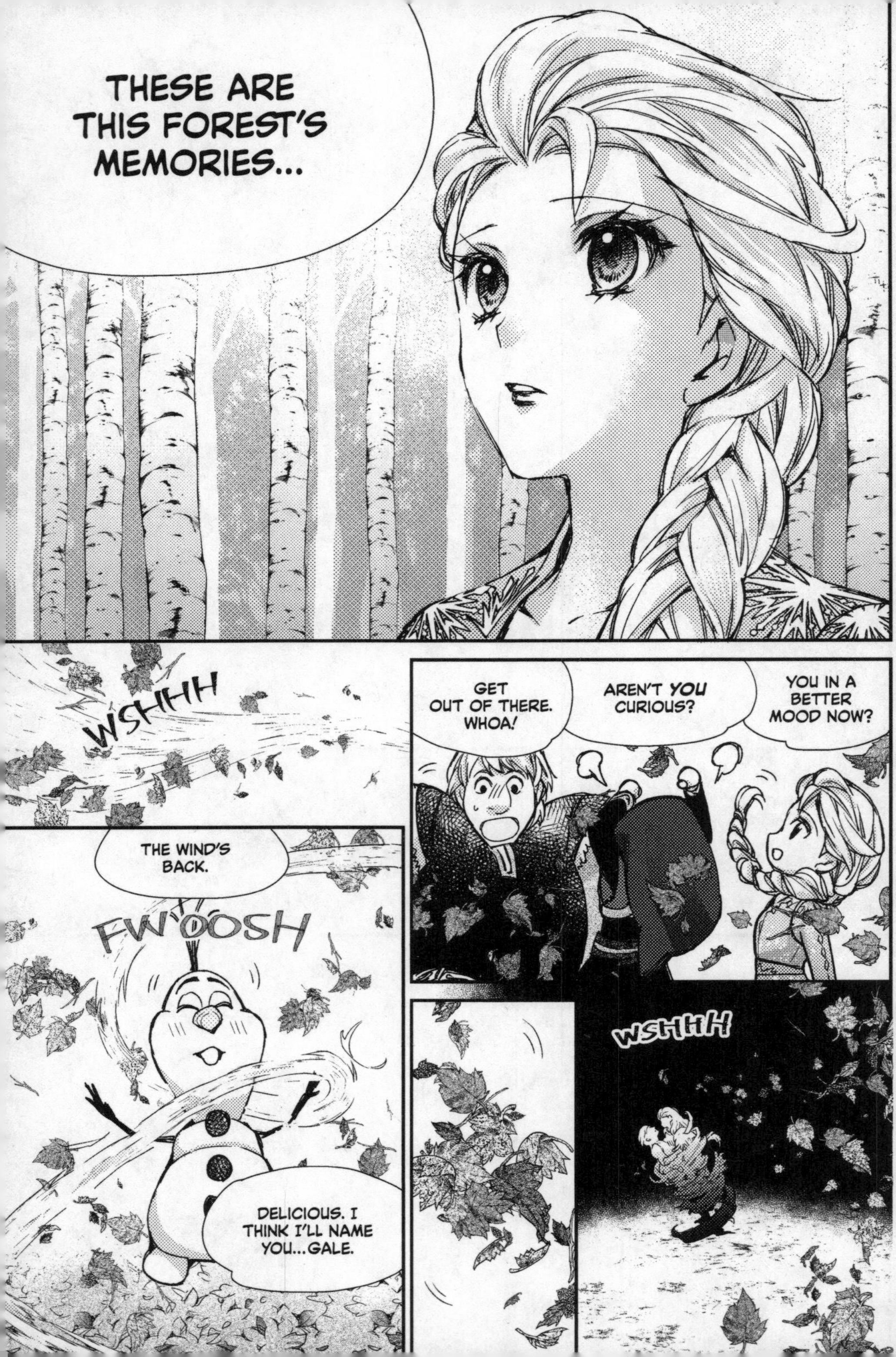
THESE ARE THIS FOREST'S MEMORIES...
WSHHH
GET OUT OF THERE. WHOA!
AREN'T *YOU* CURIOUS?
YOU IN A BETTER MOOD NOW?
THE WIND'S BACK.
FWOOSH
DELICIOUS. I THINK I'LL NAME YOU...GALE.
WSHHH

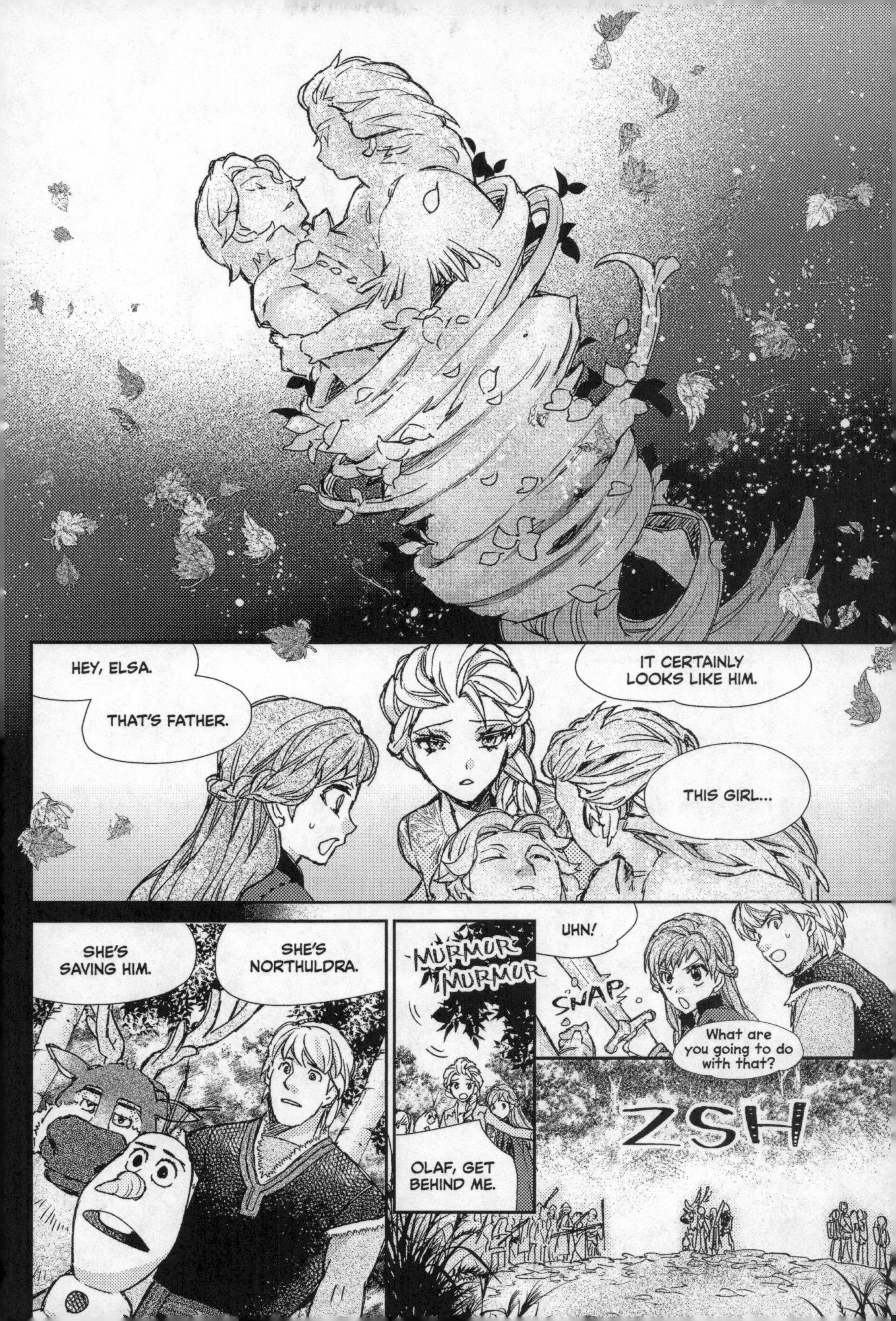
HEY, ELSA.
THAT'S FATHER.
IT CERTAINLY LOOKS LIKE HIM.
THIS GIRL...
SHE'S SAVING HIM.
SHE'S NORTHULDRA.
MURMUR MURMUR
OLAF, GET BEHIND ME.
UHN!
SNAP
What are you going to do with that?
ZSH

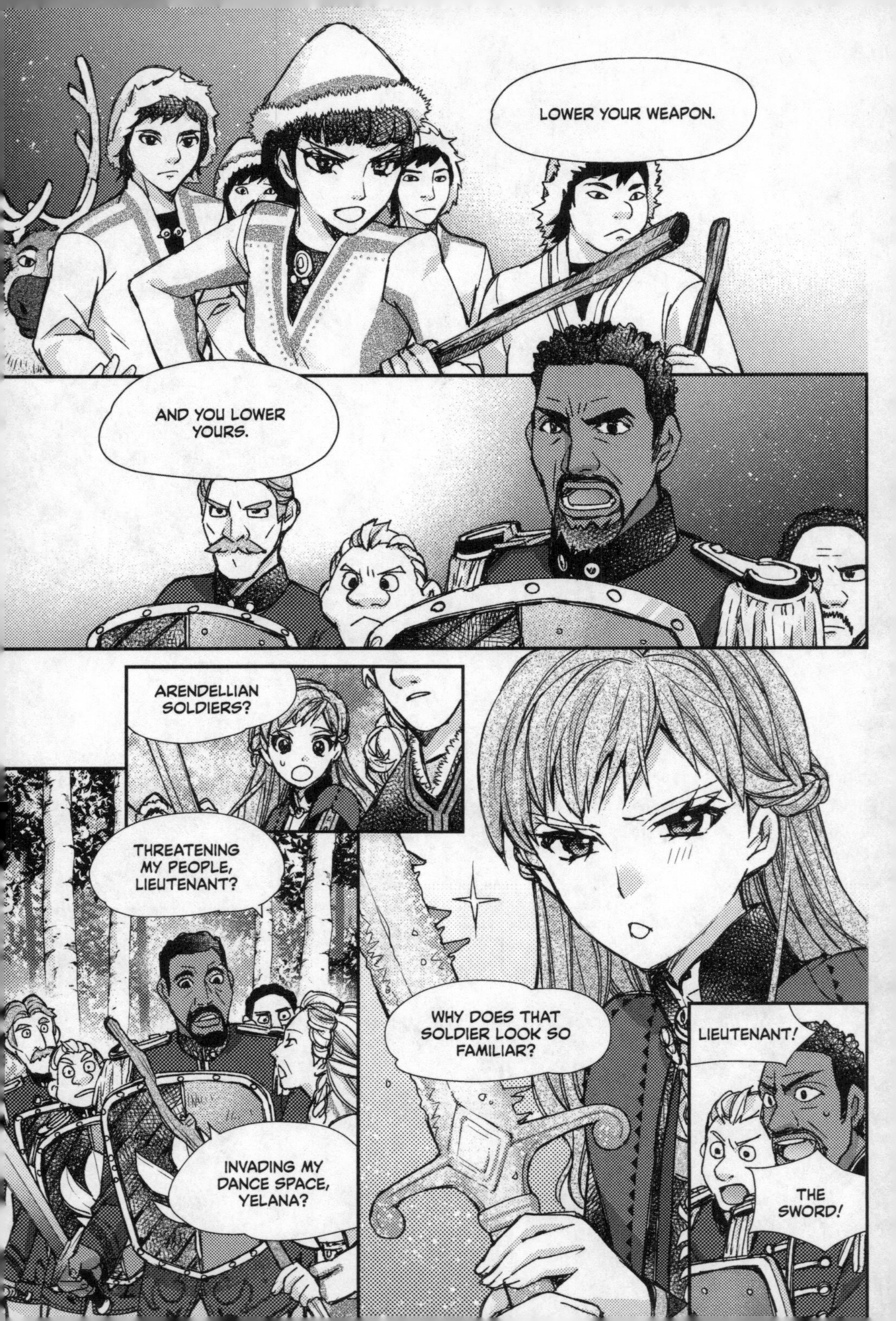
LOWER YOUR WEAPON.
AND YOU LOWER YOURS.
ARENDELLIAN SOLDIERS?
THREATENING MY PEOPLE, LIEUTENANT?
INVADING MY DANCE SPACE, YELANA?
WHY DOES THAT SOLDIER LOOK SO FAMILIAR?
LIEUTENANT!
THE SWORD!

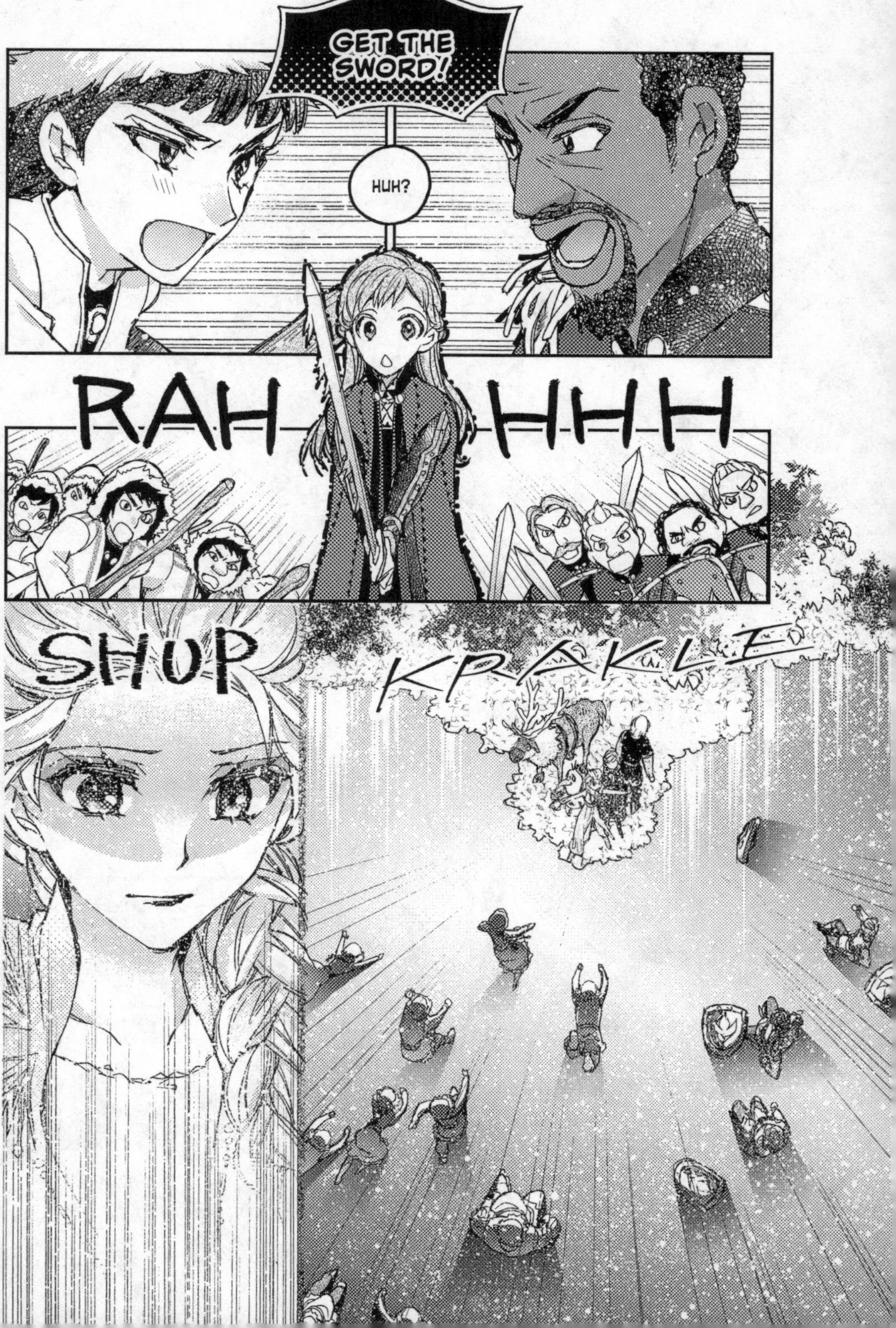
GET THE SWORD!
HUH?
RAH HHH
SHUP
KRAKLE

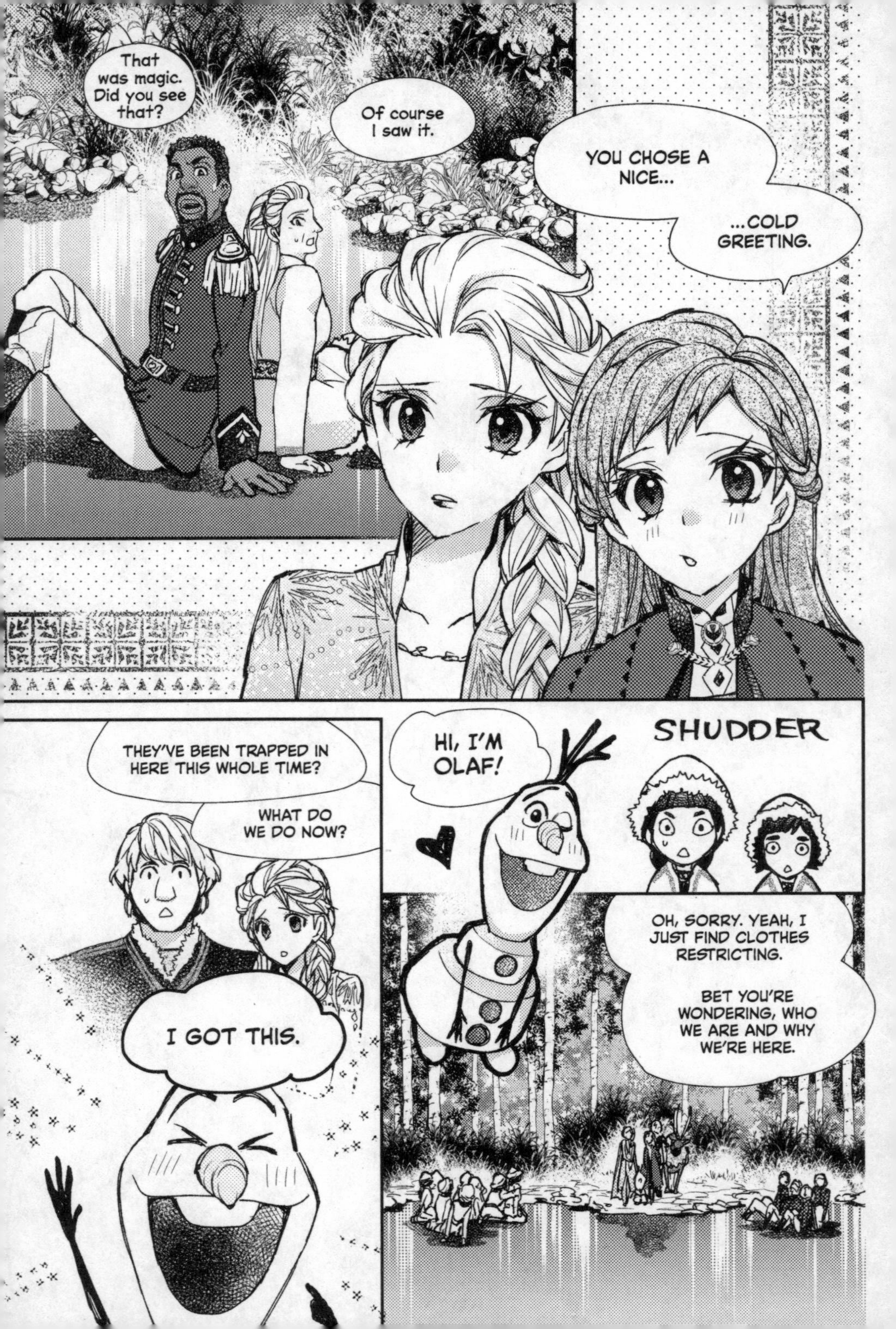
That was magic. Did you see that?
Of course I saw it.
YOU CHOSE A NICE...
...COLD GREETING.
THEY'VE BEEN TRAPPED IN HERE THIS WHOLE TIME?
WHAT DO WE DO NOW?
I GOT THIS.
HI, I'M OLAF!
SHUDDER
OH, SORRY. YEAH, I JUST FIND CLOTHES RESTRICTING.
BET YOU'RE WONDERING, WHO WE ARE AND WHY WE'RE HERE.

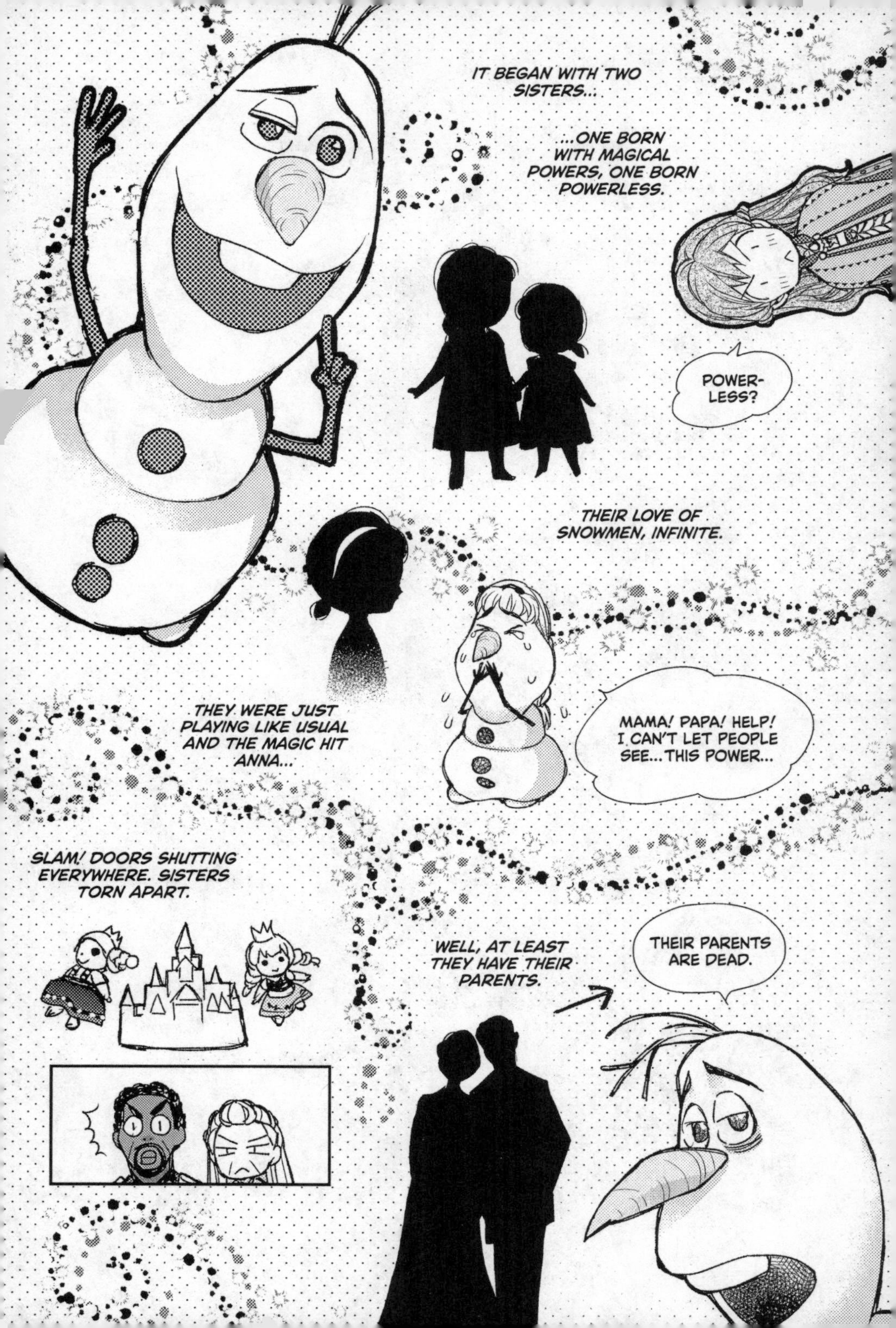
IT BEGAN WITH TWO SISTERS...
...ONE BORN WITH MAGICAL POWERS, ONE BORN POWERLESS.
POWER-LESS?
THEIR LOVE OF SNOWMEN, INFINITE.
THEY WERE JUST PLAYING LIKE USUAL AND THE MAGIC HIT ANNA...
MAMA! PAPA! HELP! I CAN'T LET PEOPLE SEE...THIS POWER...
SLAM! DOORS SHUTTING EVERYWHERE. SISTERS TORN APART.
WELL, AT LEAST THEY HAVE THEIR PARENTS.
THEIR PARENTS ARE DEAD.

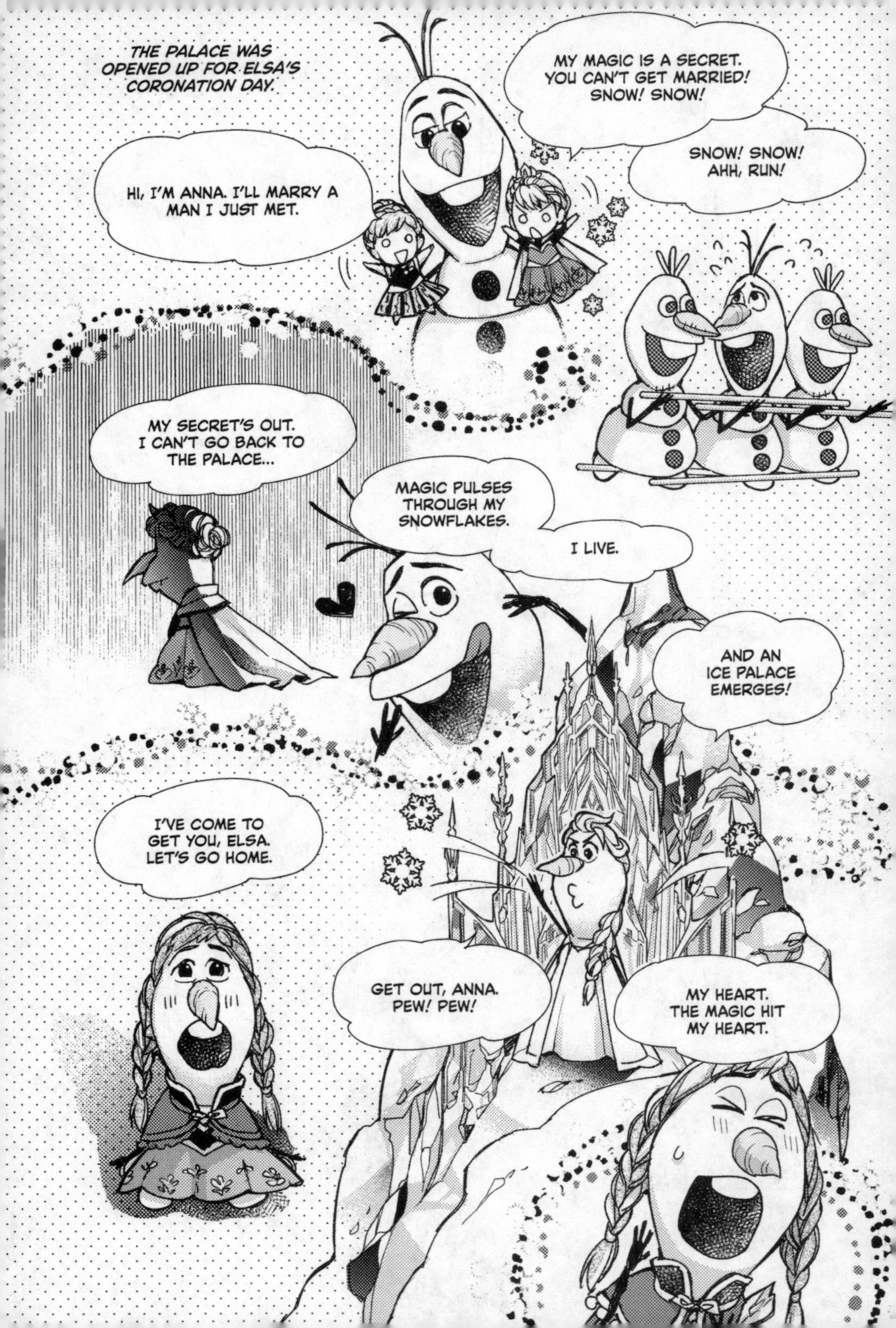
THE PALACE WAS OPENED UP FOR ELSA'S CORONATION DAY.
HI, I'M ANNA. I'LL MARRY A MAN I JUST MET.
MY MAGIC IS A SECRET. YOU CAN'T GET MARRIED! SNOW! SNOW!
SNOW! SNOW! AHH, RUN!
MY SECRET'S OUT. I CAN'T GO BACK TO THE PALACE...
MAGIC PULSES THROUGH MY SNOWFLAKES.
I LIVE.
AND AN ICE PALACE EMERGES!
I'VE COME TO GET YOU, ELSA. LET'S GO HOME.
GET OUT, ANNA. PEW! PEW!
MY HEART. THE MAGIC HIT MY HEART.

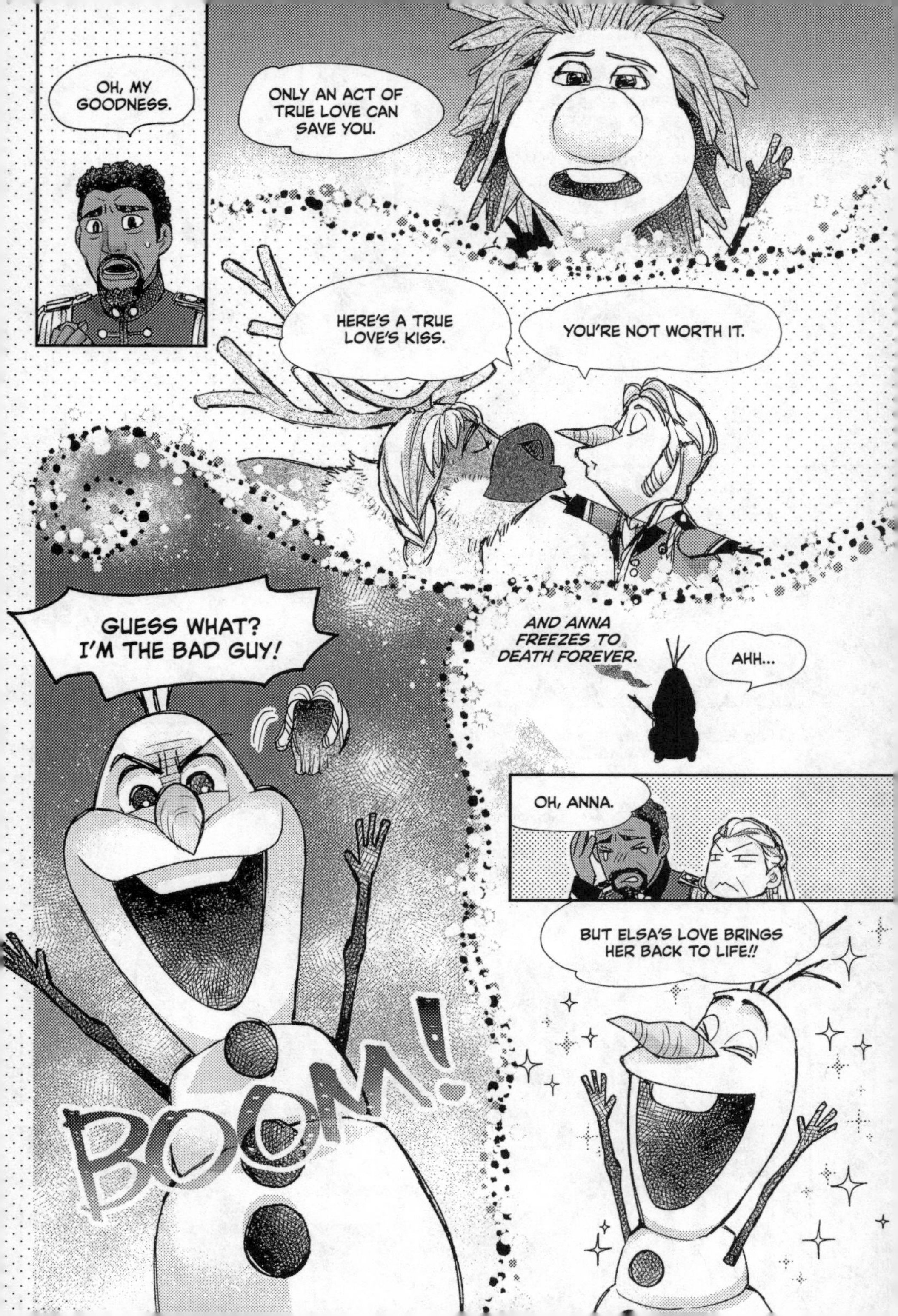
OH, MY GOODNESS.
ONLY AN ACT OF TRUE LOVE CAN SAVE YOU.
HERE'S A TRUE LOVE'S KISS.
YOU'RE NOT WORTH IT.
GUESS WHAT? I'M THE BAD GUY!
BOOM!
AND ANNA FREEZES TO DEATH FOREVER.
AHH...
OH, ANNA.
BUT ELSA'S LOVE BRINGS HER BACK TO LIFE!!

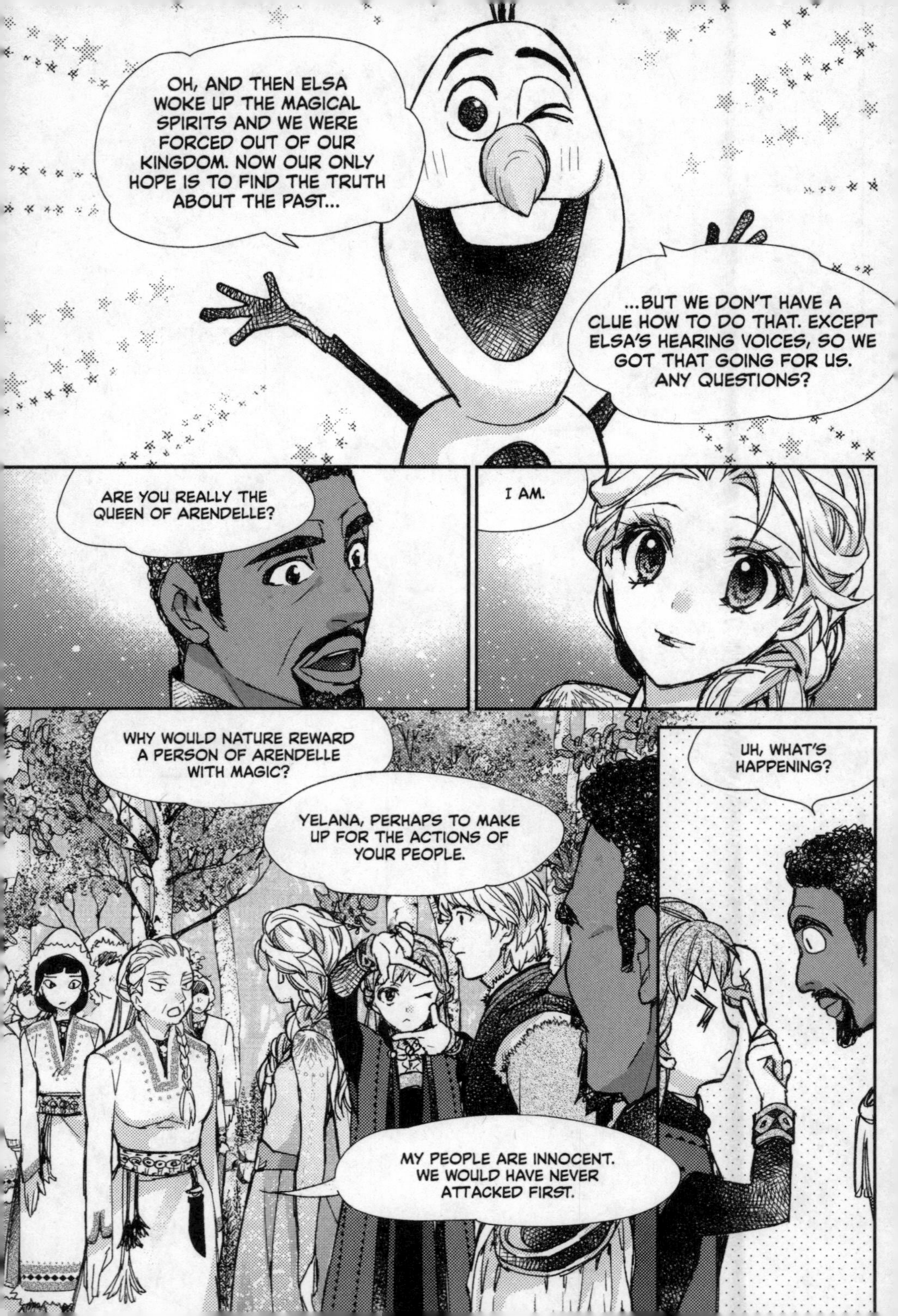
OH, AND THEN ELSA WOKE UP THE MAGICAL SPIRITS AND WE WERE FORCED OUT OF OUR KINGDOM. NOW OUR ONLY HOPE IS TO FIND THE TRUTH ABOUT THE PAST...
...BUT WE DON'T HAVE A CLUE HOW TO DO THAT. EXCEPT ELSA'S HEARING VOICES, SO WE GOT THAT GOING FOR US. ANY QUESTIONS?
ARE YOU REALLY THE QUEEN OF ARENDELLE?
I AM.
WHY WOULD NATURE REWARD A PERSON OF ARENDELLE WITH MAGIC?
YELANA, PERHAPS TO MAKE UP FOR THE ACTIONS OF YOUR PEOPLE.
MY PEOPLE ARE INNOCENT. WE WOULD HAVE NEVER ATTACKED FIRST.
UH, WHAT'S HAPPENING?

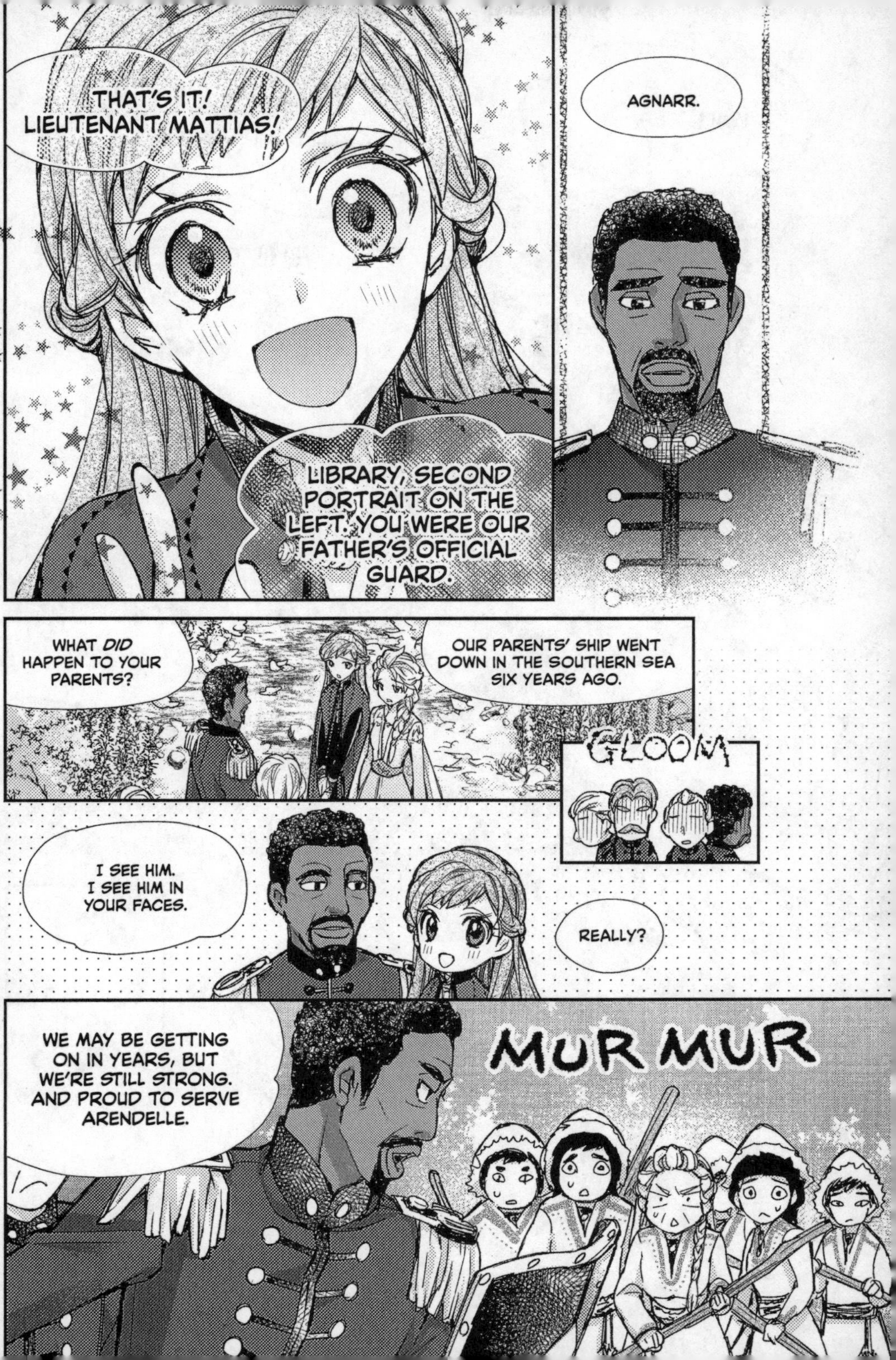
THAT'S IT! LIEUTENANT MATTIAS!
LIBRARY, SECOND PORTRAIT ON THE LEFT. YOU WERE OUR FATHER'S OFFICIAL GUARD.
AGNARR.
WHAT DID HAPPEN TO YOUR PARENTS?
OUR PARENTS' SHIP WENT DOWN IN THE SOUTHERN SEA SIX YEARS AGO.
GLOOM
I SEE HIM. I SEE HIM IN YOUR FACES.
REALLY?
WE MAY BE GETTING ON IN YEARS, BUT WE'RE STILL STRONG. AND PROUD TO SERVE ARENDELLE.
MUR MUR

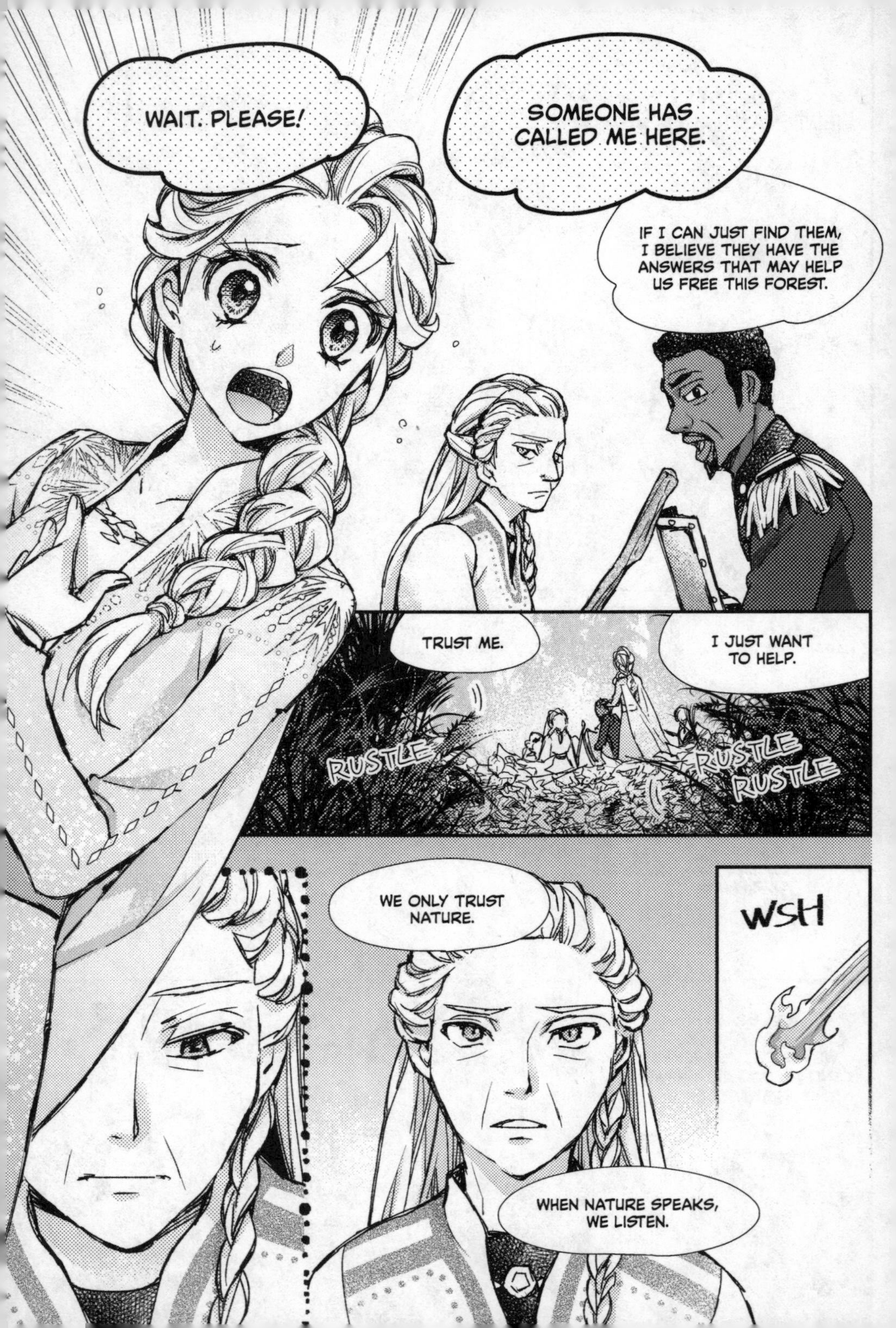
WAIT. PLEASE!
SOMEONE HAS CALLED ME HERE.
IF I CAN JUST FIND THEM, I BELIEVE THEY HAVE THE ANSWERS THAT MAY HELP US FREE THIS FOREST.
TRUST ME.
I JUST WANT TO HELP.
RUSTLE
RUSTLE RUSTLE
WE ONLY TRUST NATURE.
WHEN NATURE SPEAKS, WE LISTEN.
WSH

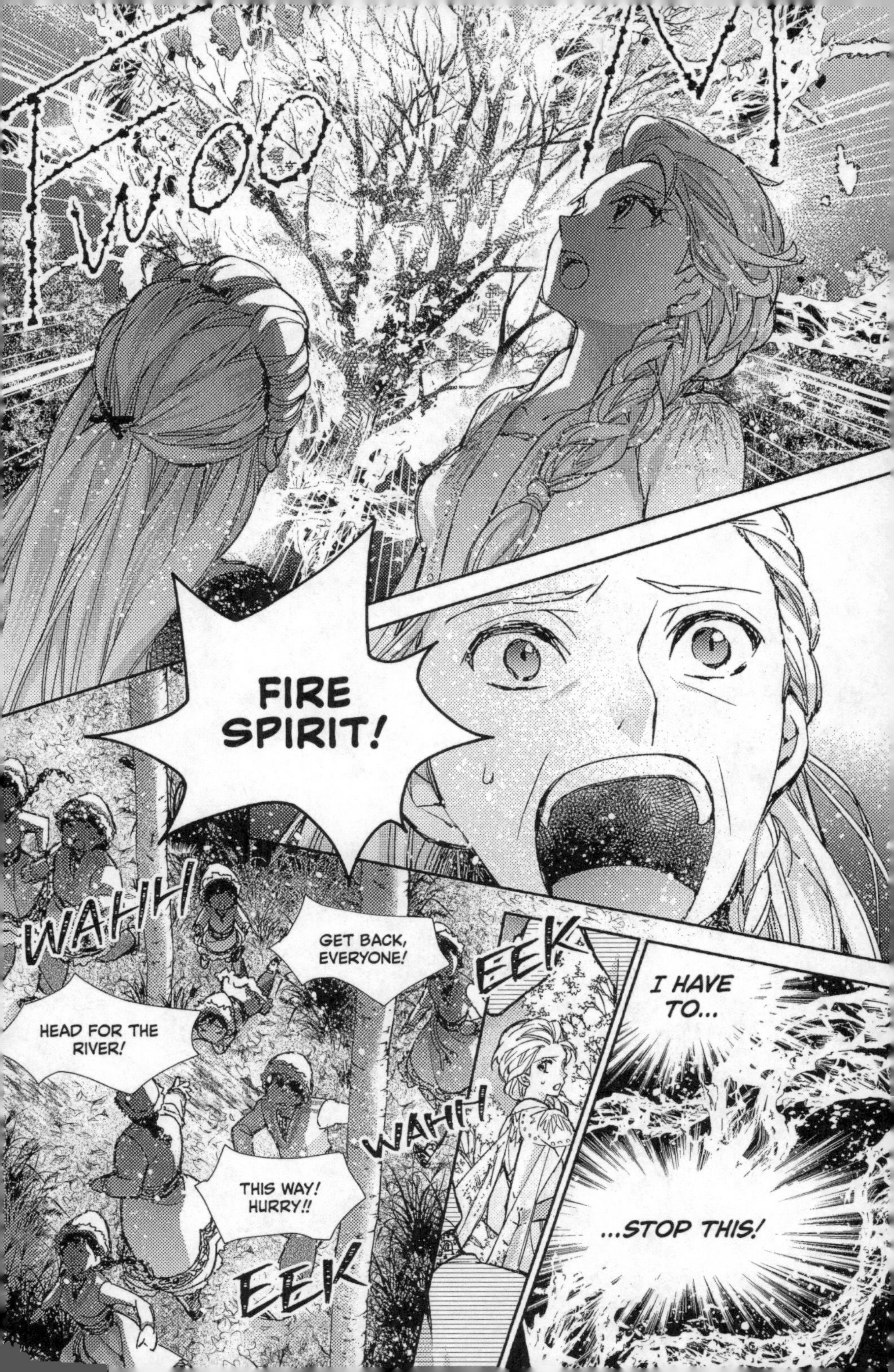
FWOOO
FIRE SPIRIT!
WAHH
GET BACK, EVERYONE!
HEAD FOR THE RIVER!
THIS WAY! HURRY!!
EEK
WAHH
EEK
I HAVE TO...
...STOP THIS!

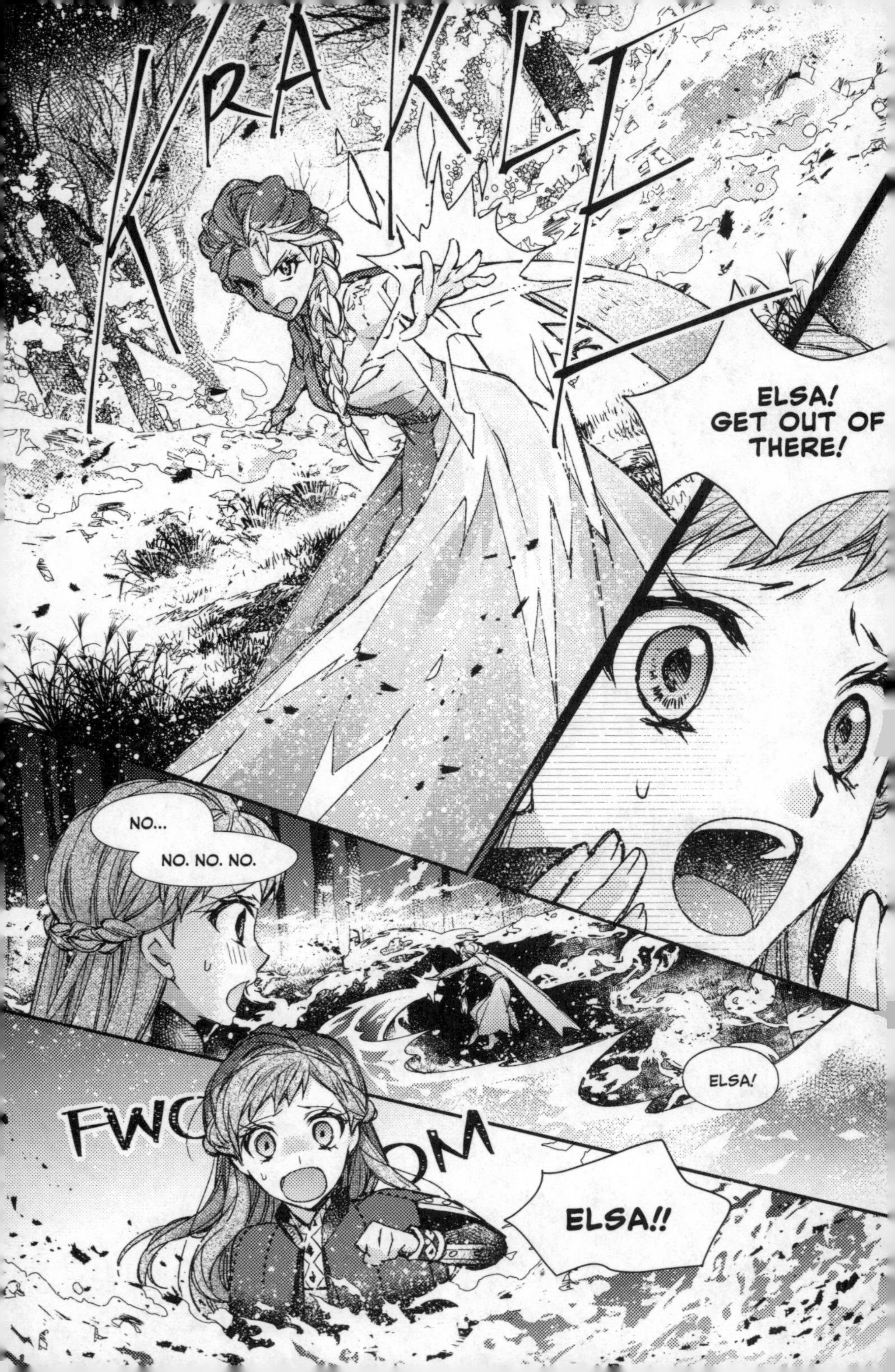
KRAKT
ELSA! GET OUT OF THERE!
NO... NO. NO. NO.
ELSA!
FWO OM
ELSA!!

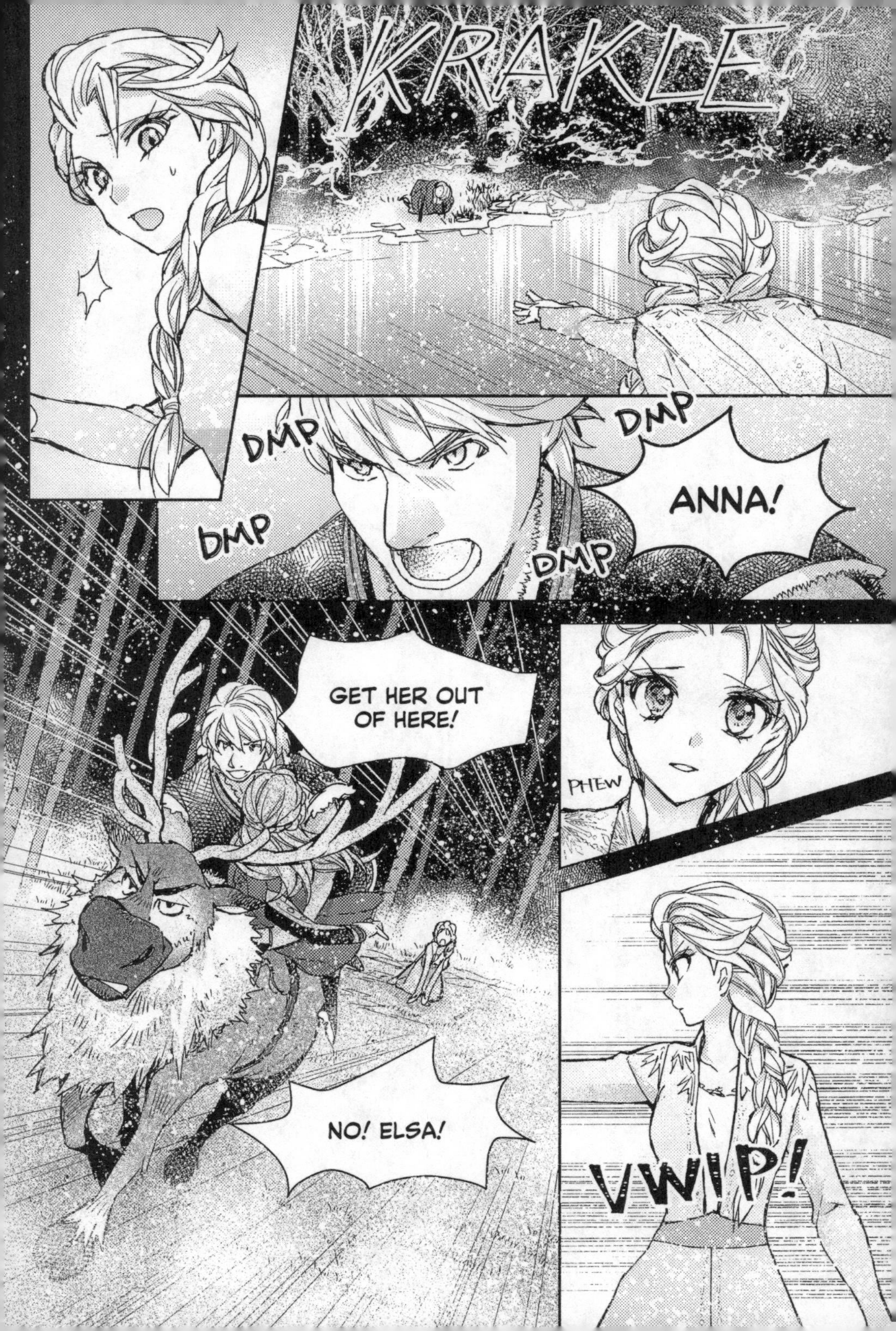
KRAKLE
DMP
DMP
DMP
DMP
ANNA!
GET HER OUT OF HERE!
NO! ELSA!
PHEW
VWIP!

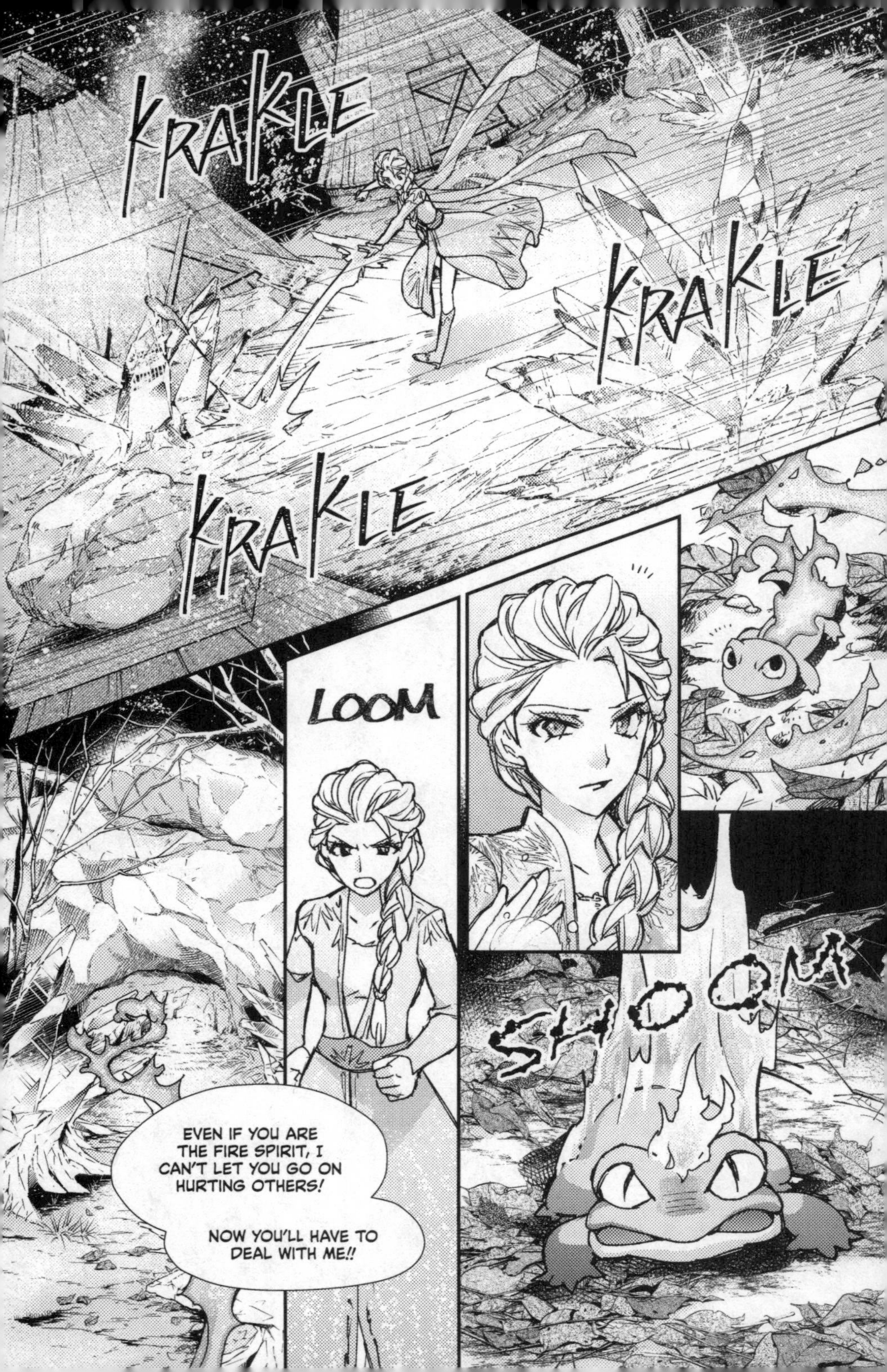
KRAKLE
KRAKLE
KRAKLE
LOOM
EVEN IF YOU ARE THE FIRE SPIRIT, I CAN'T LET YOU GO ON HURTING OTHERS!
NOW YOU'LL HAVE TO DEAL WITH ME!!
SHOOM

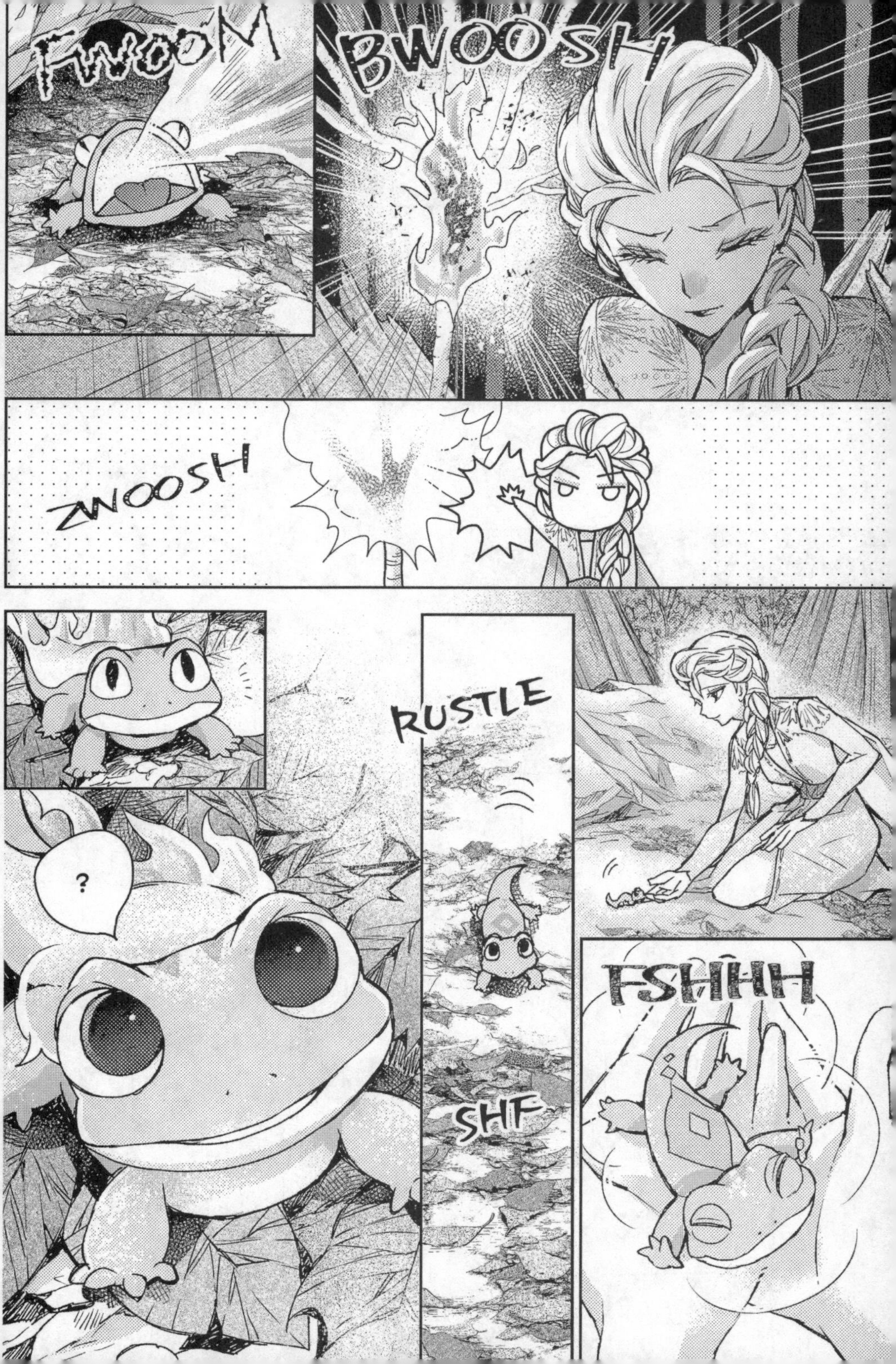
FWOOM
BWOOSH
ZWOOSH
?
RUSTLE
SHF
FSHHH

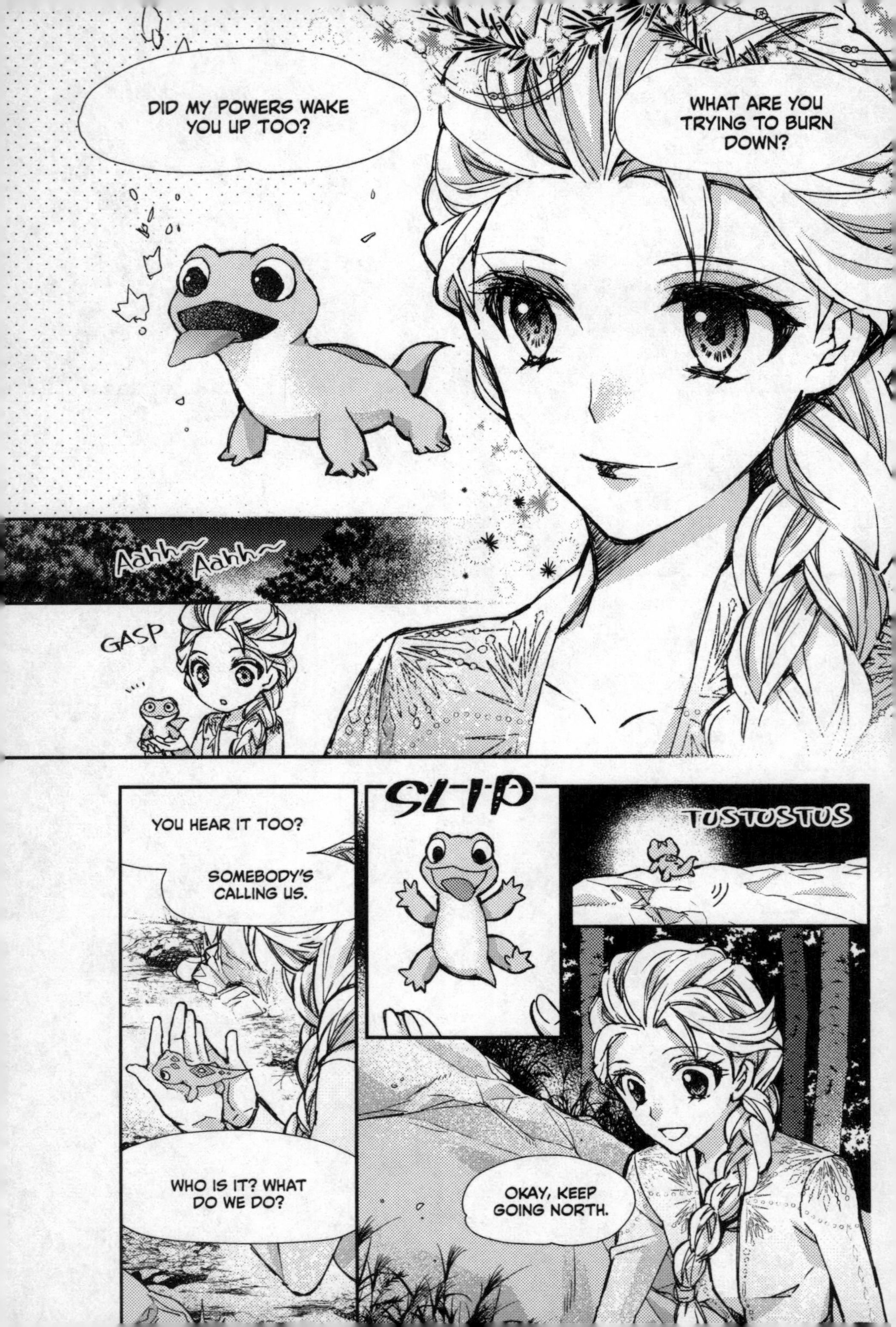
DID MY POWERS WAKE YOU UP TOO?
WHAT ARE YOU TRYING TO BURN DOWN?
Aahh~ Aahh~
GASP
...
YOU HEAR IT TOO?
SOMEBODY'S CALLING US.
WHO IS IT? WHAT DO WE DO?
SLIP
TUSTUSTUS
OKAY, KEEP GOING NORTH.

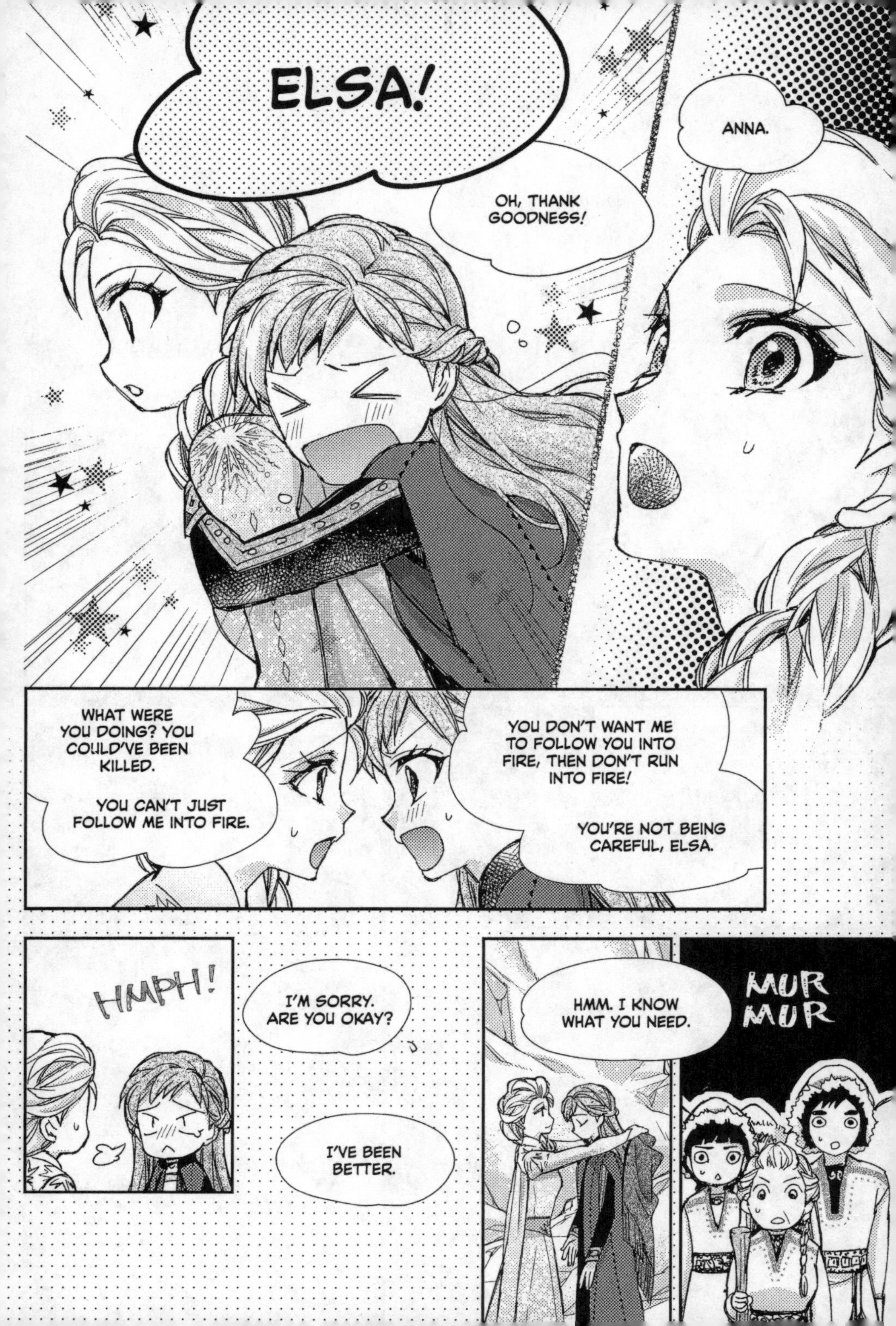
ELSA!
OH, THANK GOODNESS!
ANNA.
WHAT WERE YOU DOING? YOU COULD'VE BEEN KILLED.
YOU CAN'T JUST FOLLOW ME INTO FIRE.
YOU DON'T WANT ME TO FOLLOW YOU INTO FIRE, THEN DON'T RUN INTO FIRE!
YOU'RE NOT BEING CAREFUL, ELSA.
HMPH!
I'M SORRY. ARE YOU OKAY?
I'VE BEEN BETTER.
HMM. I KNOW WHAT YOU NEED.
MUR MUR

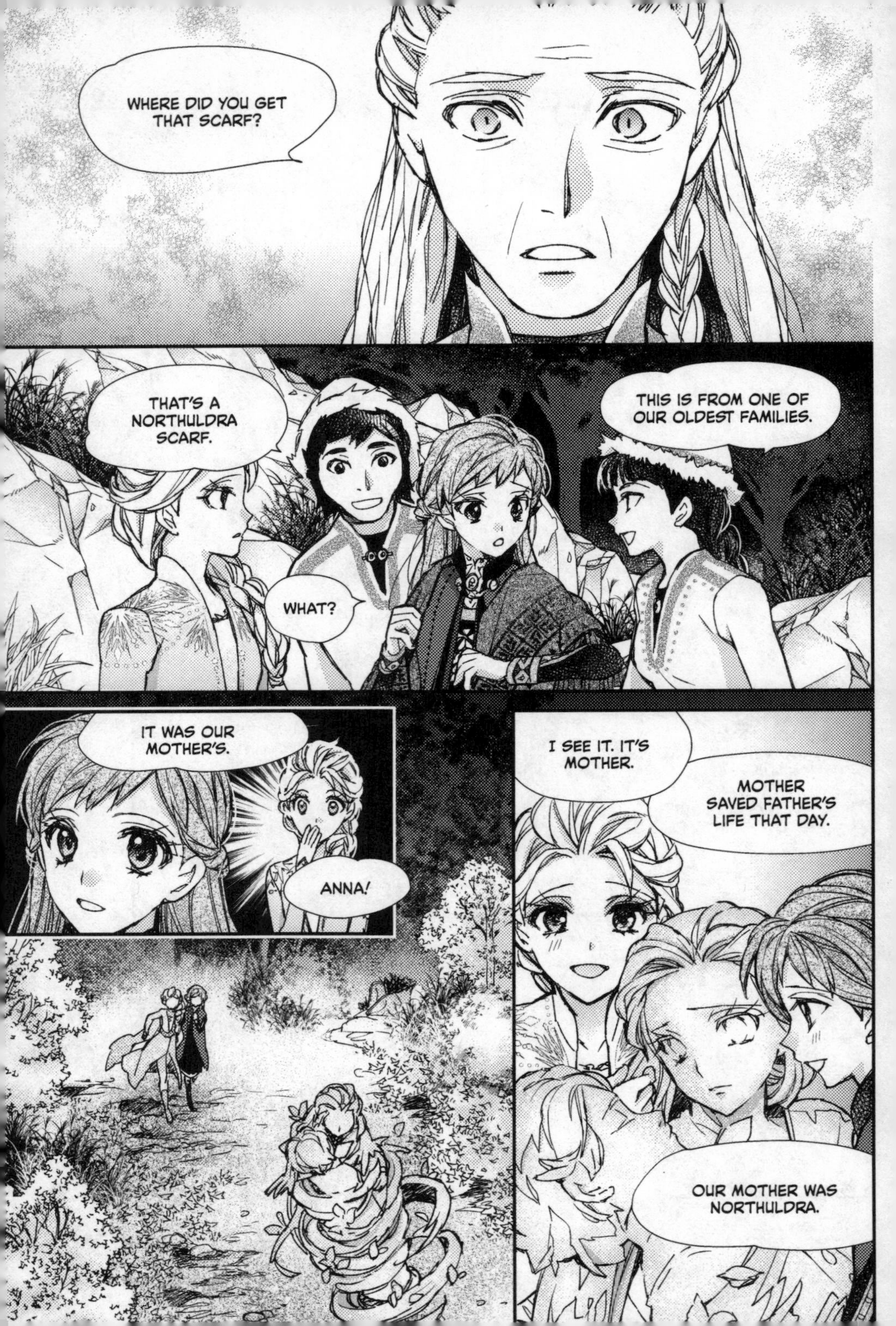

WHERE DID YOU GET THAT SCARF?
THAT'S A NORTHULDRA SCARF.
THIS IS FROM ONE OF OUR OLDEST FAMILIES.
WHAT?
IT WAS OUR MOTHER'S.
ANNA!
I SEE IT. IT'S MOTHER.
MOTHER SAVED FATHER'S LIFE THAT DAY.
OUR MOTHER WAS NORTHULDRA.

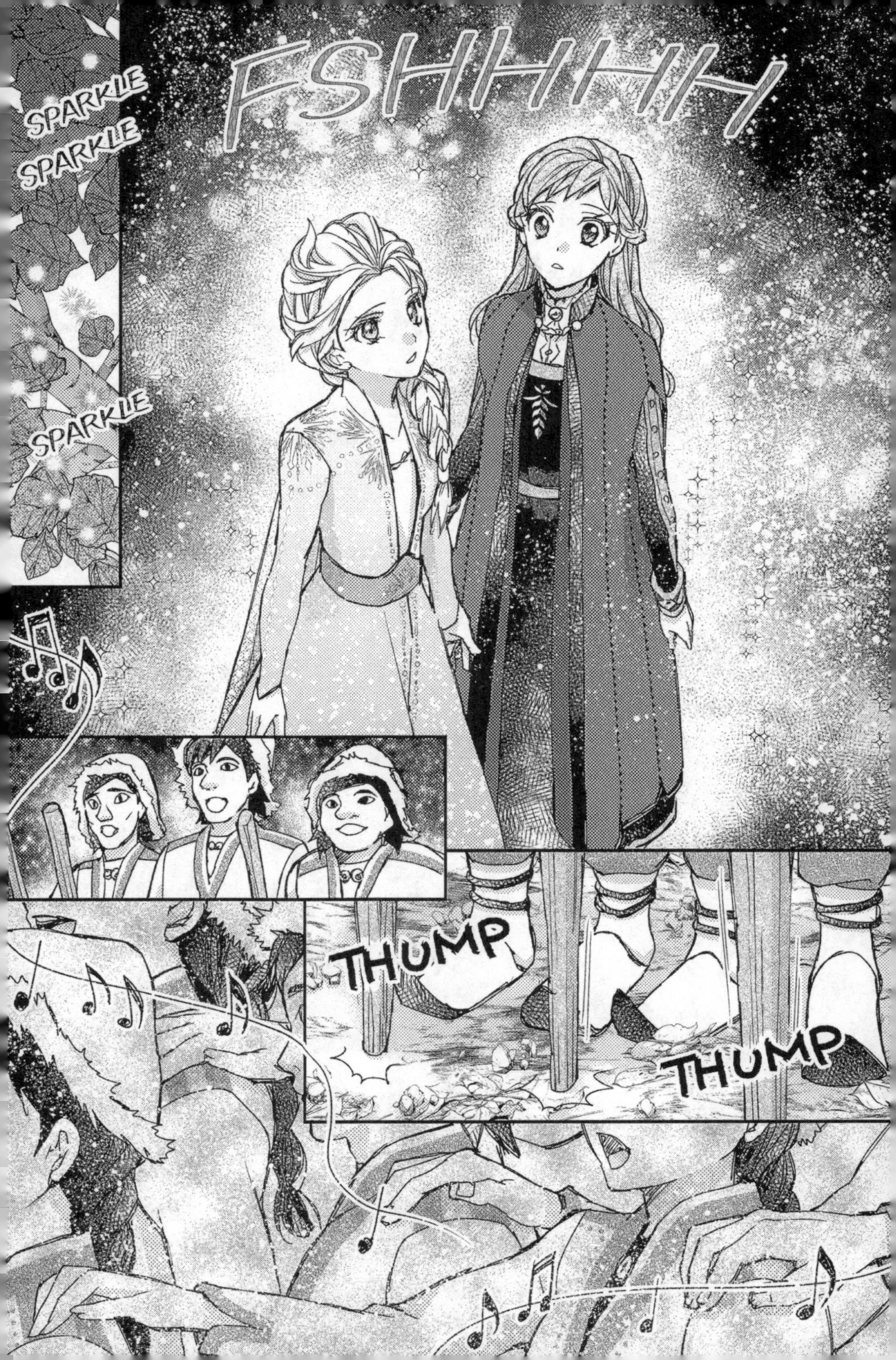
FSHHHHH
SPARKLE SPARKLE
SPARKLE
THUMP
THUMP

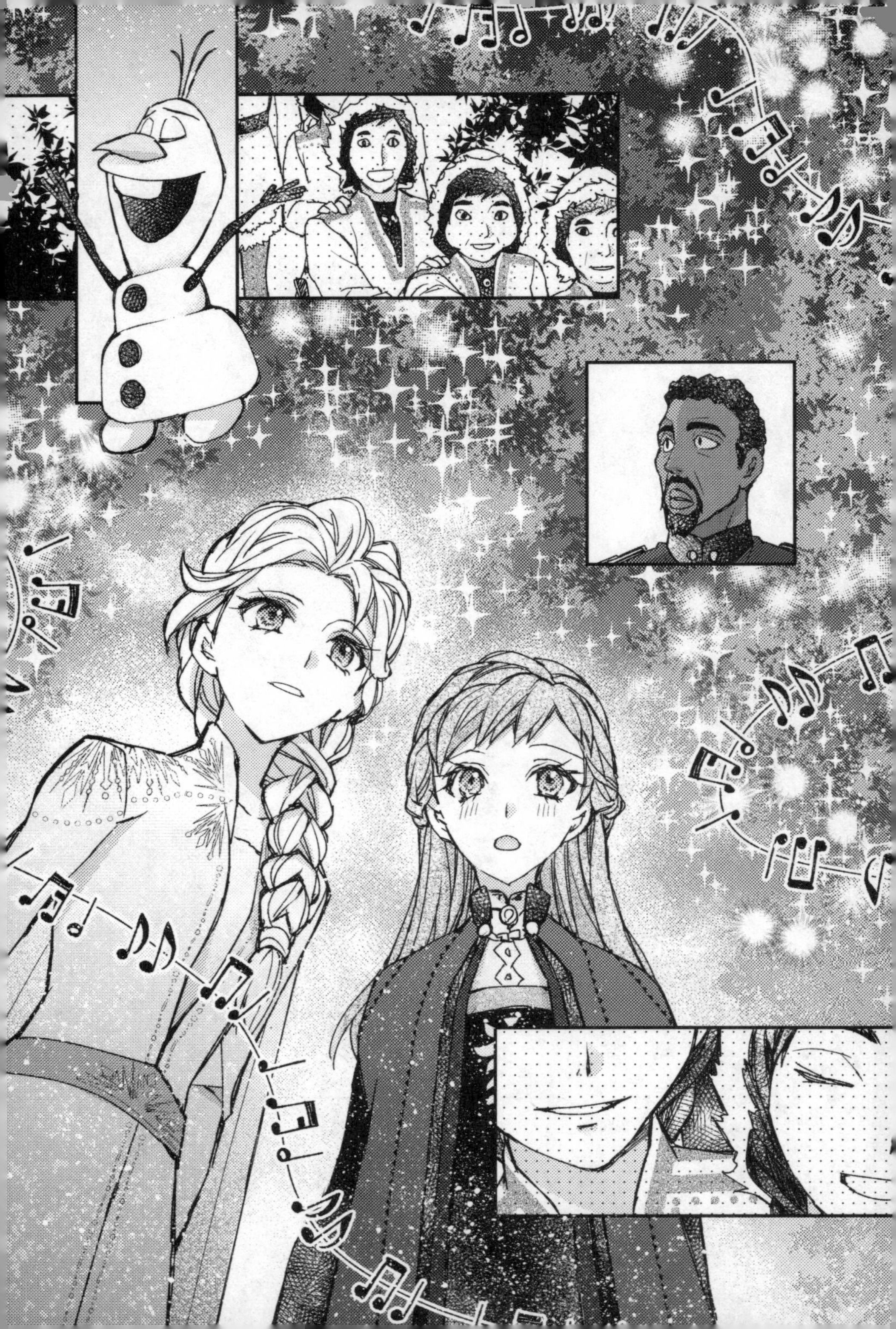

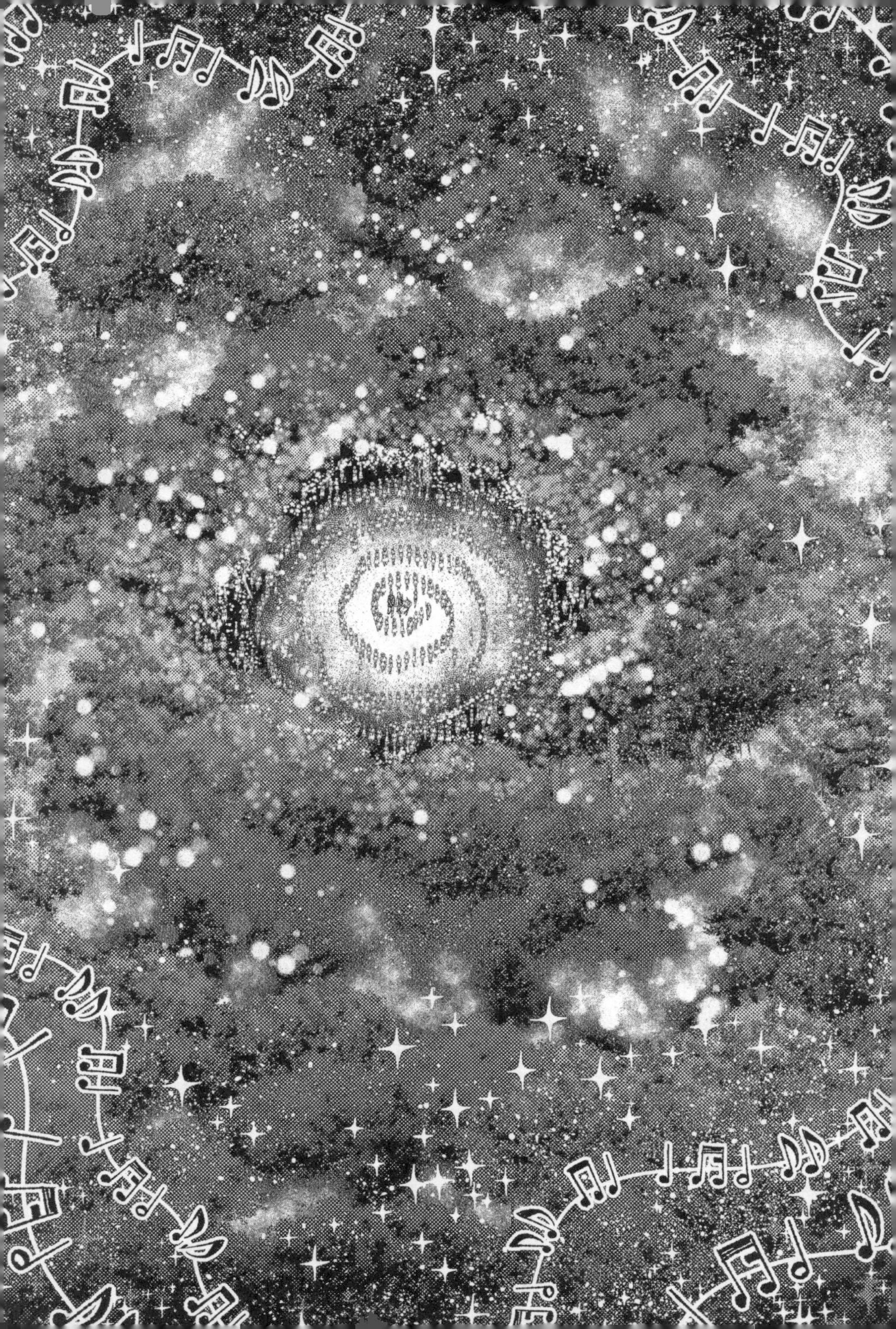

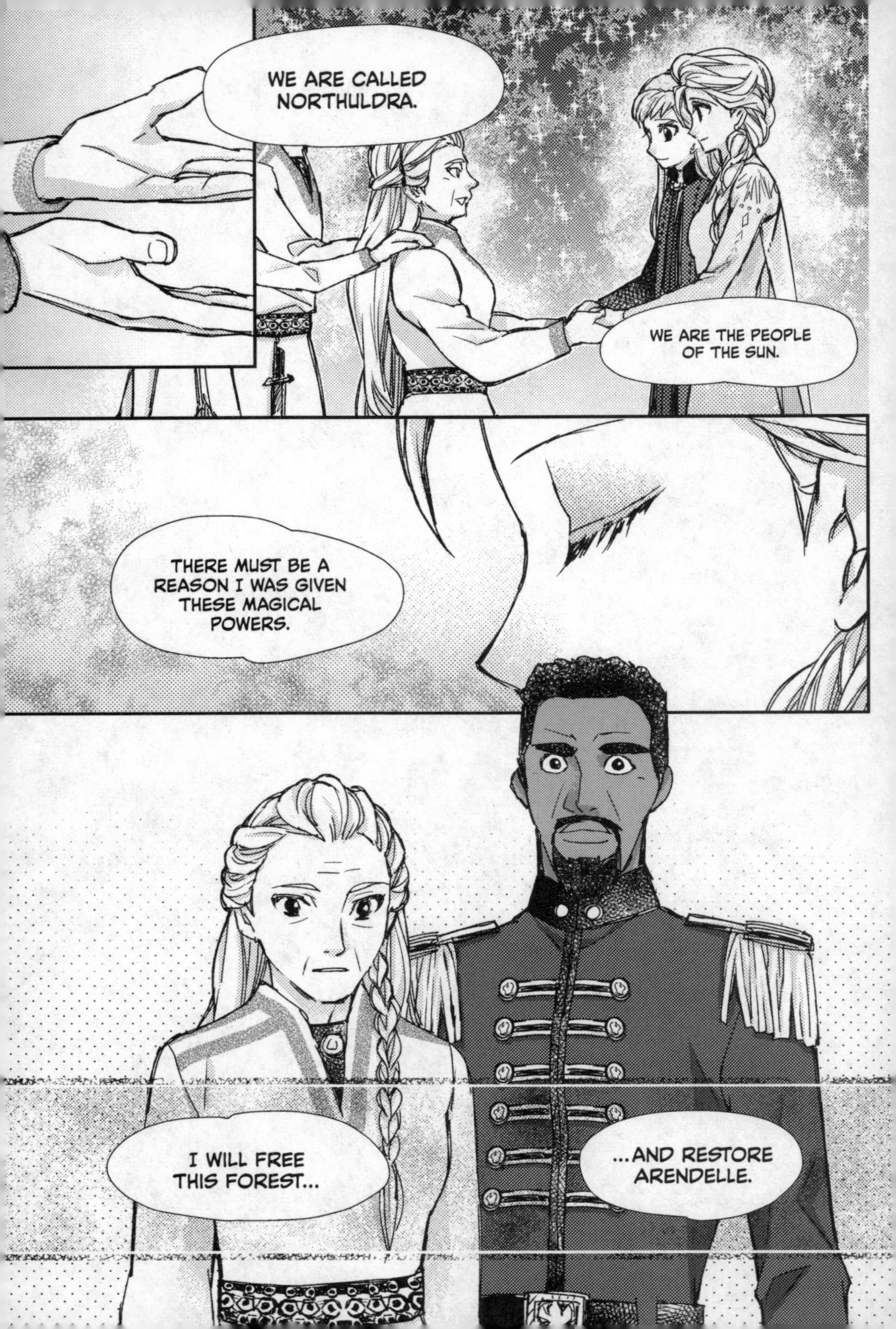
WE ARE CALLED NORTHULDRA.
WE ARE THE PEOPLE OF THE SUN.
THERE MUST BE A REASON I WAS GIVEN THESE MAGICAL POWERS.
I WILL FREE THIS FOREST...
...AND RESTORE ARENDELLE.

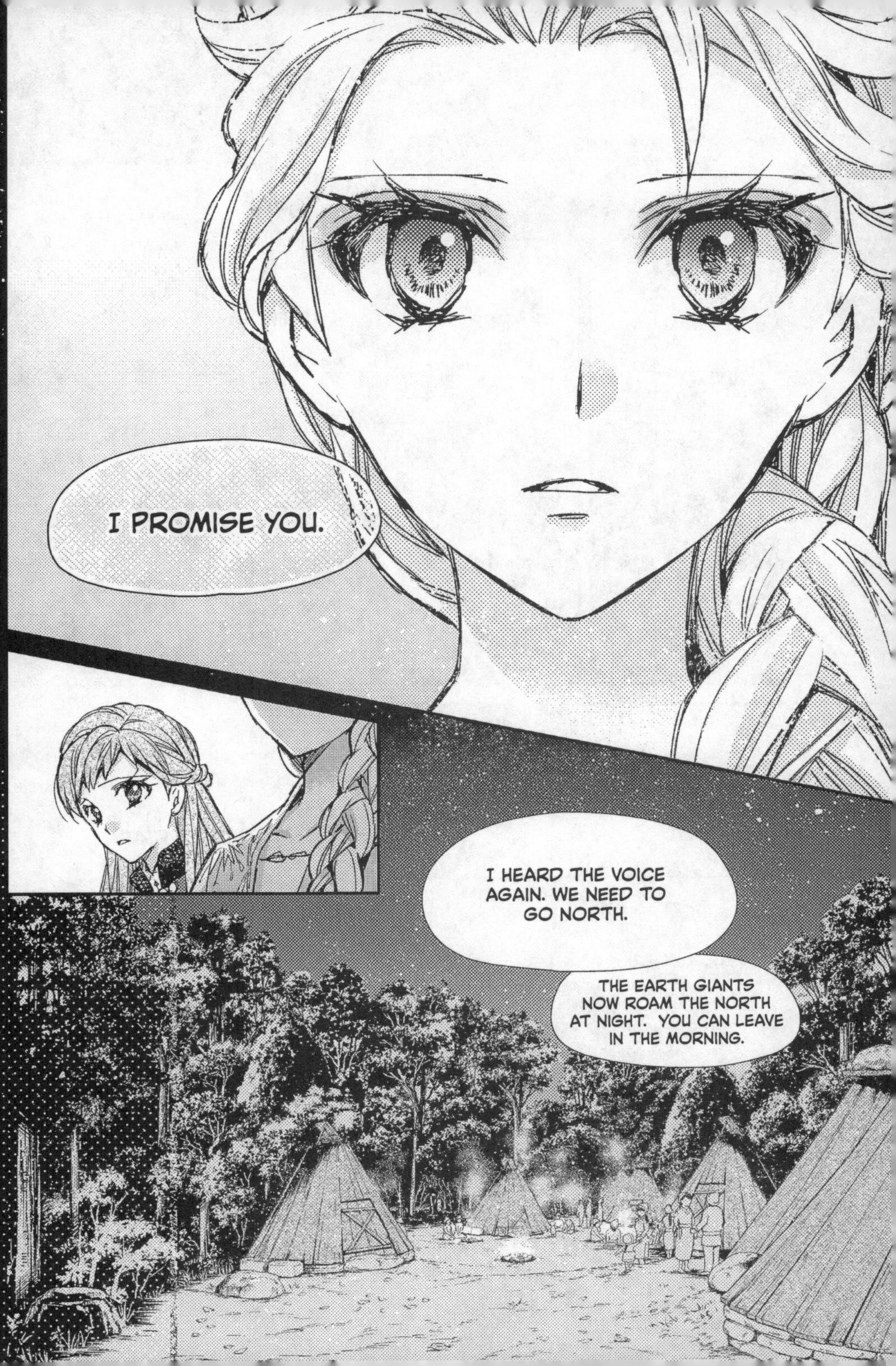
I PROMISE YOU.
I HEARD THE VOICE AGAIN. WE NEED TO GO NORTH.
THE EARTH GIANTS NOW ROAM THE NORTH AT NIGHT. YOU CAN LEAVE IN THE MORNING.

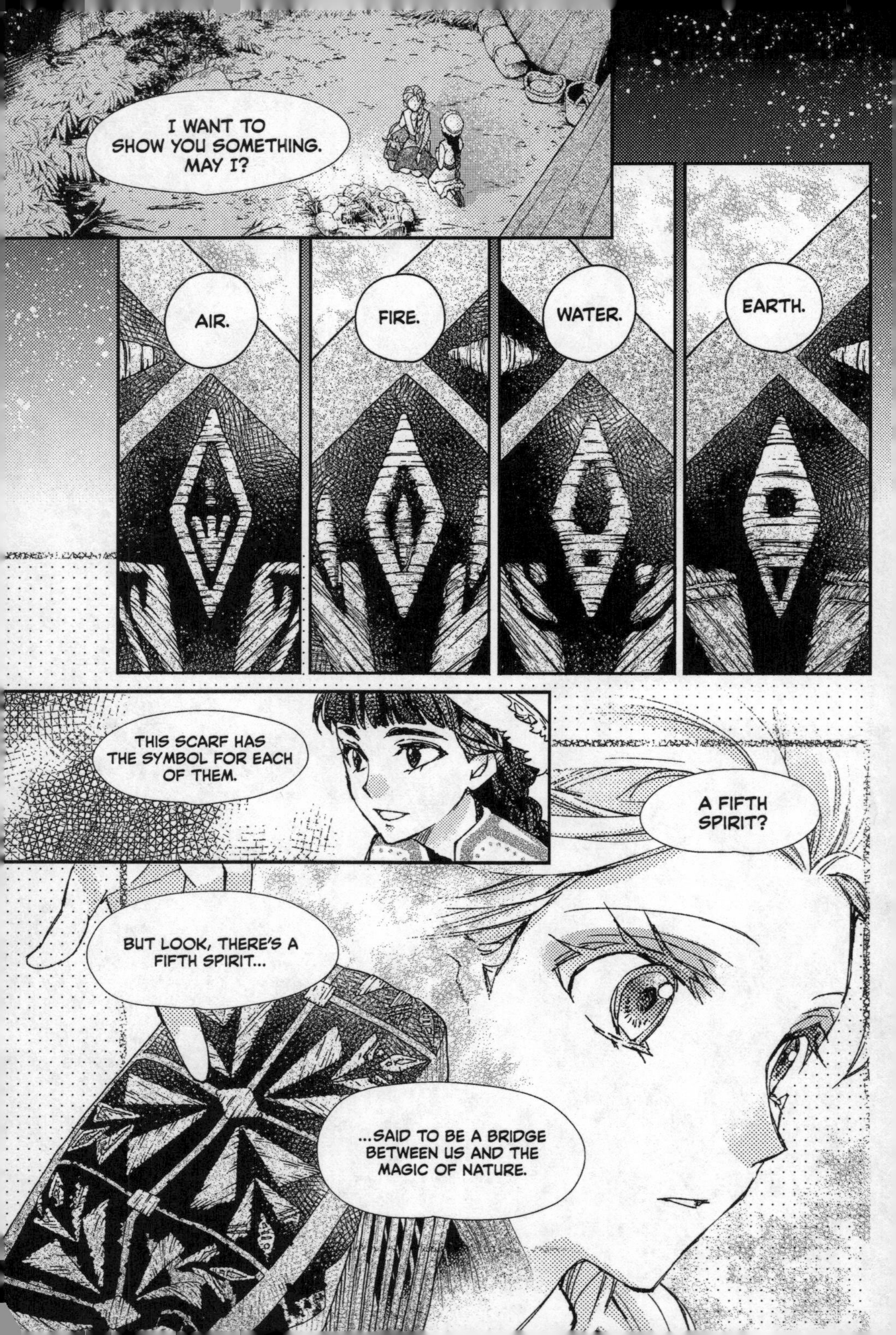
I WANT TO SHOW YOU SOMETHING. MAY I?
AIR.
FIRE.
WATER.
EARTH.
THIS SCARF HAS THE SYMBOL FOR EACH OF THEM.
A FIFTH SPIRIT?
BUT LOOK, THERE'S A FIFTH SPIRIT...
...SAID TO BE A BRIDGE BETWEEN US AND THE MAGIC OF NATURE.

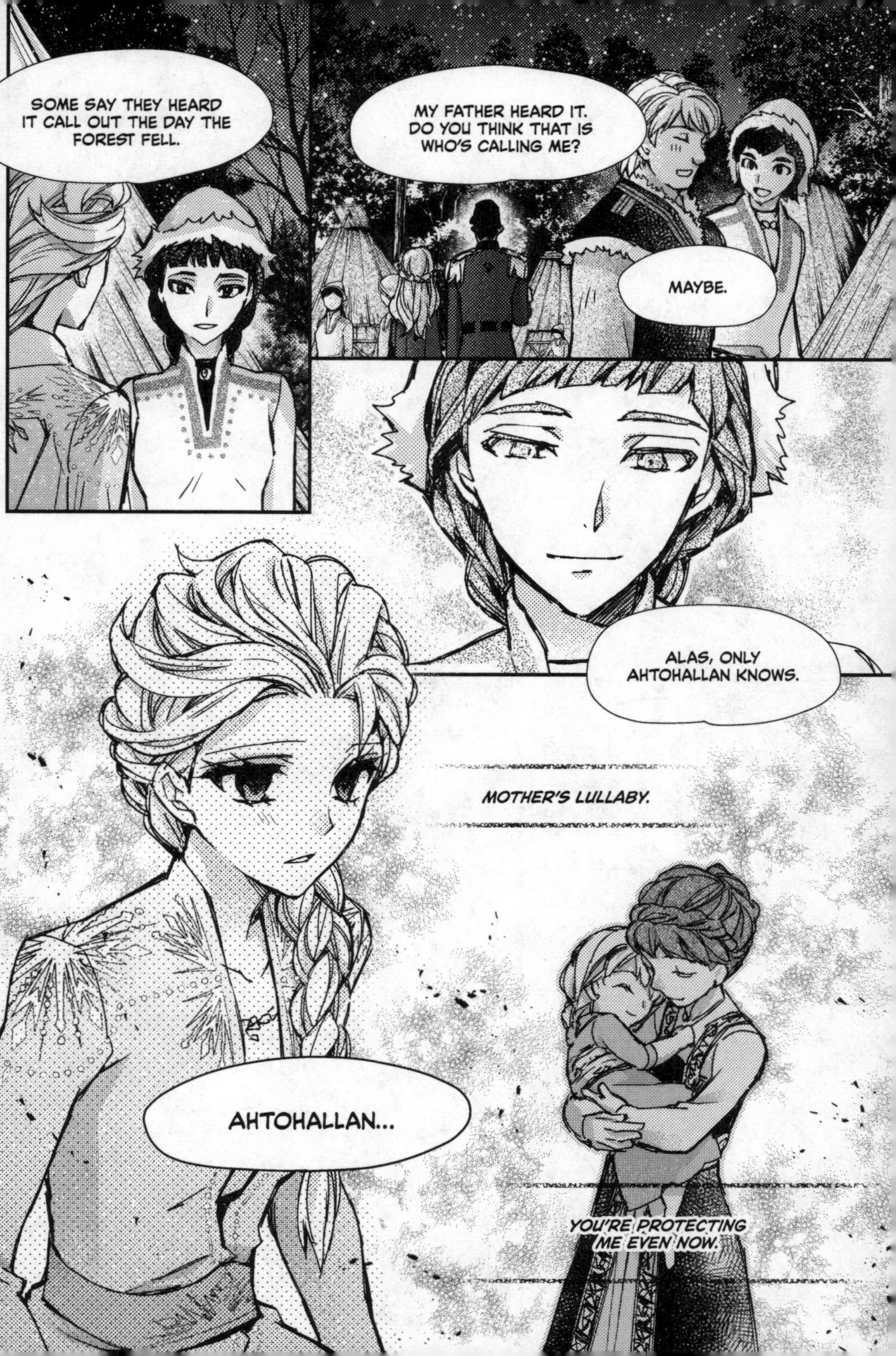
SOME SAY THEY HEARD IT CALL OUT THE DAY THE FOREST FELL.
MY FATHER HEARD IT. DO YOU THINK THAT IS WHO'S CALLING ME?
MAYBE.
ALAS, ONLY AHTOHALLAN KNOWS.
MOTHER'S LULLABY.
AHTOHALLAN...
YOU'RE PROTECTING ME EVEN NOW.

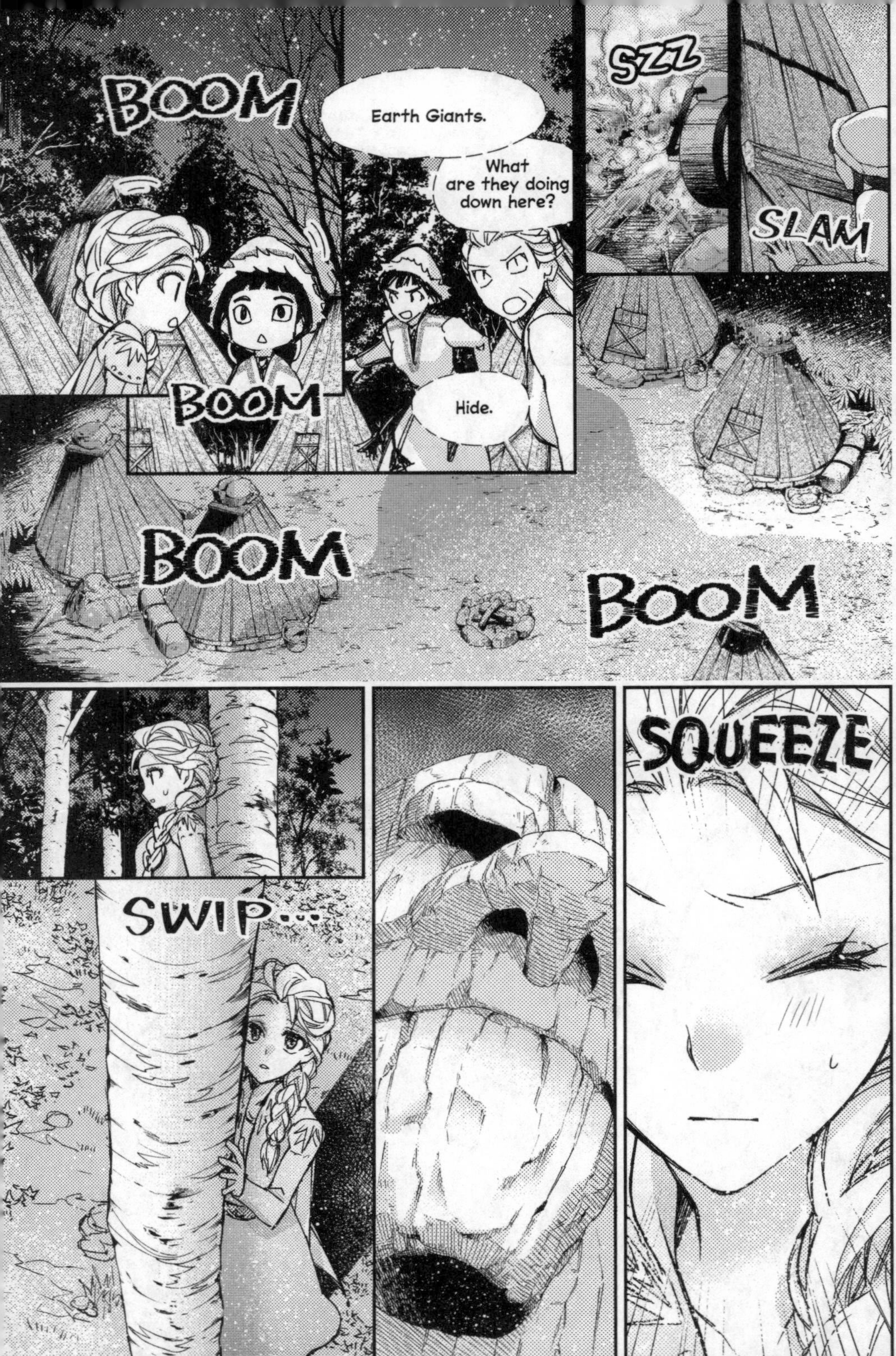
BOOM
Earth Giants.
What are they doing down here?
BOOM
Hide.
SZZ
SLAM
BOOM
BOOM
SWIP...
SQUEEZE

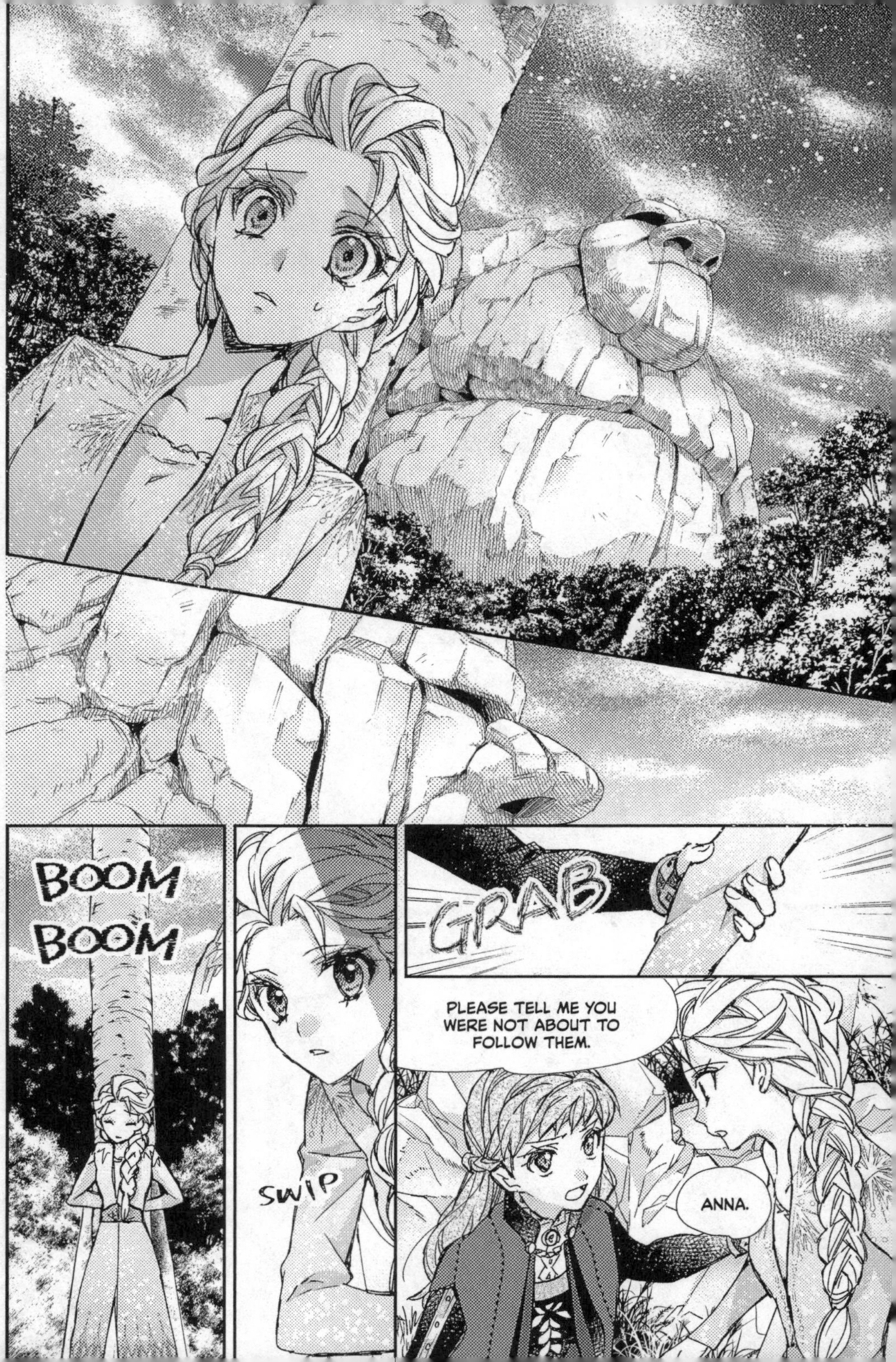
BOOM
BOOM
GRAB
PLEASE TELL ME YOU WERE NOT ABOUT TO FOLLOW THEM.
SWIP
ANNA.

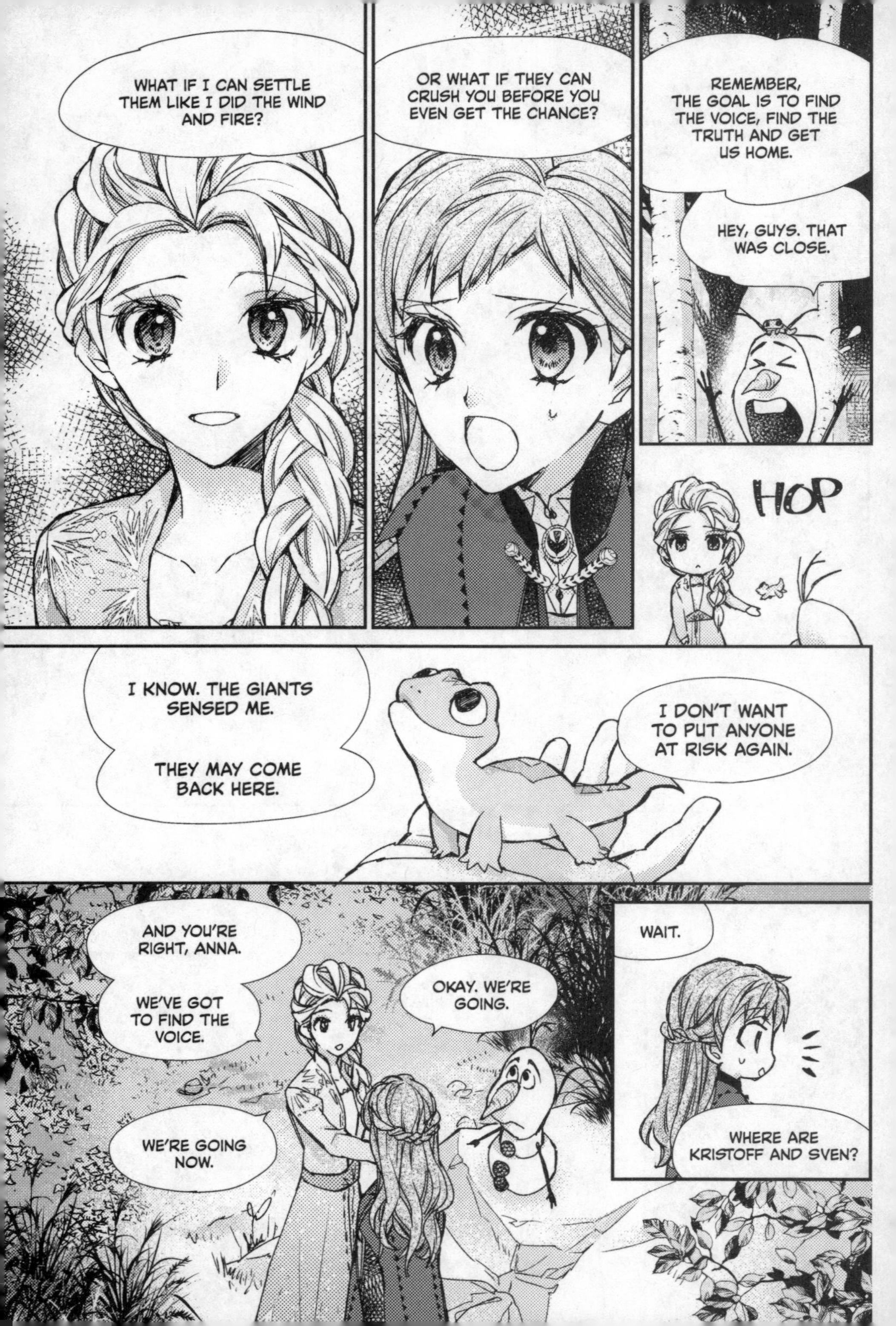
WHAT IF I CAN SETTLE THEM LIKE I DID THE WIND AND FIRE?
OR WHAT IF THEY CAN CRUSH YOU BEFORE YOU EVEN GET THE CHANCE?
REMEMBER, THE GOAL IS TO FIND THE VOICE, FIND THE TRUTH AND GET US HOME.
HEY, GUYS. THAT WAS CLOSE.
HOP
I KNOW. THE GIANTS SENSED ME.
THEY MAY COME BACK HERE.
I DON'T WANT TO PUT ANYONE AT RISK AGAIN.
AND YOU'RE RIGHT, ANNA.
WE'VE GOT TO FIND THE VOICE.
OKAY. WE'RE GOING.
WE'RE GOING NOW.
WAIT.
WHERE ARE KRISTOFF AND SVEN?

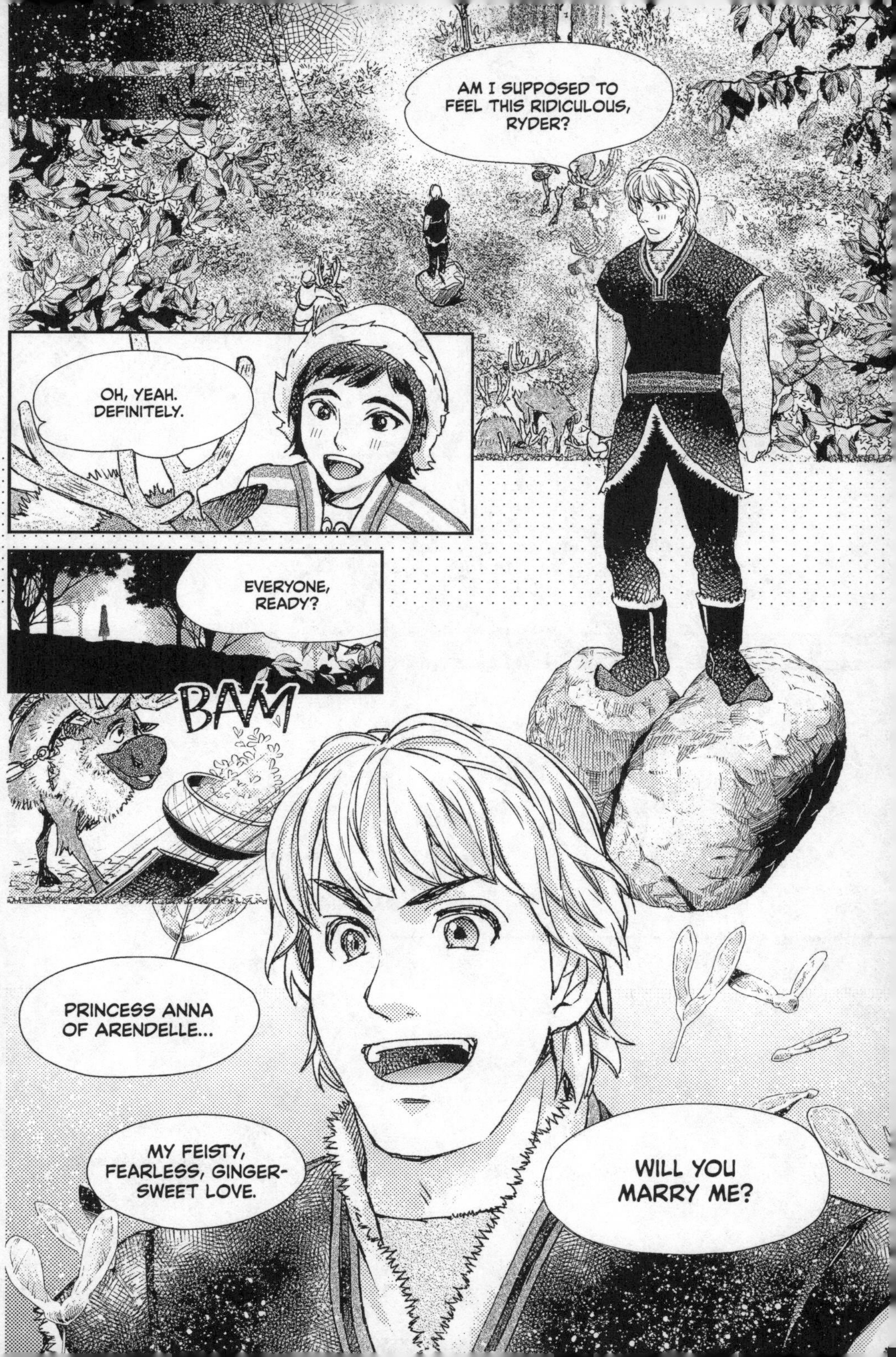
AM I SUPPOSED TO FEEL THIS RIDICULOUS, RYDER?
OH, YEAH. DEFINITELY.
EVERYONE, READY?
BAM
PRINCESS ANNA OF ARENDELLE...
MY FEISTY, FEARLESS, GINGER-SWEET LOVE.
WILL YOU MARRY ME?

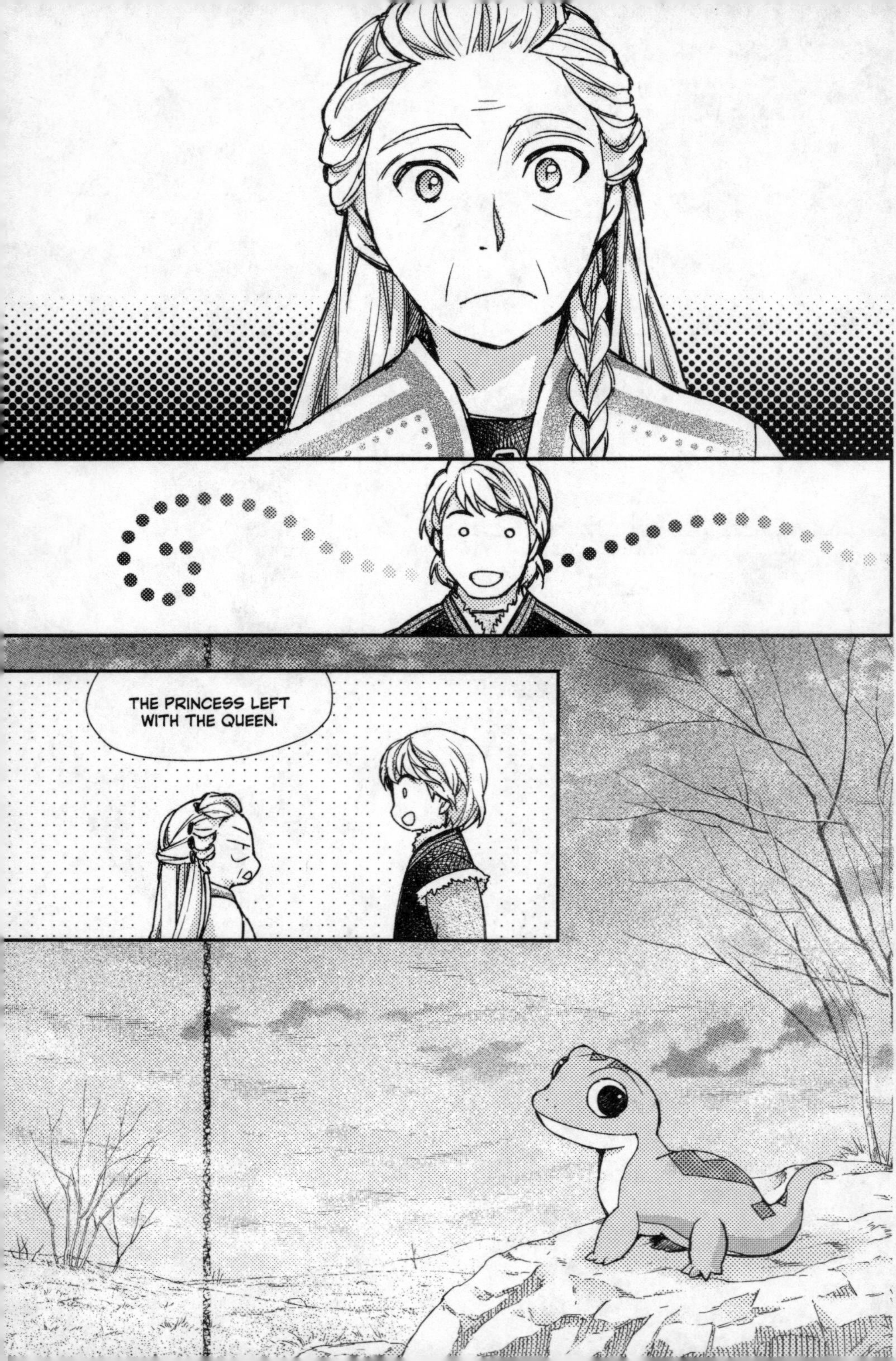
THE PRINCESS LEFT WITH THE QUEEN.

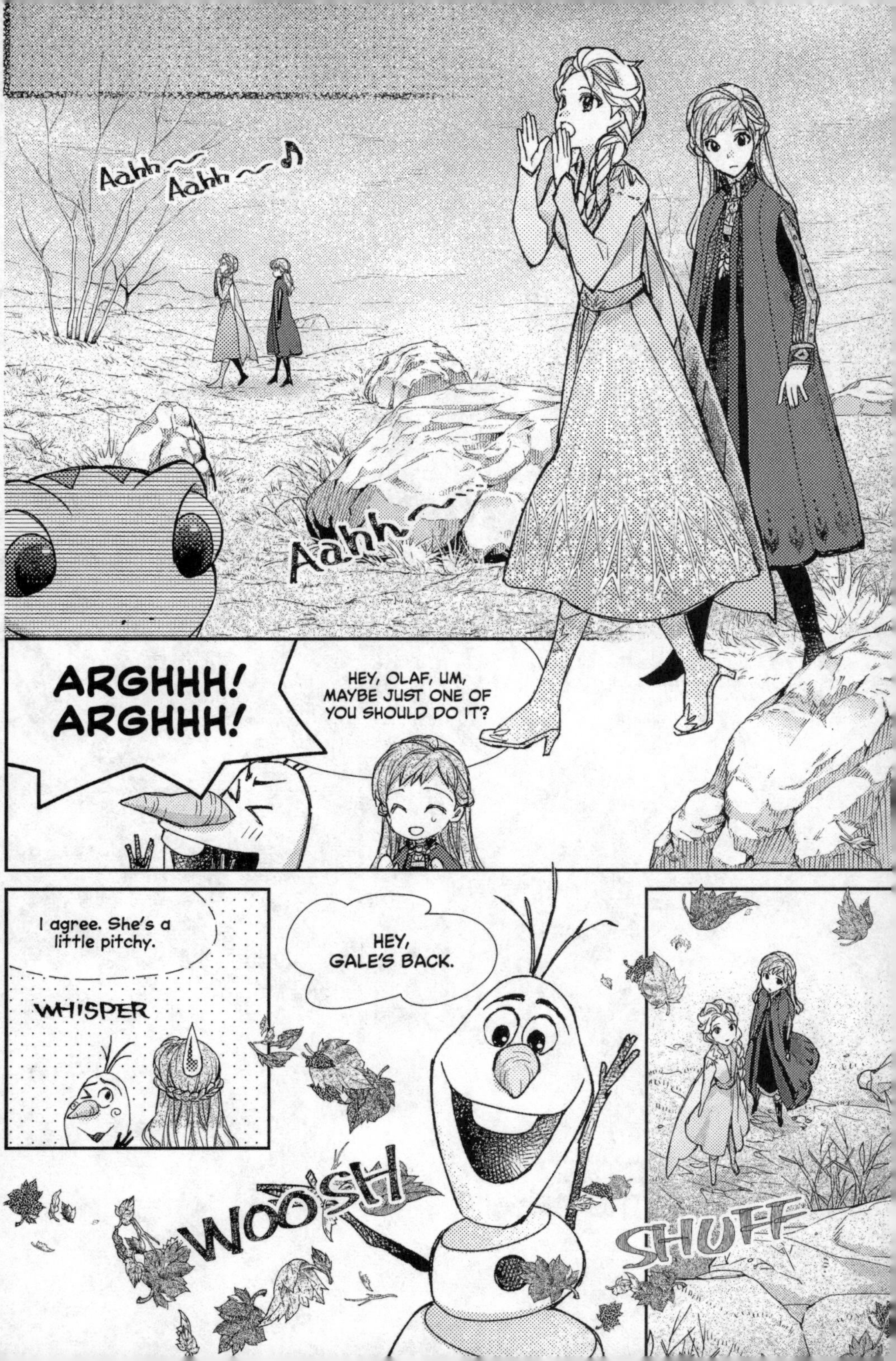
Aahh~~ Aahh~~♪
Aahh~~
ARGHHH! ARGHHH!
HEY, OLAF, UM, MAYBE JUST ONE OF YOU SHOULD DO IT?
I agree. She's a little pitchy.
WHISPER
HEY, GALE'S BACK.
WOOSH
SHUFF

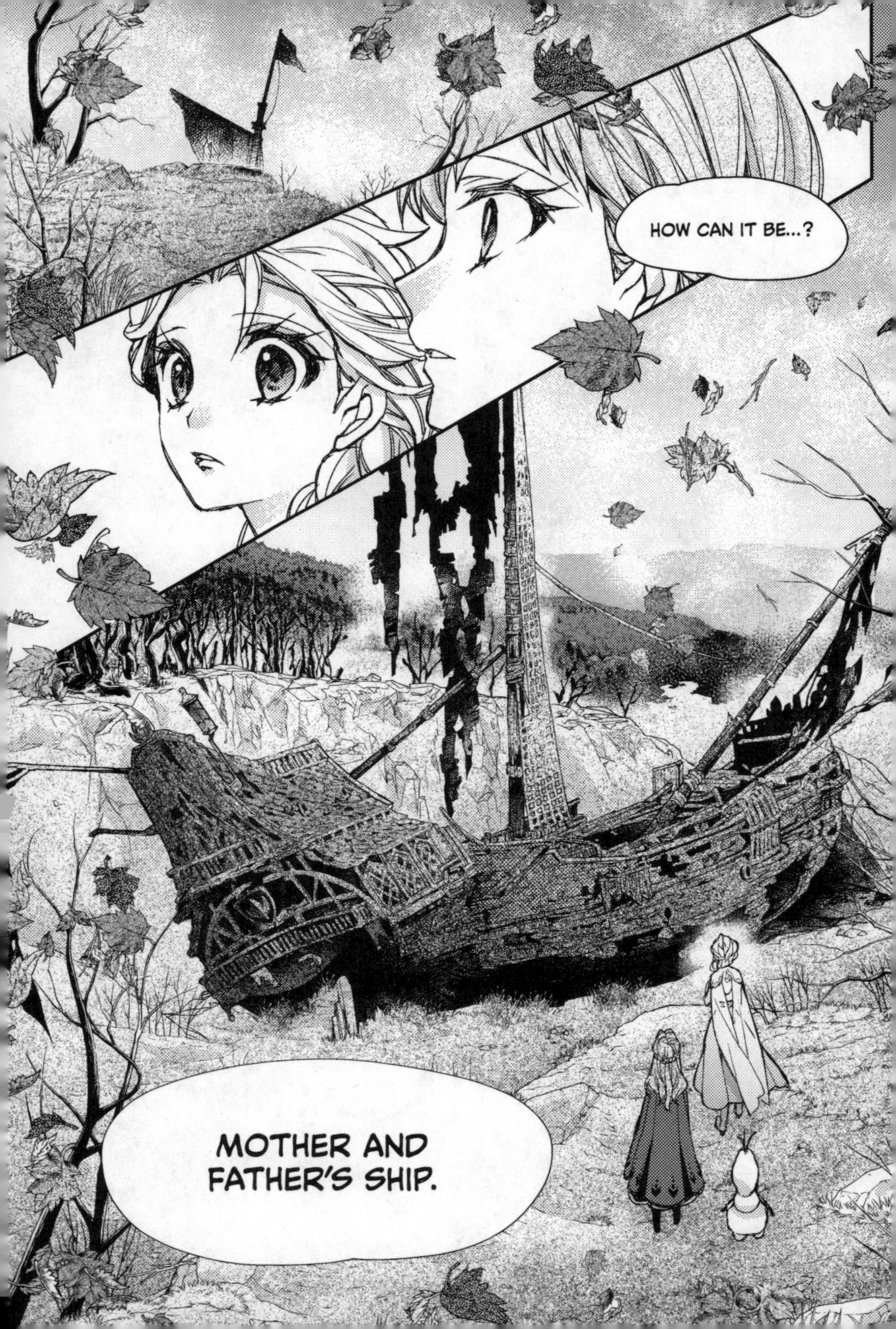
HOW CAN IT BE...?
MOTHER AND FATHER'S SHIP.

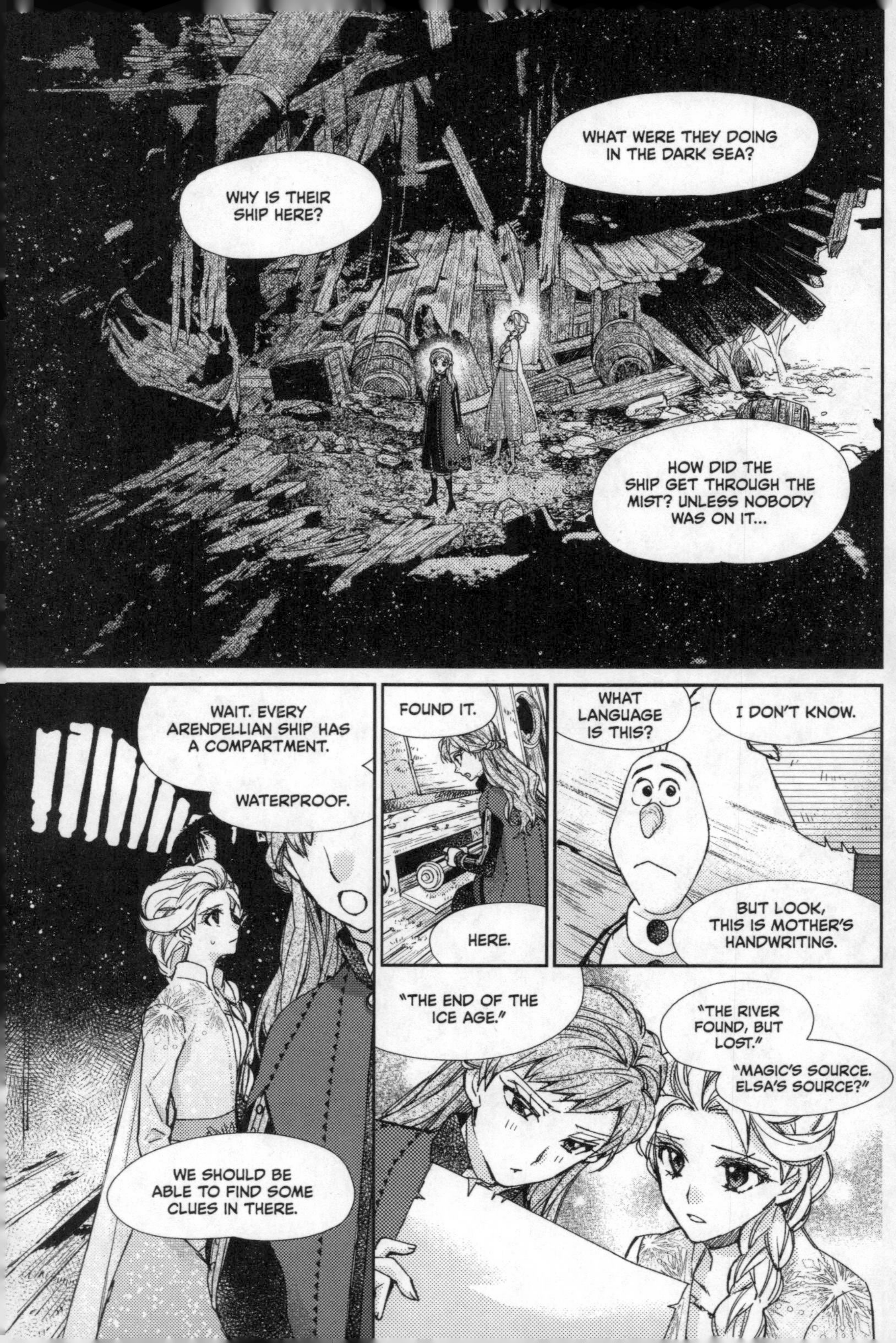
WHY IS THEIR SHIP HERE?
WHAT WERE THEY DOING IN THE DARK SEA?
HOW DID THE SHIP GET THROUGH THE MIST? UNLESS NOBODY WAS ON IT...
WAIT. EVERY ARENDELLIAN SHIP HAS A COMPARTMENT.
WATERPROOF.
WE SHOULD BE ABLE TO FIND SOME CLUES IN THERE.
FOUND IT.
HERE.
WHAT LANGUAGE IS THIS?
I DON'T KNOW.
BUT LOOK, THIS IS MOTHER'S HANDWRITING.
"THE END OF THE ICE AGE."
"THE RIVER FOUND, BUT LOST."
"MAGIC'S SOURCE. ELSA'S SOURCE?"

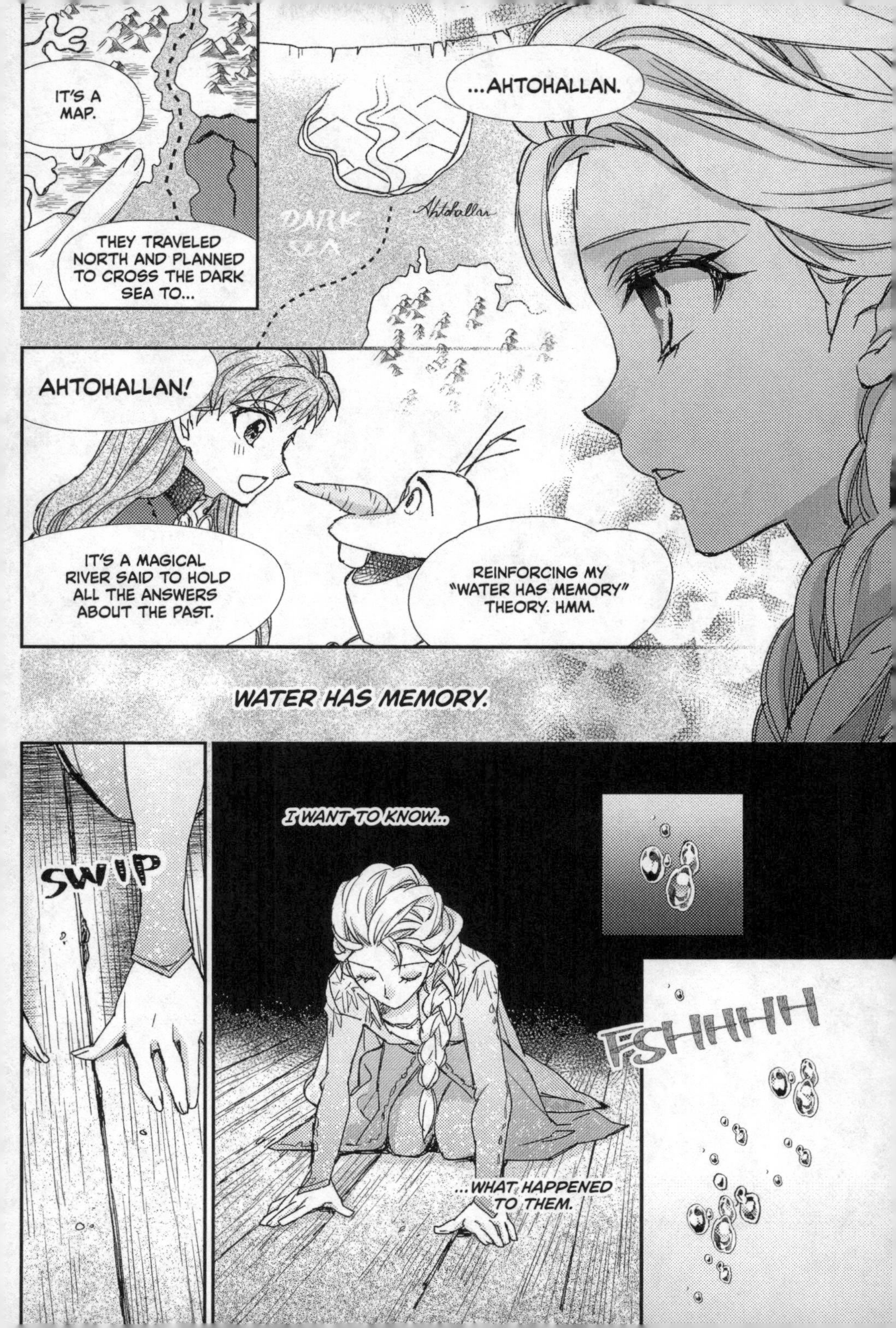
IT'S A MAP.
THEY TRAVELED NORTH AND PLANNED TO CROSS THE DARK SEA TO...
DARK SEA
Ahtohallan
...AHTOHALLAN.
AHTOHALLAN!
IT'S A MAGICAL RIVER SAID TO HOLD ALL THE ANSWERS ABOUT THE PAST.
REINFORCING MY "WATER HAS MEMORY" THEORY. HMM.
WATER HAS MEMORY.
SWIP
I WANT TO KNOW...
...WHAT HAPPENED TO THEM.
FSHHHH

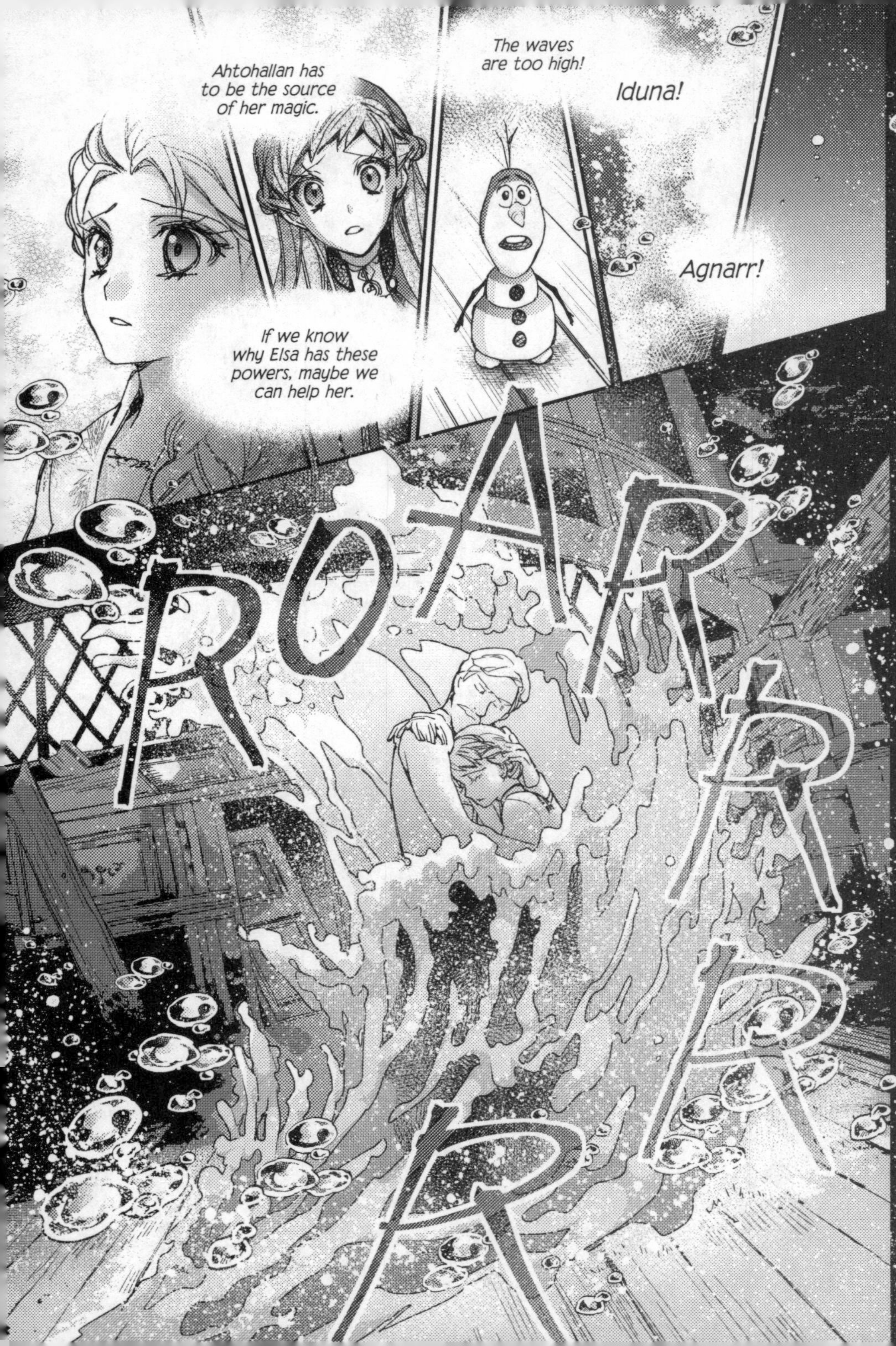
Ahtohallan has to be the source of her magic.
If we know why Elsa has these powers, maybe we can help her.
The waves are too high!
Iduna!
Agnarr!
ROARRRR

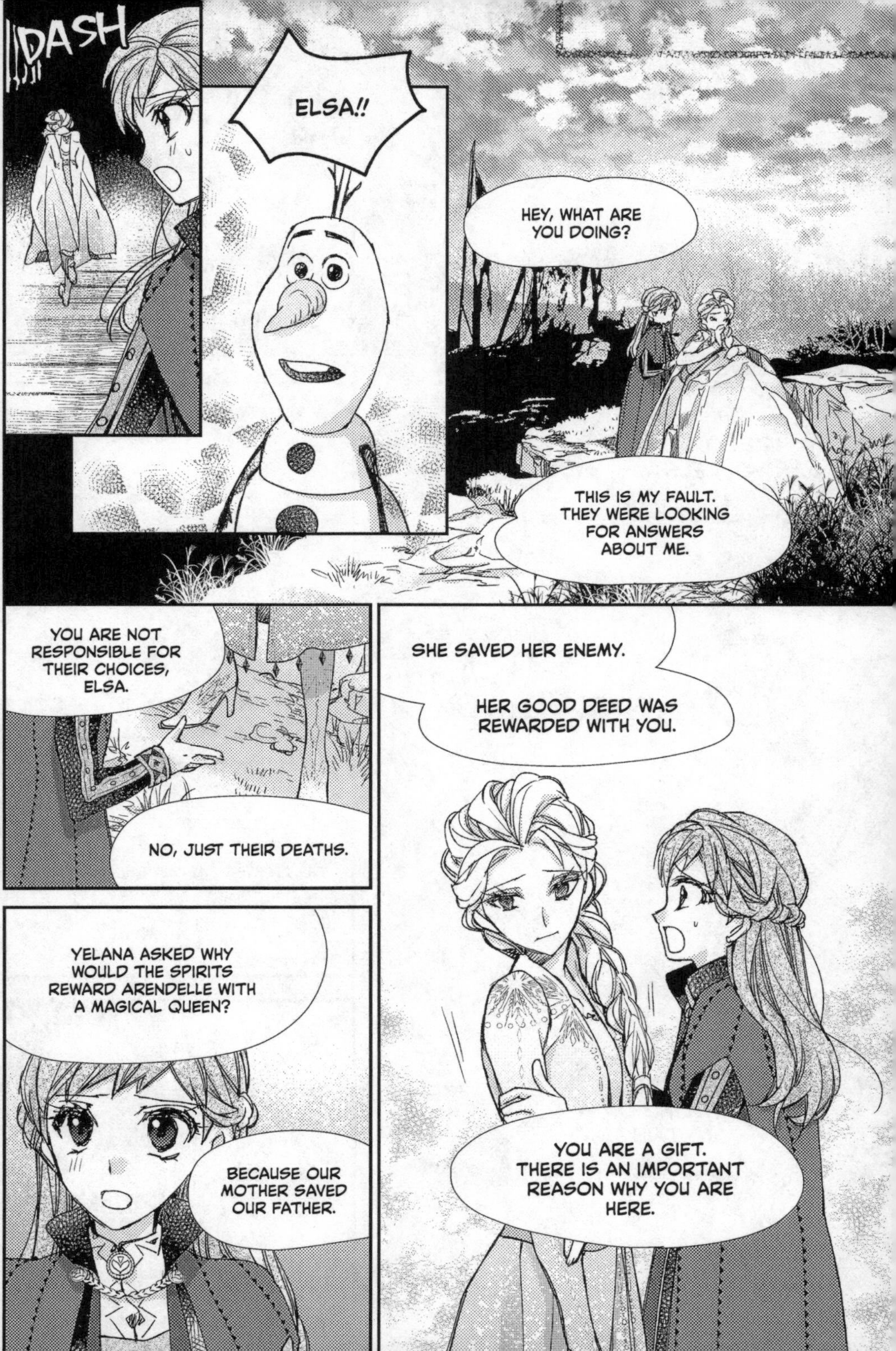

DASH
ELSA!!
HEY, WHAT ARE YOU DOING?
THIS IS MY FAULT. THEY WERE LOOKING FOR ANSWERS ABOUT ME.
YOU ARE NOT RESPONSIBLE FOR THEIR CHOICES, ELSA.
NO, JUST THEIR DEATHS.
YELANA ASKED WHY WOULD THE SPIRITS REWARD ARENDELLE WITH A MAGICAL QUEEN?
BECAUSE OUR MOTHER SAVED OUR FATHER.
SHE SAVED HER ENEMY.
HER GOOD DEED WAS REWARDED WITH YOU.
YOU ARE A GIFT. THERE IS AN IMPORTANT REASON WHY YOU ARE HERE.

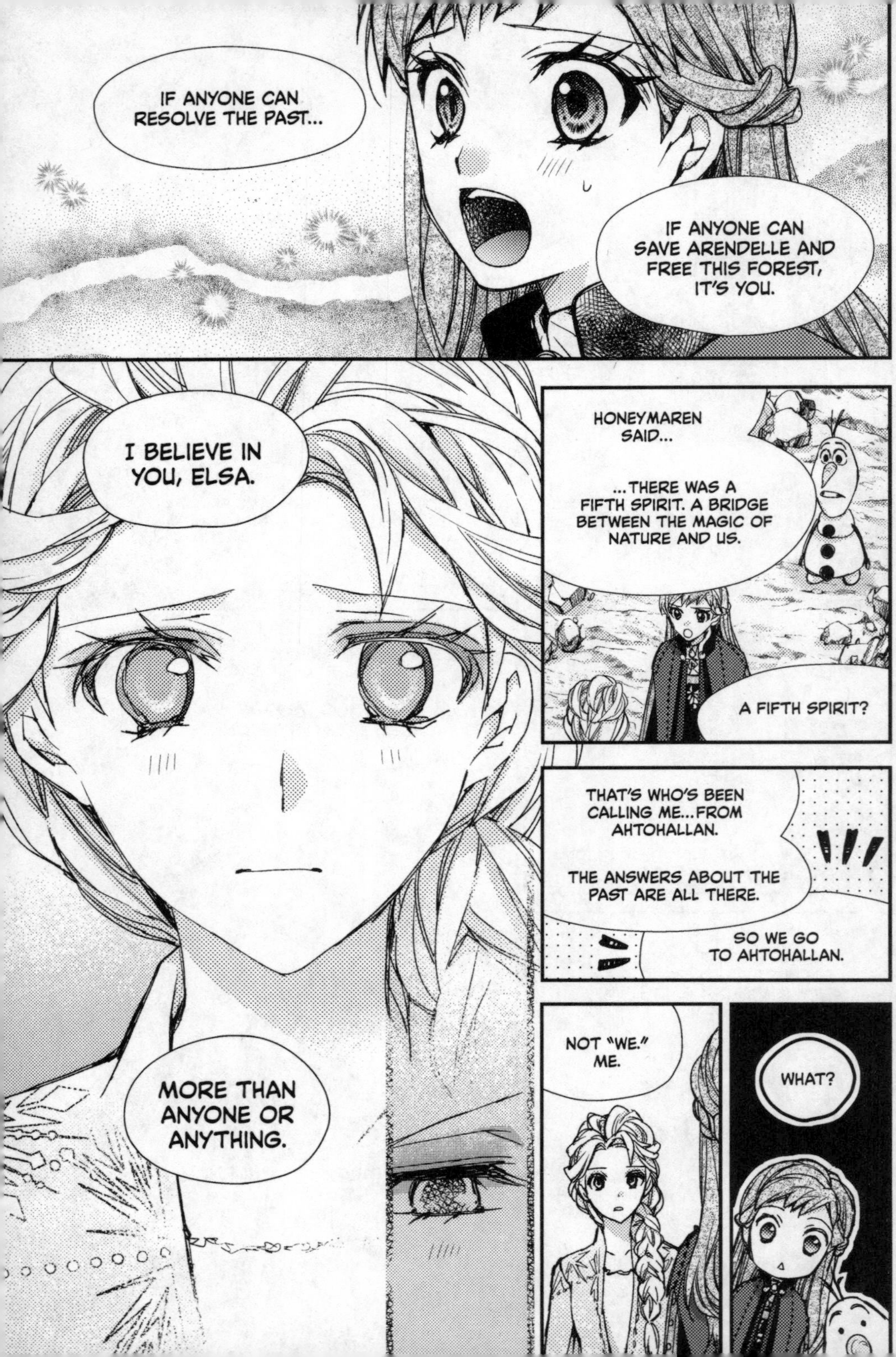
IF ANYONE CAN RESOLVE THE PAST...
IF ANYONE CAN SAVE ARENDELLE AND FREE THIS FOREST, IT'S YOU.
I BELIEVE IN YOU, ELSA.
MORE THAN ANYONE OR ANYTHING.
HONEYMAREN SAID...
...THERE WAS A FIFTH SPIRIT. A BRIDGE BETWEEN THE MAGIC OF NATURE AND US.
A FIFTH SPIRIT?
THAT'S WHO'S BEEN CALLING ME...FROM AHTOHALLAN.
THE ANSWERS ABOUT THE PAST ARE ALL THERE.
SO WE GO TO AHTOHALLAN.
NOT "WE." ME.
WHAT?

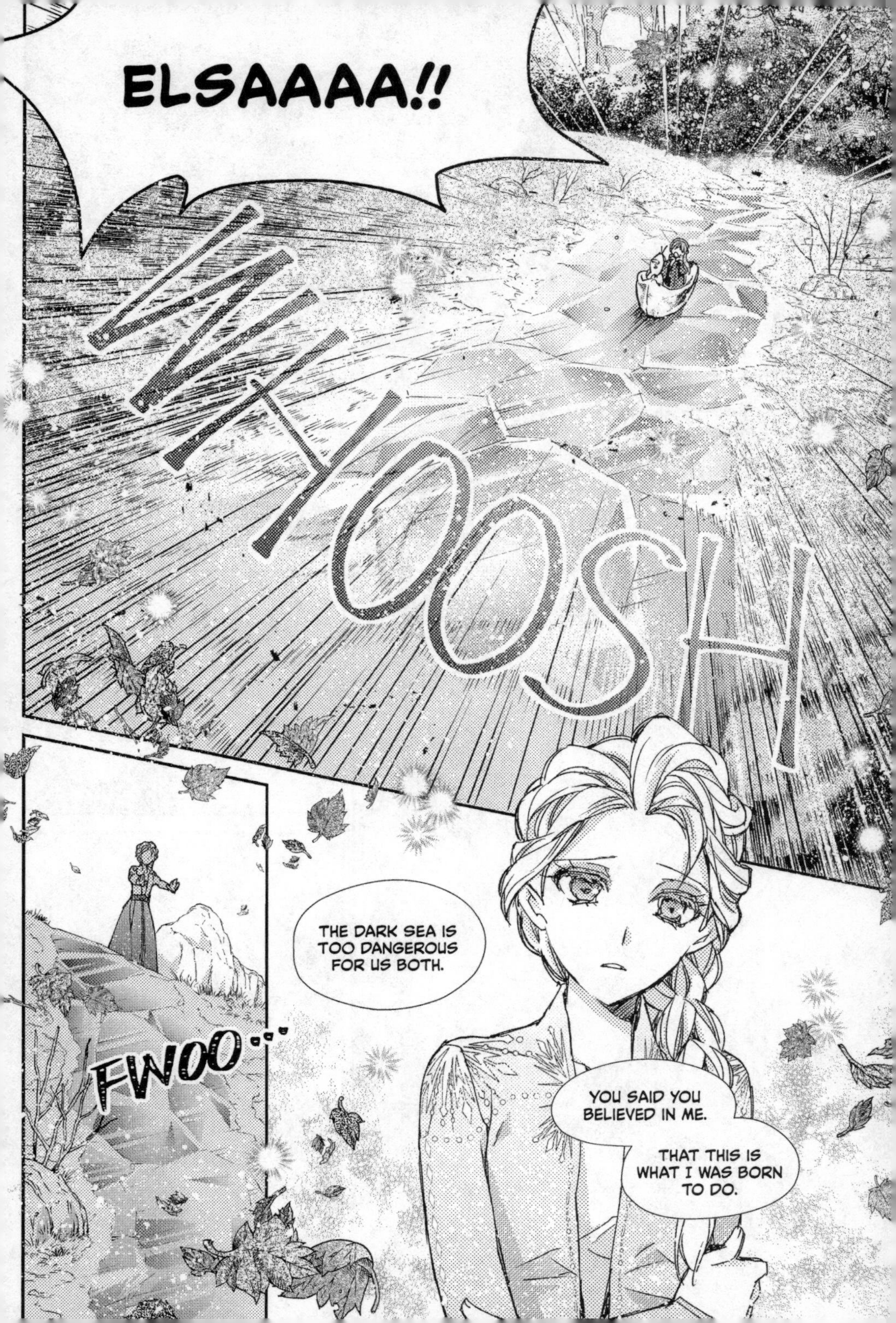
ELSAAAA!!
WHOOSH
FWOO...
THE DARK SEA IS TOO DANGEROUS FOR US BOTH.
YOU SAID YOU BELIEVED IN ME.
THAT THIS IS WHAT I WAS BORN TO DO.

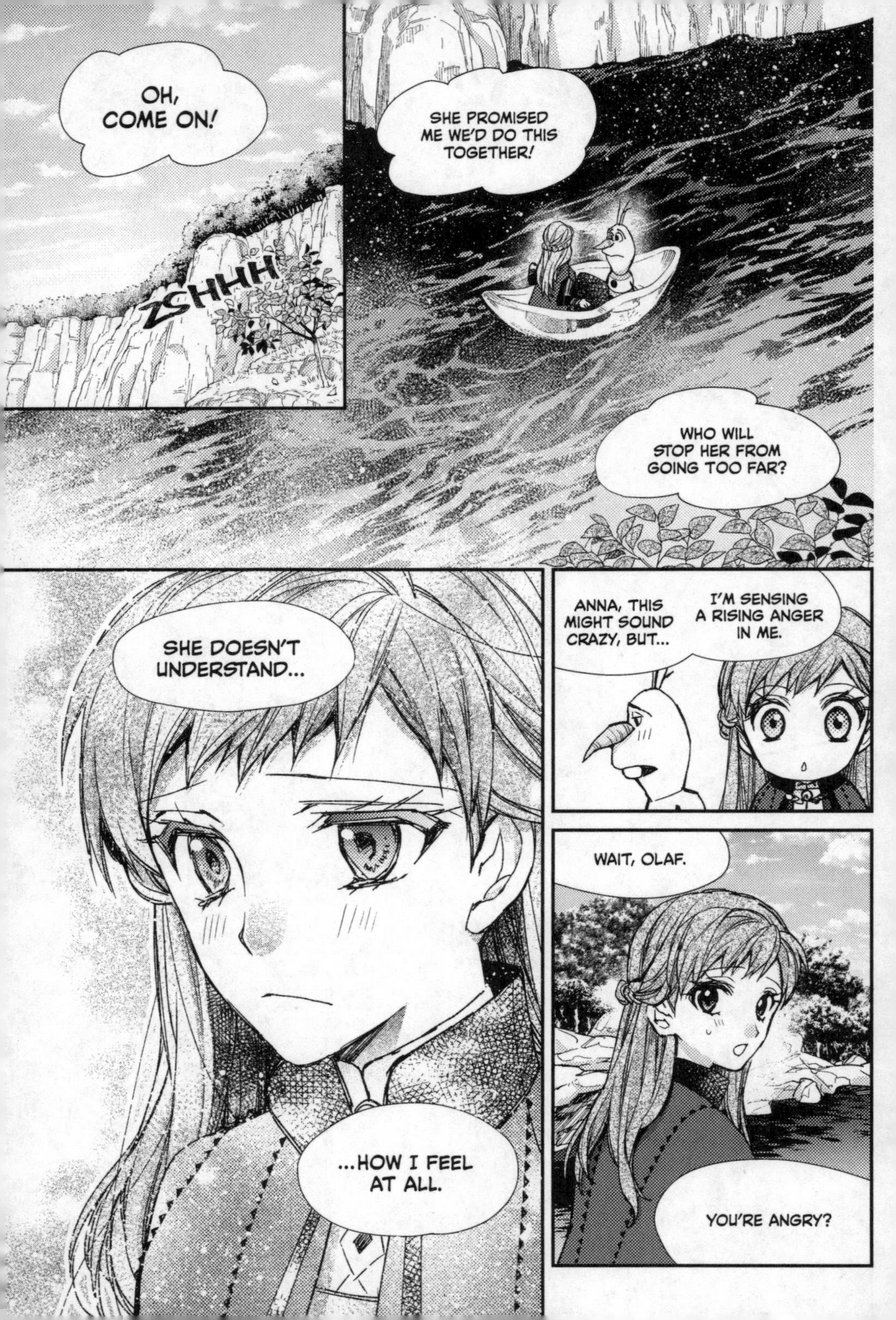
OH, COME ON!
ZSHHH
SHE PROMISED ME WE'D DO THIS TOGETHER!
WHO WILL STOP HER FROM GOING TOO FAR?
SHE DOESN'T UNDERSTAND...
...HOW I FEEL AT ALL.
ANNA, THIS MIGHT SOUND CRAZY, BUT...
I'M SENSING A RISING ANGER IN ME.
WAIT, OLAF.
YOU'RE ANGRY?

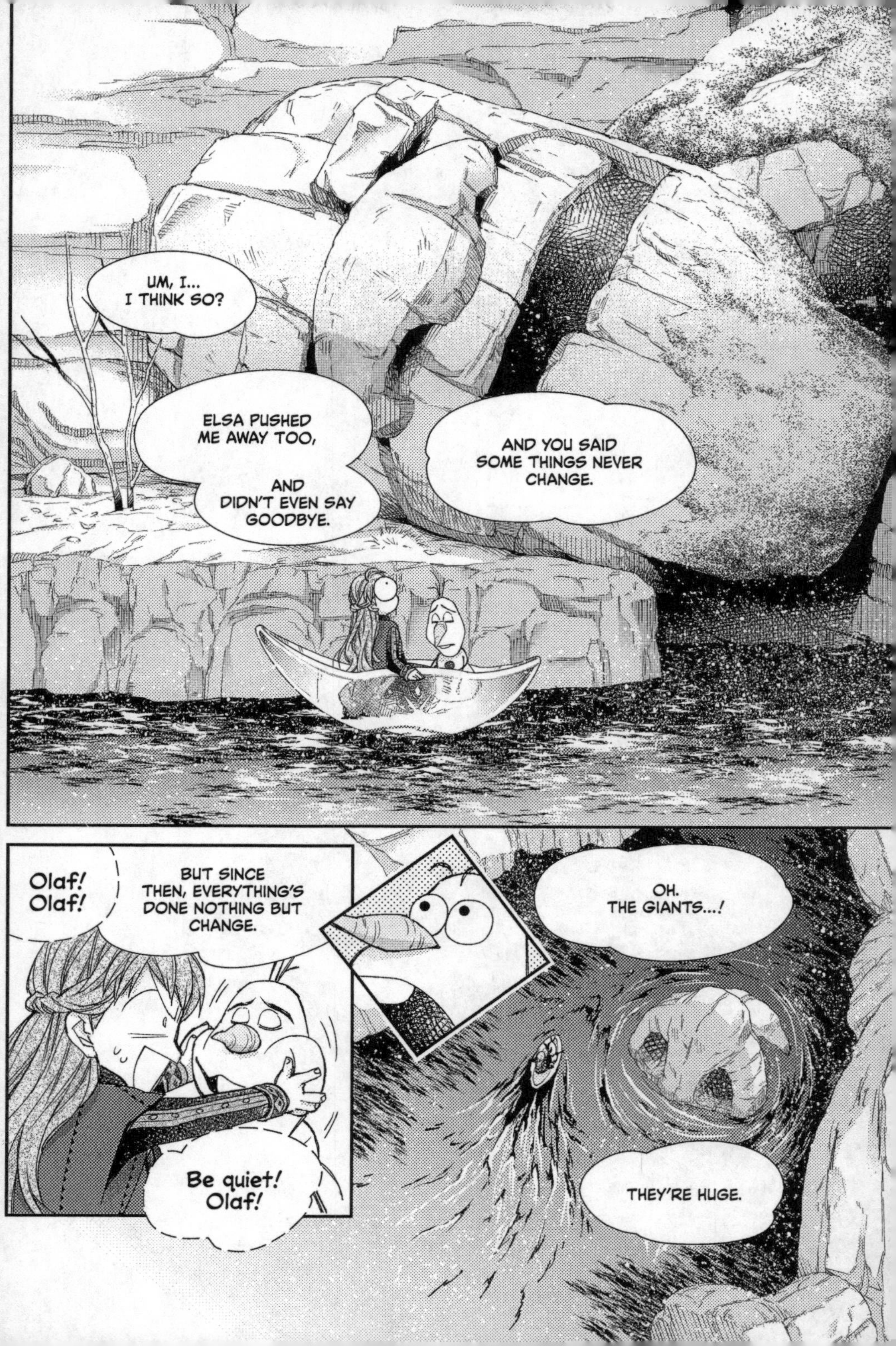
UM, I... I THINK SO?
ELSA PUSHED ME AWAY TOO,
AND DIDN'T EVEN SAY GOODBYE.
AND YOU SAID SOME THINGS NEVER CHANGE.
Olaf! Olaf!
BUT SINCE THEN, EVERYTHING'S DONE NOTHING BUT CHANGE.
Be quiet! Olaf!
OH. THE GIANTS...!
THEY'RE HUGE.

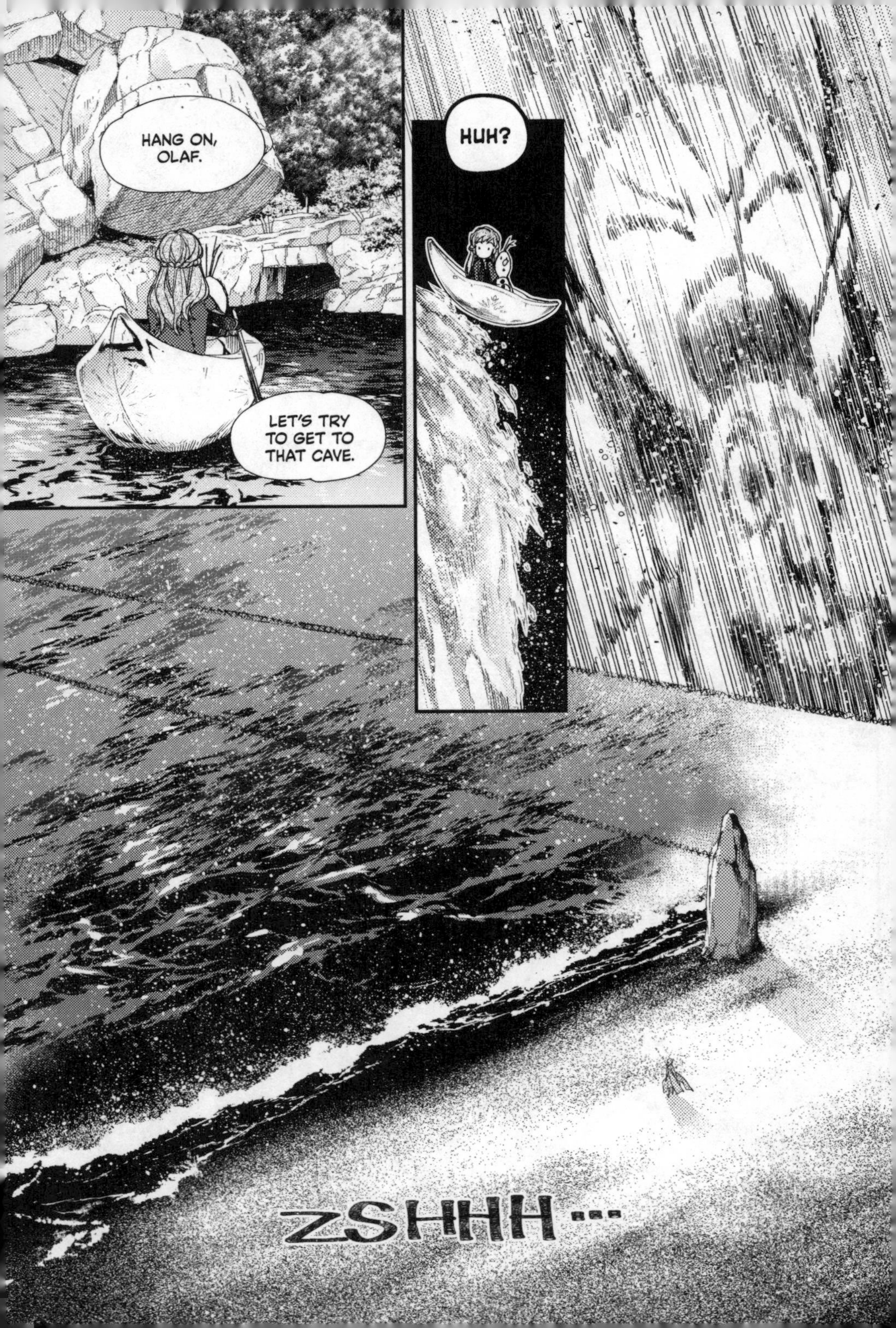
HANG ON, OLAF.
LET'S TRY TO GET TO THAT CAVE.
HUH?
ZSHHH...

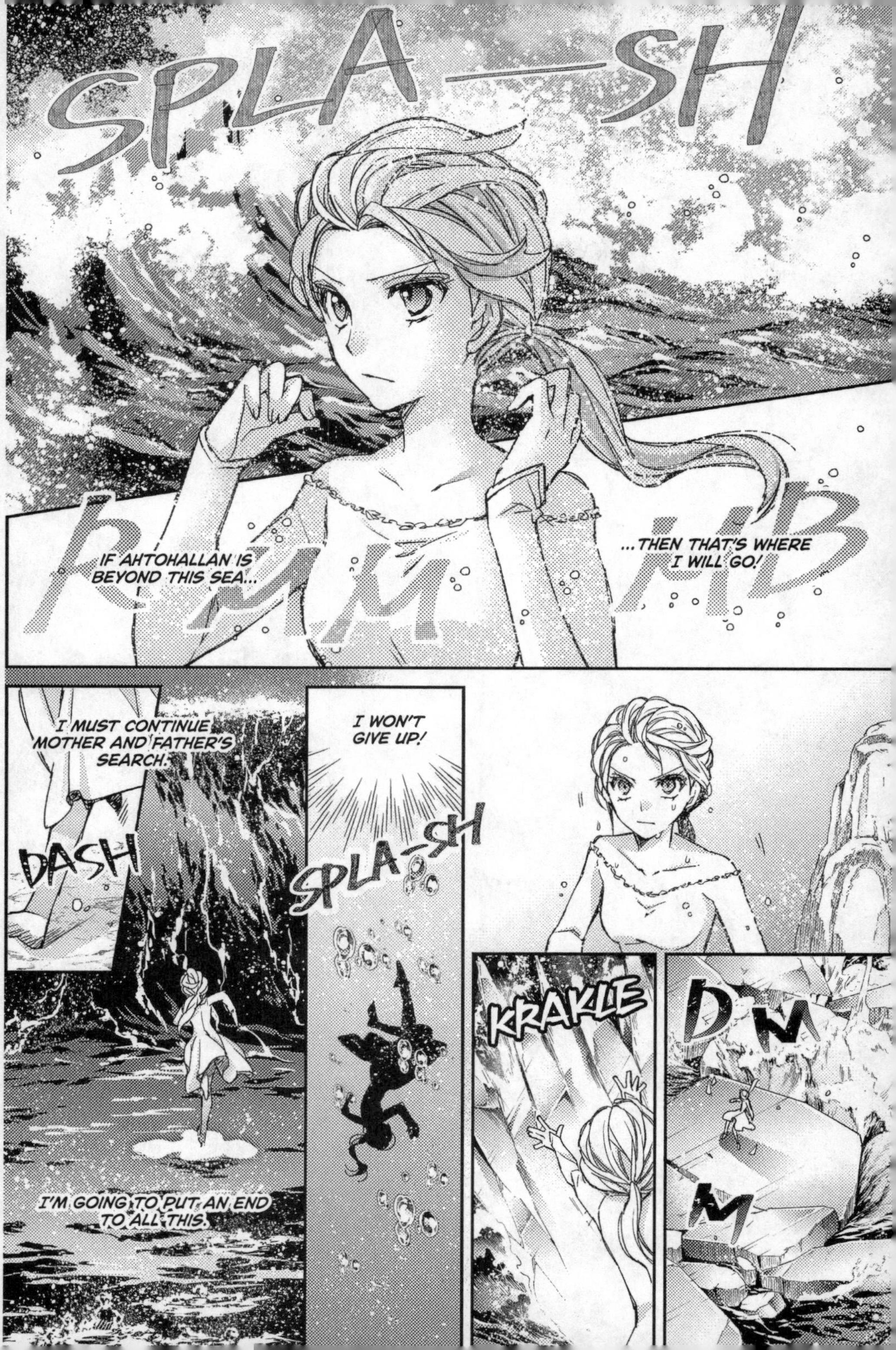
SPLA—SH
IF AHTOHALLAN IS BEYOND THIS SEA...
...THEN THAT'S WHERE I WILL GO!
I MUST CONTINUE MOTHER AND FATHER'S SEARCH.
DASH
I'M GOING TO PUT AN END TO ALL THIS.
I WON'T GIVE UP!
SPLA-SH
KRAKLE
DM
M

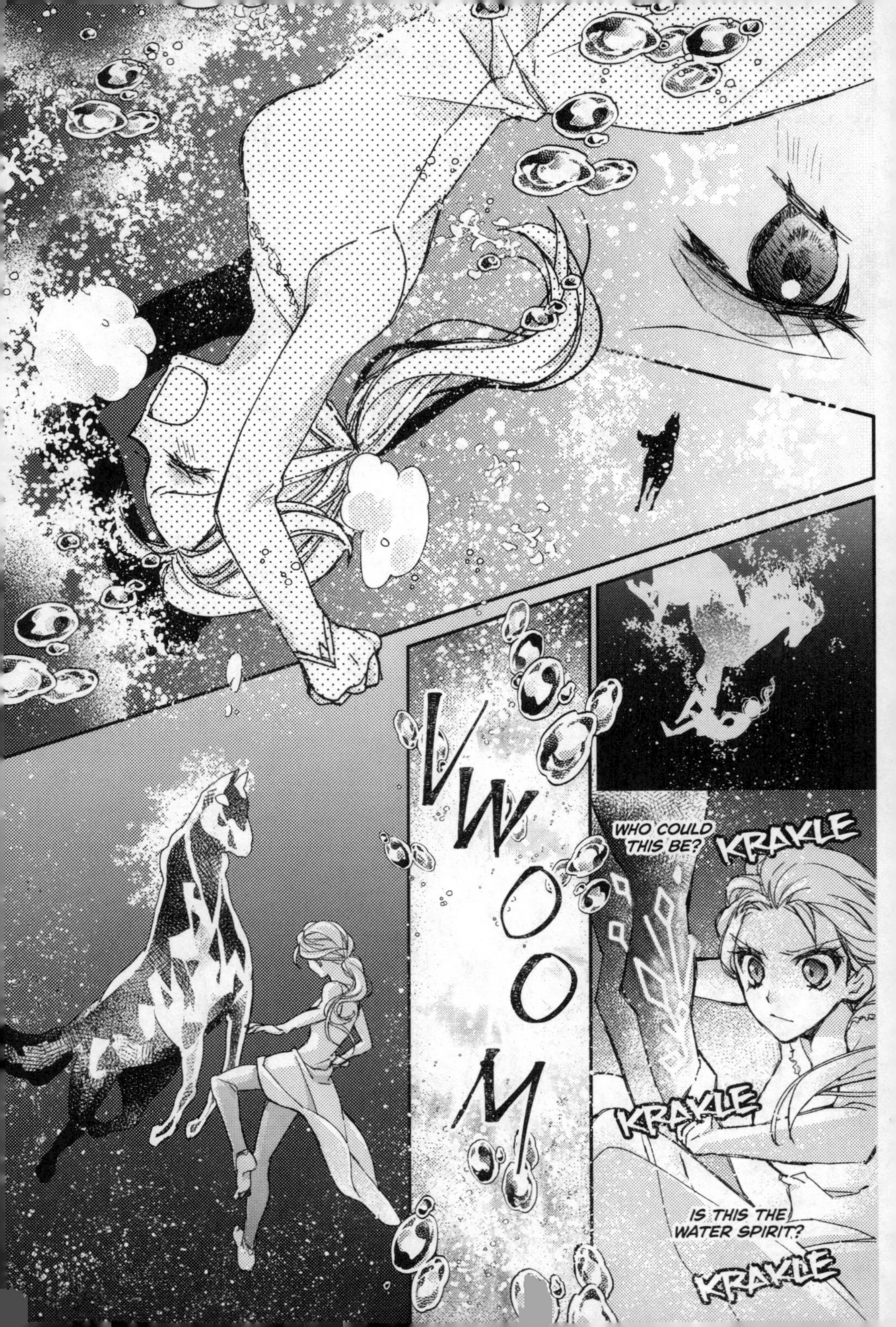
VWOOOM
WHO COULD THIS BE?
KRAKLE
KRAKLE
IS THIS THE WATER SPIRIT?
KRAKLE

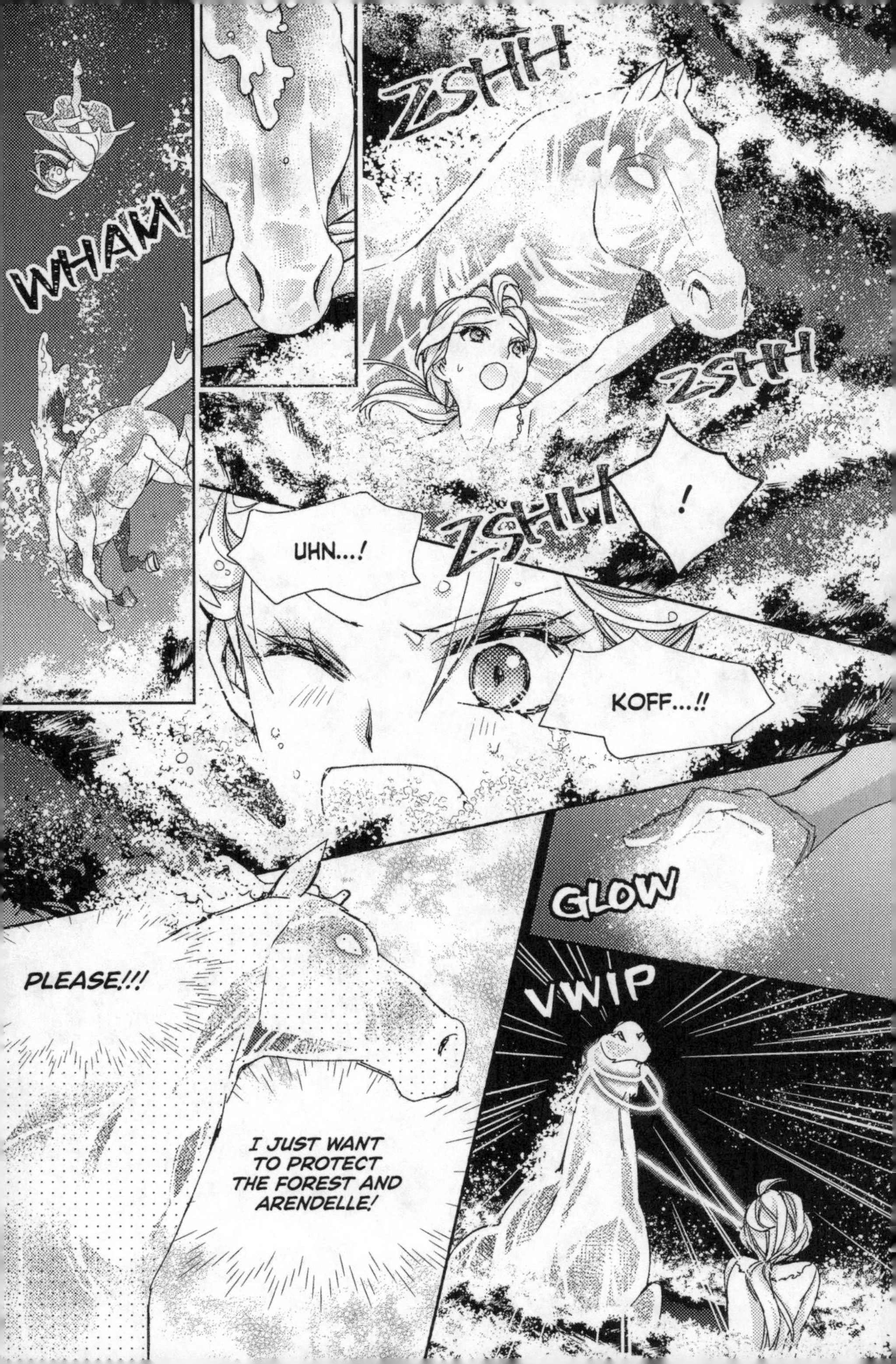
WHAM
ZSHH
ZSHH
ZSHH
!
UHN...!
KOFF...!!
PLEASE!!!
I JUST WANT TO PROTECT THE FOREST AND ARENDELLE!
GLOW
VWIP

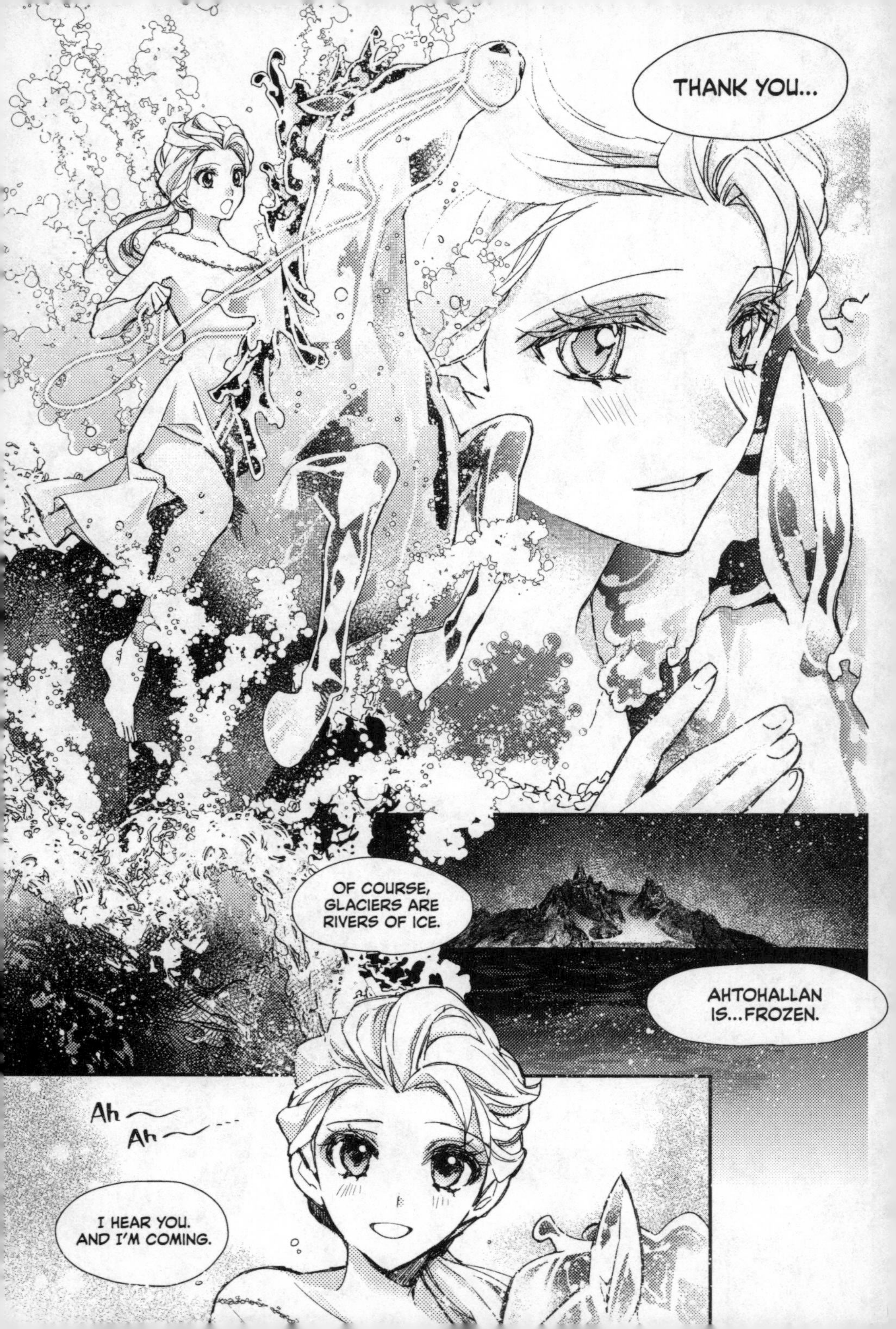
THANK YOU...
OF COURSE, GLACIERS ARE RIVERS OF ICE.
AHTOHALLAN IS...FROZEN.
Ah~ Ah~...
I HEAR YOU. AND I'M COMING.

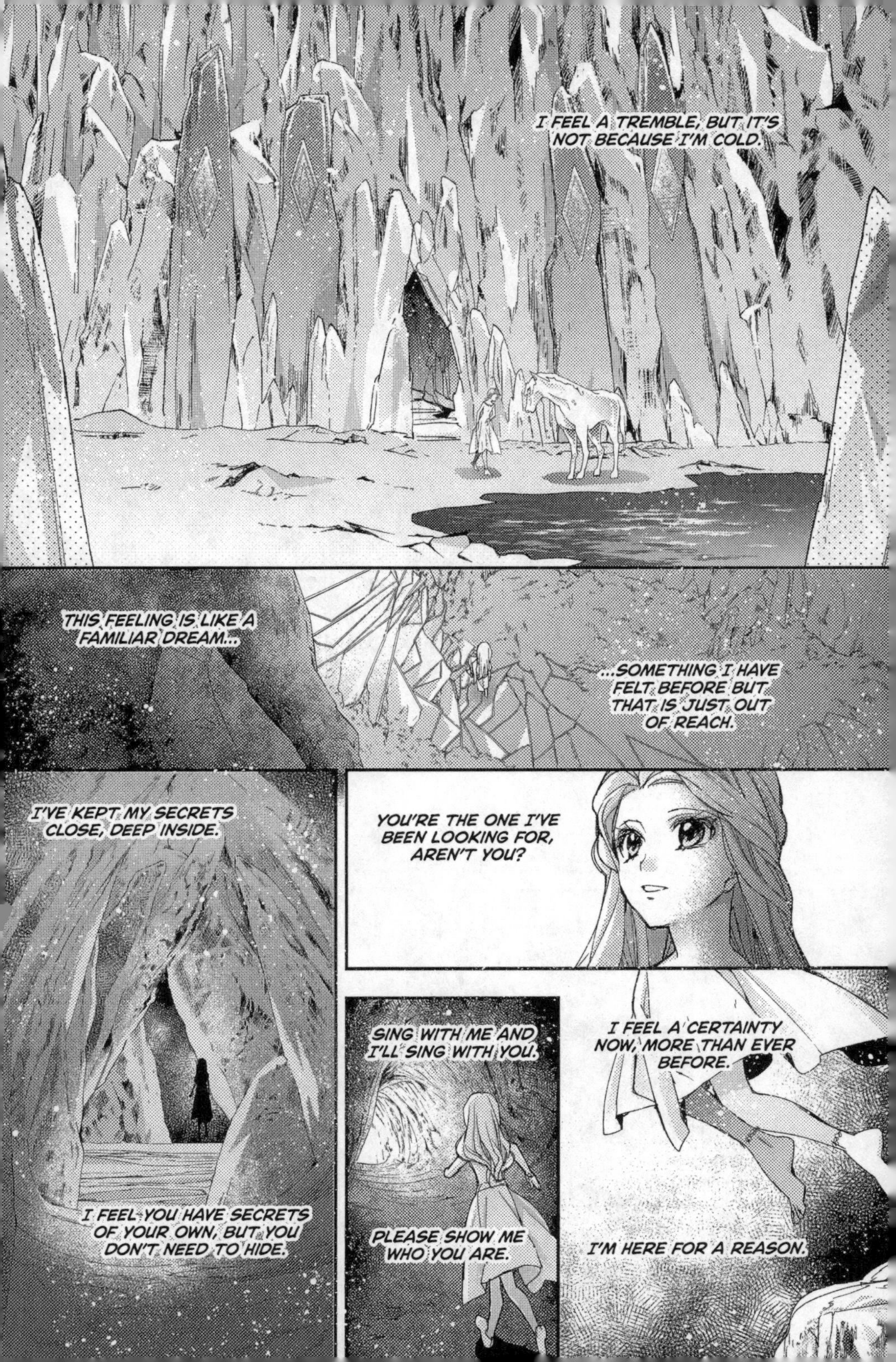
I FEEL A TREMBLE, BUT IT'S NOT BECAUSE I'M COLD.
THIS FEELING IS LIKE A FAMILIAR DREAM...
...SOMETHING I HAVE FELT BEFORE BUT THAT IS JUST OUT OF REACH.
I'VE KEPT MY SECRETS CLOSE, DEEP INSIDE.
I FEEL YOU HAVE SECRETS OF YOUR OWN, BUT YOU DON'T NEED TO HIDE.
YOU'RE THE ONE I'VE BEEN LOOKING FOR, AREN'T YOU?
SING WITH ME AND I'LL SING WITH YOU.
PLEASE SHOW ME WHO YOU ARE.
I FEEL A CERTAINTY NOW, MORE THAN EVER BEFORE.
I'M HERE FOR A REASON.

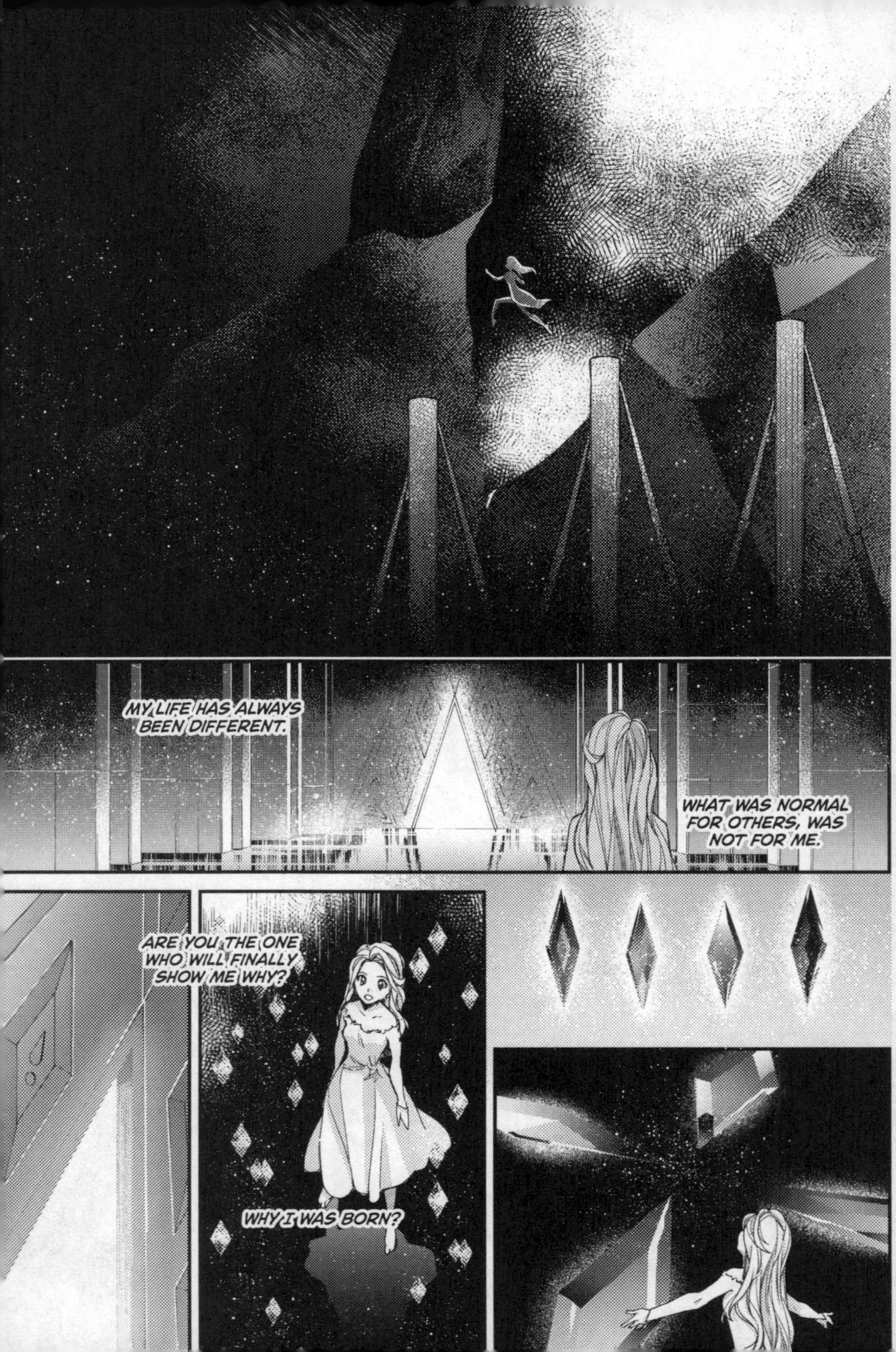
MY LIFE HAS ALWAYS BEEN DIFFERENT.
WHAT WAS NORMAL FOR OTHERS, WAS NOT FOR ME.
ARE YOU THE ONE WHO WILL FINALLY SHOW ME WHY?
WHY I WAS BORN?

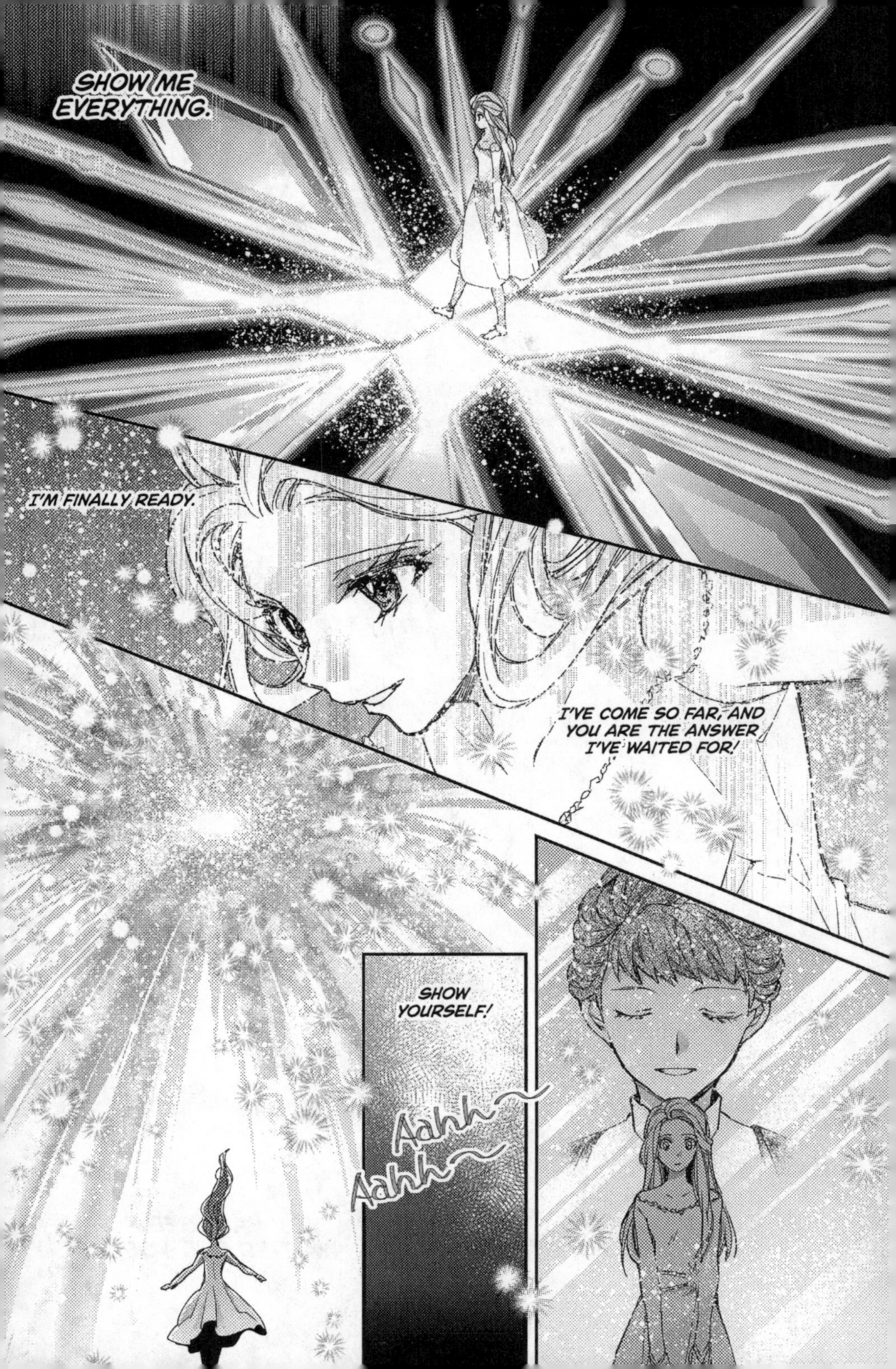
SHOW ME EVERYTHING.
I'M FINALLY READY.
I'VE COME SO FAR, AND YOU ARE THE ANSWER I'VE WAITED FOR!
SHOW YOURSELF!
Aahh~
Aahh~

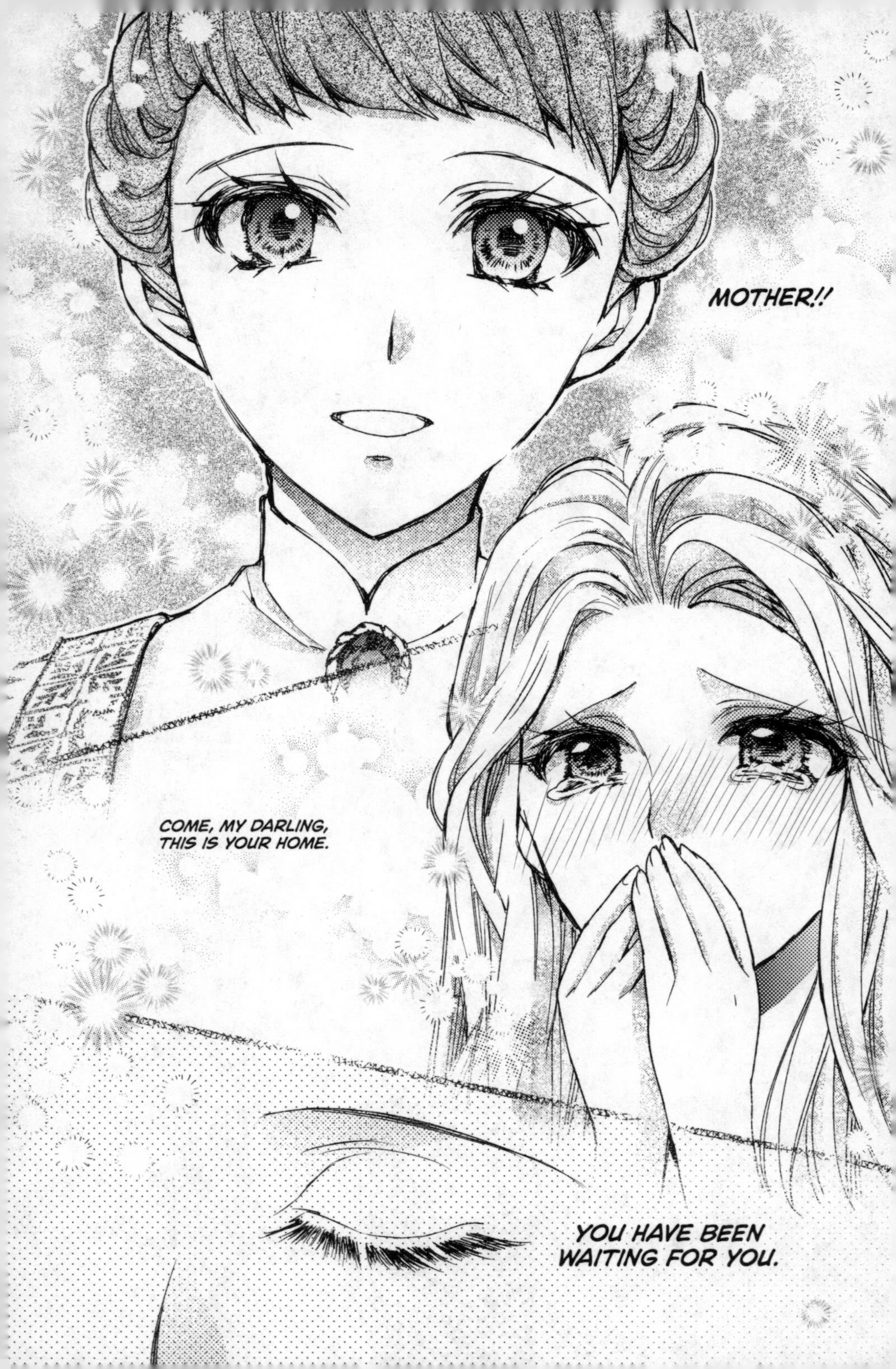
MOTHER!!
COME, MY DARLING, THIS IS YOUR HOME.
YOU HAVE BEEN WAITING FOR YOU.

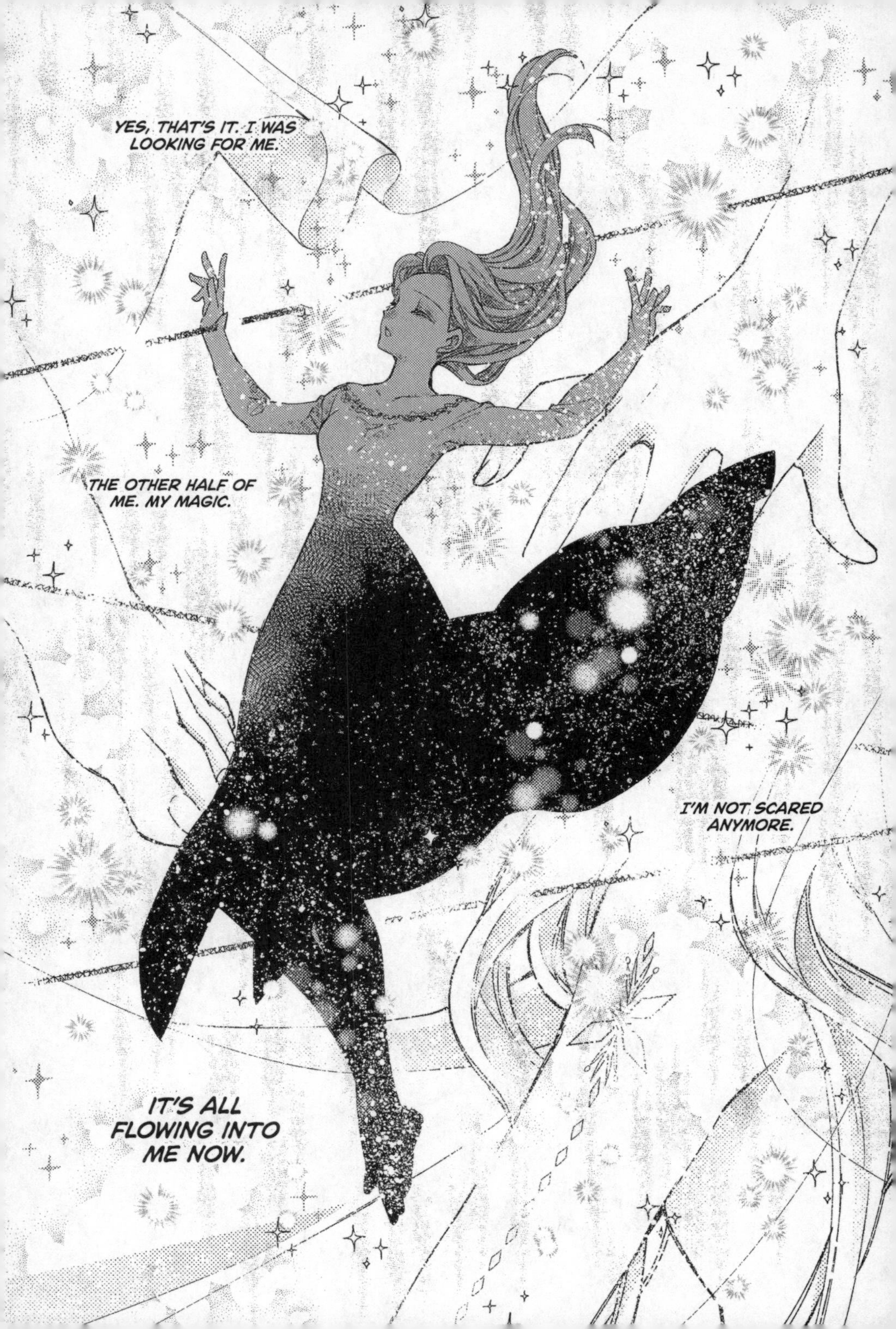
YES, THAT'S IT. I WAS LOOKING FOR ME.
THE OTHER HALF OF ME. MY MAGIC.
I'M NOT SCARED ANYMORE.
IT'S ALL FLOWING INTO ME NOW.

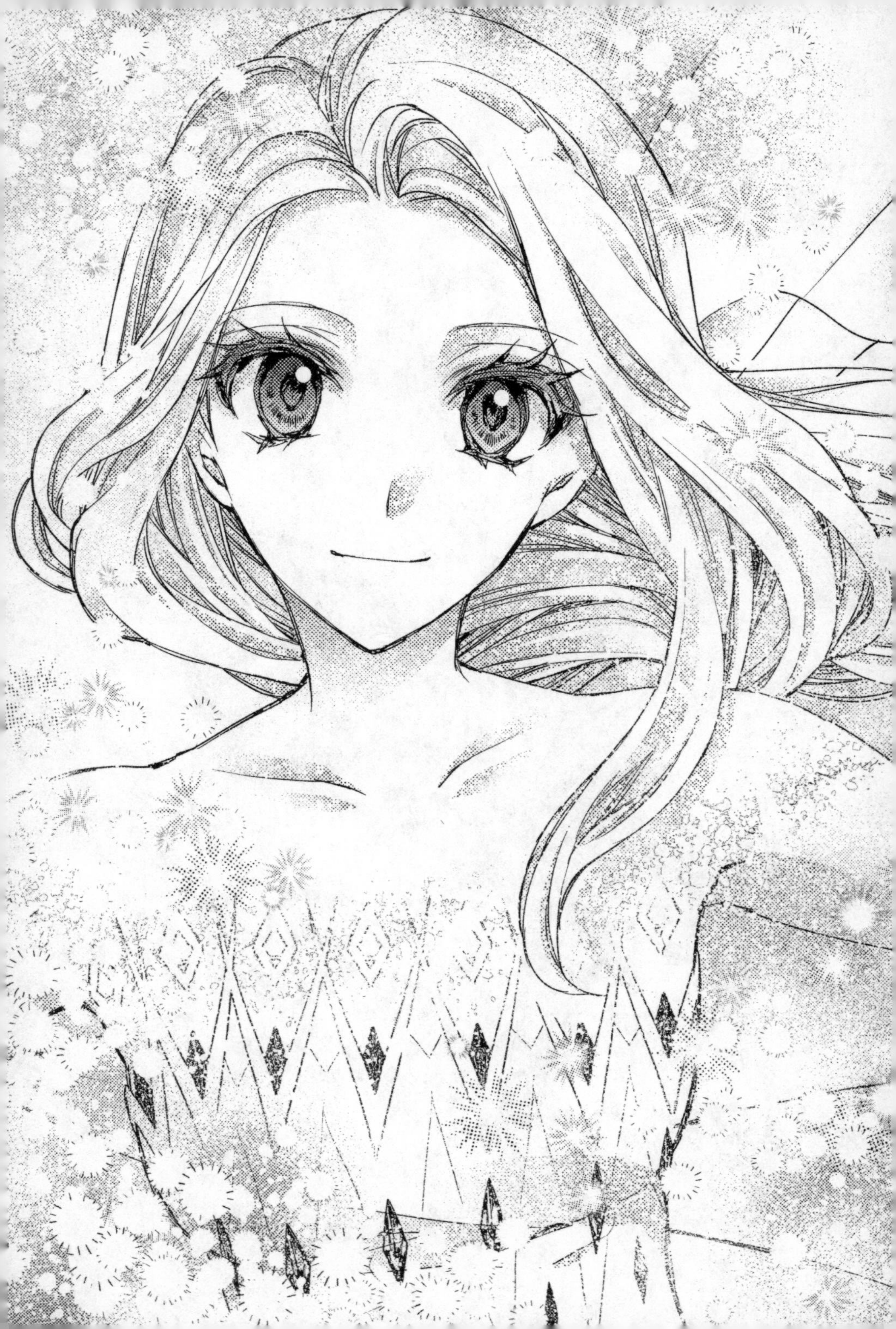

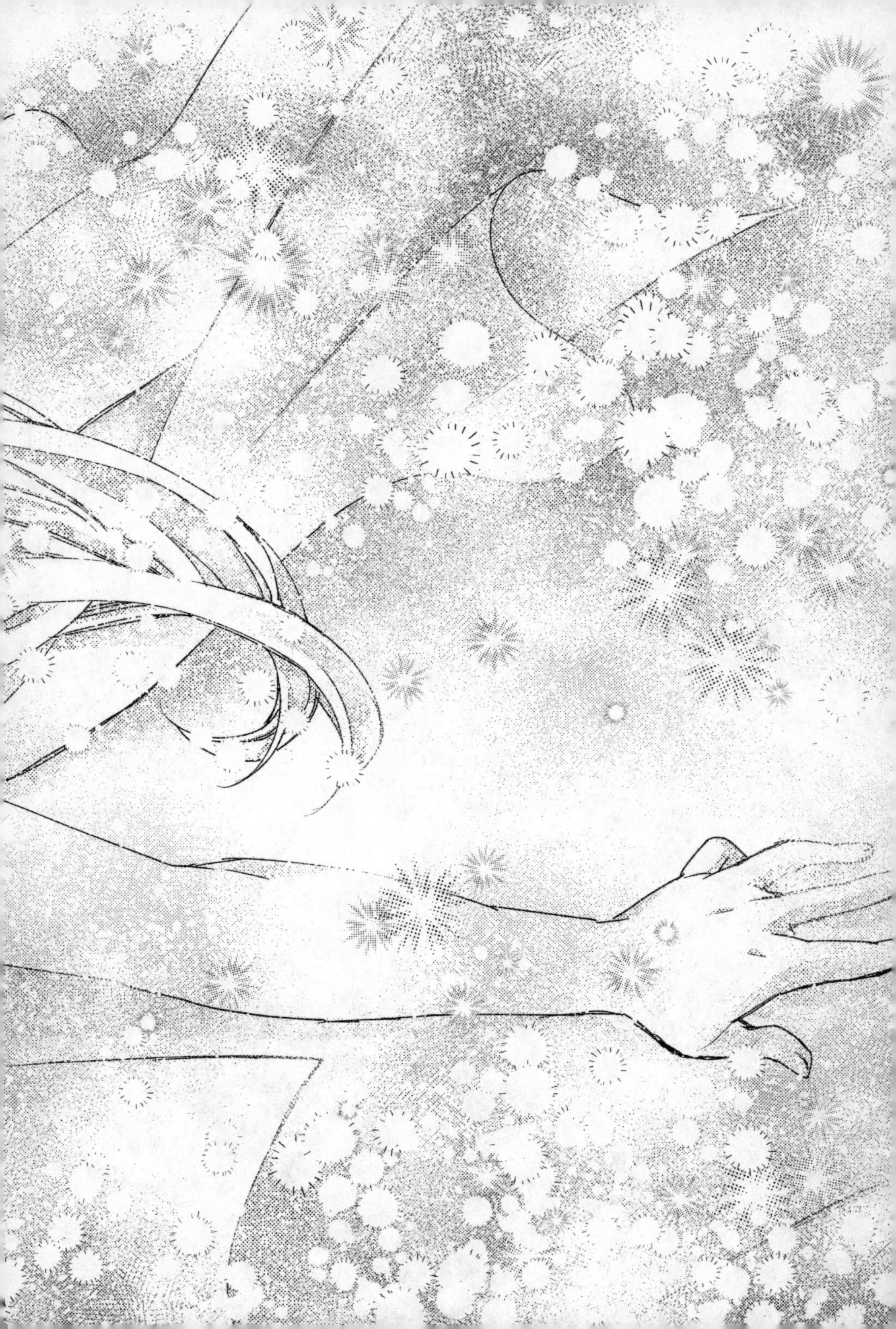

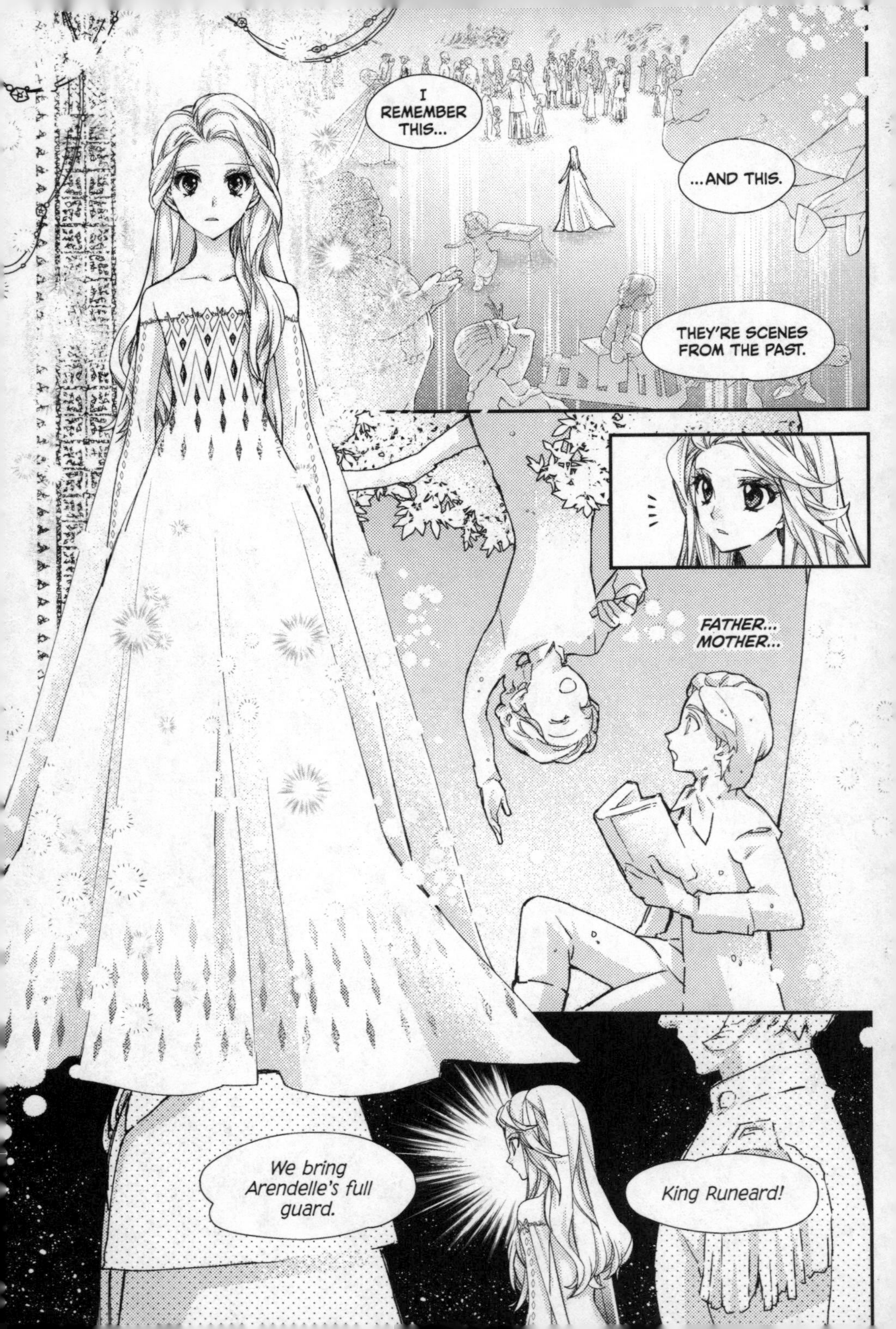
I REMEMBER THIS...
...AND THIS.
THEY'RE SCENES FROM THE PAST.
FATHER... MOTHER...
King Runeard!
We bring Arendelle's full guard.

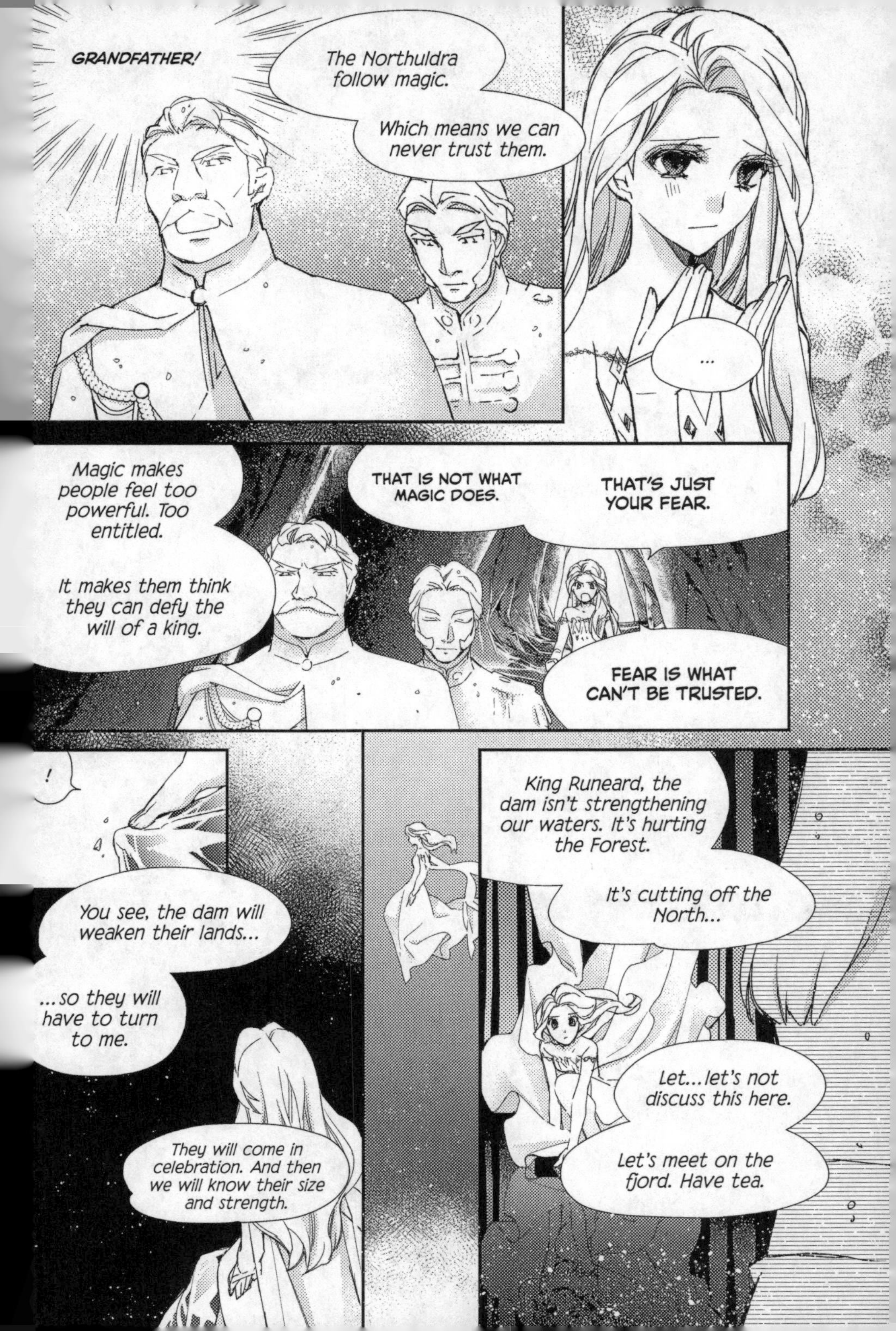
GRANDFATHER!
The Northuldra follow magic.
Which means we can never trust them.
...
Magic makes people feel too powerful. Too entitled.
It makes them think they can defy the will of a king.
THAT IS NOT WHAT MAGIC DOES.
THAT'S JUST YOUR FEAR.
FEAR IS WHAT CAN'T BE TRUSTED.
!
You see, the dam will weaken their lands...
...so they will have to turn to me.
They will come in celebration. And then we will know their size and strength.
King Runeard, the dam isn't strengthening our waters. It's hurting the Forest.
It's cutting off the North...
Let...let's not discuss this here.
Let's meet on the fjord. Have tea.

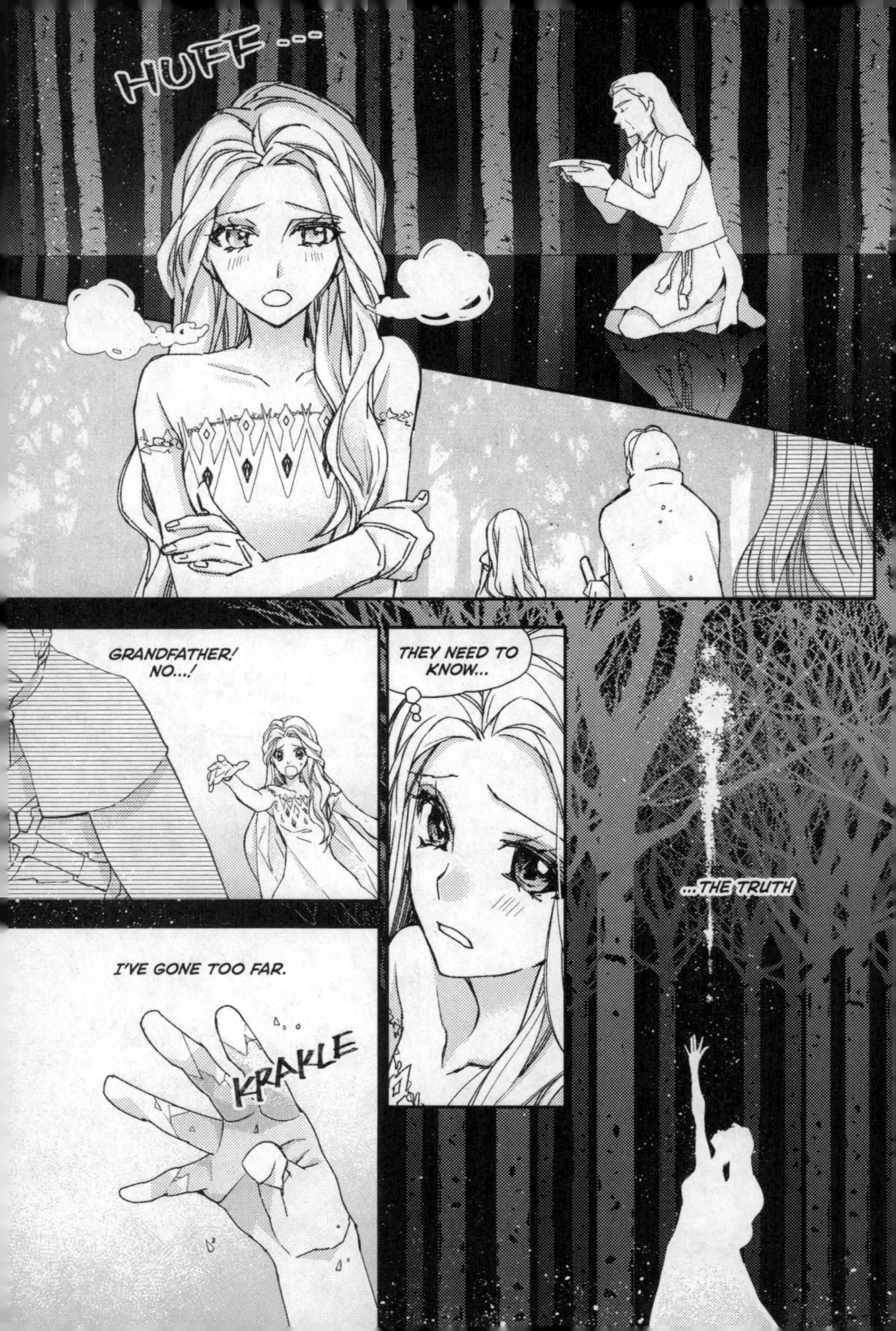
HUFF ...
GRANDFATHER! NO...!
I'VE GONE TOO FAR.
KRAKLE
THEY NEED TO KNOW...
...THE TRUTH

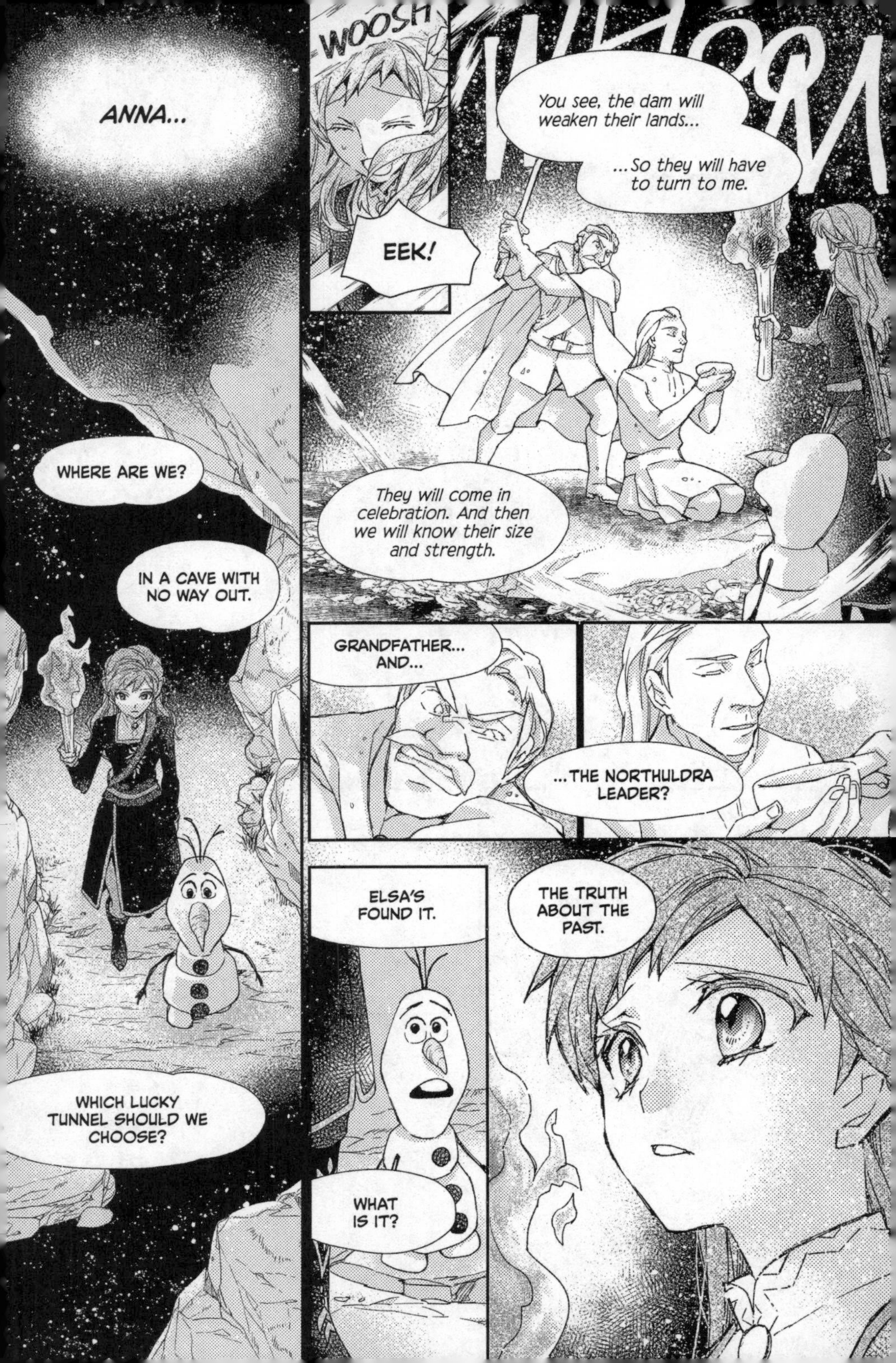
ANNA...
WHERE ARE WE?
IN A CAVE WITH NO WAY OUT.
WHICH LUCKY TUNNEL SHOULD WE CHOOSE?
WOOSH
EEK!
You see, the dam will weaken their lands...
...So they will have to turn to me.
They will come in celebration. And then we will know their size and strength.
GRANDFATHER... AND...
...THE NORTHULDRA LEADER?
ELSA'S FOUND IT.
WHAT IS IT?
THE TRUTH ABOUT THE PAST.

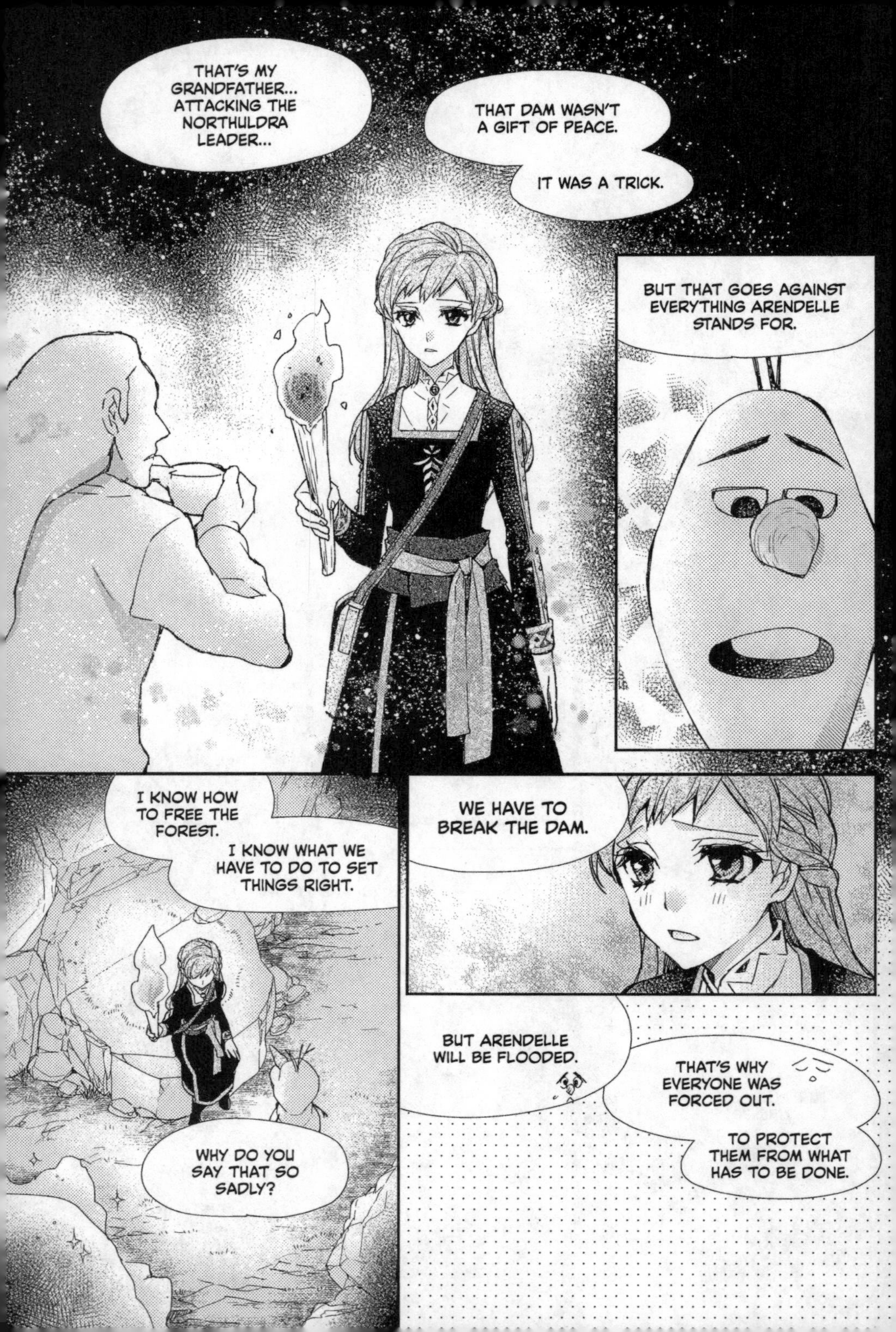
THAT'S MY GRANDFATHER... ATTACKING THE NORTHULDRA LEADER...
THAT DAM WASN'T A GIFT OF PEACE.
IT WAS A TRICK.
BUT THAT GOES AGAINST EVERYTHING ARENDELLE STANDS FOR.
I KNOW HOW TO FREE THE FOREST.
I KNOW WHAT WE HAVE TO DO TO SET THINGS RIGHT.
WHY DO YOU SAY THAT SO SADLY?
WE HAVE TO BREAK THE DAM.
BUT ARENDELLE WILL BE FLOODED.
THAT'S WHY EVERYONE WAS FORCED OUT.
TO PROTECT THEM FROM WHAT HAS TO BE DONE.

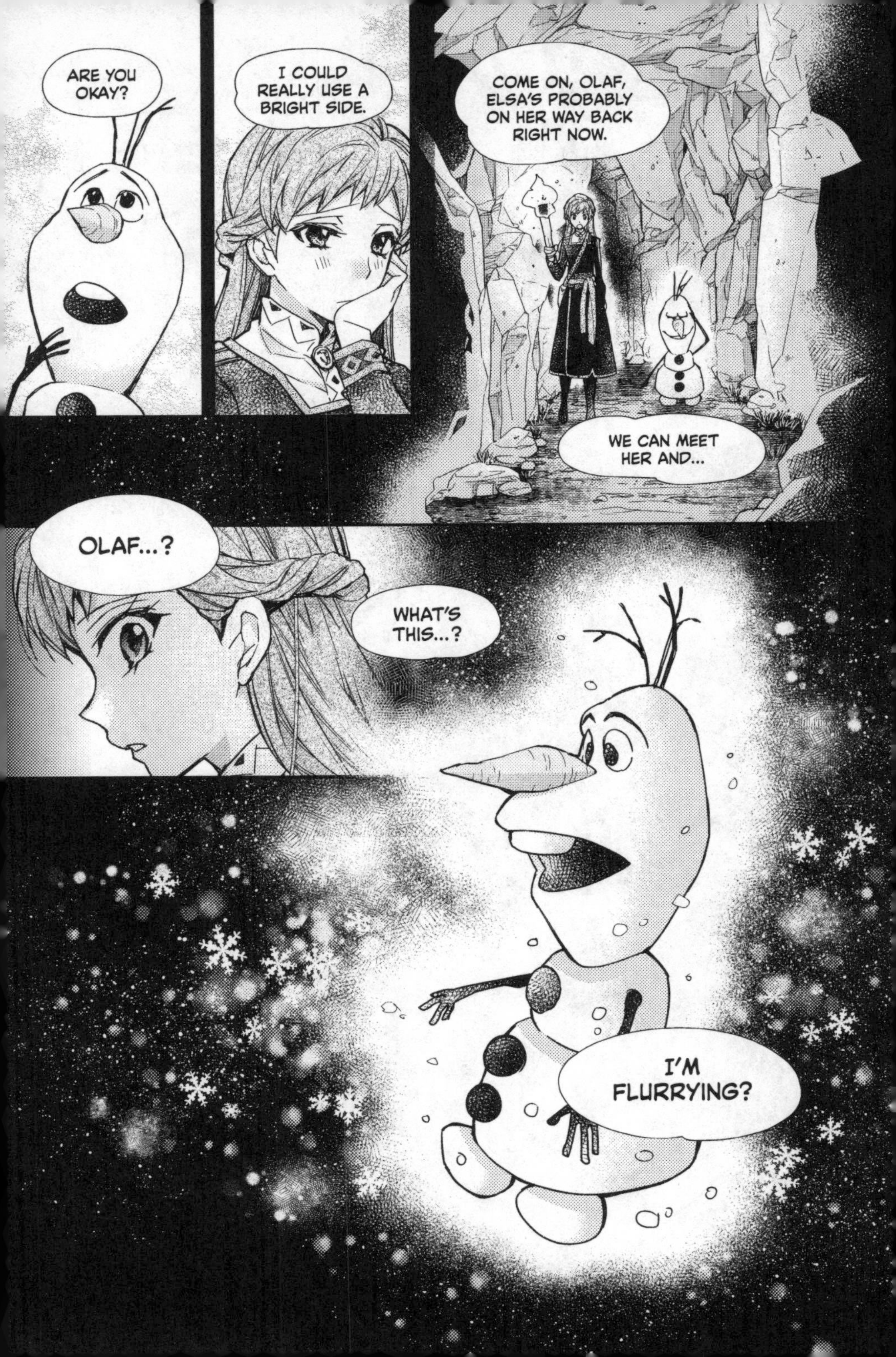
ARE YOU OKAY?
I COULD REALLY USE A BRIGHT SIDE.
COME ON, OLAF, ELSA'S PROBABLY ON HER WAY BACK RIGHT NOW.
WE CAN MEET HER AND...
OLAF...?
WHAT'S THIS...?
I'M FLURRYING?

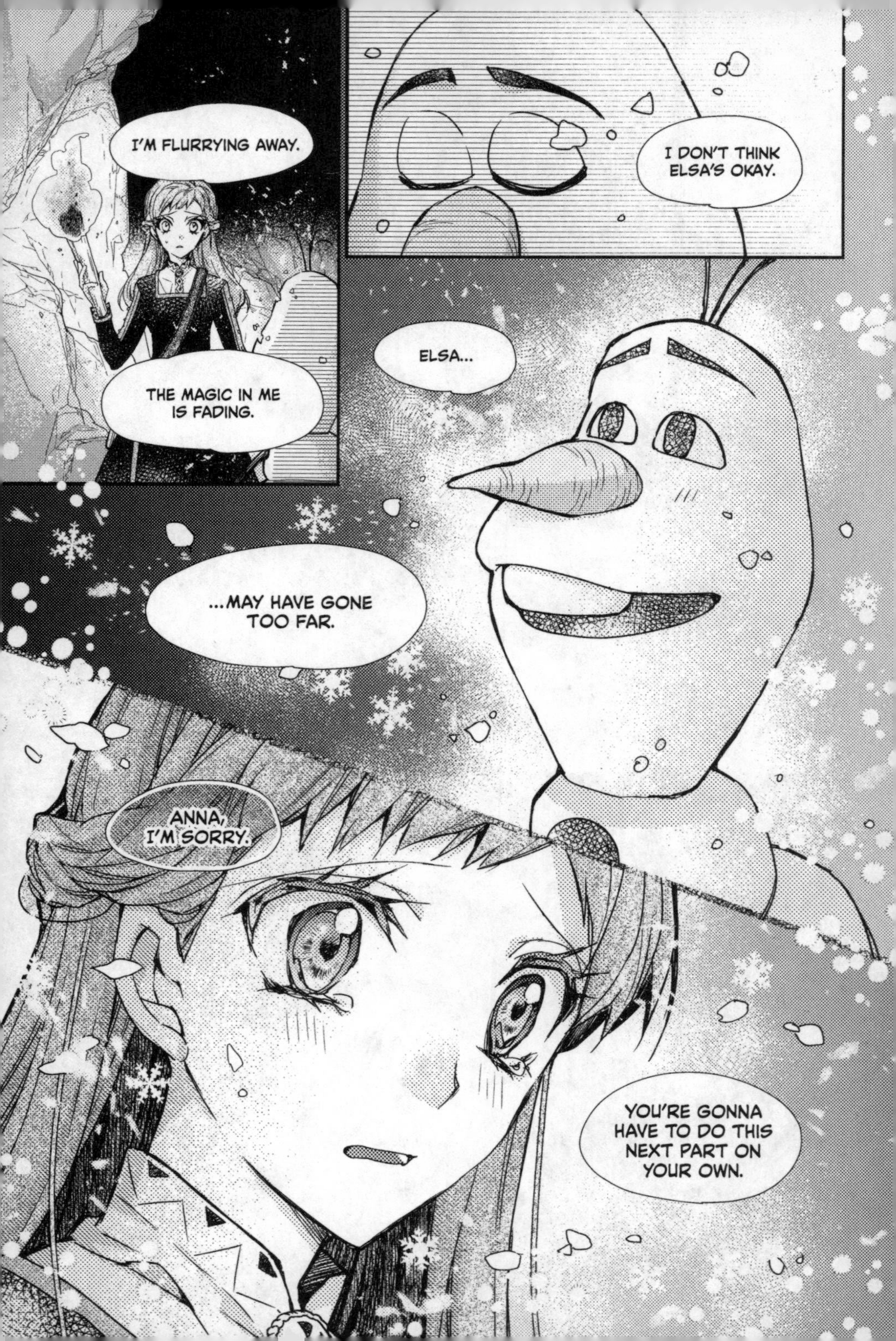
I'M FLURRYING AWAY.
THE MAGIC IN ME IS FADING.
I DON'T THINK ELSA'S OKAY.
ELSA...
...MAY HAVE GONE TOO FAR.
ANNA, I'M SORRY.
YOU'RE GONNA HAVE TO DO THIS NEXT PART ON YOUR OWN.

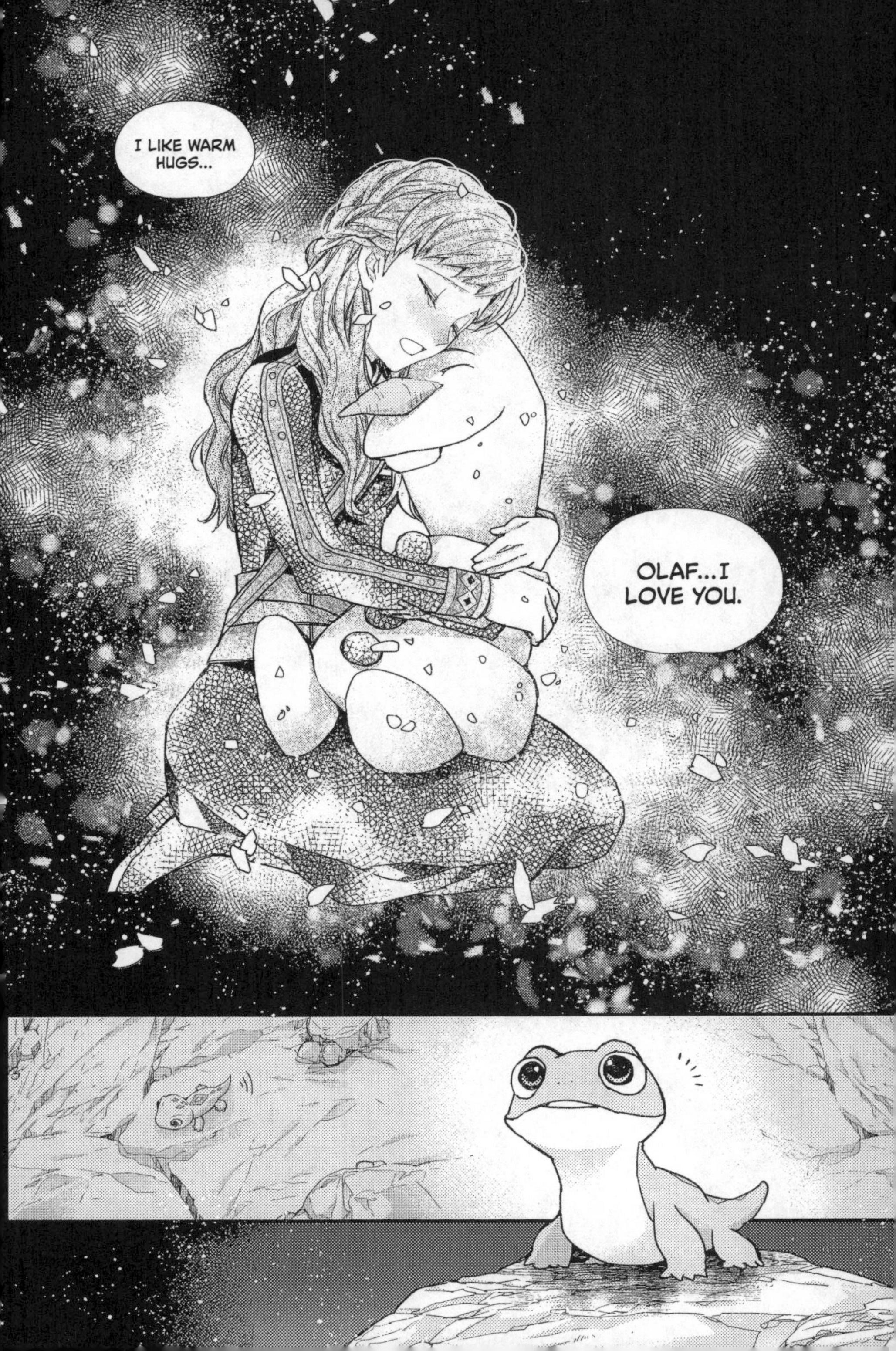
I LIKE WARM HUGS...
OLAF...I LOVE YOU.

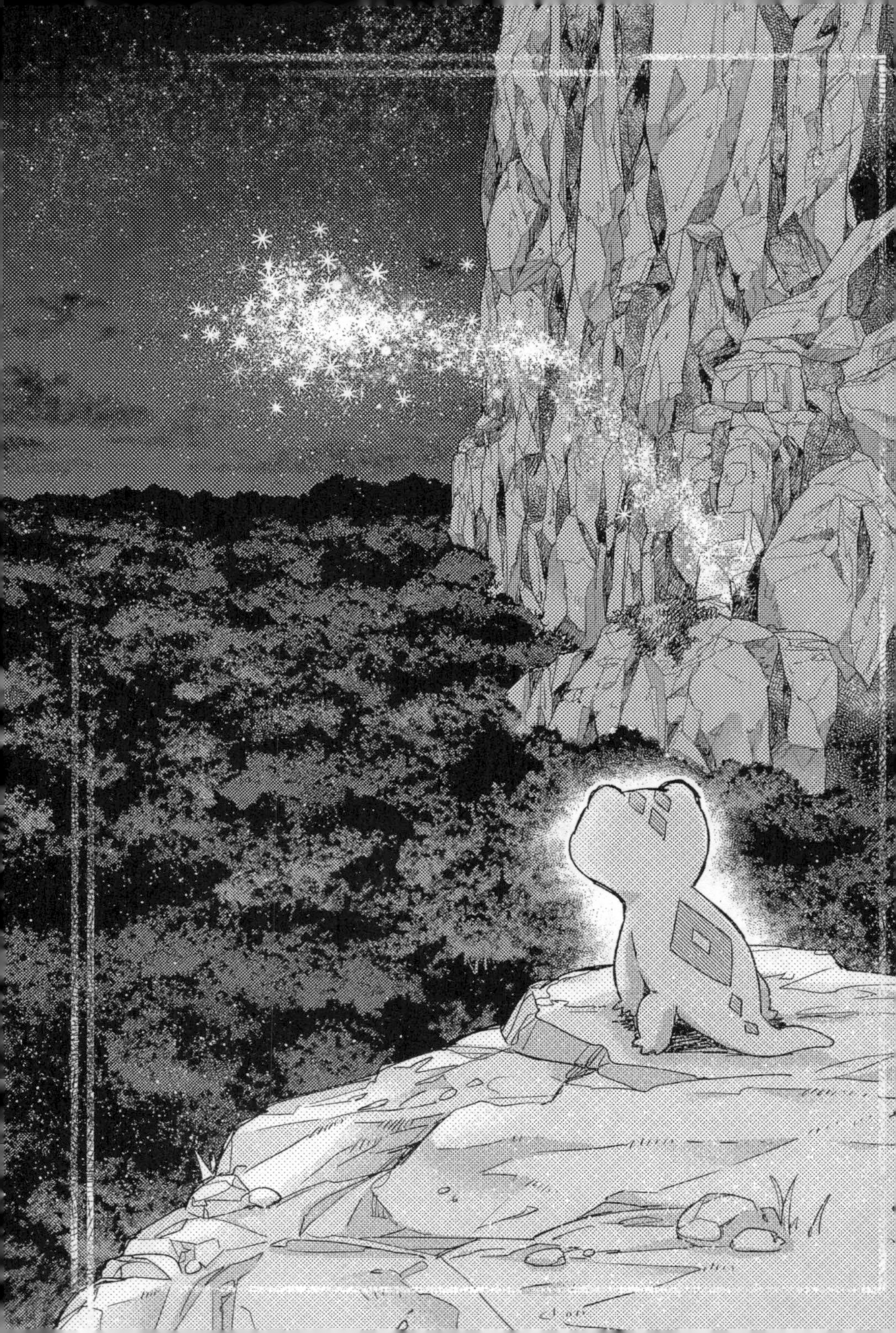

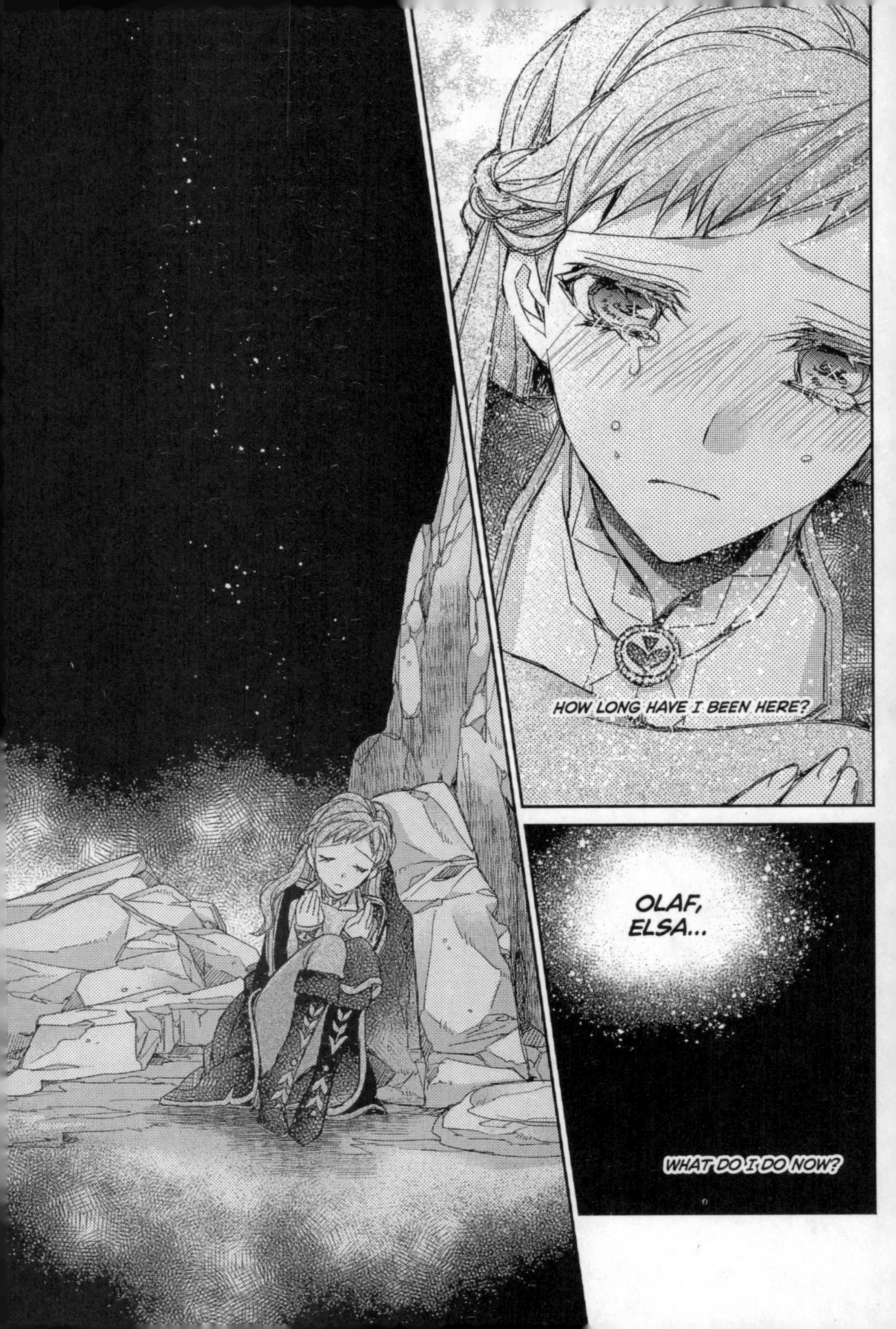
HOW LONG HAVE I BEEN HERE?
OLAF, ELSA...
WHAT DO I DO NOW?

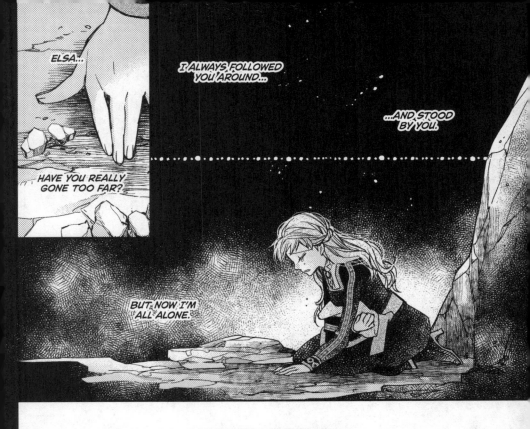

ELSA...

I ALWAYS FOLLOWED YOU AROUND...

...AND STOOD BY YOU.

HAVE YOU REALLY GONE TOO FAR?

BUT NOW I'M ALL ALONE.

I HAVE TO DO THIS ON MY OWN.

HOW CAN I GO ON...

...WHEN THE ONE PERSON WHO GUIDED ME IS GONE?

BUT...

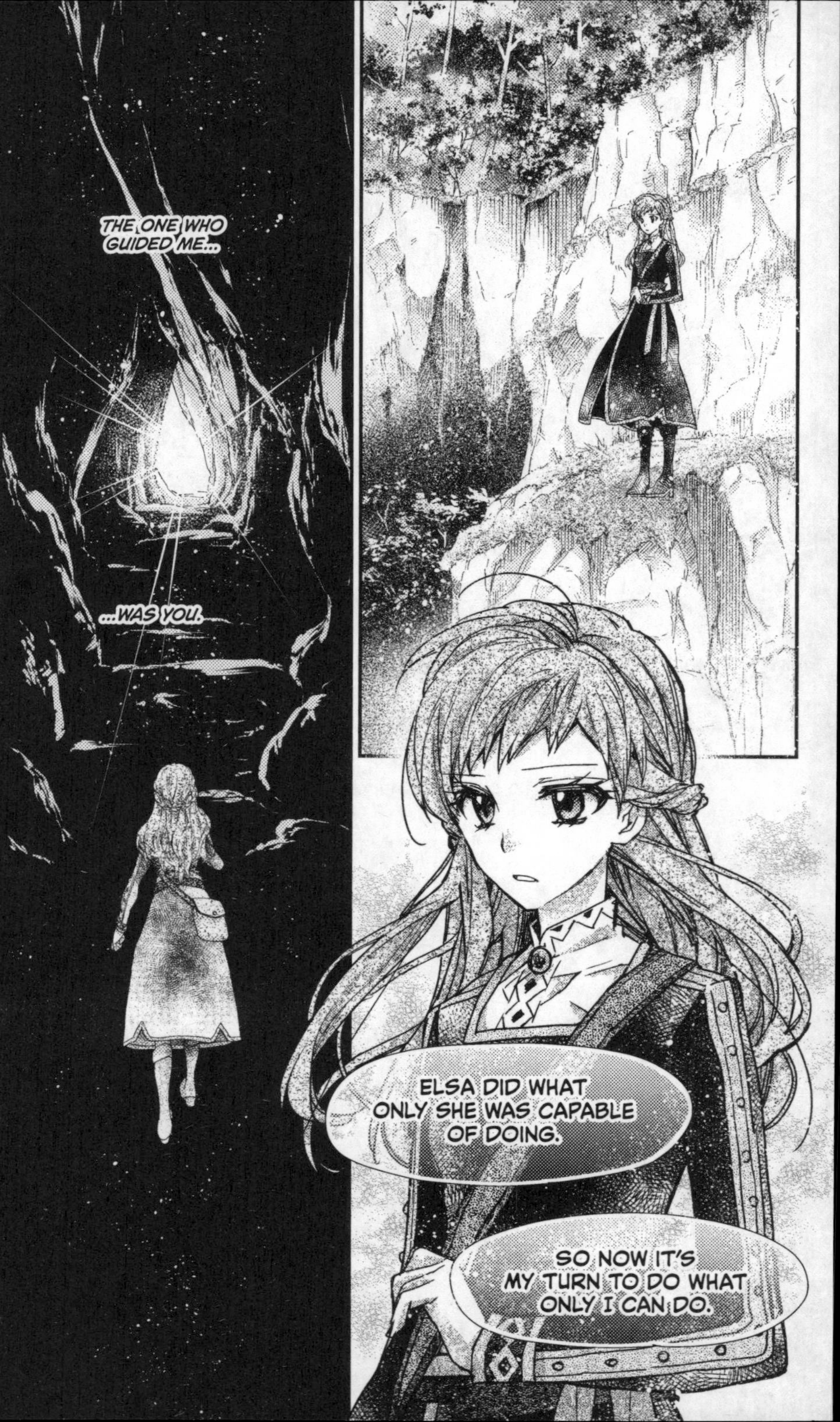
THE ONE WHO GUIDED ME...
...WAS YOU.
ELSA DID WHAT ONLY SHE WAS CAPABLE OF DOING.
SO NOW IT'S MY TURN TO DO WHAT ONLY I CAN DO.

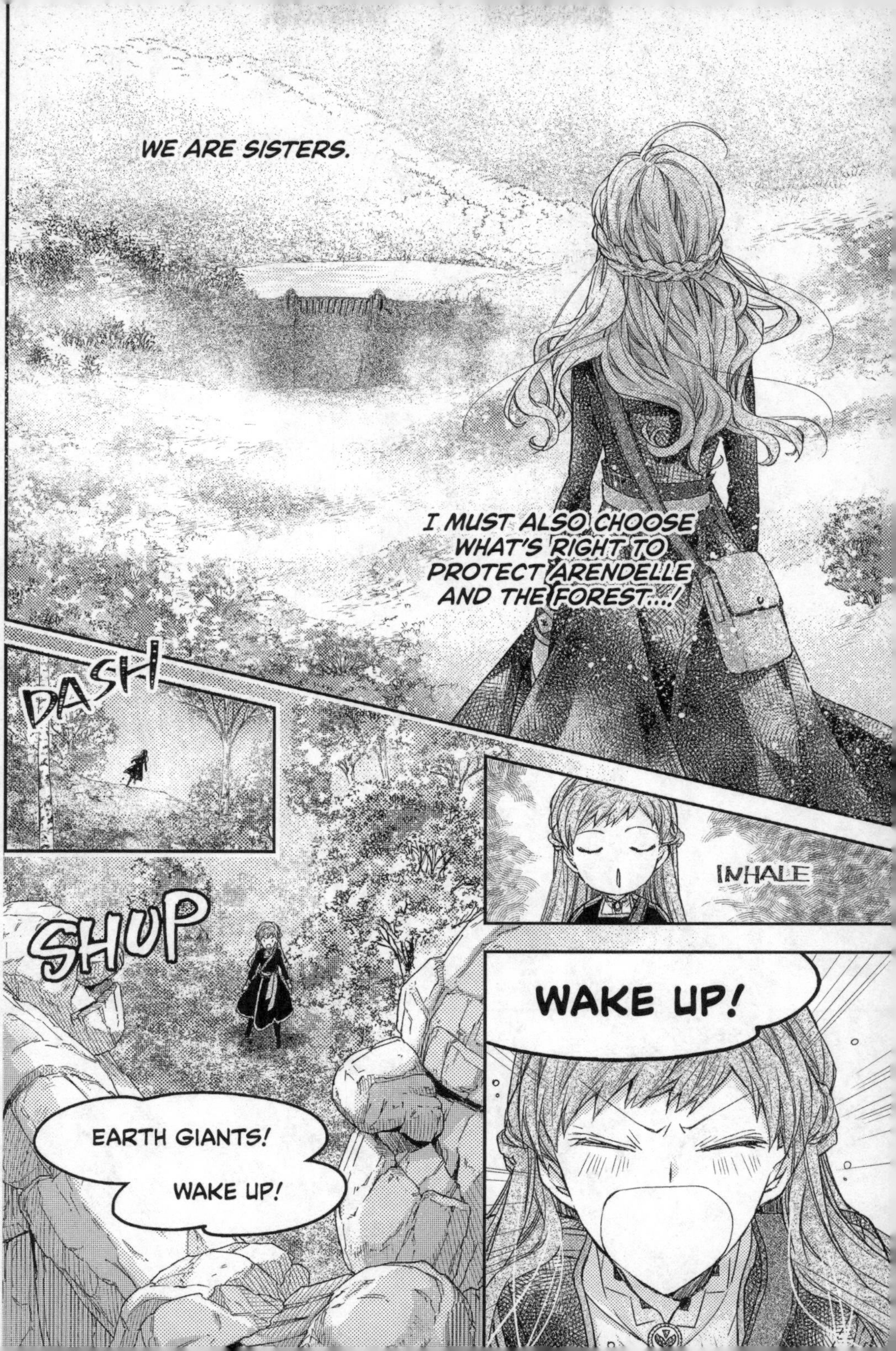
WE ARE SISTERS.
I MUST ALSO CHOOSE WHAT'S RIGHT TO PROTECT ARENDELLE AND THE FOREST...!
DASH
SHUP
EARTH GIANTS!
WAKE UP!
INHALE
WAKE UP!

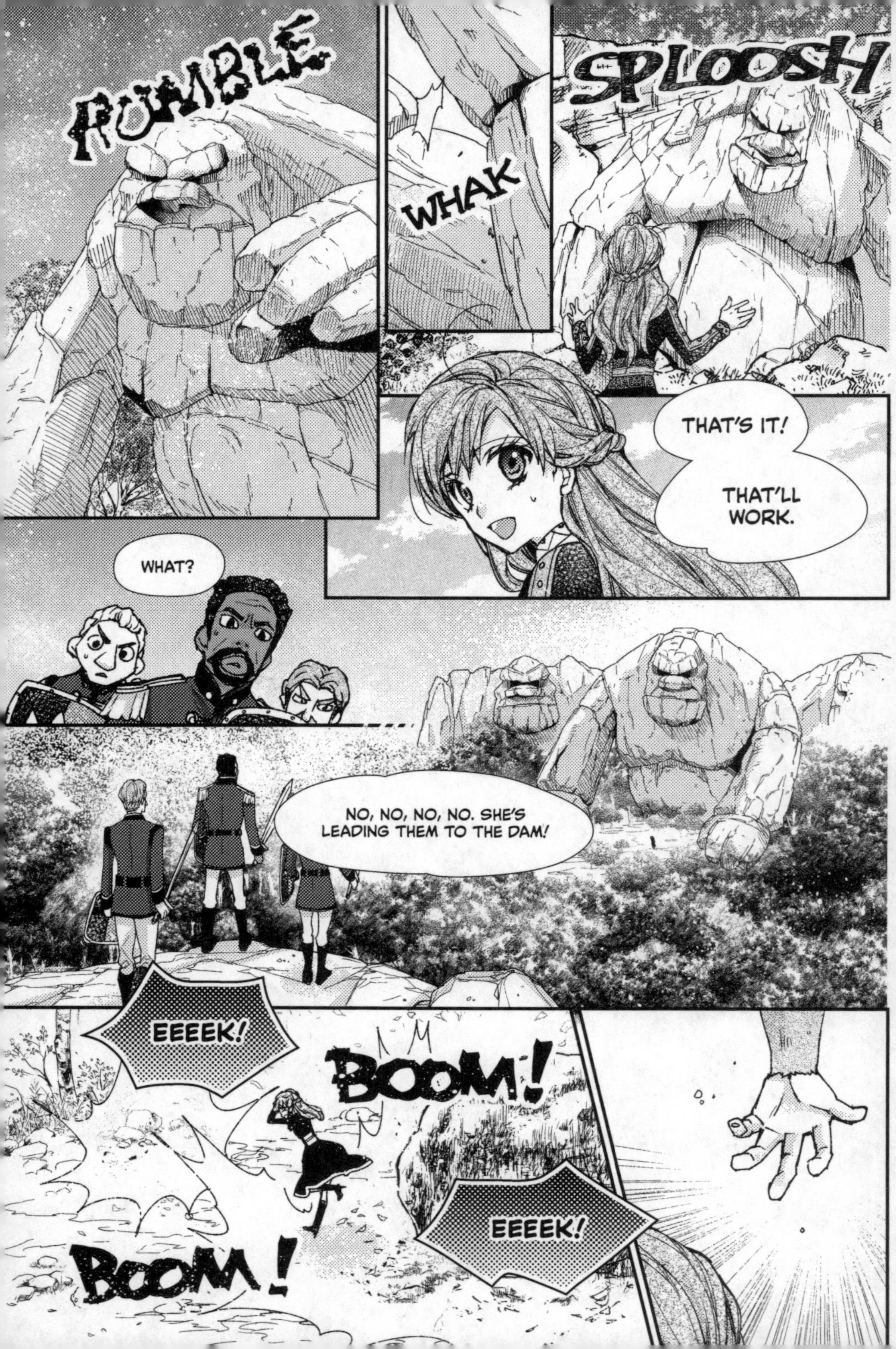
RUMBLE
WHAK
SPLOOSH
THAT'S IT!
THAT'LL WORK.
WHAT?
NO, NO, NO, NO. SHE'S LEADING THEM TO THE DAM!
EEEEK!
BOOM!
BOOM!
EEEEK!

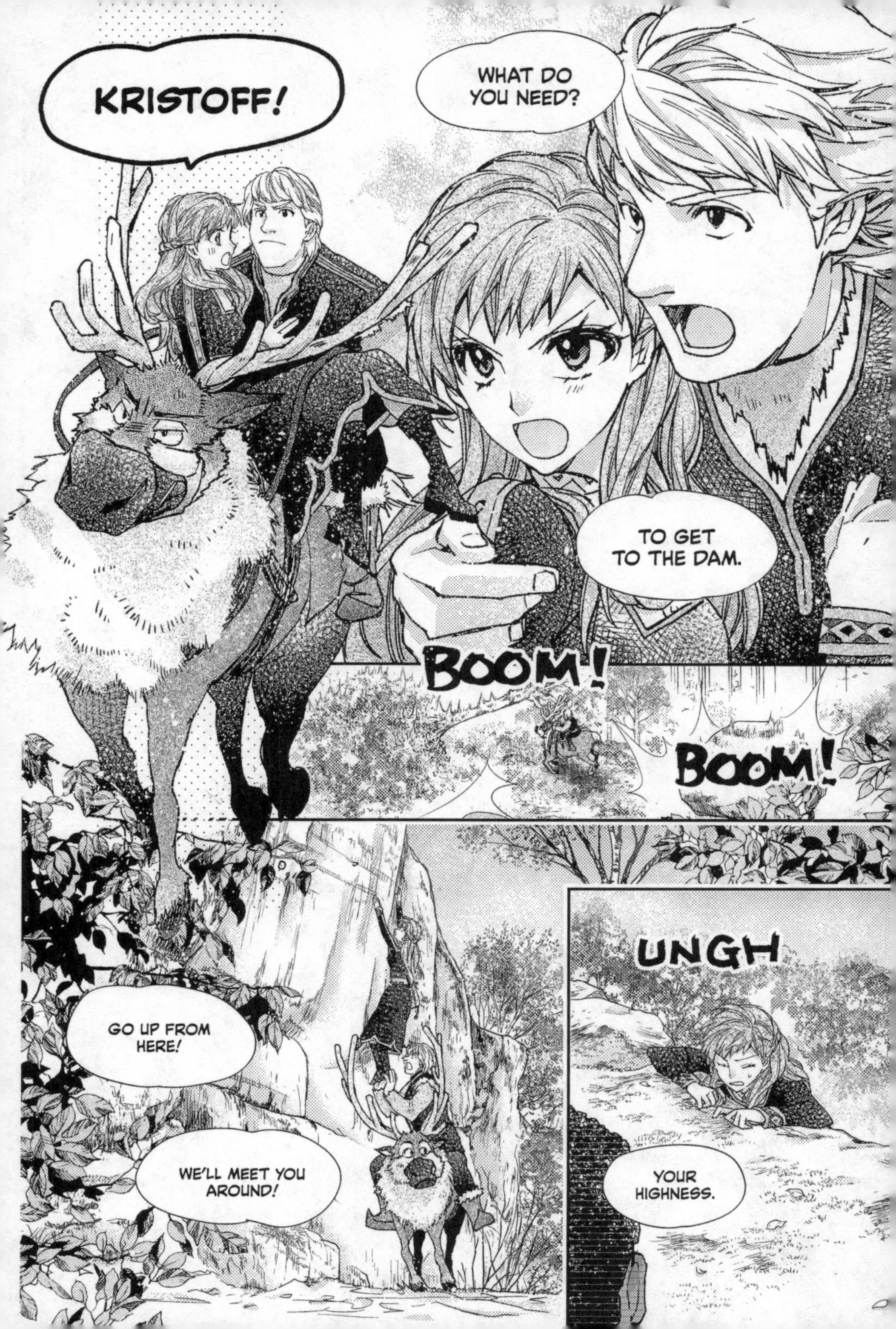
KRISTOFF!
WHAT DO YOU NEED?
TO GET TO THE DAM.
BOOM!
BOOM!
GO UP FROM HERE!
WE'LL MEET YOU AROUND!
UNGH
YOUR HIGHNESS.

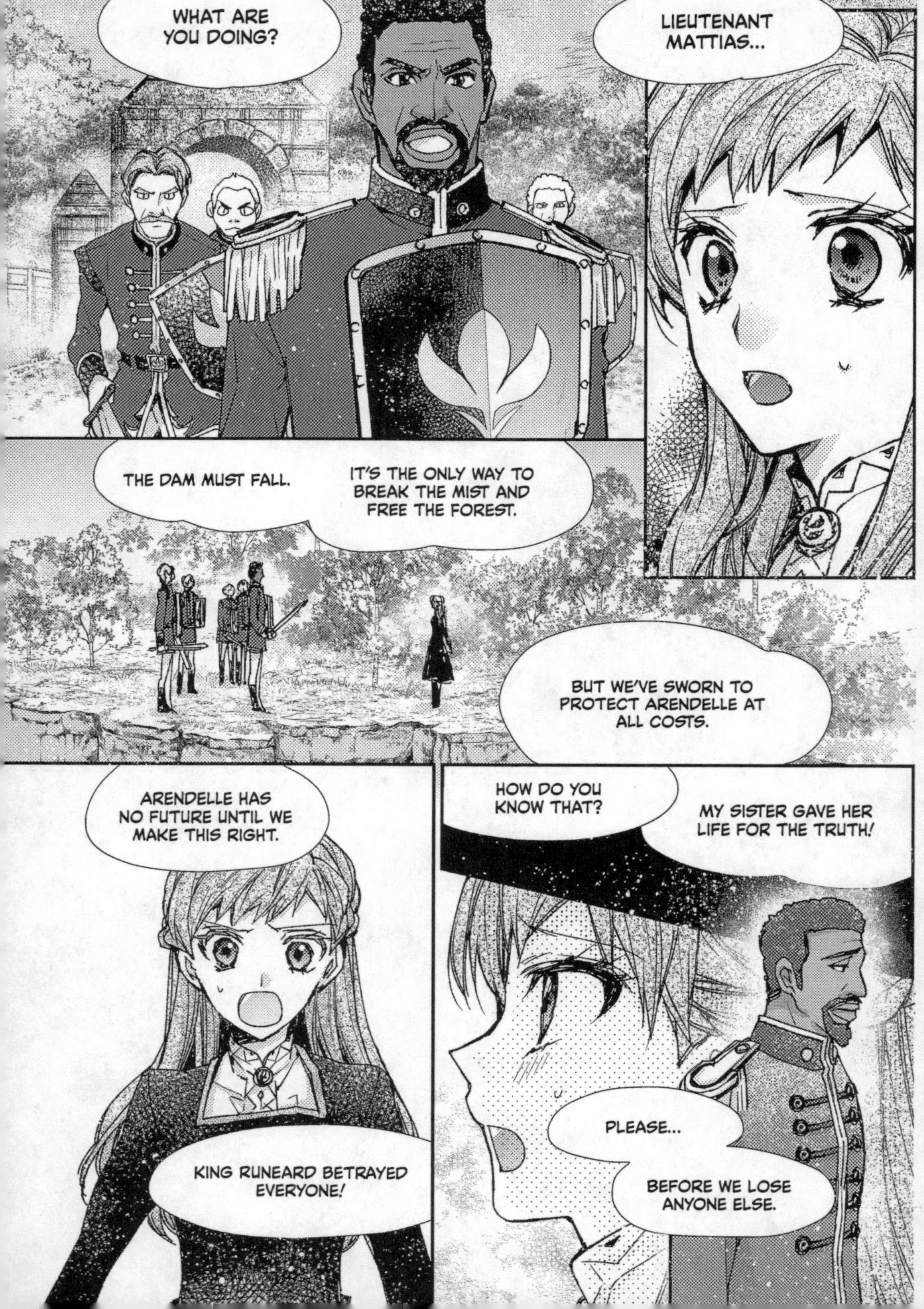
WHAT ARE YOU DOING?
LIEUTENANT MATTIAS...
THE DAM MUST FALL.
IT'S THE ONLY WAY TO BREAK THE MIST AND FREE THE FOREST.
BUT WE'VE SWORN TO PROTECT ARENDELLE AT ALL COSTS.
ARENDELLE HAS NO FUTURE UNTIL WE MAKE THIS RIGHT.
KING RUNEARD BETRAYED EVERYONE!
HOW DO YOU KNOW THAT?
MY SISTER GAVE HER LIFE FOR THE TRUTH!
PLEASE...
BEFORE WE LOSE ANYONE ELSE.

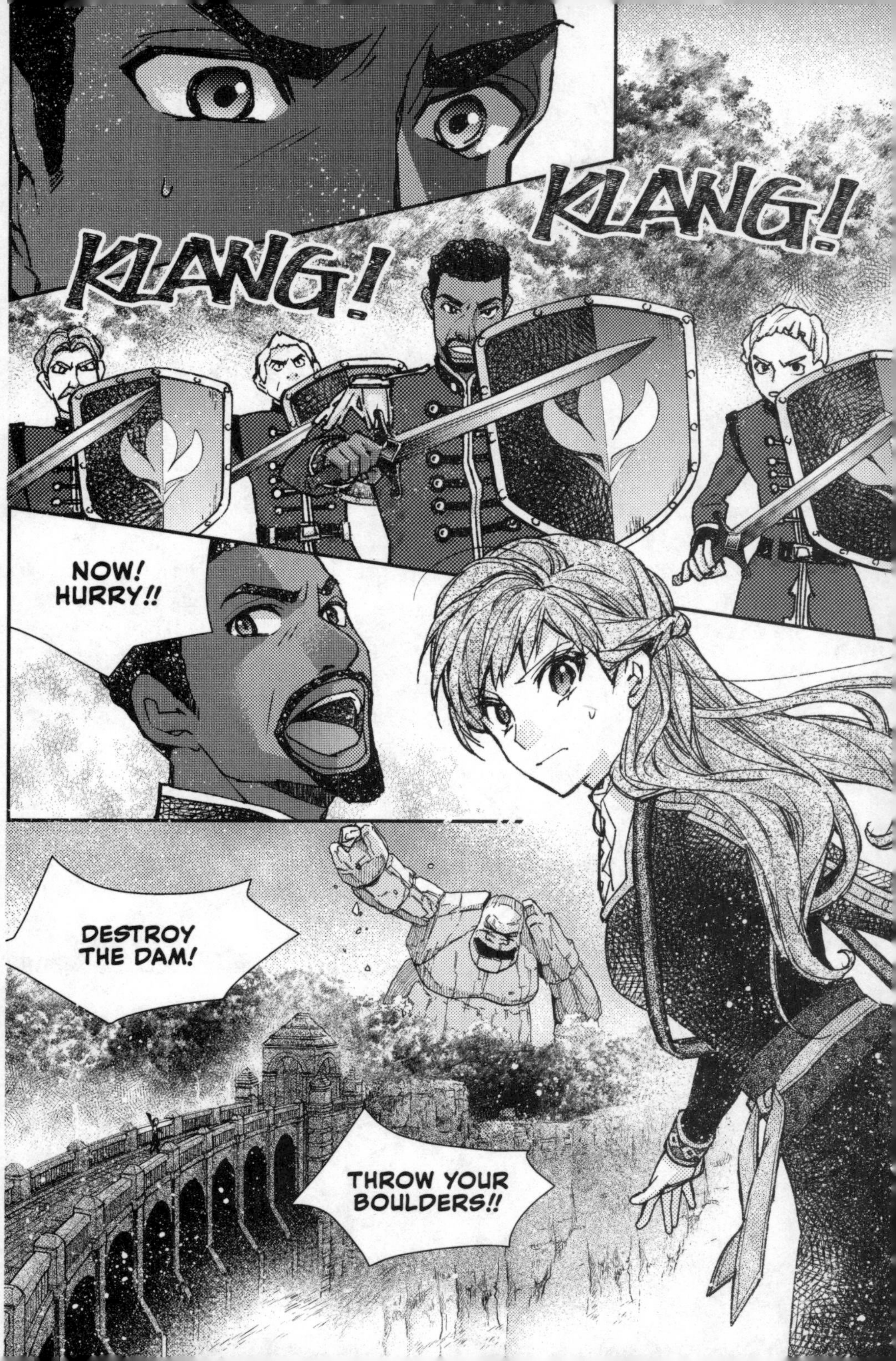
KLANG!
KLANG!
NOW! HURRY!!
DESTROY THE DAM!
THROW YOUR BOULDERS!!

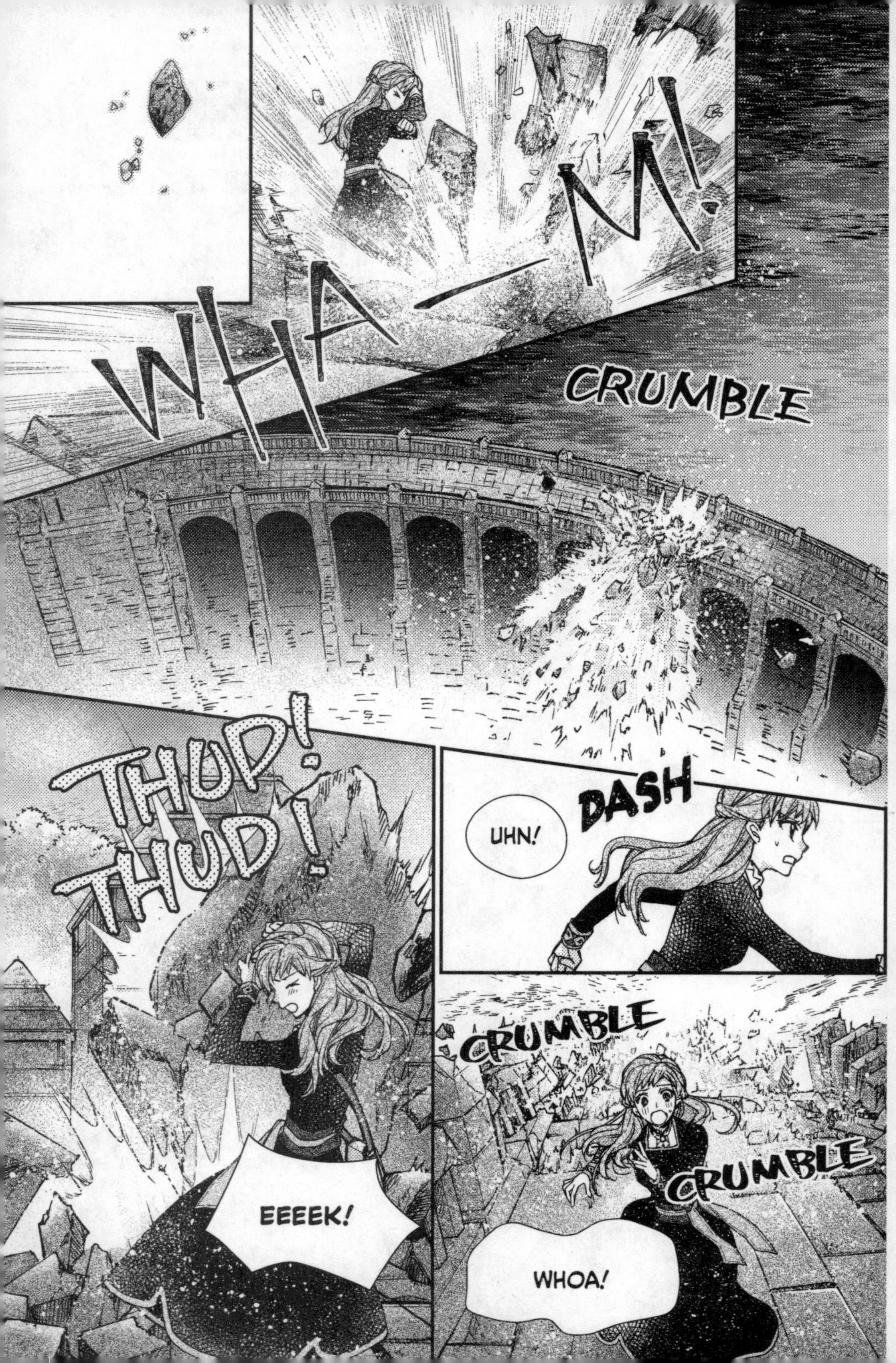
WHA—M!
CRUMBLE
THUD! THUD!
EEEEK!
DASH
UHN!
CRUMBLE
CRUMBLE
WHOA!

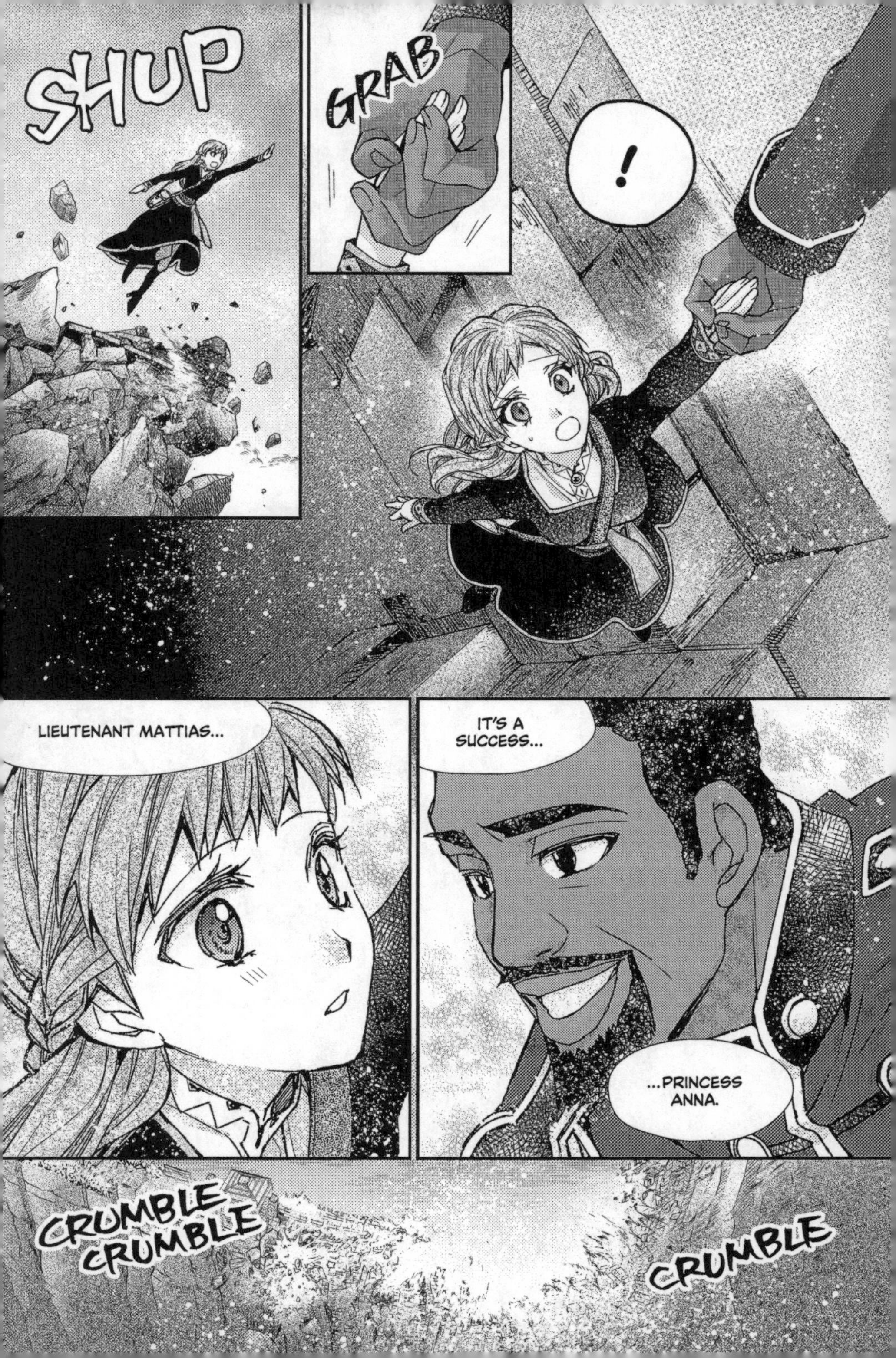
SHUP
GRAB
!
LIEUTENANT MATTIAS...
IT'S A SUCCESS...
...PRINCESS ANNA.
CRUMBLE CRUMBLE
CRUMBLE

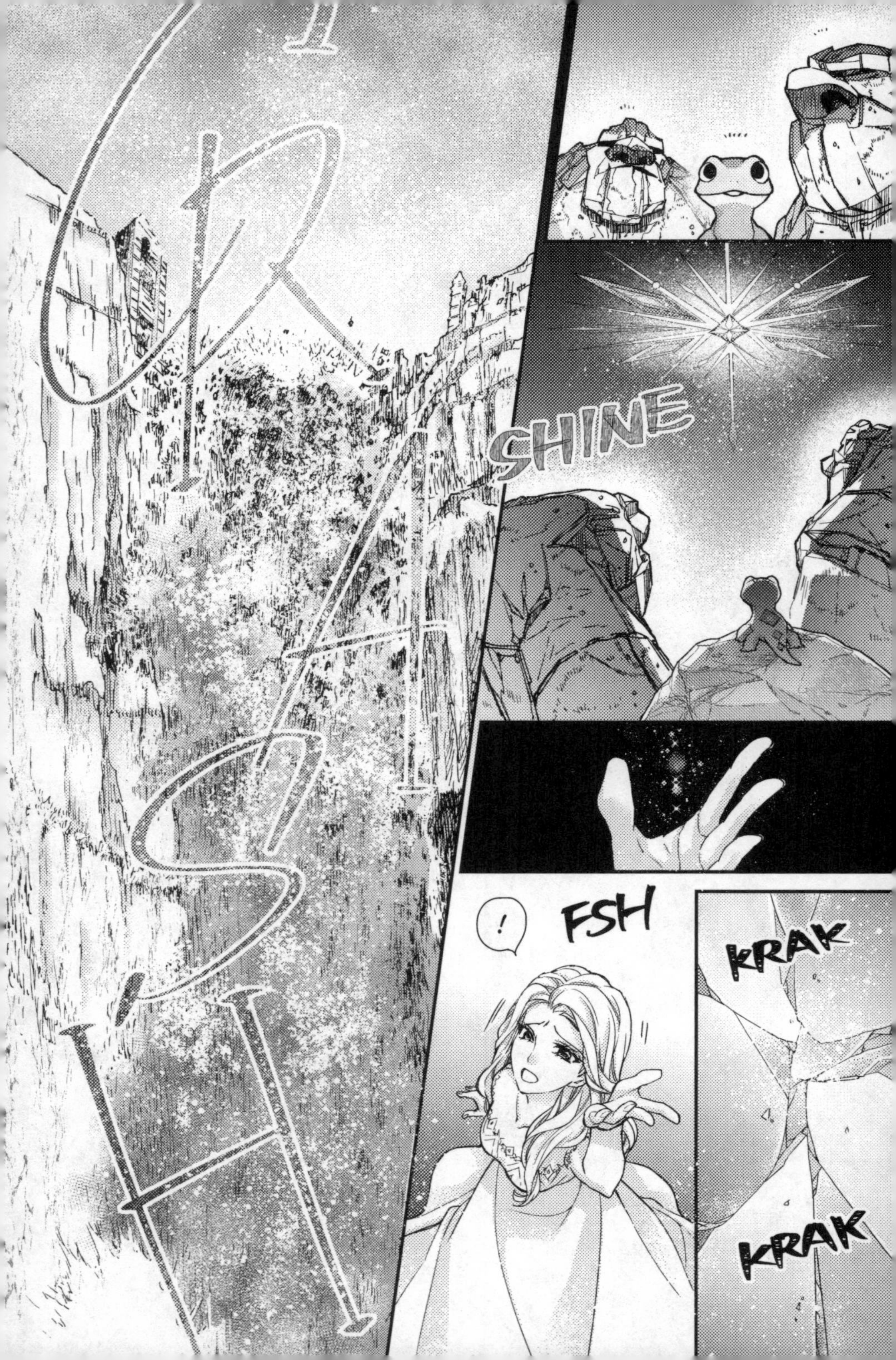
CRASH
SHINE
!
FSH
KRAK
KRAK

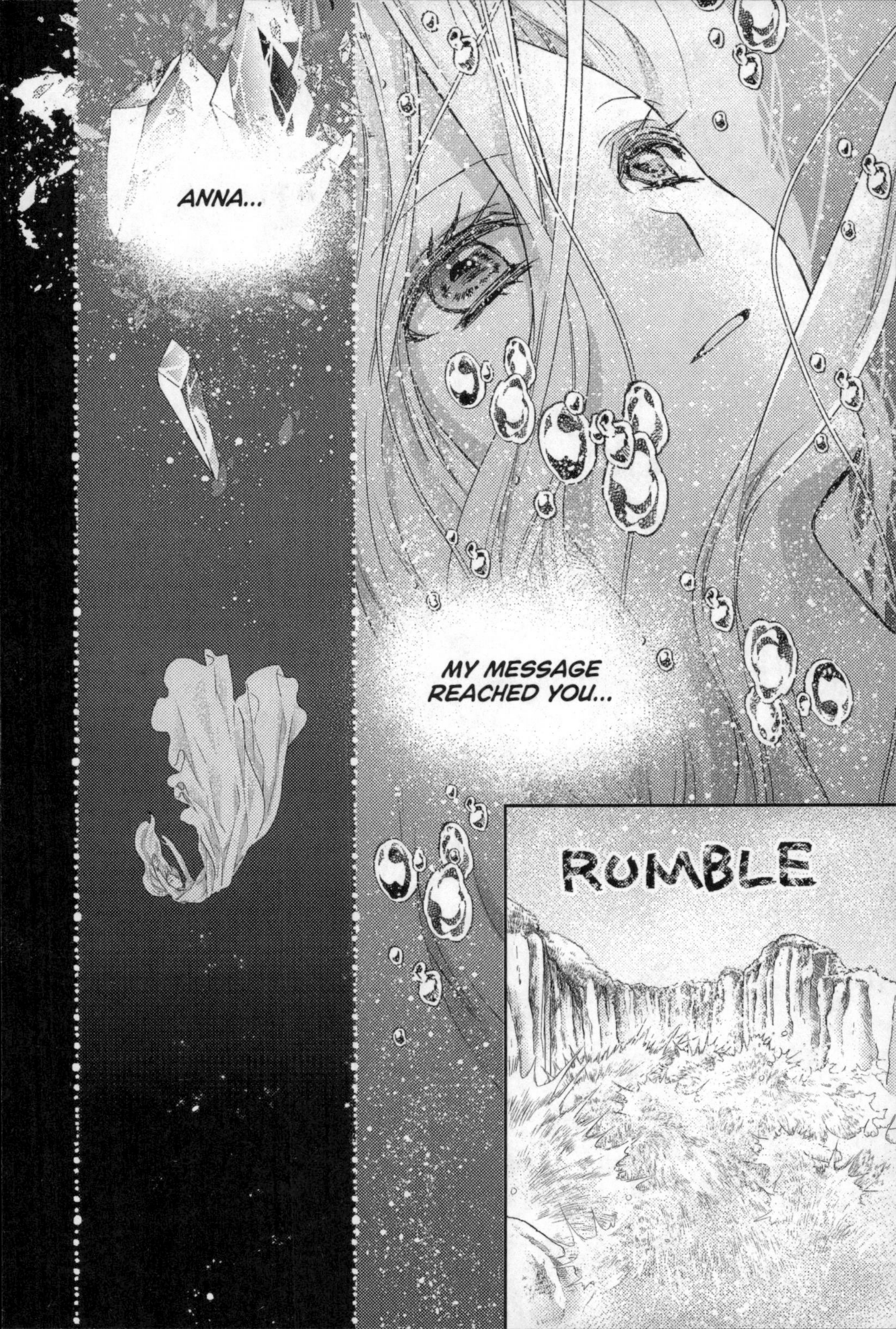
ANNA...
MY MESSAGE REACHED YOU...
RUMBLE

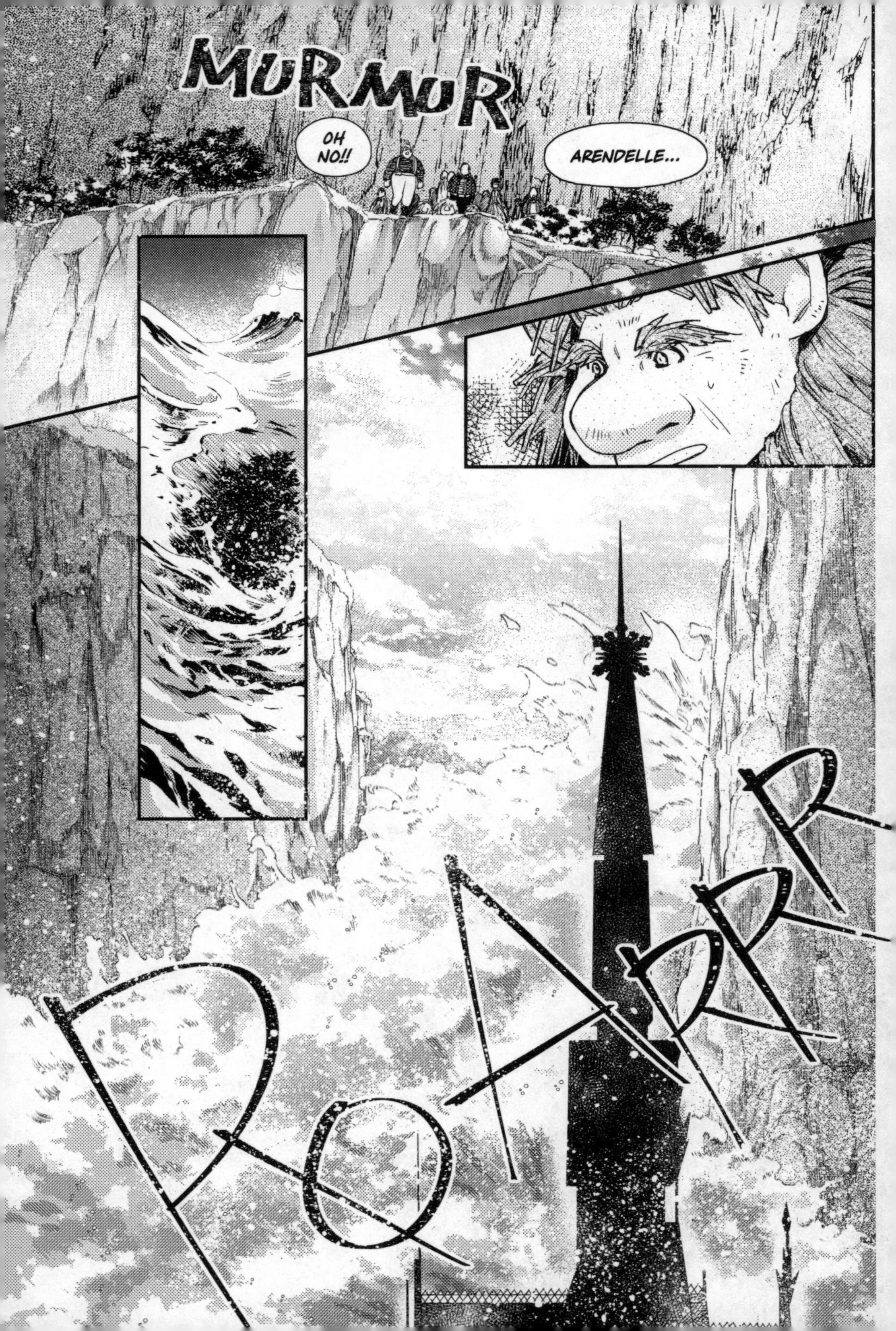
MURMUR
OH NO!!
ARENDELLE...
ROARRR

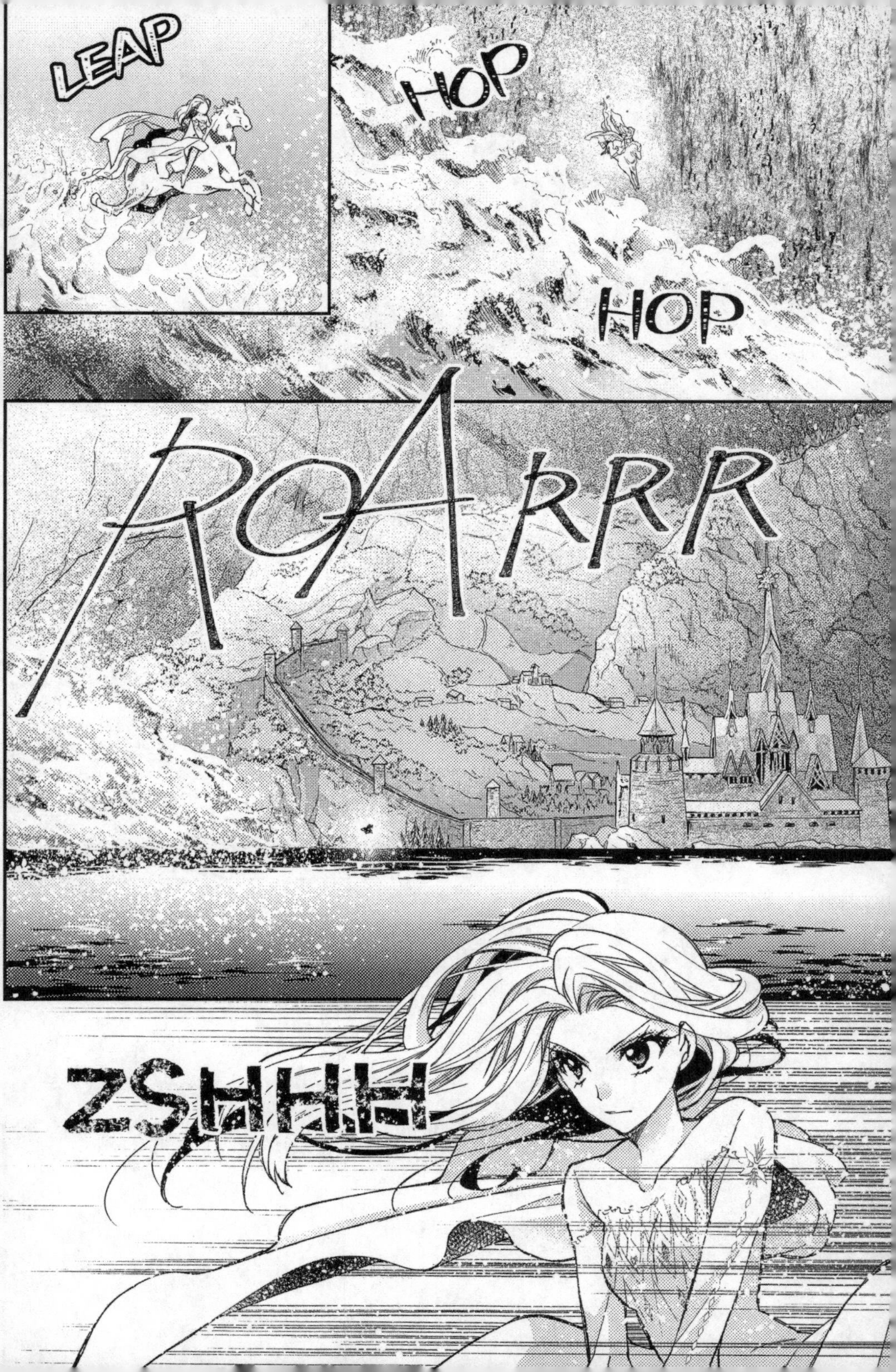
HOP
HOP
LEAP
ROARRR
ZSHHH

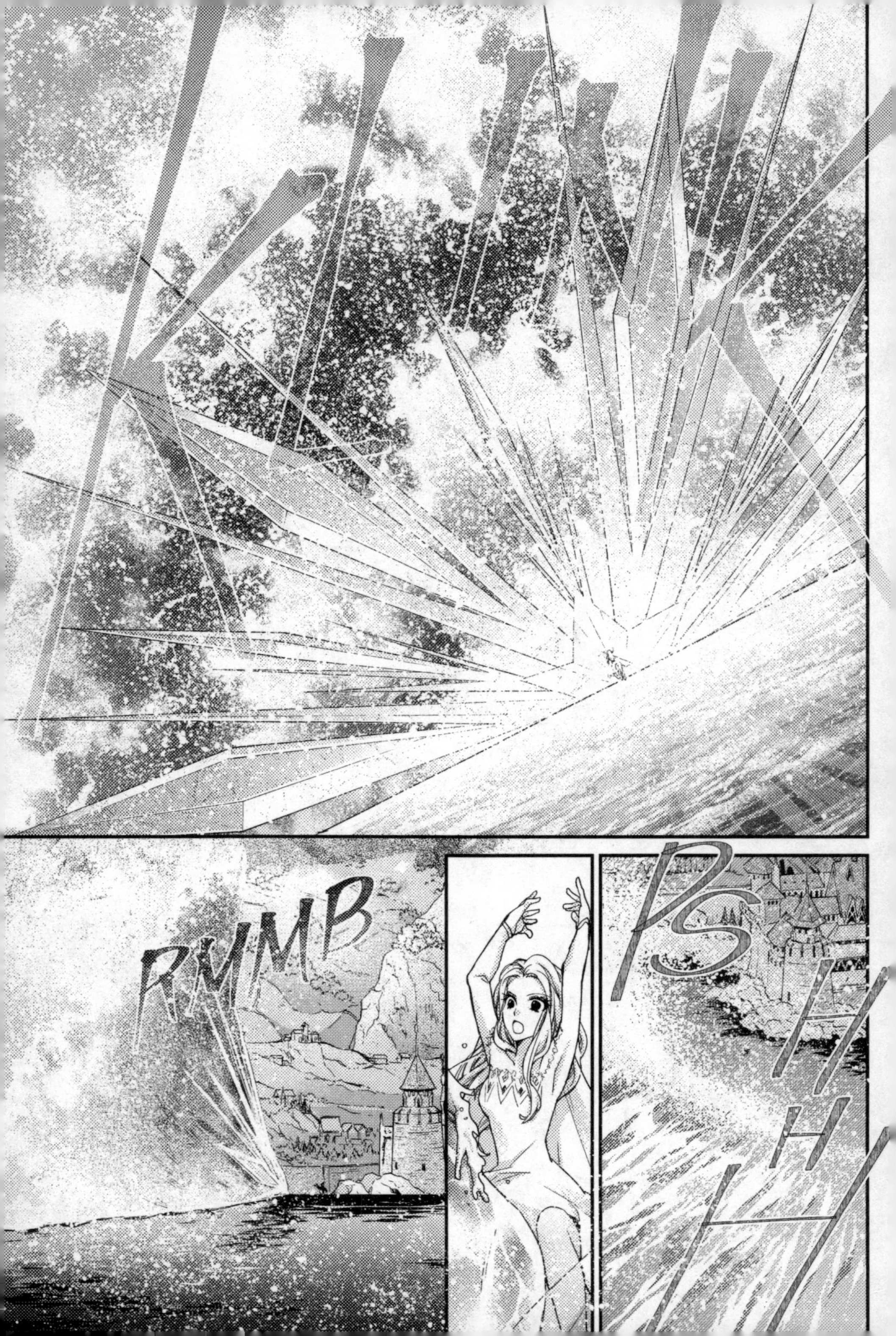
RUMB
PSHHH

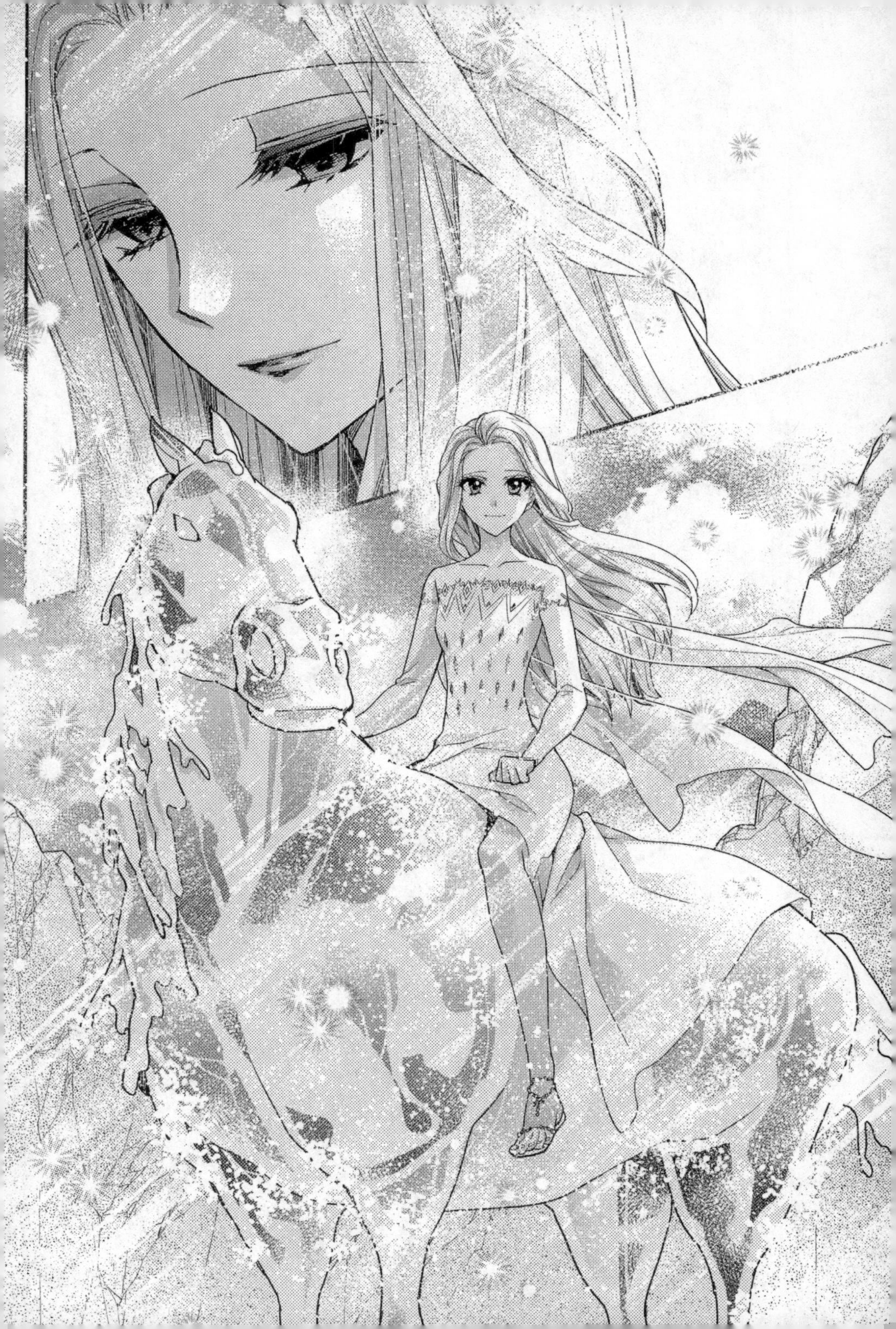

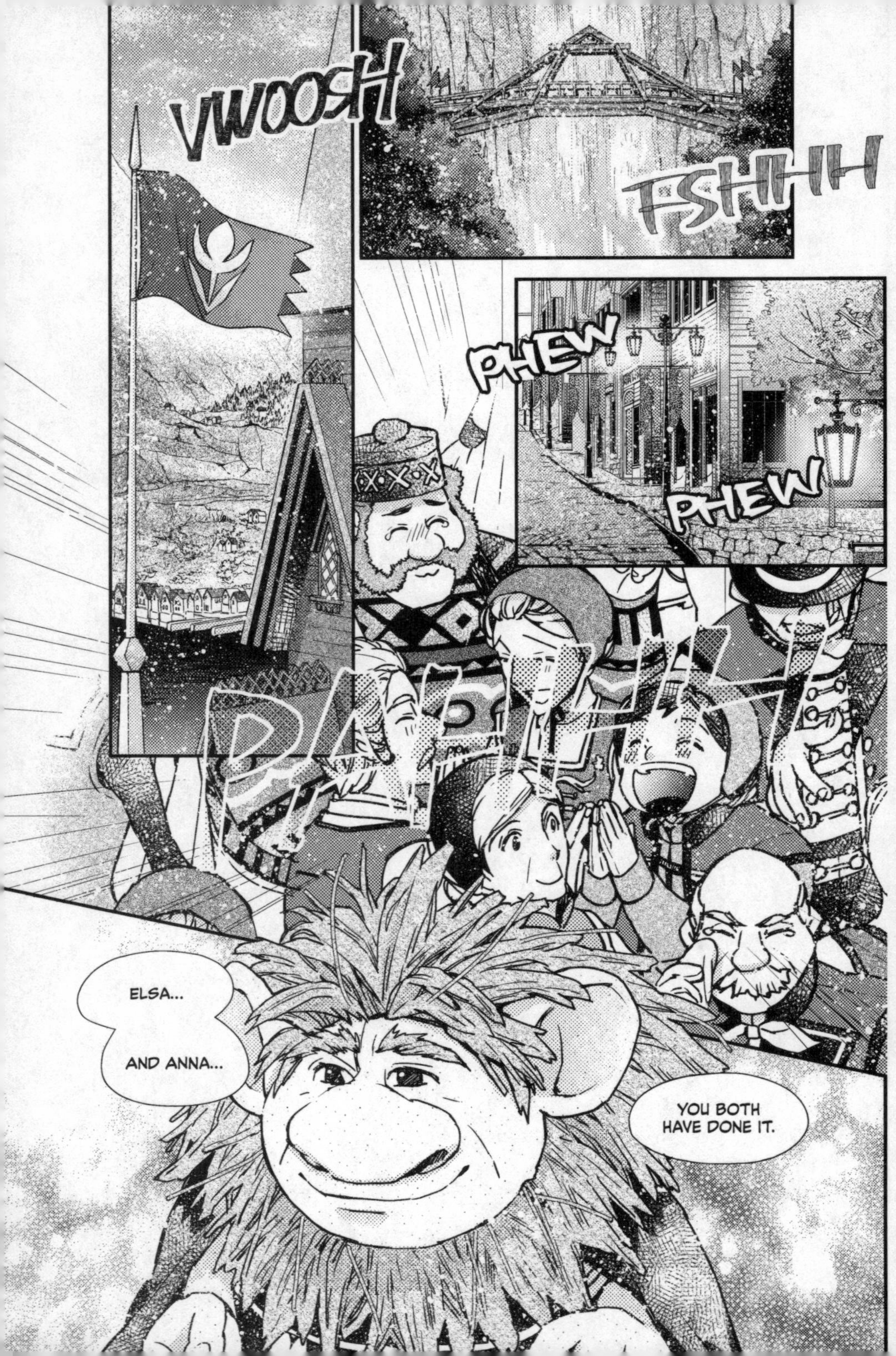
VWOOSH
FSHHH
PHEW
PHEW
PAHHH
ELSA...
AND ANNA...
YOU BOTH HAVE DONE IT.

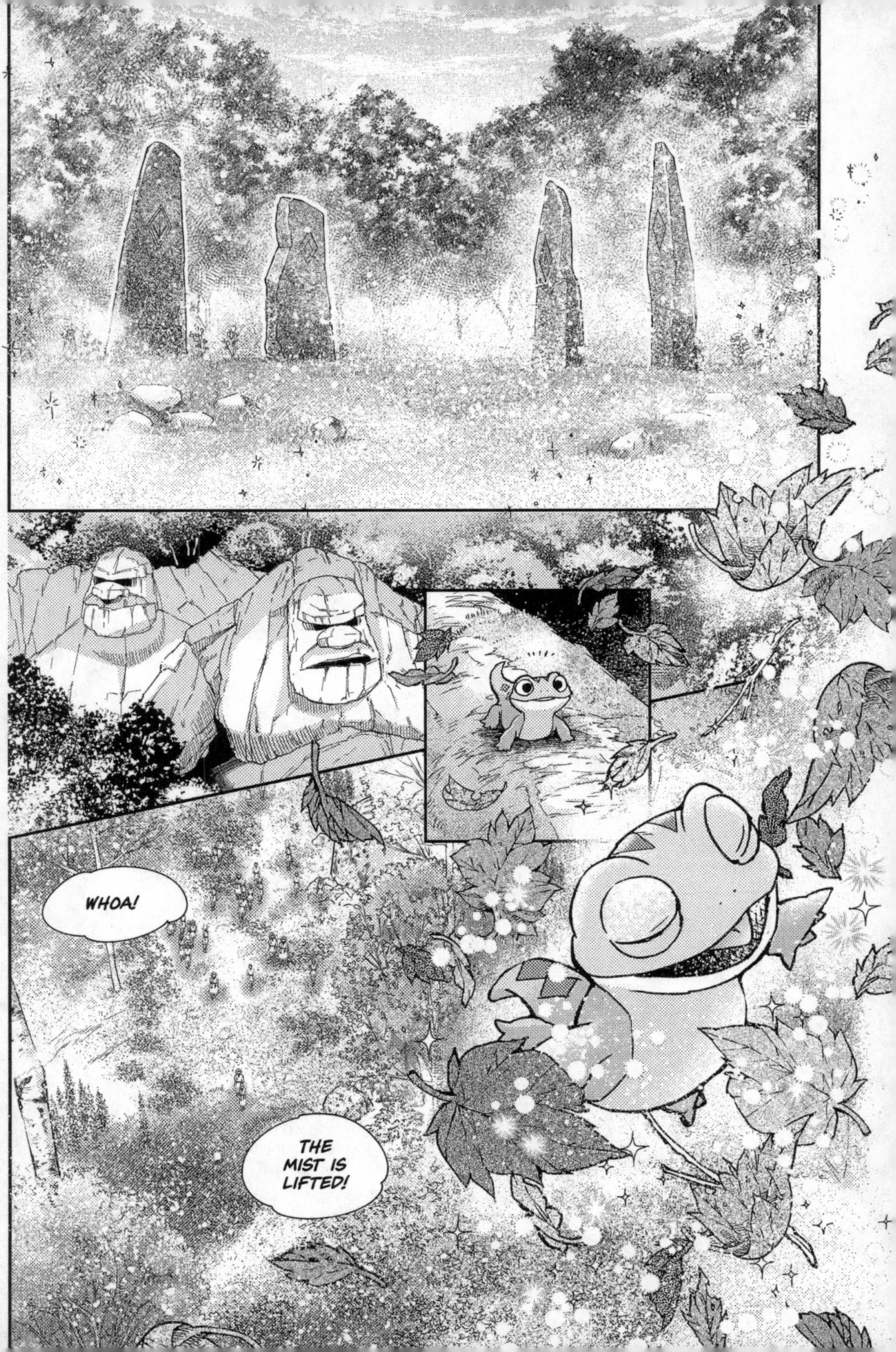
WHOA!
THE MIST IS LIFTED!

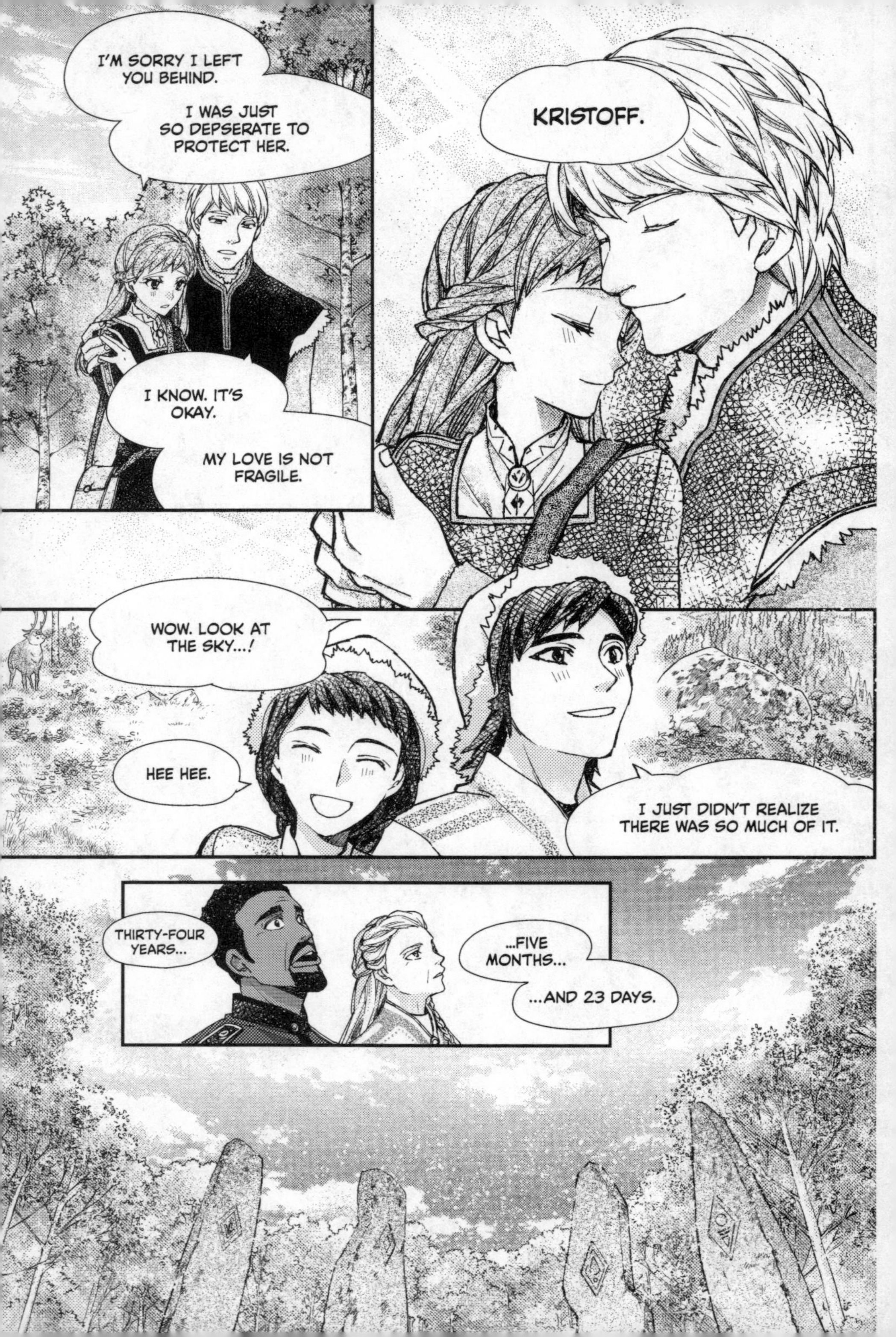
I'M SORRY I LEFT YOU BEHIND.
I WAS JUST SO DEPSERATE TO PROTECT HER.
I KNOW. IT'S OKAY.
MY LOVE IS NOT FRAGILE.
KRISTOFF.
WOW. LOOK AT THE SKY...!
HEE HEE.
I JUST DIDN'T REALIZE THERE WAS SO MUCH OF IT.
THIRTY-FOUR YEARS...
...FIVE MONTHS...
...AND 23 DAYS.

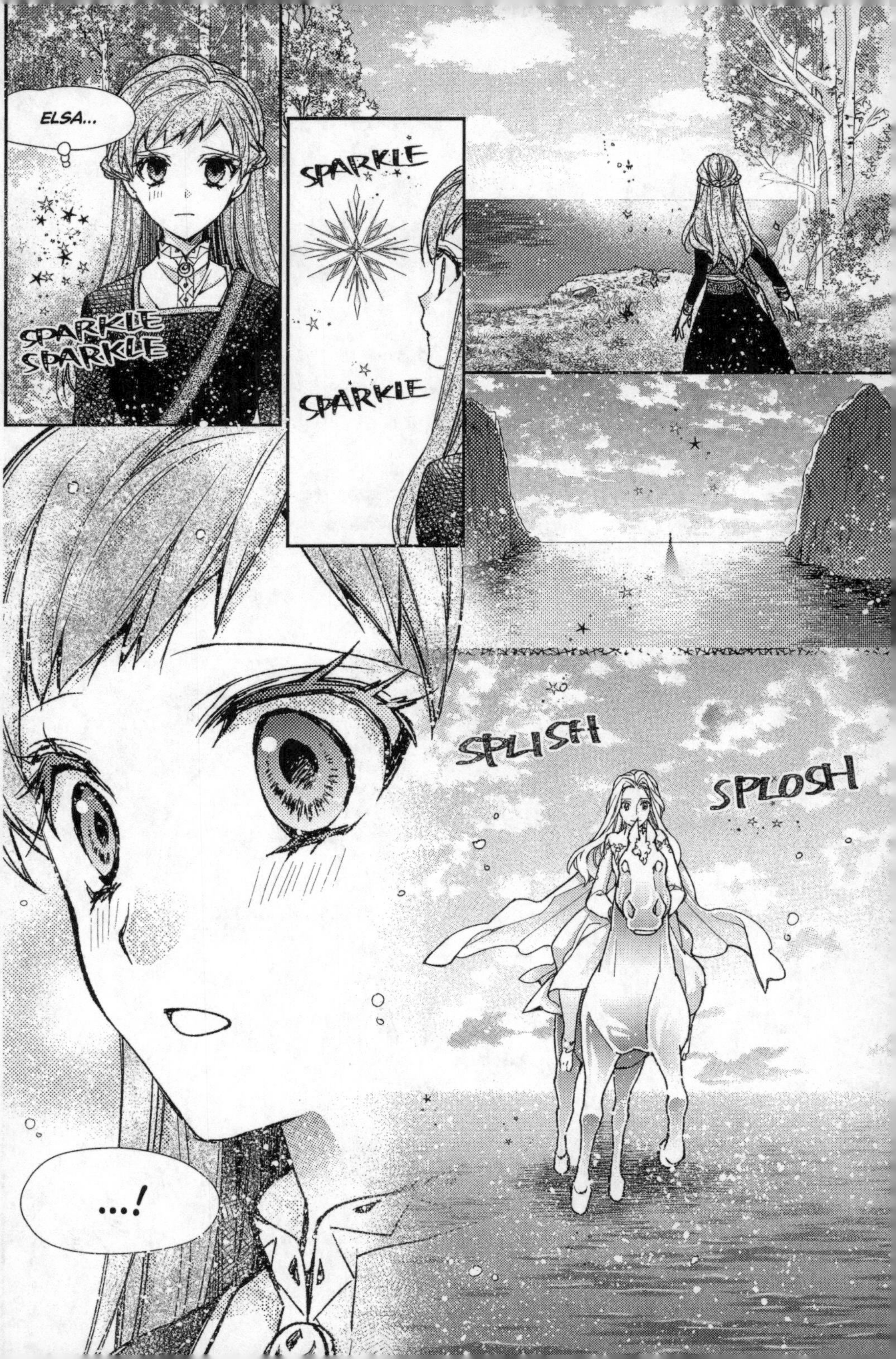
ELSA...
SPARKLE SPARKLE
SPARKLE
SPARKLE
...!
SPLISH
SPLOSH

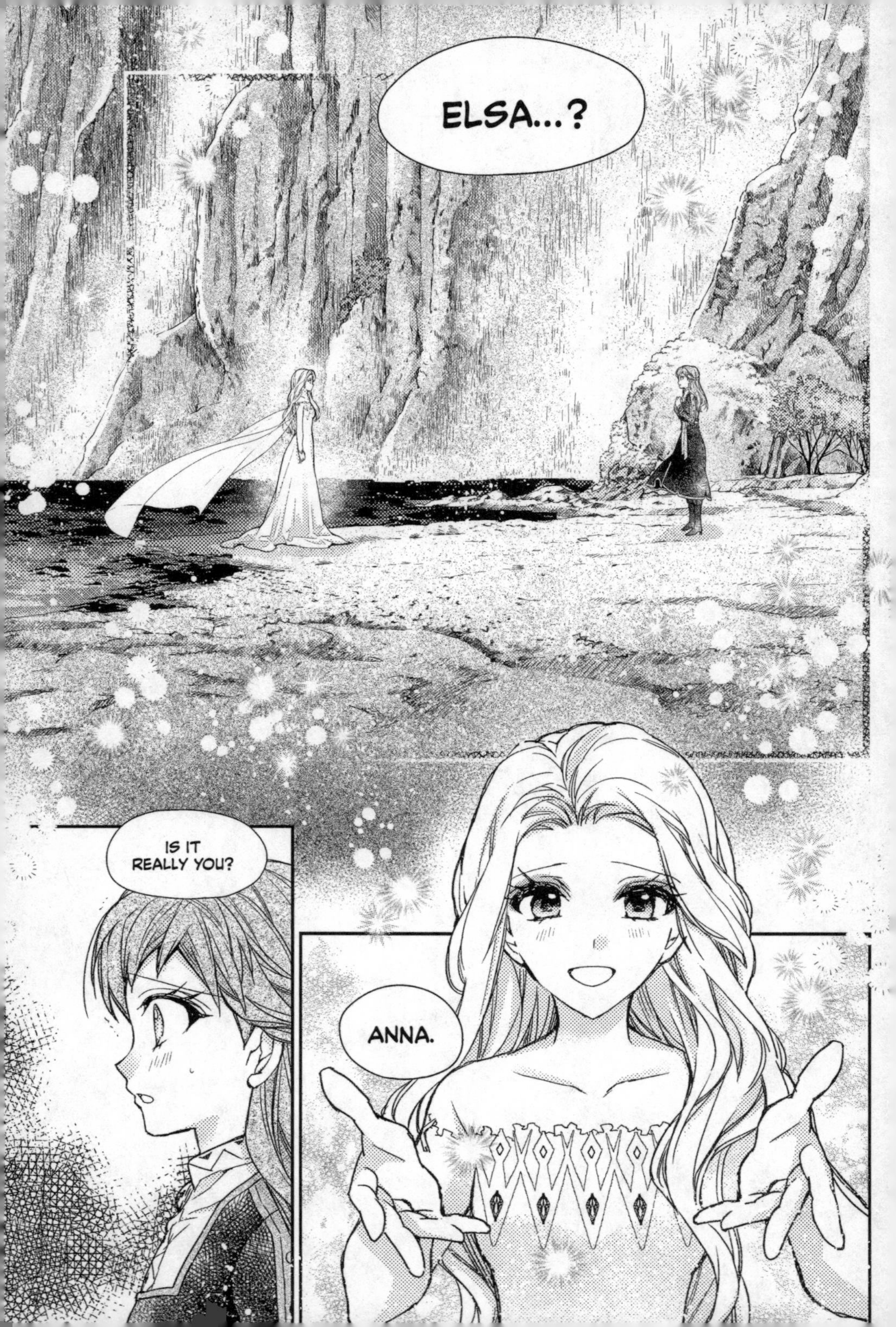
ELSA...?
IS IT REALLY YOU?
ANNA.

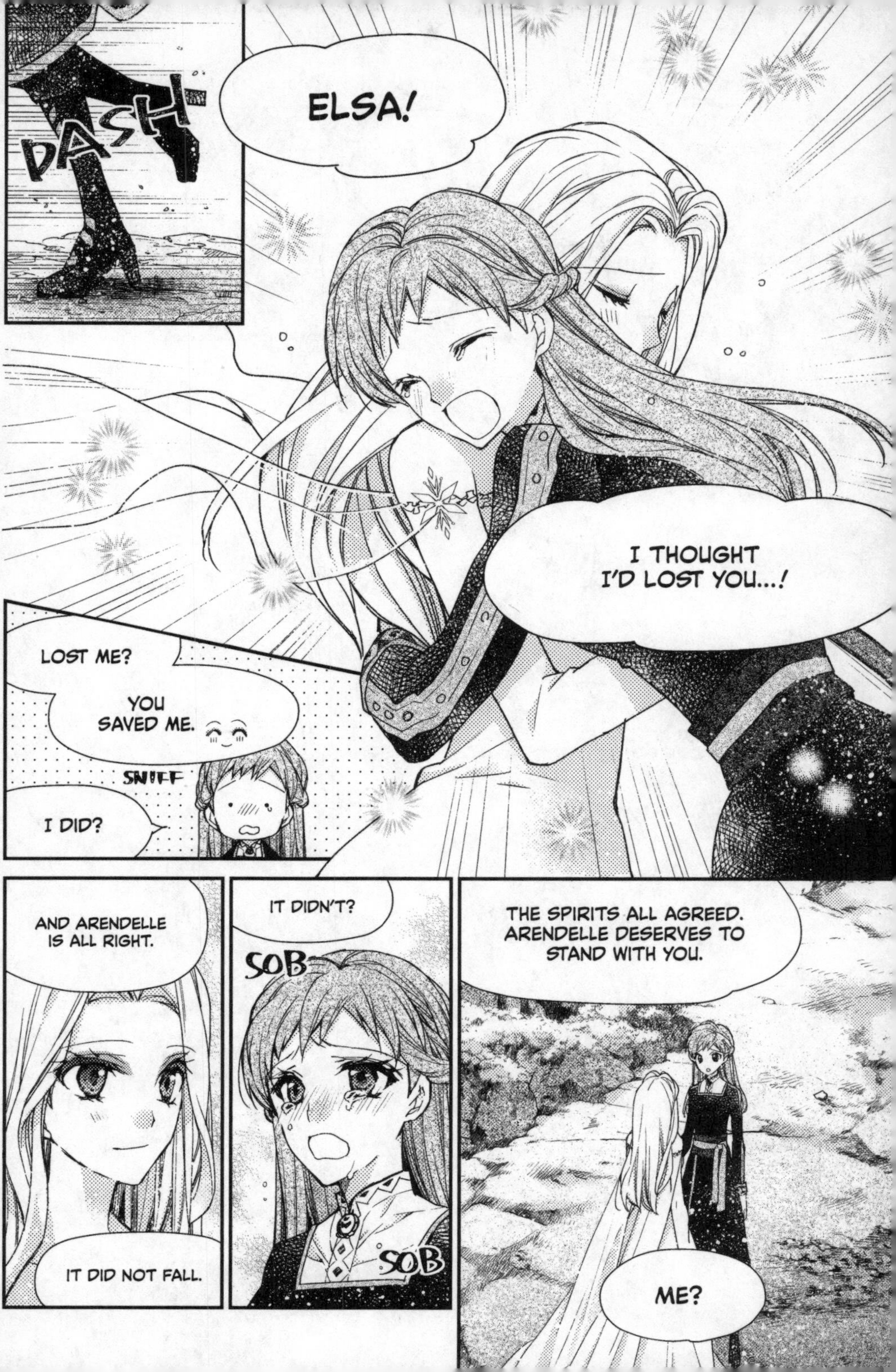
DASH
ELSA!
I THOUGHT I'D LOST YOU...!
LOST ME?
YOU SAVED ME.
SNIFF
I DID?
AND ARENDELLE IS ALL RIGHT.
IT DID NOT FALL.
IT DIDN'T?
SOB
SOB
THE SPIRITS ALL AGREED. ARENDELLE DESERVES TO STAND WITH YOU.
ME?

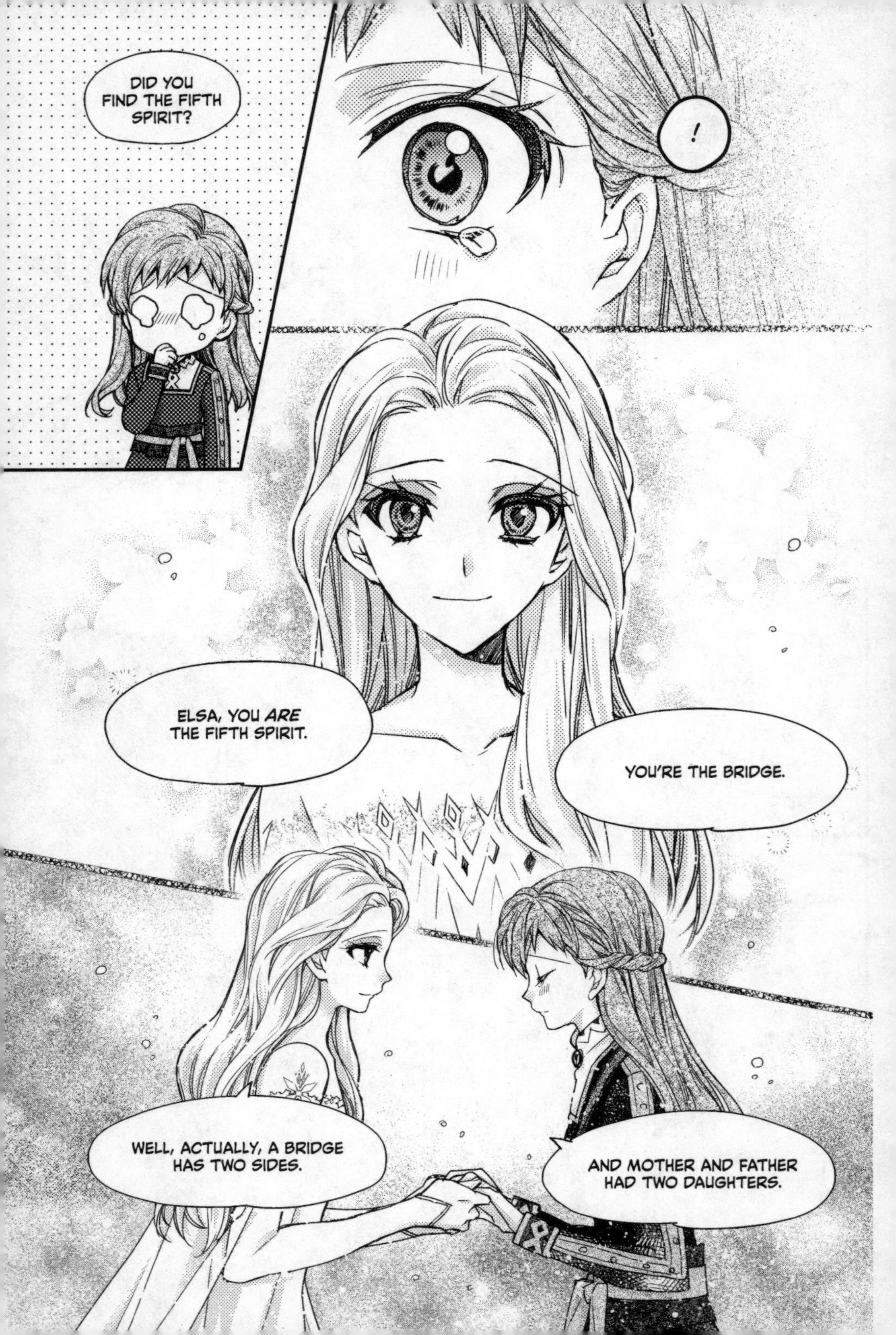
DID YOU FIND THE FIFTH SPIRIT?
!
ELSA, YOU *ARE* THE FIFTH SPIRIT.
YOU'RE THE BRIDGE.
WELL, ACTUALLY, A BRIDGE HAS TWO SIDES.
AND MOTHER AND FATHER HAD TWO DAUGHTERS.

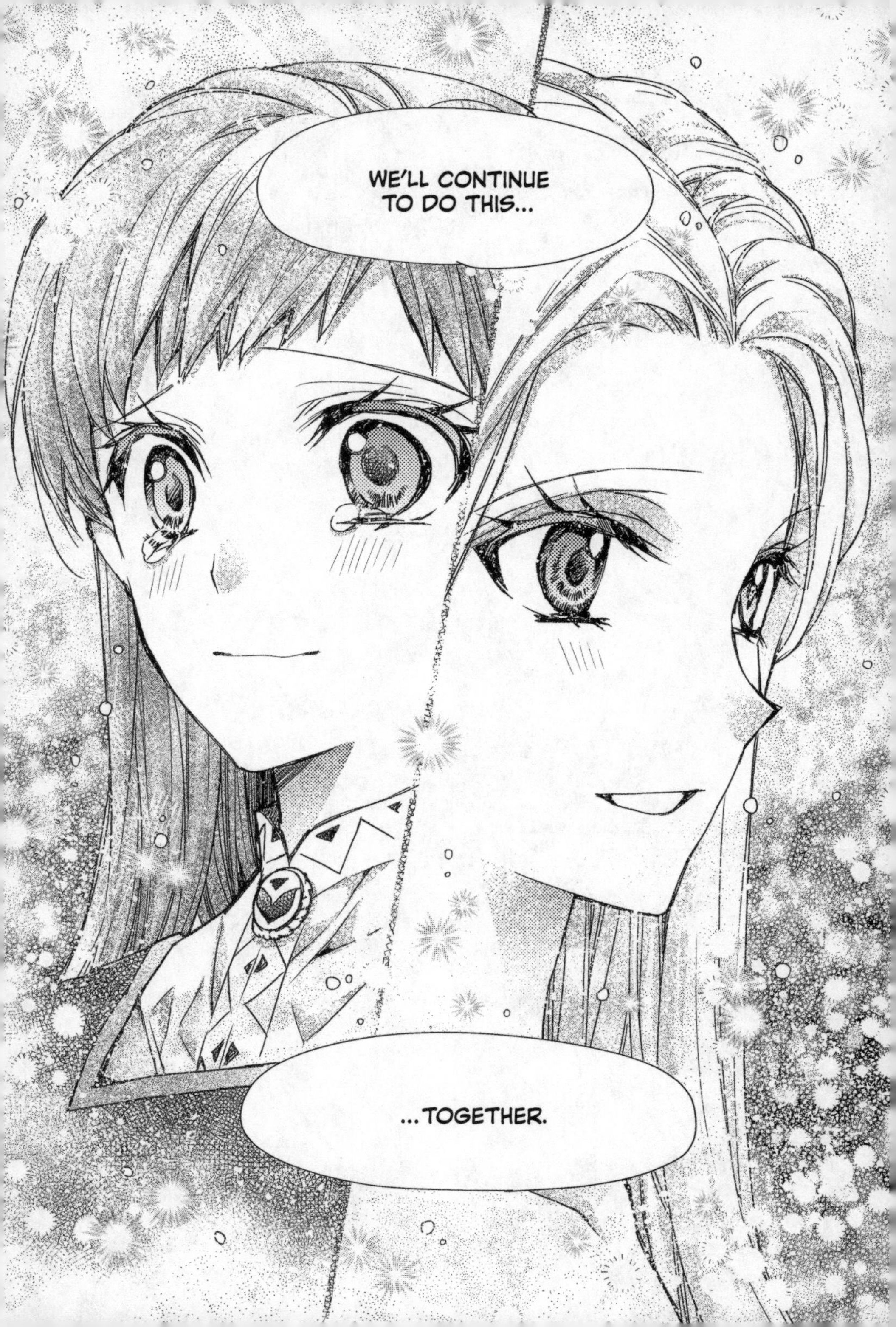
WE'LL CONTINUE TO DO THIS...
...TOGETHER.

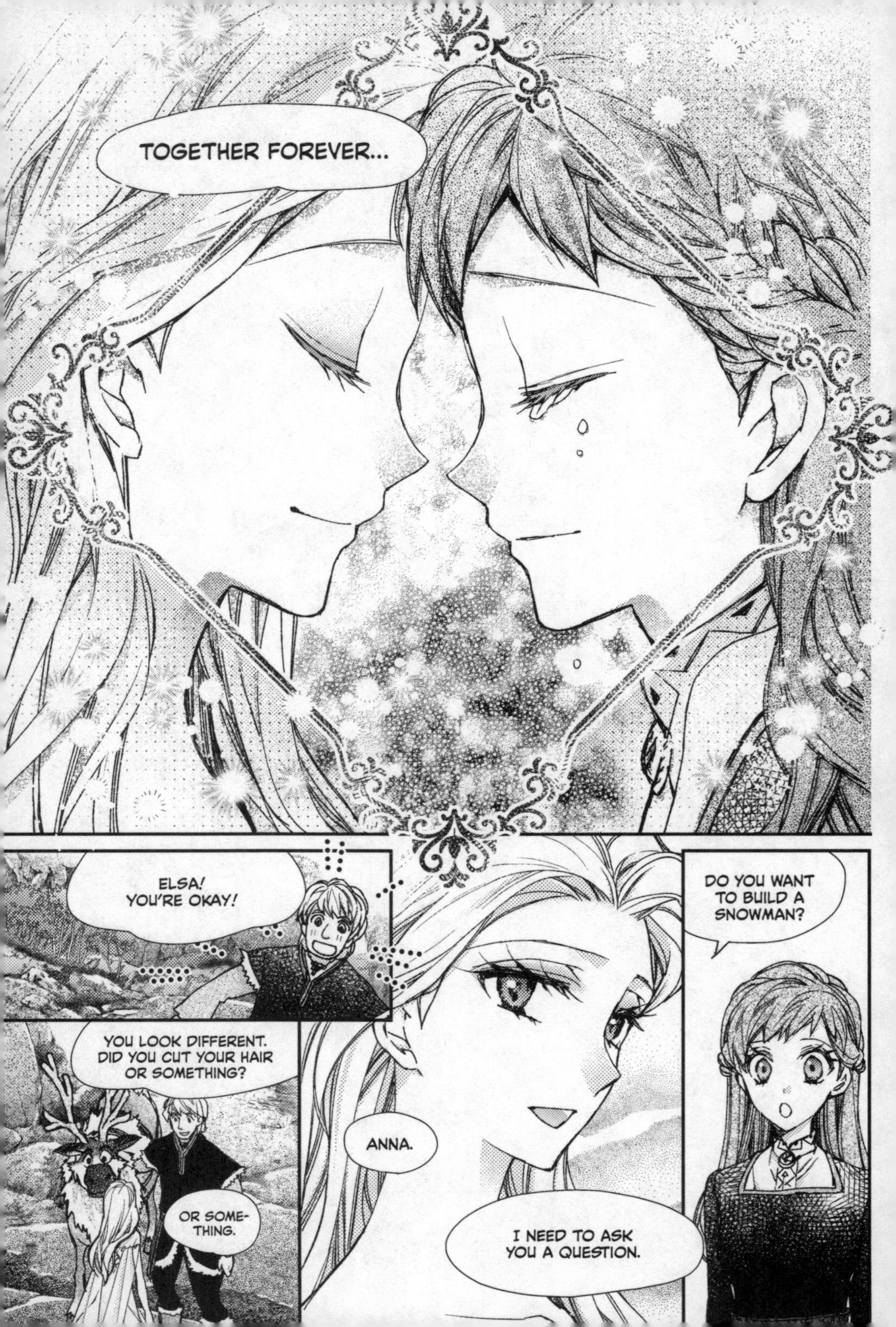
TOGETHER FOREVER...
ELSA! YOU'RE OKAY!
YOU LOOK DIFFERENT. DID YOU CUT YOUR HAIR OR SOMETHING?
OR SOME-THING.
ANNA.
I NEED TO ASK YOU A QUESTION.
DO YOU WANT TO BUILD A SNOWMAN?

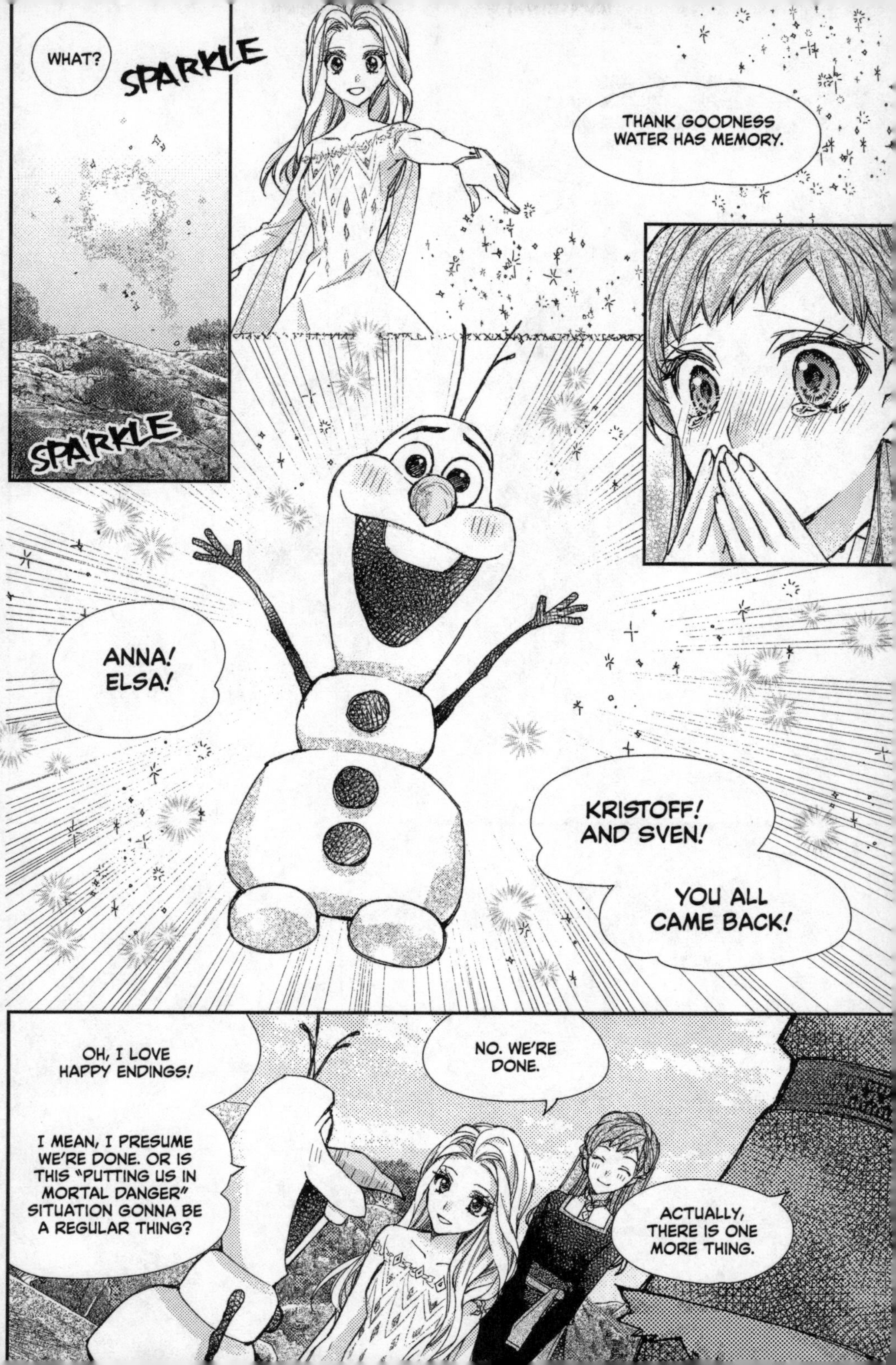

WHAT?
SPARKLE
SPARKLE
THANK GOODNESS WATER HAS MEMORY.
ANNA! ELSA!
KRISTOFF! AND SVEN!
YOU ALL CAME BACK!
OH, I LOVE HAPPY ENDINGS!
I MEAN, I PRESUME WE'RE DONE. OR IS THIS "PUTTING US IN MORTAL DANGER" SITUATION GONNA BE A REGULAR THING?
NO. WE'RE DONE.
ACTUALLY, THERE IS ONE MORE THING.

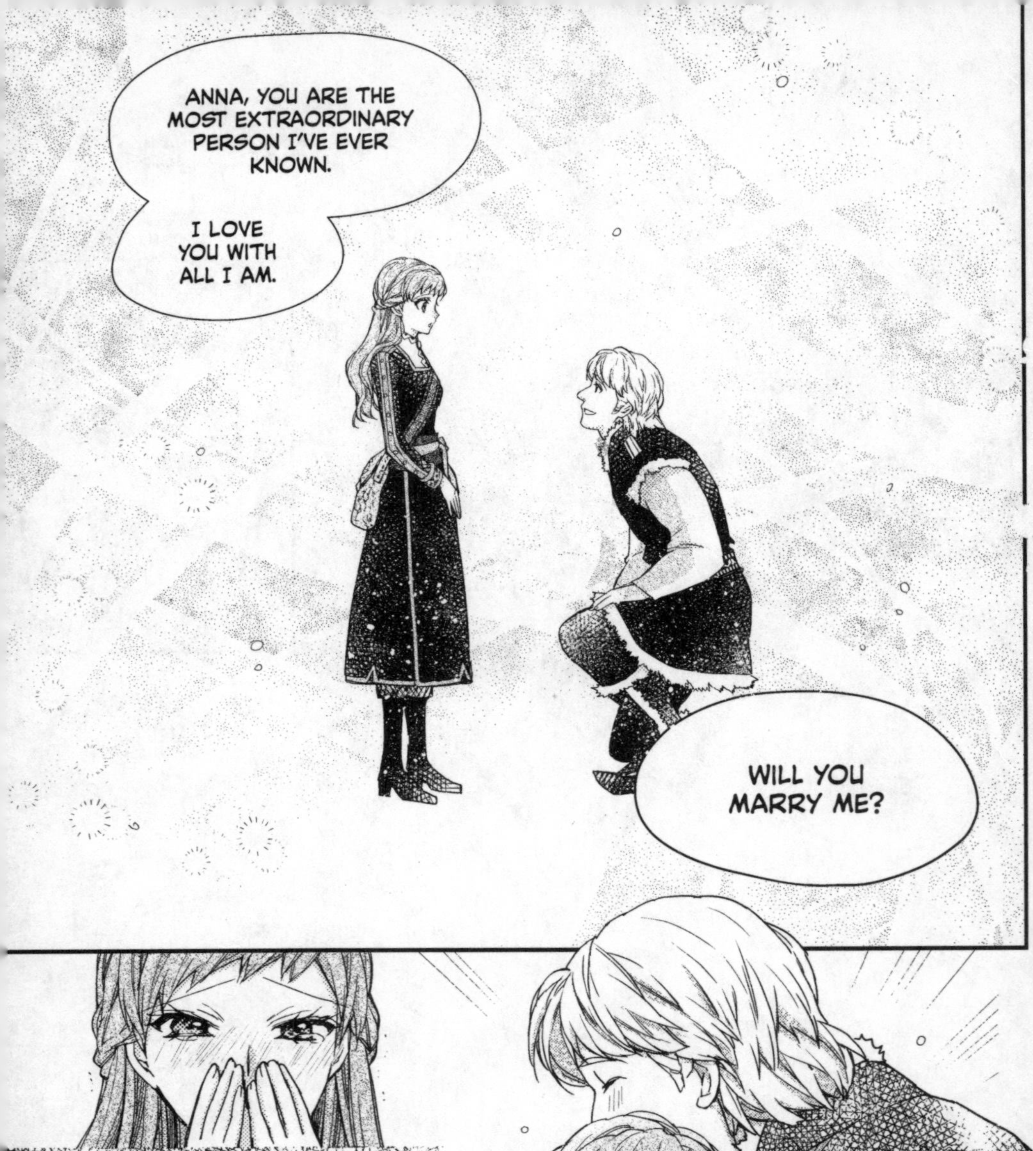
ANNA, YOU ARE THE MOST EXTRAORDINARY PERSON I'VE EVER KNOWN.
I LOVE YOU WITH ALL I AM.
WILL YOU MARRY ME?
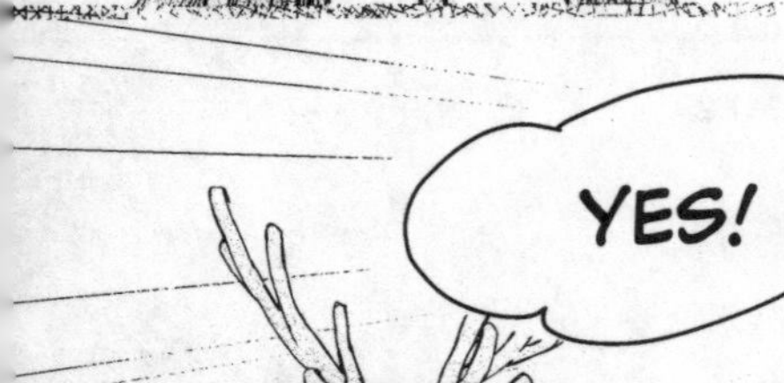
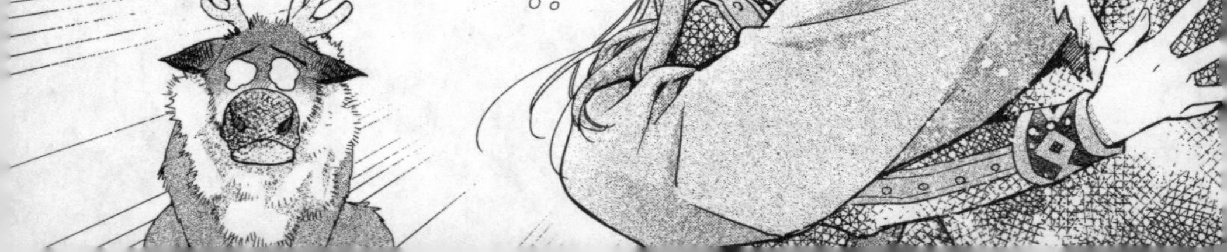
YES!

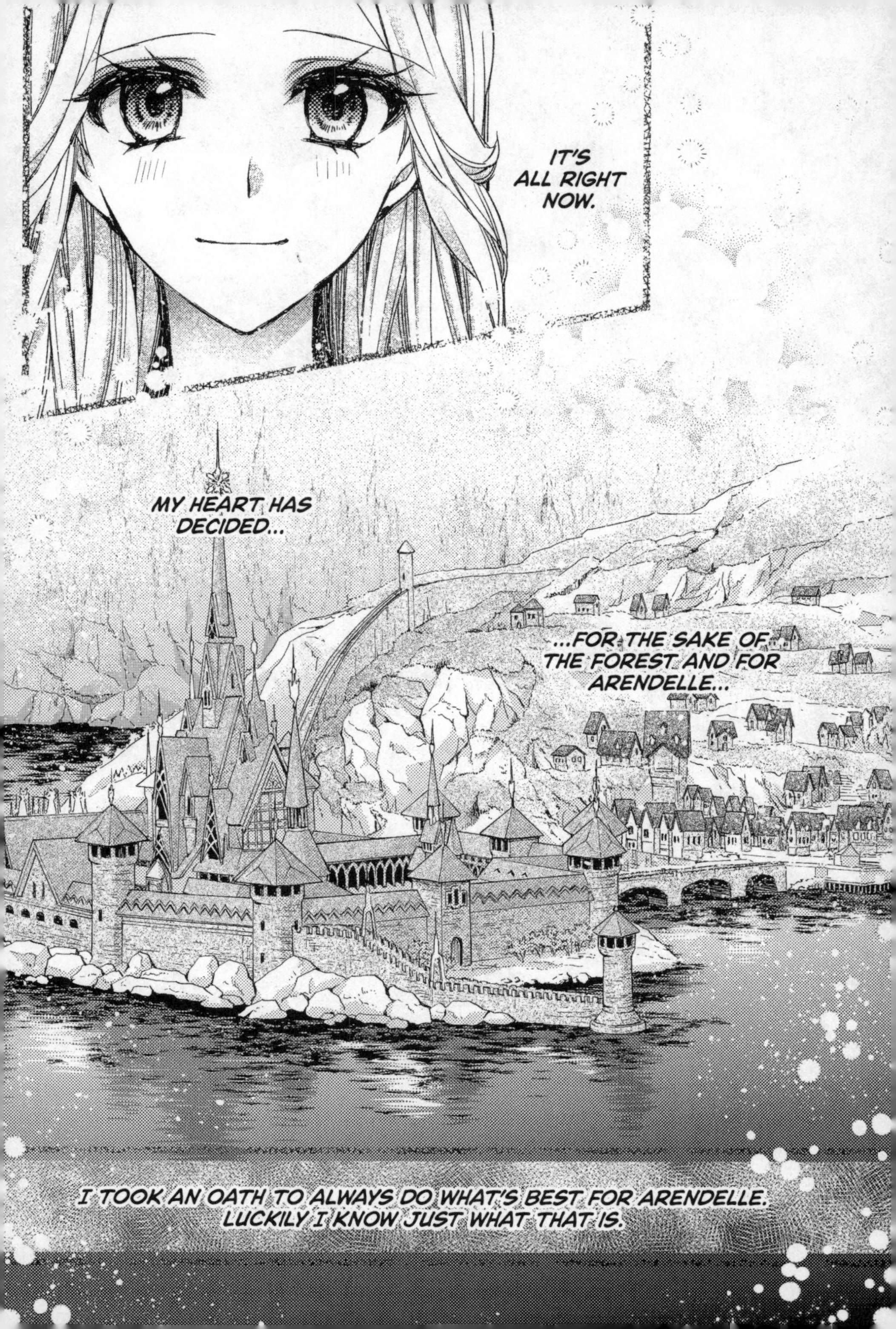
IT'S ALL RIGHT NOW.
MY HEART HAS DECIDED...
...FOR THE SAKE OF THE FOREST AND FOR ARENDELLE...
I TOOK AN OATH TO ALWAYS DO WHAT'S BEST FOR ARENDELLE. LUCKILY I KNOW JUST WHAT THAT IS.

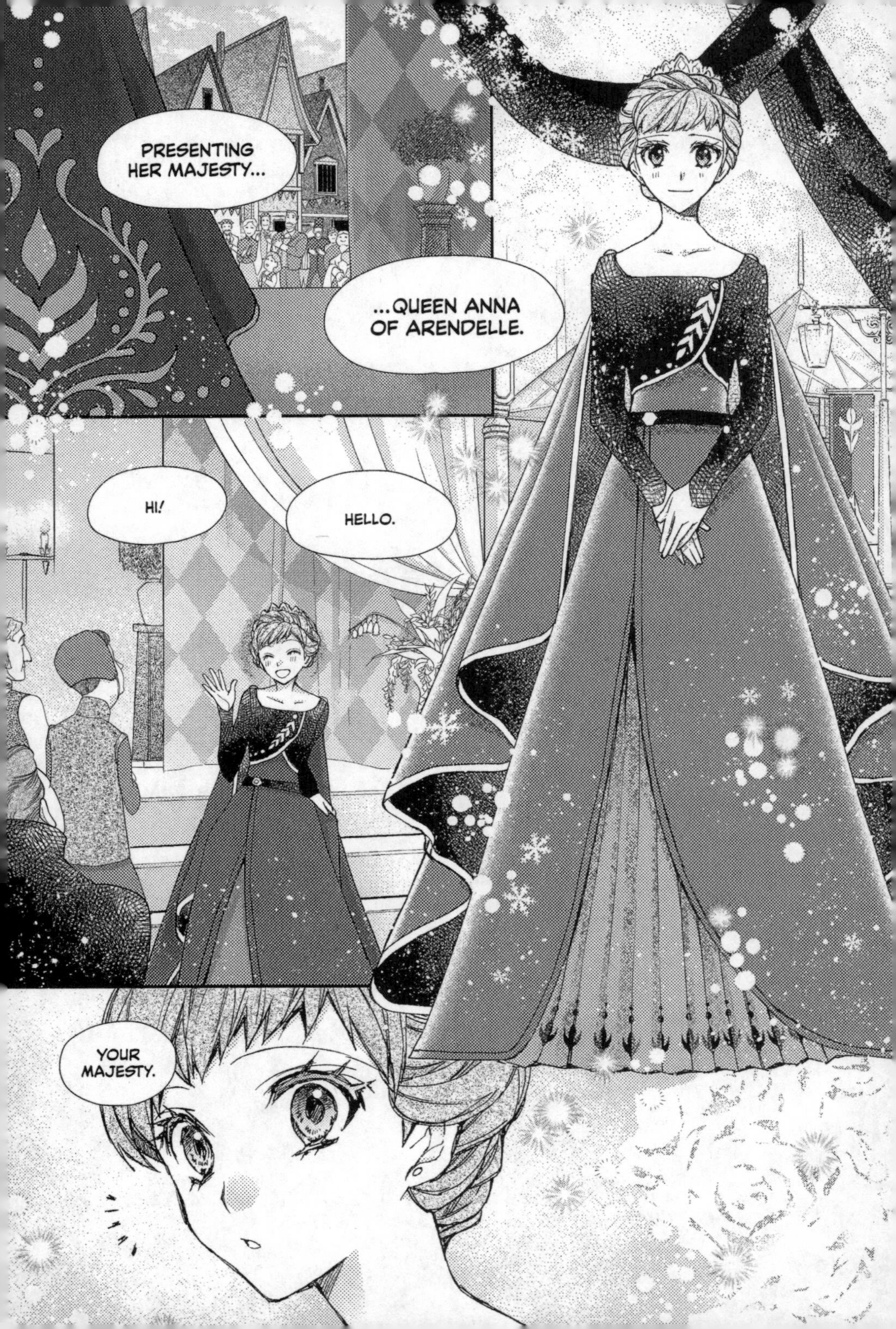
PRESENTING HER MAJESTY...
...QUEEN ANNA OF ARENDELLE.
HI!
HELLO.
YOUR MAJESTY.

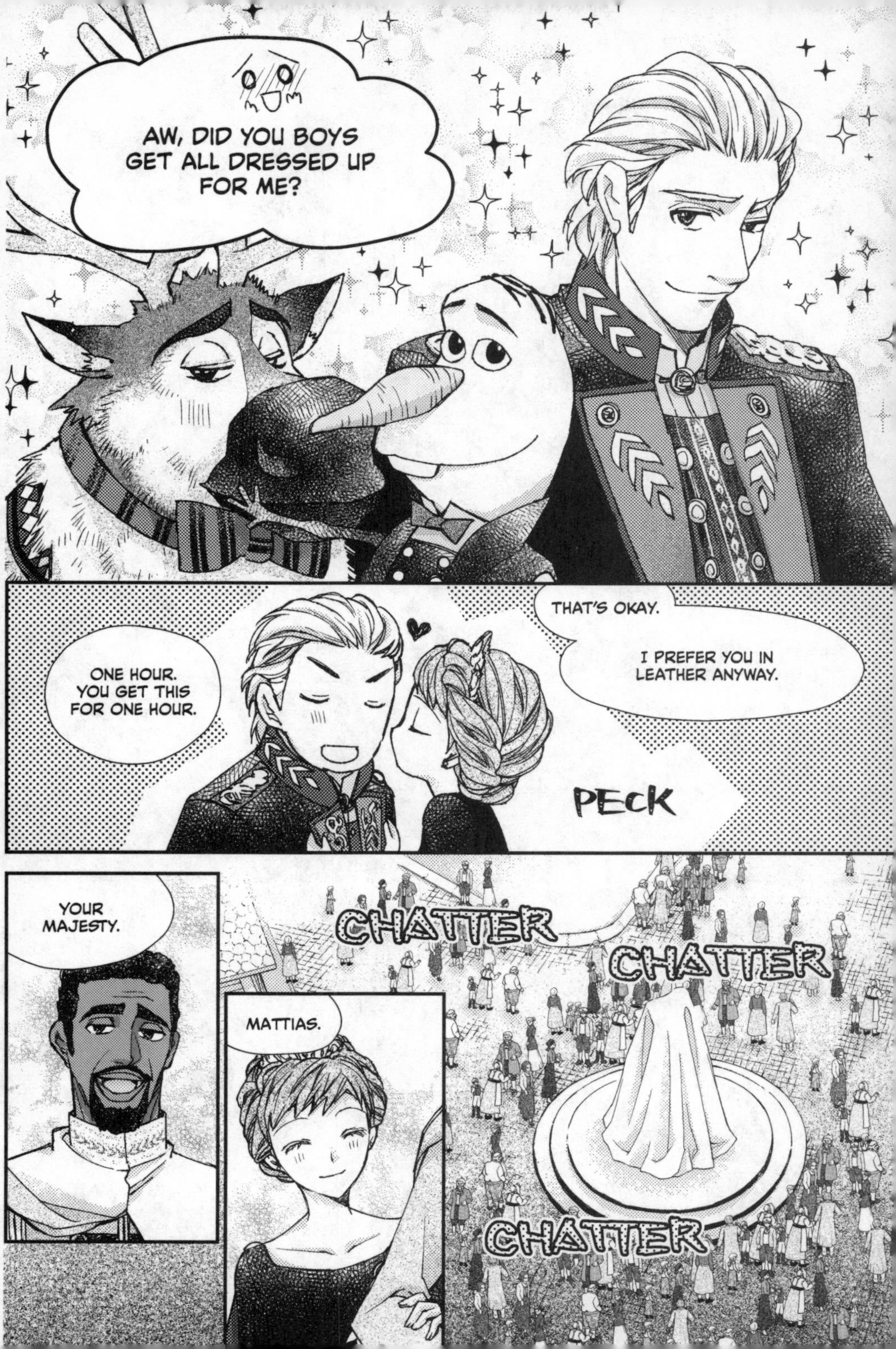
AW, DID YOU BOYS GET ALL DRESSED UP FOR ME?
ONE HOUR. YOU GET THIS FOR ONE HOUR.
THAT'S OKAY.
I PREFER YOU IN LEATHER ANYWAY.
PECK
YOUR MAJESTY.
MATTIAS.
CHATTER
CHATTER
CHATTER

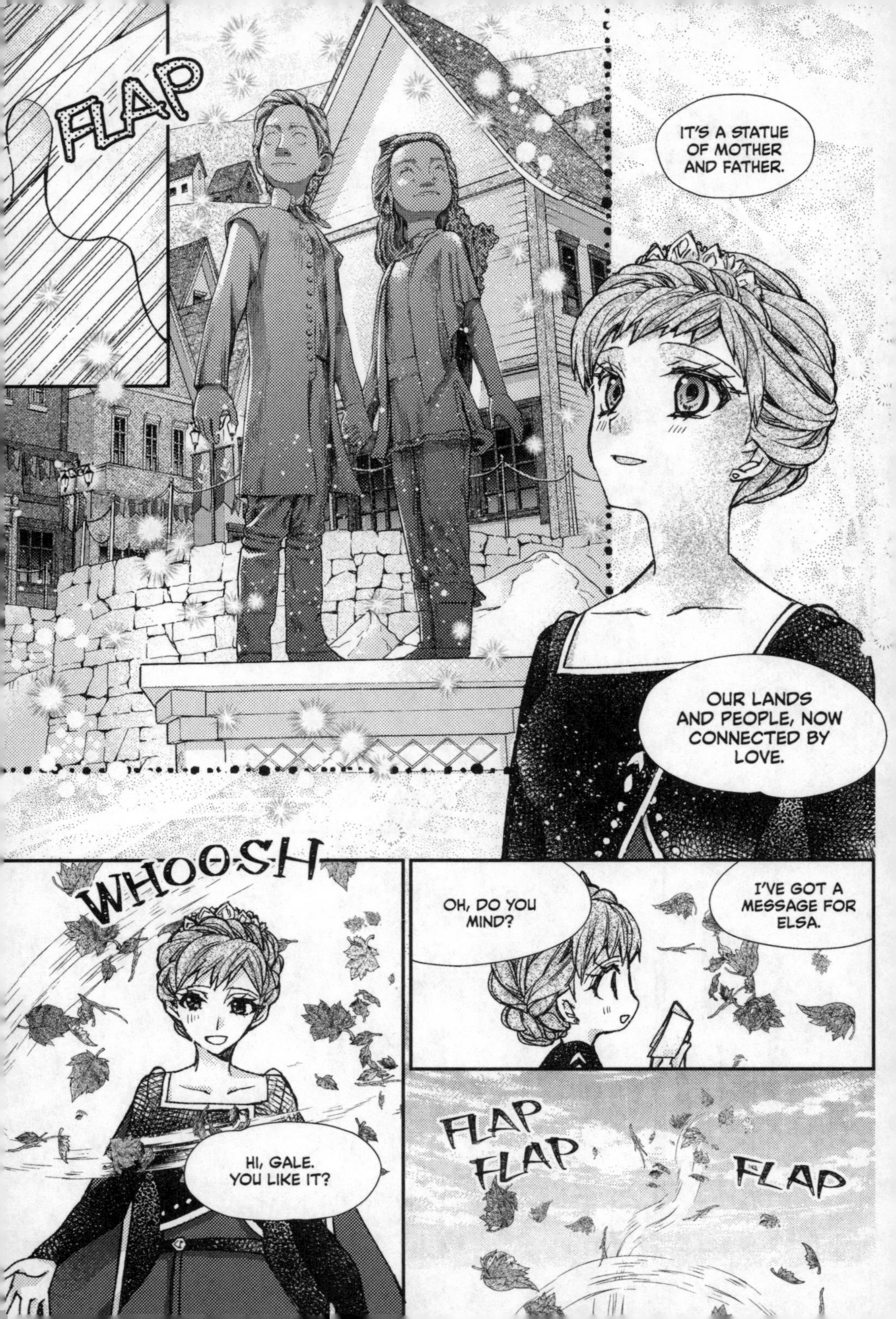
FLAP
IT'S A STATUE OF MOTHER AND FATHER.
OUR LANDS AND PEOPLE, NOW CONNECTED BY LOVE.
WHOOSH
HI, GALE. YOU LIKE IT?
OH, DO YOU MIND?
I'VE GOT A MESSAGE FOR ELSA.
FLAP
FLAP
FLAP

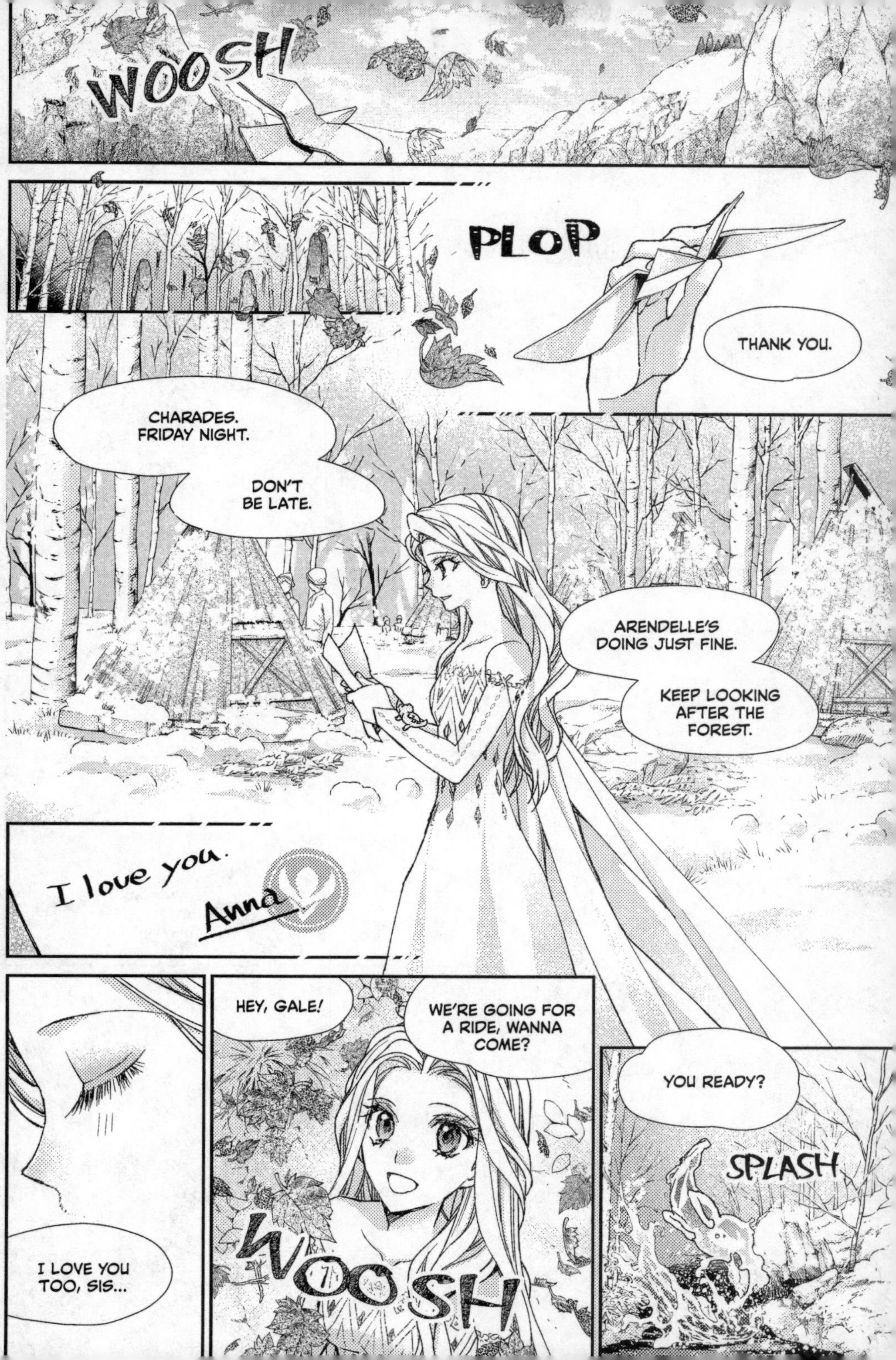
WOOSH
PLOP
THANK YOU.
CHARADES. FRIDAY NIGHT.
DON'T BE LATE.
ARENDELLE'S DOING JUST FINE.
KEEP LOOKING AFTER THE FOREST.
I love you.
Anna
I LOVE YOU TOO, SIS...
HEY, GALE!
WE'RE GOING FOR A RIDE, WANNA COME?
WOOSH
YOU READY?
SPLASH

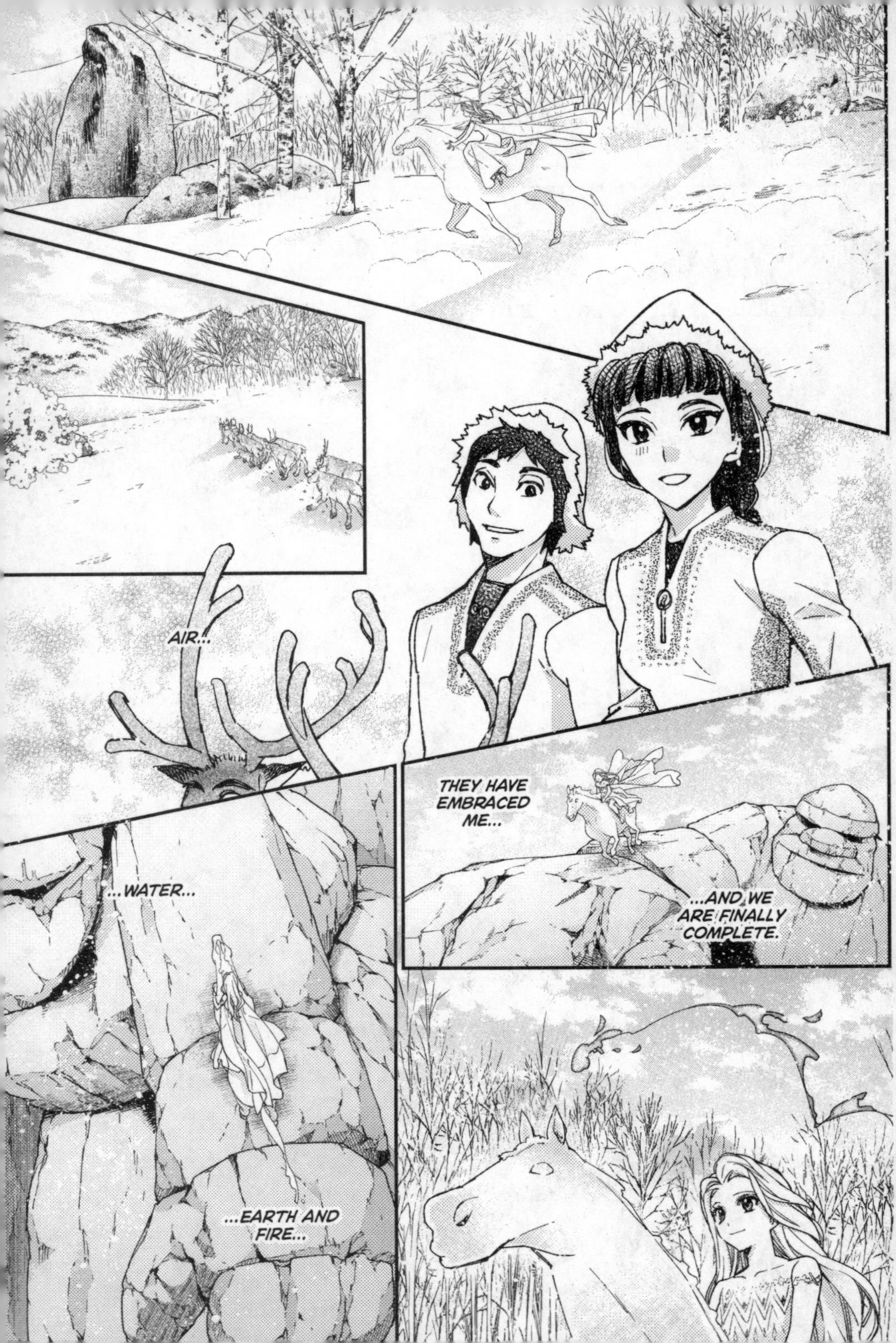
AIR...
...WATER...
...EARTH AND FIRE...
THEY HAVE EMBRACED ME...
...AND WE ARE FINALLY COMPLETE.

I HAVE FINALLY FOUND MY PLACE IN THE WORLD...

I NOW, LIVE FREELY AS THE FIFTH SPIRIT.

I UNDERSTAND MY PURPOSE.

MY POWER PROTECTS...

...AND CONNECTS EVERYONE.

SIZZLE

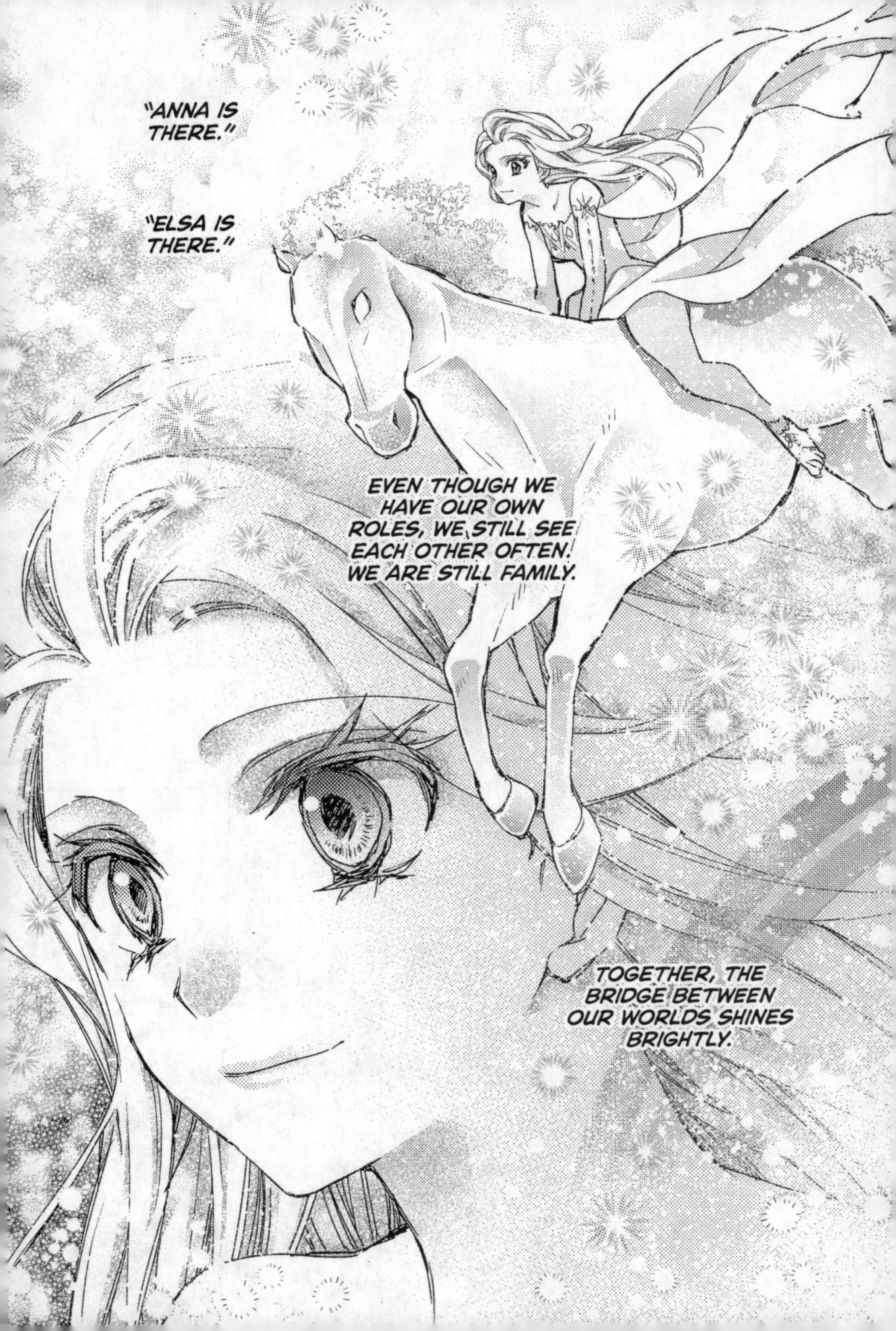
"ANNA IS THERE."
"ELSA IS THERE."
EVEN THOUGH WE HAVE OUR OWN ROLES, WE STILL SEE EACH OTHER OFTEN. WE ARE STILL FAMILY.
TOGETHER, THE BRIDGE BETWEEN OUR WORLDS SHINES BRIGHTLY.

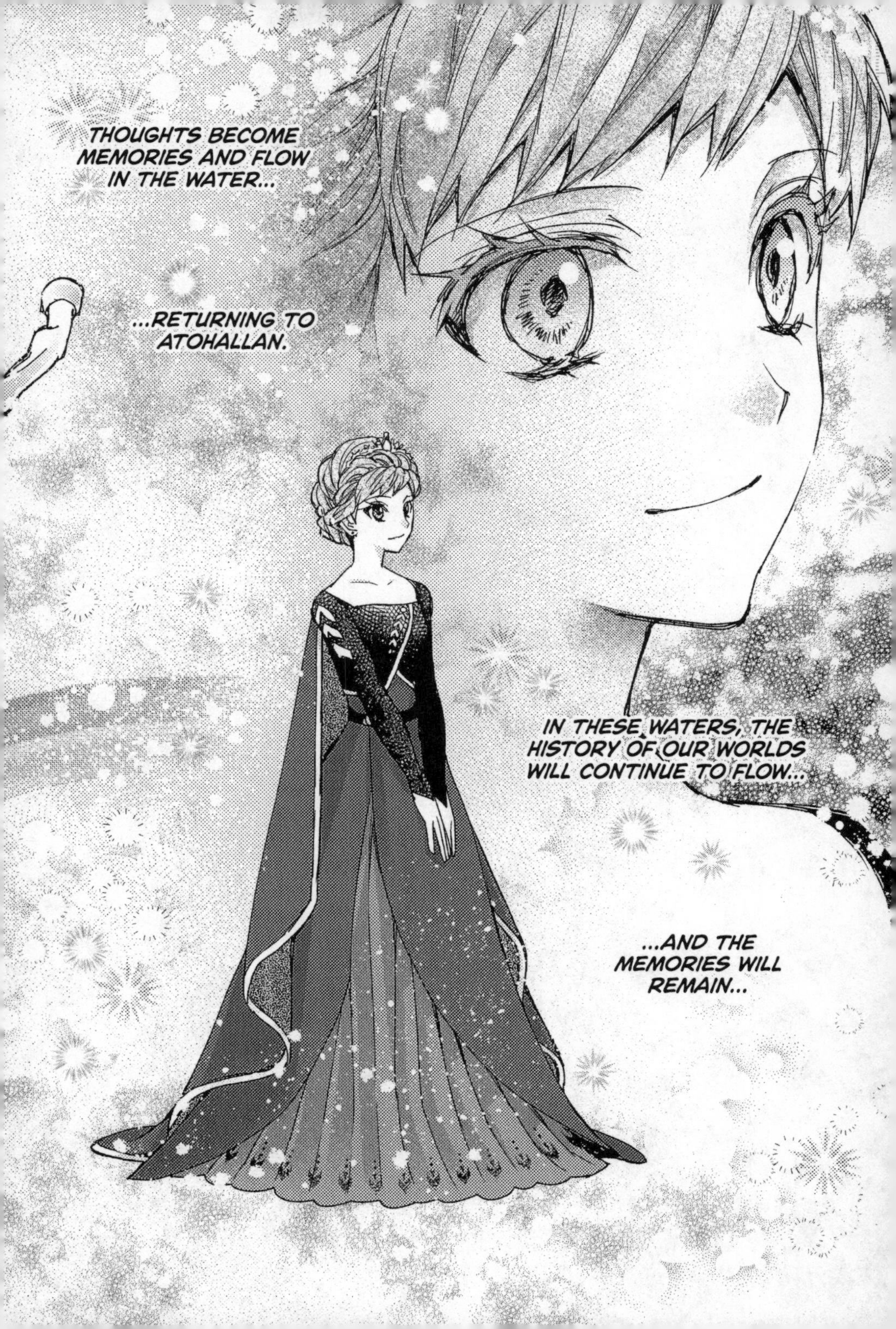
THOUGHTS BECOME MEMORIES AND FLOW IN THE WATER...
...RETURNING TO ATOHALLAN.
IN THESE WATERS, THE HISTORY OF OUR WORLDS WILL CONTINUE TO FLOW...
...AND THE MEMORIES WILL REMAIN...

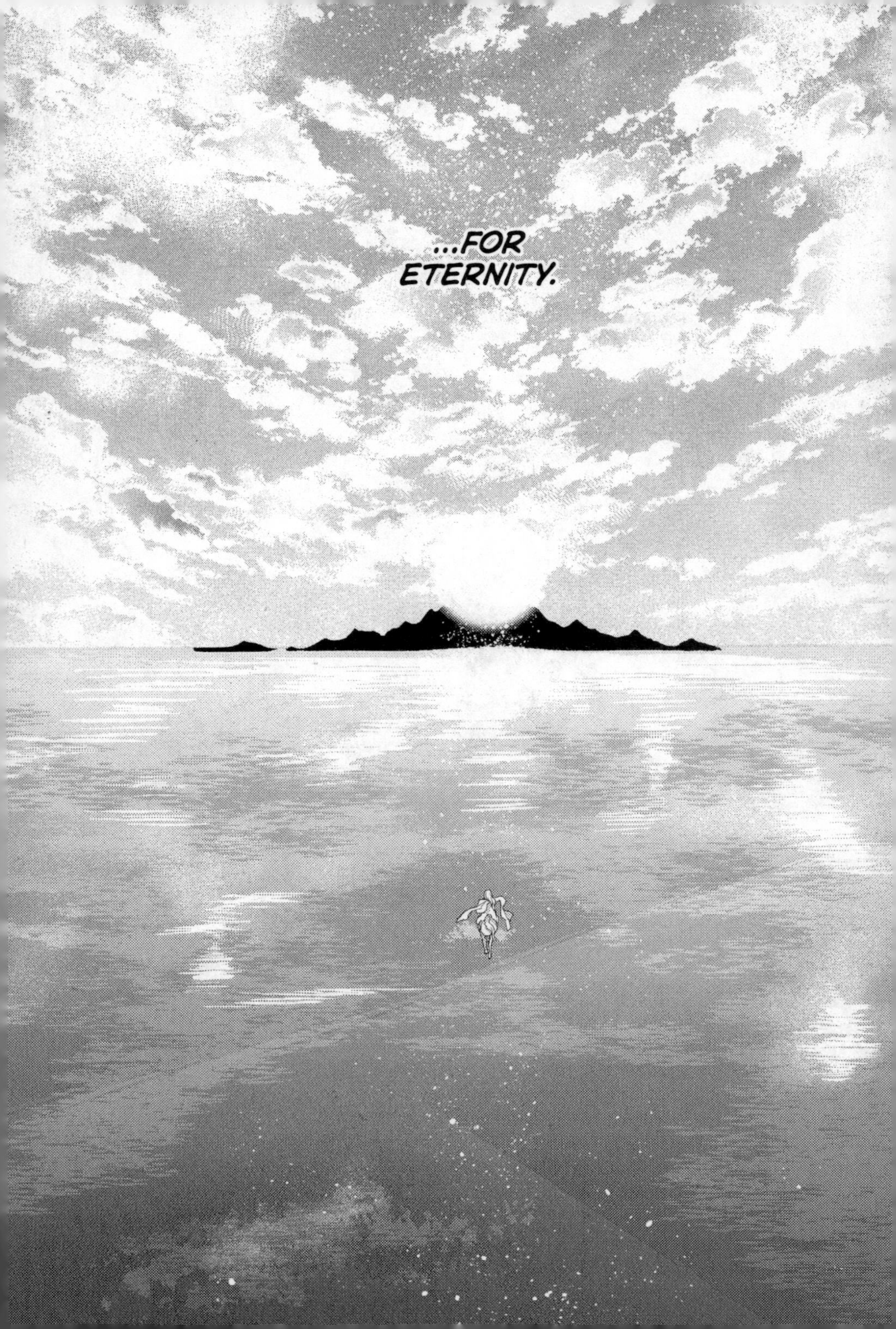
...FOR ETERNITY.

ARINA TANEMURA

Arina Tanemura began her manga career in 1996 when her short stories debuted in *Ribon Original* magazine. She gained fame with the 1997 publication of *I.O.N.* Since her debut, Tanemura has been a major force in shojo manga, with her popular series *Phantom Thief Jeanne, Time Stranger Kyoko, Full Moon, The Gentlemen's Alliance †, Sakura Hime: The Legend of Princess Sakura,* and most recently *Idol Dreams.* Both *Phantom Thief Jeanne* and *Full Moon* have been adapted into animated TV series.

SPECIAL THANKS TO

Momoko
Yukana Takada
Yuka Y. Takei
Atsuko A.
Makiko Hayashi
Ricchan
Mami Odaka
Makoto Naruse
Motoi Otsubo
Richia Kiseki
Saori Ito
Ayumi Takakura
Akane K. Mitadera
Miyuki Ochi
Chiyomi Sakuraba
Yumi Ouchi
Miho Murakami

DISNEY
FROZEN II

THE MANGA

VIZ MEDIA EDITION

MANGA ADAPTATION BY
Arina Tanemura

SPECIAL THANKS TO
Christopher Troise, Eugene Paraszczuk, Julie Dorris, Manny Mederos,
Behnoosh Khalili, Shiho Tilley, Alison Giordano, Jeff Clark, Grace Lee,
Peter Del Vecho, Mike Giaimo, Nobu Fudetani (JVTA), Luka Maeda

MANGA TRANSLATION **Yuki Murashige**
ADDITIONAL TRANSLATION **Satsuki Yamashita, Isabelle Huang, Sachiko Imai (JVTA)**
LETTERING **Erika Terriquez**
COVER & INTERIOR DESIGN **Francesca Truman**
EDITORS **Mayuko Hirao, Fawn Lau**

Copyright © 2021 Disney Enterprises, Inc. All rights reserved.

The stories, characters and incidents mentioned in this
publication are entirely fictional.

No portion of this book may be reproduced or transmitted in any form or by
any means without written permission from the copyright holders.

Printed in the U.S.A.

PUBLISHED BY VIZ MEDIA, LLC
P.O. Box 77010
San Francisco, CA 94107

10 9 8 7 6 5 4 3 2 1
First printing, February 2021

PARENTAL ADVISORY
DISNEY FROZEN 2: THE MANGA
is rated T for Teen and is
recommended for ages 13 and up.

viz.com